The Première

*A case of the Ridiculous
and the Sublime*

by

Stephen P. E. Lees. LL. B.

Other books by Stephen Lees

Visions of Architecture
Published by Bloomsbury in New York and London
ISBN No. 978-1-4081-2881-7

A fascinating study of the development of western architecture focusing on a unique selection of 54 buildings, examining why they have been designed in a particular way, the method and materials used to construct them and their impact on the *Construction Process*.

The Iron Mausoleum - A case of Sherlock Holmes and the Titanic.
ISBN No. 978-0-9571629-0-7

The Iron Vault - A case of Sherlock Holmes and Professor Moriarty.
ISBN No. 978-0-9571629-1-4

The Iron Soul - A case of Sherlock Holmes and the Napoleon of Crime.
ISBN No. 978-0-9571629-2-1

The Iron Titan - A case of Sherlock Holmes and the Invisible Presence.
ISBN No. 978-0-9571629-3-8

The Iron Metropolis - A case of Sherlock Holmes and the Titans of Valhalla.
ISBN No. 978-0-9571629-4-5

All five novels are brand-new adventures set in a fog-bound London. During the course of the stories, Holmes and Watson visit numerous places in their quest to find an explanation for the continuing mysteries surrounding the apparent sinking of the '*Titanic*'. As Holmes and Watson progress through their investigation they encounter numerous characters from different backgrounds and find themselves in various interesting locations throughout a fog-bound London, creating an atmospheric tension throughout all five volumes.

This paperback edition published in 2012 by SPEL
prodev@globalnet.co.uk

Edited by Patricia Lamb

ISBN No. 978-0-9571629-5-2

A CIP catalogue record of this book is available from the British
Library.

Book and Cover design by SPEL

Typeset in Garamond

Printed and bound in the United States

The author acknowledges the kind permission from Bloomsbury
Publisher to reproduce some images from 'Visions of Architecture' ISBN
978-1-4081-2881-7 by the same author.

Contents

Chapter 1 The Dash Through the Night

Chapter 2 The Arrival at the St. Pancras Hotel

Chapter 3 The Royal Albert Hall of Arts & Sciences

Chapter 4 The Exhibition Hall at Earl's Court

Chapter 5 The Encounter with the Fourth Estate

Chapter 6 The Green Baize Doors

Chapter 7 The Rehearsal

Chapter 8 The Café Royal - Polemic Part I

Chapter 9 The Fiasco at the Necropolis

Chapter 10 The Titan Symphony - Polemic Part II

Chapter 11 The Ballet Mecanique - Polemic Part III

Chapter 12 The Pantheon of the Gods – Polemic Part IV

Chapter 13 The Secessionists - Polemic Part V

Chapter 14 The Première

Chapter 15 The Solace and Despair

Chapter 16 The Visit to Devonshire Place

Chapter 17 The Curious Individual

Chapter 18 The Re-action

Chapter 19 The Triumph at the Bechstein Hall

Chapter 20 The Invitation

Chapter 21 The House in Bergen Avenue

Chapter 22 The Royal Aquarium Building

Chapter 23 The Mid Hour at Night

Chapter 24 The Criterion Bar

Chapter 25 The Final Reckoning - Polemic Part VI

Chapter 26 The Vision and the Passion

Index

Synopsis

The Première, narrated by Mahler's friend Friedrich Löhr, comprises a series of incidents leading up to the London *Première*, at the Queen's Hall in 1910, of Gustav Mahler's Eighth Symphony.

The symphony was not received well by the critics at its world *Première* in München in September, 1910. Accordingly, the reason for the London *Première* is to restore, hopefully, Mahler's reputation as a composer of symphonies which expanded intellectual aspiration at the time.

However, just before the *Première*, a chance meeting occurs between the intense and introspective Mahler; and the renowned writer and *raconteur*, Oscar Wilde, brimming with self-confidence and an excess of reckless wit.

Gradually a monumental argument develops between these two ego-centric Titans of the creative arts. Upon meeting for the first time in the Café Royal, they despise each other, with a detestation that increases by the minute, as the vitriolic exchanges between them intensify.

Irrespective of the vicious argument, Mahler finds time to indulge in restrained and reasonable discourse with other artists from the era. People such as Sickert, Beardsley, Stanford, Kandinsky, Whistler, Sargent and even the deranged Rossetti, though, with composers as Antheil and Zemlinsky this is certainly not the case.

The Première is ostensibly about Mahler's Eighth Symphony, but considers the arts, architecture, music, philosophy, politics and religion which influenced Mahler profoundly when composing his symphonies.

In considering Mahler's symphonies, Stephen Lees brings them to life in an interesting and fascinating way by exploring facts which are not well known, making **The Première** informative, humorous and written with affection.

Dedicated to
Marina Mahler
the Grand-daughter of
Gustav Mahler

Chapter 1

The Dash Through the Night

Our train had just blasted its way through the town of München, located in the valley of the Isar. Majestic as the river Isar is, as it flows serenely down to the Black Sea, we had no desire to visit München again.

My friend, Gustav Mahler, was just recovering, rather precariously, from a disastrous performance of the *première* of his monumental work in his Eighth Symphony, in the Bavarian capital of München some two months previously in September. Gustav and I had spent the intervening few weeks at his retreat in Lower Austria, at Maiernigg, a three-storey villa on the Wörthersee. Whilst there, he attempted, with my help, to recover his self-esteem and confidence; at the best of times in a fragile state, to say nothing of his mental and physical health, both of which were shattered.

The critics from both Vienna and München were united in their dismissal of his symphony and had subjected it to inordinately harsh treatment, pouring doubt on the structure and content of the choral elements of the work. It is a well known axiom, attendant on the act of creation, that artists, be they sculptors, painters, musicians or architects, could expect some level of criticism, fair or unfair, harsh or gentle, as the case may be. This fact has never been understood nor accepted by Mahler; who views any criticism with hostility. Criticism is, in his opinion, often motivated by prejudice or an inability to comprehend or sympathize with artistic innovation or creation.

On numerous occasions I have discussed this perpetual dilemma with Mahler, but have never succeeded in convincing him otherwise, in that adverse criticism may in some cases be justified. The implication being, one learns from it, and accordingly, adjusts one's artistic endeavors. Mahler's personality was at best individualistic but subject to hypersensitive and temperamental episodes which could augment emotional instability.

Predictably, Mahler would explode about the integrity of his work and his firm belief in the sanctity of it. He would go on to cite the circumstances surrounding Arnold Schönberg's innovative Twelve Tone system of musical expression and of his having to defend it from numerous onslaughts upon it by disaffected critics.

The Eighth Symphony had just been *premièred* at München in the recently completed metallic exhibition hall, built for that, and other performances. It was our intention to organize the London *première* of the symphony, in the hope of recovering Mahler's reputation. This was no easy task, given his predilection for monomania, as expressed by his clinical depression, isolated by Sigmund Fraud, the great commentator on nervous disease and hysteria, whom Mahler had consulted previously. Unfortunately, that consultation had the effect of confirming our worse suspicions, and given unequivocal expression in the maxim purporting: 'every silver lining has a dark cloud'!

In an attempt to publicize the *première* of the Eighth Symphony, the manager of the Ausstellungs Halle, in München, had assigned the rather fanciful *sobriquet*, to the work of being a '*Symphonie der Tausend*'. Accordingly, newspapers across Europe had repeated this somewhat preposterous exaggeration, which the critics seized upon immediately, especially in München, as an attempt by Mahler to lend verisimilitude and inordinate importance to his symphony.

The symphony is undoubtedly a major *tour de force* in symphonic composition, requiring huge orchestral forces and a substantial choir in order to perform the work. However, to suggest that a thousand persons were needed to perform the work must be seen as an exaggeration. Though this *sobriquet* was never Mahler's invention, it has added a pomposity that has irritated critics instinctively. This fact alone, may then not endear the work to the Fourth Estate in England, nor imbue confidence in Mahler that his symphony would be accepted in London. Indeed I am reminded of our experience in München as being the appropriate indicator of what would testify readily to this fact.

I was considering my friend's condition whilst in our 1st. Class compartment, and began to reminisce about the earlier years, when Mahler's meteoric rise and reputation appeared to sweep all before him. I distinctly remembered listening to his hopes and ideas for the future, whilst on a train from München to Berlin to witness a *première* of his Symphony No. 2 in C minor, *Die Auferstehungs Symphonie,* 1 in Berlin.

I remember all too well the despair attending the creation of that Second Symphony and how his inability to complete it nearly shook his confidence to the core. As with a lot of incidents in Mahler's life; triumph was inevitably attended by irretrievable despair.

On that occasion it concerned Mahler's search for a suitable subject for the *finale* to his *Auferstehungs Symphonie*.

At the time, it looked as if the symphony would remain in a deficient fragmentary state, if not consigned to oblivion, for no musical thoughts presented themselves to him. Then, in that winter of 1894, Hans von Bülow, the great conductor and exponent of the music of Richard Wagner, unexpectedly died in Cairo. His body was later brought back to Hamburg for interment at the Ohlsdorf cemetery. The news of the death of von Bülow affected Mahler, as indeed it did the musical fraternity far and wide.

We resolved to attend the funeral, which was to be held in the church of St. Michael in the Hanseatic Quarter of the city. Predictably members of the musical establishment turned out to express their farewells at the *requiem*, which was a dignified, if solemn occasion. However, during the *requiem*, the chorale from Friedrich Gottlieb Klopstock's Messias was sung:

'Arise, my dust, rise again from your brief repose;
He who has called thee will grant thy soul immortal life!'

It was here in those words specifically, that Mahler found the genesis for the inspiration he was searching for his *finale* to the Second Symphony. By transposing this *plaintif chant*, my friend was able to bring the symphony to a triumphant climax manifested in a powerful orchestral and choral *crescendo* expressing all the exuberance of life that gives perpetual purpose. Rather like the redemption found amongst the wreckage and cataclysm in the *finale* to Wagner's opera *'Götterdämmerung'*.

The Second Symphony, of course now, has met with considerable acclaim and justifiable recognition for the composer, and still remains a standard in the symphonic *repertoire* of many leading established orchestras. However, the symphony still has the power to move Mahler into deep retrospection, as if he has somehow gained by von Bülow's death and the subsequent inspiration derived from the *requiem*.

I have never asked him outright, but suspect this may have been one of the contributing reasons why, in 1900, Mahler embraced the Catholic faith; by being baptized at the church of St. Ansgar in Hamburg. It was not out of convention, that I do know, but because he sincerely sympathizes with the Christian teachings on redemption and suffering. It was for this reason that Mahler had not given his consent to have the Second Symphony played whilst we were to be in London. Instead only the first symphony, *Der Titan,* was to be performed during our *sojourn* to Metropolitan England.

Again, this particular triumph of the Second Symphony was, a few weeks later, made all too *Pyrrhic* by the fact that Mahler's twenty-two years old brother, whilst in despair, took his own life. It is as though success was fated with tragedy, as *spectres* and demons vied to control his destiny, whilst they haunted him in his thoughts. It is to be remembered death was a constant companion to my friend Mahler. He was born one of fourteen children, of whom eight died in infancy, and this fact is often reflected in his musical works, especially in his song cycle, *Das Klagende Lied.*[2]

The same forces of destiny were marshaled against him on another occasion in 1897. He had just been appointed to the prestigious *rôle* of conductor at the Vienna Opera. Marvelous as this news was, it was immediately over-shadowed by the news, following on quickly, of the death of another friend and composer, Johannes Brahms. Despite triumph at his appointment, the deep sadness attended Mahler's feelings for some considerable time after-ward.

Gustav Mahler 1860 - 1911

Though their friendship had been bitter sweet, there was, at times, a genuine and often profound affection between them. I am reminded of an incident related to me by the music critic of the *Neues Pestor Journal,* Victor von Herzfeld, who, with another critic, Hans Kössler, invited the ageing composer, Johannes Brahms, to witness Mahler's conducting a performance of Mozart's *Don Giovanni* at the Budapest Opera.

'I would not dream of attending the performance,' Brahms is reported to have replied to the invitation. 'No one can conduct *Don Giovanni* correctly for me. I enjoy reading it much more directly from the score. I have never heard a good *Don Giovanni* performed yet. We would be better off going to the *bier-keller!*'

Accordingly, Herzfeld and Kössler arranged with Brahms to visit a *bier-keller,* but in so doing, deliberately went via a circuitous route that took them past the Opera House.

'It will be probably too early; the beer will not have been going long. Come into the Opera House for just half an hour,' Kössler said to Brahms.

'Alright then,' replied Brahms, 'but is there a sofa in the opera box?'

'Of course,' replied Herzfeld.

'Good. That is alright then, I shall sleep through it!'

Despite this apparent slight at Mahler's conducting of *Don Giovanni*, not limited to Mahler alone of course, Brahms had invited Mahler to send him the score in manuscript of his fated Second Symphony! That done, we waited with bated breath for the *Maestro's* re-action. It was not long in coming.

'Up to now I thought Rickard Strauss was the chief of the iconoclasts, but now,' Brahms said, 'I see that Mahler is the king of the revolutionaries!'[3]

All this of course was some years past, in fact in December 1895. For the present in 1910, however, things were a little different. Huddled before me, in the corner of our railroad carriage and wearing a large wide-brimmed blue felt hat, was the eminent composer, Gustav Mahler. I had spent the summer with him at his retreat, a villa at Maiernigg am Wörthersee, in order to lend support and help in the creation of his monumental work the Eighth Symphony. I had assisted in its genesis by playing on the *piano forte*, the various symphonic sections, as Mahler composed them. From my *piano forte* accompaniment, Mahler might adjust or revise his symphonic composition. Often, I might experiment with a particular melodic progression by subjecting it to a piano transcription or paraphrase to see if we could derive more thematic material from the existing score Mahler had composed.

We had caught our train at Klagenfurt, the nearest town to Maiernigg am Wörthersee, and though I did not feel disposed to telling Mahler, I knew from the outset that this journey would be a mistake.

I had tried to dissuade Gustav from accepting an invitation, received from Henry Wood the director of the Queen's Hall Orchestra in London, to conduct his Eighth Symphony at the Queen's Hall, at what they call a *Promenade Concert*, whatever that might be. I had advised Mahler to decline this offer, for fear the strain might induce a relapse in his recovery. Honored as the invitation was, to conduct the Queen's Hall Orchestra, it was in my opinion, an invitation to court disaster. Should the concert meet with the opprobrium of the critics, it would have catastrophic consequences for Mahler, whose nerves, at this very moment, were frayed and shattered. Though one would not suspect this to be the case it looking at his reposing self, but I knew he was on the edge of a precipice and further critical rebuff would precipitate a major mental collapse.

I remember Bruno Schlesinger's[4] description of Mahler on first meeting him, but whose features now, some years later, were not entirely dissimilar. 'There Mahler was standing there in person in the theater office as I emerged from my introductory call upon Director Pollini: pale, thin of small stature, with a long head, his high forehead frames in black, keen eyes behind a pair of *pince-nez*, with lines of suffering and humor in a face that exhibited, when he talked to someone, the most amazing changes of expression! Never before had I encountered such an intense personality or dreamed how a sharp, pointed word, an imperious gesture, a concentration of will-power, could throw others into anxiety and terror and force them to blind obedience.'

Villa at Maiernigg am Wörthersee

I was pondering these thoughts as our train took on more steam and pounded remorselessly the steel railroad line below us in a syncopated rhythm, sympathetic with the railroad carriage rolling and rocking from side to side.

We had left Austria and were now steaming through southern Germany on a late November afternoon. I did not engage Mahler in conversation, for I felt at any rate, he would not reciprocate; such were his private concerns searing through his mind. I contented myself in watching the beautiful countryside this part of Germany has to offer those travelling through it. Indeed, my delight was increased further when our train began to slow down in order to negotiate the steep curve of the railroad as it approaches Regensburg. I had traveled many times to Regensburg by train from München or Linz, and knew exactly what to expect during the next few minutes. Even more so now, as the sun was setting low in the sky, creating that soft light one only experiences during the autumnal Fall.

Then I saw it! I beheld the sight through the railroad carriage window as it came into view and resplendent in the sunlight, crowning the hillside upon which is constructed, Valhalla! Though located in the distance on the other side of the Donau River, it appeared even more majestic, rising above the red and golden hues of the forest in its autumnal splendor. Even Mahler smiled at the vision of this beautiful classical temple based clearly upon the Parthenon that dominates the Acropolis at Athens of which it forms an integral part.

We pressed on to Nürnburg and after waiting for several minutes at the station, progressed on to Frankfurt-am-Main. We skirted round the huge Grünewald, that defines Frankfurt and onwards relentlessly to the ancient city of Köln and its tremendous Gothic cathedral on the Trankgasse overlooking the railroad station. The *Dom*, dedicated to Ste. Peter and Mary, was outlined against the evening sky, dominating the locality. This impressive structure, complete with its myriad of turrets, and pronounced massive flying buttresses, was capped with pinnacles decorated extravagantly with crockets emulating foliage. Those details were all subject to the dominating splendor of the cathedral's two tall crenellated spires.

It was here in 1904 that Mahler's Fifth Symphony received its *première*, but which left our friend Bruno

The Acropolis

Schlesinger most unsatisfied; in that the instrumentation failed to bring out clearly the complicated contrapuntal fabric of the elements, as a result of a self-confessed inability of Mahler to master the control of the orchestra. Such admissions indicated a progression, which affected my friend's confidence, to the extent that the symphony was later revised substantially.

I recall the structure of the Fifth Symphony as that of being taut and wound up, due to its tonality which progresses from C sharp minor, to the point of creating tension. Commencing with a *trauer marsch*, introducing the *fate motif*, that tension is given substance and is increased continually throughout the symphony by the expression in key of A minor of the second movement. Then by the key of F major, conveying the reflective and serenely beautiful *adagietto – sehr langsam*, scored for strings and harp. This was composed at the time as a deep expression of love for Alma Schindler, whom he was then to marry in March 1902. This slow movement reflects the melodic structure, later, in 1905, to be given a more profound expression in the sublime *lieder*, based on the poems by Rückert, *'Ich bin der Welt abhanden gekommen'*.[5] This *adagietto* movement then careers into the parody of the combination of the *ländler* [6] and *waltz* that comprise the thematic material of the *scherzo* progressing into the *finale* both of which share the key of D major.

Eventually, we steamed into the ancient Belgian city of Brügge. I remembered the occasion well, because Mahler and I attended in this city the *première* of Erich Korngold's opera, *'Die Tote Stadt'*,[7] during which we met and spoke with the composer for several minutes. Curiously, Mahler had asked him then, why he had particularly set the opera in that town of Brügge, to which, Korngold merely replied, 'go visit the place!'

Well here we were doing just that. One did not need to leave the train and walk about the town; it was patently obvious what Korngold was referring to. Even from our railroad carriage, I could smell the stench of decay and still waters rising up to the viaduct that our train was travelling along. From this vantage point, one could see quite clearly the all-pervasive aspect of destruction as though the town and its ancient gloomy buildings were falling apart, but in slow motion. To add to this feeling of helplessness and forlorn aspect, muted church bells could be heard, in the near distance, sounding out the hours, but for whom to hear, in their despair?

It was with relief that our train took on more steam and thundered along the elevated railroad viaduct and out of this *'Dead City'* as Korngold aptly depicts in his opera. Eventually our train reached the coast on its way to the port of Calais. The German ocean looked threatening as its turbulent and dark waters heaved up and down in great swells. It was upon this very sea, that Mahler and I would be sailing presently, when we arrive at Calais to take passage on a steam packet boat to Dover, in England.

1 Symphony No. 2 in C minor the *Resurrection*
2 The Songs of Lament.
3 Quoted by the critic Kössler, who noted at the time Mahler appeared put out by Brahms' words.
4 Known as Bruno Walter, the conductor.
5 *I have lost my way in the world*
6 A German dance and true origin of the Waltz.
7 '*The Dead City*', and premièred in 1920'

Chapter 2

The Arrival at the St. Pancras Hotel

Mahler to date had written eight symphonies. The First, called *The Titan* followed by the so-called *Wunderhorn Symphonies*, which number, Two, Three and Four. They incorporate religious songs from a collection of folk-poetry called *Das Knaben Wunderhorn*, to augment what would have been only the orchestral version, adding further dimension. He then reverted to this symphonic structure with voice when creating the Eighth. The *Wunderhorn Symphonies* and the Eighth are concerned with man's search for a light by which he can find salvation in God from the peril of an all too mortal transition on earth. This is very much the subject of the *finale* of the Second Symphony, incorporating another reference from the *Das Knaben Wunderhorn*, that of Klopstock's Resurrection Hymn, *Auferstehen*. The Third Symphony was fully completed in 1902 but the Fourth was completed earlier in 1901. The Fifth was completed in 1902, Sixth in 1905 and the Seventh in 1905 and now his Eighth in this present year of 1910.

After some rather uncalled for discourtesy by officials in the dockside customs shed, we handed over our traveling documents in readiness to take passage to England. At length, exhausted, cold and with shattered nerves, we clambered up the gangplank to board the steam packet boat '*Princess-Louise*'. Minutes later we were underway across the English Channel for Dover and posterity or calamity. But, in my heart, I retained a nameless foreboding about the efficacy of this journey. Eventually we saw the lights of Dover and within a surprisingly short period of time found ourselves seated comfortably in a 1st. Class compartment carriage of the South Eastern Railway bound for a place called Charing Cross.

In our quest, we had crossed Europe, and now were heading toward London in order to organize a performance of Eighth Symphony that had met with failure, for a variety of reasons, at its *première* in München. Our train steamed up the railroad into London and through the extensive suburban districts, of which this great English Metropolis is comprised. As we did so our train pounded its way to the very center of London, by traversing over endless elevated railroad viaducts and bridges, straddling houses and buildings as it did so. Beneath us, I thought, were the dark brooding slums so vividly and graphically depicted in Gustave Doré's accurate reminiscences of such concentrations of humanity. At length, our train eventually clanked into a fog-bound Charing Cross Railroad Station, a seething hive of activity and noise.

Alighting from our train carriage onto the platform, we were engulfed by a tide of passengers seemingly in a hurry to vacate the station's precincts. We found ourselves being swept along in this rather unpleasant and pushing tide of people as it made its way to the gates located at the end of the platform. On reaching them, a rather perfunctory *employé* of the South Eastern Railway, wearing his black velveteen uniform with red piping, demanded to see our travel papers and tickets. Again, after some uncalled for discourteous words were exchanged, we tried to make our way out into the station's forecourt in an attempt to avail ourselves of a carriage.

We did manage to quit the station, and headed straight for the cab rank where there were various carriages waiting. We climbed into a Brougham four-wheeler with roof to afford us some degree of protection from the pervasive acridity of the fog that was swirling around.

Of course, in Vienna we are used to the fog, but here in London, though much denser, it had an acrid taste and smell to it, as though impressed with coal and wood smoke emanating from the numerous chimneys ranged across this Metropolis. Within minutes of leaving the train our eyes were itching with irritation brought about by the fog.

"Well, Gustav here we are in London to re-launch your Eighth Symphony; are you confident?" I asked my friend.

"At the moment Friedrich, I feel quite apprehensive with attendant feelings of vulnerability!" replied Mahler.

"Why? After some rehearsals the symphony should be ready to be released upon an expectant and grateful audience," I replied.

"No, Friedrich, the vulnerability I refer to is of being scared of large cities, including such a huge Metropolis as London, especially shrouded in dense fog, it can release feelings of claustrophobia, and probably other phobias which plague me constantly."

Mahler had uttered these words whilst we were *en-route* to the St. Pancras Hotel and of course I realized that he had only lived in Vienna and Hamburg, neither being anywhere near the size of London!

It was with an irrational trepidation that we both ascended the broad granite steps leading up in to this magnificent red brick High Victorian decorated Neo-

St. Pancras Hotel

Gothic edifice to ostentatious monumentalism. We entered the Hotel through the *Porte Cochere* to the west wing leading to the main Entrance Hall through the honey colored Ancaster stone framed doorway flanked by columns of polished green and pink limestone.

Nothing could have prepared us for the sheer feeling of beauty emanating from its lavish decoration and opulence including murals that decorated the main Entrance Hall beneath several bright and glittering acetylene gas-fuelled *chandeliers*. An impressive cantilevered Grand Staircase progressed dramatically into the vaulted ceiling of the fifth floor and the walls were covered with maroon coloured wallpaper punctuated with golden *fleurs de lys* integral designs.

In order to complete our checking in to this Hotel, we approached the *concièrge* reception desk, and in particular to a person behind it, who was dressed, in a red tail-coat and black top hat and blue rosette to the side. He immediately looked at Mahler's rather tired apparel, but seemed to focus more on his large, wide brimmed, blue felt hat, before diverting his gaze to look down on a pair of scuffed patent leather boots.

"Who did you say you were?" he asked accusingly, and without diverting his gaze from Mahler's boots.

"Friedrich Löhr and this is *Maestro* Mahler," I replied.

"Very good sir; is *'Maestro'* his Christian name?" inquired the *concièrge*, "but if you would care to complete these forms, I shall attend to your reservation." And with that, he walked off to confer with another person at the reception desk.

Presently, he came back with a sizeable register that he placed next to us on the desk.

"What did you say your names were?" he asked expectantly.

I repeated our names slowly and deliberately, as though addressing a person whose hearing was less than perfect. The *concièrge* moved his index finger up and down written entries over several pages. He then looked at us with a faint hint of pleasure in his facial expression.

"We do not appear to have a reservation for either a Mr. Friedrich Löhr or a Mr. *Mastro* Mahler."

It was Mahler who intervened.

"What do you mean, you do not have reservations for us? A cablegram was dispatched to you four days ago, reserving two *suites* for us."

"Did you receive a telegram from us confirming your

reservation?" asked the *concièrge*.

Both Mahler and I looked at each other and shrugged our shoulders in mutual response.

"Wait here and I shall make inquiries to ascertain what we can do for you in the absence of your booking a room at our Hotel," said the *concièrge*.

"This is rather an inconvenient setback, but feel confident that they can find us suitable rooms, after all, this Hotel is large and well-appointed," I said, moving my arm in a wide sweep to indicate the spaciousness of the place.

We stood there for quite some time, in awe of the undoubted sumptuous beauty of the Hotel. For not only did it boast a variety of firsts in its appointment, but also the level of luxury it attained and offered, not least that the Hotel was built onto the new and innovative iron frame which allowed the creator of the building to span wide spaces to form large rooms and openings within the structure. The Hotel, I noticed, included new hydraulically operated elevator carriages, acetylene gas-fuelled *chandeliers* and electrically operated bells.

The Hotel also provided bedrooms with an antechamber, in which a whole bathtub was located, and a considerable army of servants and chambermaids to wait on every needs and fads of the guests. One particular innovative piece of equipment, I observed, was an electro-phone that linked Hotel guests by wire to music being played at various London concert halls, including the Aëolian Hall in Bond Street and the Queen's Hall in Portland Place, where we were to *première* the Eighth Symphony. In the main Entrance Hall were several elaborate murals, impressed into the plaster with which the walls are lined. The traditional and ubiquitous indoor palm tree was, as usual, much in evidence, as a peculiarly

English Victorian vernacular.

Eventually the red tail-coated *concièrge* re-appeared and informed us that they had found rooms for us. At that moment a porter, wearing a black and red striped waistcoat, materialized at our side with his small trolley onto which he began loading our *portmanteaus* and *valises*.

We followed him through the main Entrance Hall to what looked like an ornate bronze door set flush into the polished limestone wall. He pulled at a bell rope and a few seconds later the bronze doors slid apart revealing a small room paneled in mahogany, and a bell-boy.

Moments later the door closed behind us and the bell-boy pushed the operating lever to its full extent, and immediately the room in which we were standing began moving up through the floors. Instantly I felt as if my stomach had dropped.

With a hissing noise accompanied by a grinding feeling, the elevator carriage in which we stood came to an abrupt stop. The bell-boy opened the doors and we stepped out into a corridor that seemed to be in the eaves of the roof and the floor of which was covered with a length of brown linoleum. Following our porter, we went clattering along the corridor, down a flight of steps and passed several chambermaids, bearing vessels of hot water and clean linen. We then veered into a doorway that lead through into another corridor, the ceiling of which literally formed part of the apex of the the roof. We were obviously in the attic of the Hotel, and no doubt being shown to the cheaper rooms.

At length the porter stopped at one door and with a key opened it and invited either of us to enter. Mahler elected to do so and walked in to the room. The porter showed me to my room on the other side of the corridor, and then abandoned us.

I surveyed what bedroom there was that I had been allocated, whilst pushing down onto the bed to test its softness, or rigidity, as was the case here. Walking over to the *quarter foil* window reveal, I looked out onto fog, framed by a few roof tiles adjacent to my ornate stone window surround. I left my bedroom and went to Mahler's, knowing that he would be quite incensed at his being relegated to inferior quarters. I knocked on his open door and walked in only to see him sitting on the bed looking at the wall with a blank expression upon his face, beneath his large brim, blue felt hat. The small window of his room looked out onto the underside of a vast iron and glass roof of the station under which the noise coming up from the platforms and locomotives was tremendous.

Beneath the extensive iron and glass canopy of the station roof were suspended enormous town gas light globes. Though not of the *chandelier* type, they did illuminate the scene of chaos beneath, as various trade wagons, pantechnicons and other delivery carts competed for precedence for their horse drawn vehicles amongst the piles of luggage.

I stood there transfixed by the concentrated commotion emanating from the platforms below, which were teeming with people in search of their trains or departing from them. The scene was one of utter chaos, as one train after another clanked noisily into St. Pancras Railroad Station, disgorging their passengers; whilst other trains departed along platforms with a great show of steam and even more noise. Amongst the chaos were flitting shunting engines, hissing steam fiercely, while marshalling carriages to large locomotives, painted in purple livery and eager to depart hauling their passengers.

Amongst this vicissitude of transportation and commerce, children played with their dogs; dodging, miraculously, cumbersome wagons that paid them no heed. Some children were of the street urchin type, whilst others, wearing boots, were clearly passing through the station or waiting for a train. The expression upon their faces proclaimed as much, as they stood there, wrapped up tightly in their high quality travelling coats. Some gazed awestruck amid these new experiences.

Within this concentration of the travelling public were other persons, some, conducting the business of commerce, pointed accusingly to delivery orders or shipping manifests; and then in the direction of where none existent goods ought to be. Other people were appealing, in the last resort, to unconvinced servants of the railroad. Others merely watched, including nurses pushing their perambulators, oblivious in which direction they did, among the general chaos.

The smell of choking smoke from railroad engines was appalling; and even from the Hotel room window from which I looked down. I now understood why some people were walking rather quickly along the platform in their bid to leave the station. In so doing one person was unfortunate to be passing a locomotive engine at the very instance it evacuated its surplus steam straight into his pathway. That instant a steam fog enveloped his person, making him momentarily vanish! When he did emerge he was frantically wiping from his face the sticky residue with a handkerchief.

Then I saw something which left me quite aghast. It was a seasoned pick-pocket; he was in full action, but oblivious to an observant railroad servant upon the platform who was watching him perform his delicate action. Then suddenly he shouted at the pick-pocket, and then gave chase.

"Quick! Gustav, come to the window and look at this!"

I beckoned, but to no avail.

Below me, on the station platform, pandäemonium was let loose. A sheaf of papers and a bowler hat erupted into the air. From beneath this plume of papers and headdress, I noticed that the pickpocket had crouched down and was removing himself quickly from the *mêlée*. However, in his haste he collided with a railroad pantechnicon with London Midland & Scottish Railway Co. Ltd. emblazoned on its side panelling. This however, did not impede his egress from what was I think, a concerted attempt to apprehend his person. By now of course the view-halloa was in full cry, as both uniformed representatives of the law and the observant railroad *employé* dressed in his velveteen uniform, if hatless, gave chase in the hue and cry. I also observed in the corner of my eye, that another pickpocket, a true cannon, was clearly taking advantage of the commotion, and advised Mahler accordingly!

Surprisingly enough, a woman of quite stout demeanor, wearing a frilly bonnet, and several bellowing and voluminous mauve and purple silk skirts, intercepted the pickpocket and quite literally fell upon him and very nearly succeeded in frustrating his escape. However, at the last moment, she missed her footing and hit the ground, bonnet and all, with pronounced force as the fleeing fellow made good his escape out of the station and to liberty.

"We have not yet even left the precincts of the St. Pancras Hotel," I remarked to Mahler, "before we are compelled to witness behavior quite simply unacceptable in Vienna."

All this activity was taking place beneath what is a stupendous iron and glass roof, a hundred or so feet in height, which spans from wall to wall the entire collection of platforms and commotion beneath its huge arched canopy, at least one hundred feet in width. This glazed roof structure is a series of ribbed arches which comprise iron curved girders braced by cross beams and transoms, and anchored to the rear *façade* of the hotel over-looking the platforms, and from where I was looking down from Mahler's Hotel room window.

The arched glazed canopy progressed from the rear *façade* of the Hotel out along the platforms and permanent way of the railroad for a distance of at least three hundred feet in length. This canopy fulfilled another function admirably; it kept the inclement and acrid fog-laden aëther out of the station precinct, and consequently out of this Hotel room. The effect of this glazed structure was to create a massive enclosed space similar to the Hall of Machines erected at the Paris International Exposition of 1878. A place, ironically, on that occasion, Mahler liked, because, as he reminded me, the structure is expansive and does not impede sunlight and therefore uplifts the soul!

I pulled my head back into the room and turned to look at Mahler who seemed even more forlorn than when I first entered his room only a few moments before and he was still staring at a blank wall.

"It is that steel and glass structure outside that window," he finally offered.

"What about it Gustav, it is but a station roof, admittedly over particularly noisy platforms, but still only a roof?" I said, questioningly, for I could not determine the cause of his upset, since he admired a similar structure that is the Hall of Machines.

"The roof," he continued, with a tone of resignation in his voice, "reminds me of München and that entire trauma, which we had to contend with; and our very reason for travelling from it and, I suppose, being in this

Hall of Machines

room."

I looked back at the immense vitreous glazing structure, smiled and returned my gaze to Mahler.

"Come on my friend, let us go and dine, you will feel better when you have got a glass or two of Moselle inside you!" I said, at which he fell in eagerly with my suggestion.

After we had gained the elevator, Mahler suggested that we repair to the ground floor Grand Drawing Room, located in the curved west wing of the Hotel. When we had stepped into the elevator carriage I instructed the bell-boy accordingly as to the floor. Our elevator arrived some moments later at the ground floor and delivered us into the corridor, at the end of which, were two large highly polished walnut paneled doors. It was through this imposing portal that we entered into the Grand Drawing Room.

On so doing, a waiter glided into our vicinity *maneuver-*

ing his person and bending his body adeptly around items of furniture, placed between him and us, in this large and spacious Grand Drawing Room. On reaching us he offered to escort us to a low table made of exquisite deep pink *Giallo Siena* marble and surrounded by red *damask* covered sofas complemented with *antimacassars* of white lace on their fronts.

"May I get you something to drink?" asked the waiter.

"Yes," I replied, "hock and seltzer."

"And for sir?"

"Me?" replied Mahler, "*Tokay.*"

Whilst I listened to Mahler, my thoughts began to drift and I found myself admiring the ornate plaster and gilded details of the ceiling with an intricate architrave around the walls of the immense Grand Drawing Room. It was clear to me this Hotel was built using an iron frame that supports the building. Indeed one could just make out the presence of the metal frame, albeit *camouflaged* by elaborate plaster mouldings and timber encasement set in between wall panels of highly textured and patterned wallpaper.

At length we left the Grand Drawing Room and made our way to the *piano-nobile* to the Grand Dining Room. We walked down a thick red Axminster carpeted corridor that was decorated in cream paint with exquisitely raised gilded filigree patterns, to the ceiling and wall surfaces. This created a sumptuous feel of opulence for which the St. Pancras Hotel is justly famous. We entered the Grand Dining Room for dinner. Before I could utter a word of amazement as to the sumptuous *décor* of the room, a rather obsequious waiter appeared from nowhere and asked that we follow him. He guided us to a table located in a deep bay window alcove framed with purple drapes partially open to reveal a large window overlooking the main road fronting the Hotel – if we but could see it due to the folds of fog. My attention though, was on my irritable friend, not the fog and I attempted to engage him in conversation. All of a sudden a portly person with a distinctive black moustache and dressed in a black tail-coat, came into sight and with no regard for other diners spoke loudly whilst rushing across the room in our direction to take our orders.

After dinner we rode the elevator down to the ground floor and made our way again along the corridors of this magnificent structure to ostentatious Neo-Gothic excess, the vernacular of which is a very English trait. However, nothing could have prepared us for the sheer feeling of beauty emanating from one particular Gallery's lavish decoration and opulence, including murals that decorated it, beneath several bright and glittering *chandeliers*. We made our through this decorative extravagance, as though eager tourists, save we did have the time to stand and admire the pervasive beauty of the interior finished appointments, so evident everywhere.

As we entered the coffee *salon* I immediately thought it to be a misnomer. The Grand Coffee *Salon* would have been more appropriate, for it was a room of such proportions as to overwhelm any person standing within its precinct. The room was quite impressive, the proportions of which were based not on a regular rectilinear shape, but on a curved style. One curved wall that overlooked the front of the Hotel, comprised a series of Gothic pointed *trefoil* arches of stone and into it were set large windows at least twenty feet in height. However, due to the fog, no clear vision through them was possible and the windows merely took on the appearance of white *opaqueness* with only a just discernible hint of the occasional movement of shadows scuttling by.

In the background, the sound of a keys being struck on a piano could be heard, coming from what sounded more like a mechanical operated Aëolian pianola, a contraption that is all the rage in England, but not in Europe and certainly not in Austria. Whatever the case, the music emanating from it was sufficient to catch Mahler's attention, who directed his ear in the origin of the sound. It was an improvisation on the solemn work for piano, the *Bénédiction de Dieu dans la solitude,* by the *Abbé* Liszt, a pianist, for whom Mahler had the greatest respect and admiration.

However, this Aëolian pianola was, in effect, reproducing from some hidden perforated roll secreted in its machinery, an over extended and elaborate extemporization transcription with more *roberto* than considered skilful execution of *arpeggio,* which when played properly, creates sound reminiscent of diamonds *ricocheting* off a marble surface. Alas, not on this occasion, but it did remind me of an incident in 1891. It was during Mahler's tenure as conductor of the Hamburg Opera, when he played his *Totenfeier,[1]* on the *piano forte* for the acclaimed conductor Hans von Bülow.

"When you had finished playing," I said to Mahler, "von Bülow removed both hands from covering his ears, and said to you, 'well if that is music, then I know nothing about music', remember?"

"True, my good friend, Friedrich," said Mahler, "but at least we parted in a friendly manner, though at the time I had the feeling that, while von Bülow regarded me as a capable conductor, he nevertheless considered me a bad composer!"

"At the time, I thought, your reaction was one of doubt in your confidence of the possibility of your having the makings of a great composer," I replied.

Chapter 3

The Royal Albert Hall of Arts & Sciences

We were to attend a performance of my friend, Gustav Mahler's Symphony No.1 in D major *'Der Titan'* to be performed by the London Symphony Orchestra under the renowned Hans Richter at Royal Albert Hall of Arts & Sciences in the quarter called Kensington near the Hyde Park. Somewhat of concern to Mahler and myself was the fact that this orchestra was formed in 1904 when fifty or so players broke away from Queen's Hall Orchestra, during an unresolved dispute with its chief conductor, Henry Wood. Rather forebodingly, that which was left of the Queen's Hall orchestra would be performing the *première* of Mahler's Eighth Symphony.

Despite our drive being slow as it was uneventful, due to the fog, we approached the Royal Albert Hall of Arts and Sciences on time. There were several carriages of every type, Broughams, Clarences, Victorias and improved Landaus and all delivering guests. Having alighted from our humble Phäeton carriage, we dismissed it and immediately joined this large gathering on their way into the massive hall. Eventually after some lengthy searching around, we found our seats in the Dress Circle and settled down for the concert.

Mahler had elected to attend the performance of his First Symphony in D major merely as an ordinary member of the public, rather than as an honored guest, with all that entails, including advising the conductor that he may have just interpreted badly one's musical work. I also suspect, he had no wish to tempt the fates with his now-established First Symphony.

Looking at the program, I noticed the first work in this evening's concert was to be Wagner's overture to his early opera called, *'Das Liebesverbot' - eine große komische Oper*.[1] I pointed this out to Mahler and his response was quite unexpected:

"I have always preferred the profound Teutonic music over the frivolous Latin," my friend confided in me, as he sat back in his seat fingers together and his eyes closed to the world.

One thing both Mahler and I noticed was the presence of a fanatically political group called, the Nihilists,[2] who were sworn to disrupt any philharmonic concert for the sake of incommoding members of the public attending such performances. They were in attendance and looking distinctly furtive, but, I think, had been recognized by members of the audience and concert hall officials. However, they had not quite reached that critical mass in their number, to fuel the confidence needed to create and let loose that unbridled pandäemonium, their sworn intention on any occasion! Instead they merely restricted their activities to muted mutterings amongst themselves of their dreaded chant, *'be it now or never!'*

We got through Wagner's *'Das Liebesverbot'* without incident from the Nihilists, despite their ardent wish to turn the proceedings into an unmitigated disaster. What I did not know, reading the program notes, was the amusing history behind this seemingly innocuous opera, an early one, by the *Maestro*. Why Wagner had chosen to construct this particular *libretto* for the basis of his opera must remain an enigma. That Wagner conducted the *première* in 1836 is not in doubt, what was in doubt was the lead singer's ability to remember her lines, which she forgot, and had to improvise – in front of Wagner!

The opera, not surprisingly was a resounding failure. Its second performance fared no better, and had to be cancelled even before the curtain went up, as a result of a major brawl backstage between the lead tenor Ignaz Freimüller and the *prima donna*, Karoline Pollert's husband. When the opera eventually began, only three people made up the entire audience! Needless to say, the creator of such later powerful works, as *Das Ring Der Nibelungen* and the sacred music dramas of *Parsifal* and *Lohengrin*, never witnessed that opera in his lifetime again – presumably thankfully, since it's potential for failure may be found in its very title!

After some uncalled for forced coughing, a hush descended upon the hall once again. With one sweep of his baton, Hans Richter launched into the sublime opening section of Mahler's First Symphony, in which the sustained high octave A-major chord gradually unfolds a sequence of descending *fourths*.

My mind drifted with the music up into the heavens, or at least into the upper reaches of the Royal Albert Hall. Occasionally, my eyes took in the impressive classical architecture of this magnificent building. I especially appreciated the circular colonnade of columns straining up through the space of the building forming arches at the top, upon which was formed an upper perimeter where people were walking round slowly, as though promenading.

Thinking about Wagner's opera '*Das Liebesverbot*', I recall that the Master himself, conducted, here in this very hall, six concerts to mark the Wagner Festival of

1877. Even now, I regret, my not being able to attend that festival of Wagner's music.

Towards the *finale* of the symphony I could not help but think that the architecture of the hall, with its towering columns and expansive arches, reflected the soaring chords and the marshalled massive orchestral forces of Mahler's First Symphony. Both, I concluded, were architectural masterpieces in their complex construction. The symphony concluded with its rapturous hammer chords reverberating throughout the huge auditorium, and in so doing brought the music to triumphant conclusion and to ecstatic applause, which I think, awakened Mahler from his slumbers.

We made our way out of the Royal Albert Hall of Arts and Sciences along with other patrons, at an agonisingly slow pace. Eventually, on emerging into Kensington Gore, we were confronted by a scene of chaos, as the stampede for available carriages was discourteous as it was tremendous. So much so that we decided to resort to the Hyde Park on the other side of the Kensington Gore and make our way to Piccadilly only a short walk away, despite the pervasive fog still with us, rather than involve ourselves in an undignified struggle to gain a carriage.

1 *'The Ban on Love - a Great Comic Opera'.*
2 A group who are by way of being disaffected revolutionaries sworn to disrupt concerts specifically for the *bourgeoisie.*

Chapter 4

The Exhibition Hall at Earl's Court

Much as I enjoyed witnessing the performance of the First Symphony, of which I remain fond, there are still apparent, to me, weaknesses in areas of harmonic expression and continuity. These weaknesses, rising from the depths of uncertainty, are able to qualify Mahler's intention to convey joy and optimism. In particular, the transition from the third movement to the fourth does not complete the ideas developed in the third, which makes the progression into the fourth rather abrupt and unresolved. This experience of the D major Symphony, does not of course, detract from the overall integrity of the symphonic structure and counterpoint, and Mahler's ability to address our souls. It was because of my thoughts on this First Symphony that I endeavored to take Mahler's mind off his intense pre-occupation with his Eighth Symphony. Accordingly, I had persuaded him to agree to accompany me on a visit to the Imperial Austro-Hungarian Exhibition, [1] a hugely popular *extravaganza* attracting record attendances, or at least so the London *Times* newspaper informed us. Having resolved our intention to attend, we referred to the rather over confident, red tail-coated, *concièrge* in his undoubted domain, that of the reception in the foyer of the St. Pancras Hotel.

"To Earl's Court you wish to go? My advice is to ride the urban railroad to it," he replied to my friend's polite inquiry, and then promptly marched off to another part of the reception abandoning us!

I was compelled to motion away a rather indignant and reluctant Mahler from the reception desk.

"I have the solution to hand Gustav," I said, quickly thumbing through my *Baedeker's* guide to London. "His advice was not entirely erroneous, and from what I could make out of this urban railroad map it seemed the quickest way to Earl's Court was to take a train called the Metropolitan-Circle.[2] We can avail ourselves of it from below this very Hotel," I said with a flourish.

Minutes later, we had left the comfortable and opulent surroundings of our Hotel and were enveloped in swirls of the acrid fog that showed no signs of dissipating. Eventually we managed to locate the entrance to what was, I believed, the railroad station from which the Metropolitan-Circle left, *en-route* to Earl's Court. After some uncalled for discourtesy whilst purchasing our tickets, we made our way down to two parallel platforms. A signboard indicated upon which platform we must wait for the Metropolitan-Circle.

It was whilst we were waiting upon the platform, I noticed that not one square inch had escaped the attention of the advertiser. Advertisement posters of every description were plastered on every available surface, including those of railroad equipment and buildings. This plethora of gaudy advertisements made it difficult to search for useful railroad information, and indeed, almost impossible to achieve.

Not with standing this irony, Mahler and I had our attention arrested by a most blatant and preposterous advertisement, affixed to the wall opposite the platform.

My knowledge of chemistry and of the English language was not profound; but neither was it by any means insufficient for even my feeble grasp to understand the absurd claims propounded in this poster. In particular, the advertisement was promoting or exhorting some chemical compound as a veritable modern day elixir! Mahler found the bill poster to be extremely amusing, and wondered whether our *concièrge* could be prevailed upon to procure a bottle of the stuff for us.

Presently, when the Metropolitan-Circle did arrive, it came thundering down the side of the platform creating a rush of wind that blasted the fog in front of the engine out of the way. As the locomotive passed us, it created

---

SUTTON'S COMPOUND
CREAM OF AMMONIA

CLEANS AND RESTORES COLOURS TO CARPETS
ACTS AS A DISINFECTANT IN THE SICK ROOM OR
HOSPITAL HAS NO EQUAL FOR REMOVING
GREASE SPOTS FROM CLOTHES INVALUABLE TO
ENGINEERS FOR REMOVING OIL AND GREASE
MAKES LINEN WHITE AND WOOLLEN GOODS
SOFT CLEANS CULINARY UTENSILS AND PLATE
FOR LAUNDRY PURPOSES SOFTENS HARD
WATER IN YOUR MORNING BATH REMOVES THAT
TIRED FEELING !

---

an instant sensation of heat upon our faces, and from its smokestack discharged a cloud of black smuts, notably onto our topcoats. Finally as the train screeched to a stop, carriage doors were flung open in a reckless manner, allowing passengers to alight on to the platform that all of sudden seethed with humanity moving in different directions.

We attempted to make our way to an open carriage door and after some undignified pushing and determined behaviour, by others, succeeded in boarding the train. We looked about for a seat but found none and were thus compelled to stand. Neither Mahler nor I use the public urban railroad in any city normally, but I find travelling by horse drawn carriage an inefficient and slow method of traversing especially in a Metropolis as London with its unfamiliarity and in dense fog. In this respect trains are quicker if nothing else. I mentioned to Mahler that according to my *Bäedeker's* guide to London, we needed to change trains at an intermediate station called 'Baker Street'.

"'Baker Street', now, that rings a bell," said Mahler, "though for what reason, I could not say. But, I do remember the street having some importance attached to it that I became aware of when I resided in London during the summer of 1892 when I was guest conductor at the Covent Garden Opera House."

"Is there a concert hall located in that street or some other musical establishment? I inquired, becoming curious myself as to the street's significance for no other reason, except to while away the time on our train to Earl's Court.

"I remember!" shouted Mahler in my ear; "I recall the reason why Baker Street stuck in my mind. It was the home of a famous person. A certain Madame Tussauds and her chamber of *grotesque* wax *mannequins* located in the bazaar at 55 Baker Street!"

Looking about the carriage, my attention was arrested by the sight of a woman sitting on the timber cross benches reading a novelette. She wore a purple colored velvet jerkin with red sleeves, slim blue cross-gartered hose and a green cap with a falcon's feather caught in an imitation jewel of olive green chrysoberyl that turns red by lamplight.

Suddenly our train began to slow down and the syncopated clicking of the steel wheels pounding the iron track below decreased in rapidity.

Moments later we steamed into the Baker Street Station.

"We need to change for another train called the Metropolitan-District heading for a place called Wimbledon, where I believe the peculiar English sport of cricket is played, But, *en-route*, the train should call at Earl's Court Station," I said to my friend as we crossed the platform.

"I think you will find it is the game of rugby that they play at Wimbledon, not cricket," Mahler corrected me.

Whatever the sport, our Metropolitan-District did arrive at Earl's Court station. We alighted on to a particularly busy platform and made our way at an agonizingly slow pace through a *labyrinth* of corridors packed with people and up into the street, albeit a fog-bound street.

On the other side of the road was a large Victorian structure constructed of brickwork, iron columns and girders and glass window panes with which the walls and roof were covered. We walked up a wide and steep set of steps into the massive Exhibition Hall, a veritable cathedral of iron columns all stretching up to a steel glazed apex roof. The Exhibition Hall was illuminated with large coal gas-fueled lamps, in the form of clusters of white *opaque* globes, pouring out their powerful light onto a dark timber decking along which we now walked to purchase our tickets and brochure.

From what we could make out in the pamphlet, the Austria-Hungarian Exposition had several and distinct themes, including a typical 'Tyrolean Village', woodcarvers, lace-makers, cafés, essential bier-kellers and an underground salt mine.

Not that Mahler needed to be informed about any of these, since he was of course born in the Bohemian village of Kalischt in the Margravate of Moravia within the imperial territories of the Austro-Hungarian Emperor, Franz Joseph I.

The Exposition, I noted was to be opened by no less an individual in the person of the Count Lützow. I am not sure that we know this count, but however, knew for certain that we had in the recent past met with the acclaimed Josef Jindřich Šechtl, whose skill in creating silver-nitrate images without recourse to the *daguerreotype* method was legendary. Unfortunately, he was nowhere to be found, when we at length called upon him to renew our acquaintance. Instead, we spent some time walking about among what was familiar to Mahler, though not to me. I was content to view what exhibits they had on display, some of which reminded me of Vienna, the capital of our Austro-Hungarian Empire. And, if nothing else, it was a welcome respite from a fog-bound London with a rather infamous *première* to let loose upon a notoriously conservative London audience.

Having made our way around this rather gaudy collection of what, I could not really say, Mahler was moved to describe the whole experience, including the lace-makers, as more reminiscent of a trip to the circus, a feature of his childhood years and needless to say, something that he had been compelled to endure.

In order to avail ourselves of some fresh air, if such could be had in the midst of this huge Metropolis, I did manage to persuade Mahler to ride the huge Great Ferris Wheel fabricated of iron and towering three hundred feet in height, straight into the fog-laden aëther above Earl's Court.

No sooner had we commenced our cycle upwards, than a feeling of being violently sick gripped Mahler, who thereafter was compelled to stand in the corner of the carriage, facing away from other passengers, least he had to perform his sickly function. Whilst looking at Mahler, I noticed, through the adjacent carriage windows, a huge somber-looking building, more reminiscent of the upper section to an Aztec temple. The presence of this Aztec styled building constructed of massive limestone blocks, in the midst of Earl's Court seems incongruous, I thought.

However, by the time I had reconciled that incongruity, we had descended to earth, and it was all my friend could do to stagger down the steps from the Ferris apparatus and into a nearby cloakroom. Eventually he reappeared looking slightly less sallow and just perhaps more alive than dead.

We then reëntered the iron-fabricated hall and in so doing another spasm took hold of Mahler with such vehemence as to cause him to nearly pass out. It was all I could do to help him to a nearby cast iron bench. Having settled him down, and made inquiries of him, he responded slowly at first, but pointing to a position behind me. I turned around only to be confronted by a scene, an almost exact replication of the iron and glass structure that is the München Ausstellungs Halle! All exhibition halls are much the same and are built to keep

Aztec Building

the weather off the exhibitors and exhibits, whilst allowing the maximum amount of daylight to shine through large glazed areas that comprise the roof and walls of the structures.

It was a peculiarity of this hall at Earl's Court that it resembled in every detail the steel and glass hall at München. The vision of the steel and glass structure immediately brought back vivid images of the building wherein the cause of our present anxieties and tribulation were created! This building's style and architecture could not have been more reminiscent of failure, and its similarity had triggered something dormant in the subconscious of my friend and the implication of its presence I found disturbing.

We abandoned the Exhibition Hall immediately and made our way down to the Earl's Court Station. There we hoped to catch a train of the Metropolitan-District line going back to Baker Street Station. Here we would change again for the Metropolitan-Circle heading to King's Cross urban railroad station above which I knew to be the St. Pancras Hotel, a place of safety for the time being. It was probably just as well we retired early, for in the morning, part of the real business of our being in London would commence. It was an arranged meeting, at the Langham Hotel, with members of the Fourth Estate,[3] comprising correspondents from various newspapers eager to learn about Mahler's *première* of his Eighth Symphony!

1 The Imperial Austro-Hungarian Exhibition was in 1906
2 The District Railway operated by the Metropolitan Railway
3 One of the Estates of the Establishment concerned with journalism

Chapter 5

The Encounter with the Fourth Estate

The next day our Clarence carriage delivered us to the front the Langham Hotel, as instructed. Later we gathered in the *foyer* of the Langham Hotel, located conveniently opposite the Queen's Hall in Langham Place. Mahler was looking forward, though full of aspiration, but with some concern, for the opportunity of hopefully reëstablishing the Eighth Symphony and gaining its acceptance into the musical *repertoire*, thus far denied him. He was especially anxious to promote the work beyond its disappointing *première* earlier at München in the Exhibition Hall. Looking around the *foyer* we could see a large number of correspondents and accordingly, our hopes for a successful conference with these gentlemen of the press, the Fourth Estate, were reasonably high.

"Good morning Mr. Mahler, I am from the *Morning Post;* for the record do we call you *Mister* or do you prefer that we address you as *Maestro?*"

"*'Maestro'* is, I believe the appropriate title!" answered Mahler, with confidence.

"Thank you *Mahler.*"

"I represent *The Globe*, in this respect; please tell us Mahler, what do the newspaper critics call you?"

"A variety of titles, all of which are courteous!" replied Gustav.

The Daily Telegraph inquired, "Is it true you are a fanatical Bi-cyclist and quite an authority on the Rudge-Whitworth *velocipede* upon which you hope to enter the London to Brighton Bi-Cycle Tournament and, is that why you are in London, to train for the race?" [1]

"By-cycle, London to Brighton?" inquired Mahler, searchingly.

"Yes," enjoined a reporter from *The Times*, "who would you say your main competitor is, in the world of bi-cycling? Could it the sober Frenchman Pierre Delacroix, who, as a result, is reported to have reached, on his new improved aluminum *velocipede*, an unimaginable speed in excess of twelve statute miles within a continuous period of one hour?"

"Who is this sober Frenchman Pierre Delacroix?" asked Mahler.

"Do you think that you could beat that record, Gustav?" asked the correspondent from the *Daily Chronicle,* "and, will your drinking affect your chances of success against Pierre on the track?"

"Drink, by that do you mean having the occasional glass of beer of an evening, or the odd glass of Chianti or Moselle?" asked Mahler.[2]

"Yes I do," continued the *Daily Chronicle.*

"Mahler, I am from the popular best selling newspaper *"The Echo"*. Do you consider yourself as being part of a group, - as in the 'Famous Five'?"

"What are you talking about?" asked a rather confused Mahler, "are they a bi-cycling team that I ought to be aware of?"

"A bi-cycling team; I am talking about *the Famous Five* as in the Russian composers? You know, Balakirev, Cui, Borodin, Mussorgsky and Rimsky-Korsakov!"

"Who?" inquired Mahler.

"With regard to your London *première*, why do you call your Eighth Symphony the *'Symphonie der Tausend?'*" asked the reporter from the *London Chronicle*, "is that not a bit pompous?"

"That title *'Symphonie der Tausend'* is neither of my invention nor suggestion; rather it was given the *sobriquet* by an overzealous Emil Gutmann who was concert manager at the München *première"*.

"I understand you bask in the after-glow of knowledge that you are the sole surviving member of that elite group of composers known as the 'E Rs'? That is to say, all those great composers whose names end with the letters 'er'. Such as Web*er*, Bruckn*er*, Wagn*er* and of course yourself – Mahl*er*."

"Purely co-incidental; what can I say, except that I agree with it?"

"Would you say that a tragic theme pervades all your symphonic and *lieder* compositions?" inquired the correspondent from the *Daily News*.

"No, I personally would not quite put it like that," replied my friend.

"How would you put it?" continued the reporter from the *Daily News*.

"Aspects of life can be sorrowful as well as joyful," replied Mahler.

"Would that theme conveying sorrow, your distinct *métier*, be consistent with the three monumental hammer blows with which you bring your Symphony in A minor [3] to a conclusion, signifying death or despair?" continued the *Daily News*.

Mahler looked surprised at the reporter's incisive question.

"By that," continued the *Daily News*, "in the last movement you describe yourself and your destruction, or as you later said, the destruction of your hero; a hero who suffers three strokes of Fate, of which the third fells him like a tree, your words *Maestro*. Or, are you inspired by Wagner's three massive hammer blows which precede Siegfried's funeral march in Act III from *Götterdämmerung*. Or, indeed the hammer blows which rained down in concluding Act II, the real *finale,* to *Götterdämmerung?*"

"The Sixth Symphony expresses a range of emotions and responses," replied Gustav Mahler.

"Would such a range of despair include a description of your new wife Alma Schindler, the daughter of the famous painter Emil Schindler, to whom you said, 'I have tried to capture you in one of the themes in the first movement – whether I have succeeded I do not know, you will just have to put up with it, but the symphony describes you accurately!'" quoted the *Daily News* reporter.

"Mr. Mahler, what is the *sobriquet,* or the title of your A minor Symphony in which you describe your new wife?" asked the *Daily News*, in a nonchalant manner.

"Die Tragische!" Mahler answered, hesitantly.

A few of the reporters, I noticed turned away and began to giggle behind their note pads.

"But," continued Mahler in an attempt to lend *gravitas* to the proceedings, "I do hold with Goethe's dictum, that 'the artist must create what the public ought to like, not what it does like'."

"Really," replied the correspondent from the *Morning Post*, "how do you explain the remarks made by Klaus Pringsheim when commenting on your rehearsal of that Sixth Symphony in Essen in 1906? Allow me to remind you, and I paraphrase: '...when Mahler conducted an orchestra in rehearsal, it was more a question of trying the music out, rather than rehearsing it. Right up to the

last rehearsal before the *première*, he would make altera-
tions, improvements and try out new solutions. It was
as if he suffered from an inner uncertainty or a persistent
indecision regarding his own work and would canvass
opinions from a few persons close to him who were in
the auditorium. This was not always the case and Mahler
might take advice from relative strangers; one such
person was the twenty-two year old pianist Gabrilovitch.
This obscure *répétiteur* from Vienna, was given an important function, that of being allowed to 'conduct' the
off-stage cowbells!'"

"The creation of any art may involve considering other
peoples' ideas in resolving a particular *impasse;* it does not
necessarily indicate indecision or inability," replied Gustav, "nor necessarily be in conflict with Goethe's dictum."

"Would you say your earlier symphonies reveal a tragic
theme in your life and the frequent disappointment of
human aspiration?" asked the reporter from *The Echo*.
"And with regard to your Symphony No 6, the *'Tragische'*,
both Berg and Schönberg, two young composers I
believe you know, admire it and in fact allude to aspects
of classical form to it. Might you agree Mr. Mahler, that
your symphony reflects that dual and conflicting consciousness propounded by Hegel in his' *The Phenomenology
of Spirit'*, where he alludes to the concept of unhappy
consciousness'– divided between recognition of divine
providence and less than perfect self awareness?"

"The fact of both Berg and Schönberg, admire the
symphony and in fact alluding to aspects of classical form
to it, is of course a matter of their opinion," responded
Mahler.

"Both Arnold Schönberg and Alban Berg have stated
publicly that they recognise elements in your music which
they considered point the way in music development as

manifested in the post Wagnerian work. Especially in the case of Schönberg, and his composition *Gurrelieder*, and as you know, this was composed in 1901 just after his *Verkläte Nacht*. Both deploy huge orchestral and choral forces. Do you agree that these works represent a precursor of your Eighth Symphony composed nine years later, and contemporaneous with Strauss *Feuersnot* or Sigmund Freud's seminal book '*The Interpretation of Dreams?*" inquired the *Daily News*.

"One could state that easily and with equanimity about any composer addressing the great philosophies and ideas prevalent at the time. Music today is composed to express ideas, to put into musical form ideas that perhaps cannot be conveyed elsewhere," replied Mahler.

"Indeed," said the correspondent for *The Echo*, "your friend, the critic, Robert Hirschfeld, wrote in the *Wiener Abendpost* in January 1907 about your Sixth Symphony No. 6 in A minor, *Die Tragische,* 'that if you were capable of expressing tragic feelings through the power of musical sound, you could readily dispense with the hammer and its fateful blows. But, you lack that inner, genuine creative strength. So in your Tragic Symphony, at the highest peak of excitement, you reach for the hammer; where the music fails, a hammer falls!'"

This reporter from *The Echo* was being facetious; by no means could Robert Hirschfeld be considered a close or even a distant friend of Gustav Mahler's. In fact Hirschfeld was the main figure in the adverse campaign that was constantly waged against Mahler.

"The symphony must be like the world. It must embrace everything, as I remarked to the Finish composer, Jean Sibelius on meeting him in Helsinki and to Eliel Saarinen in the Fall of 1907. I also had cause to repeat this injunction when, a few days later, discussing with Saarinen

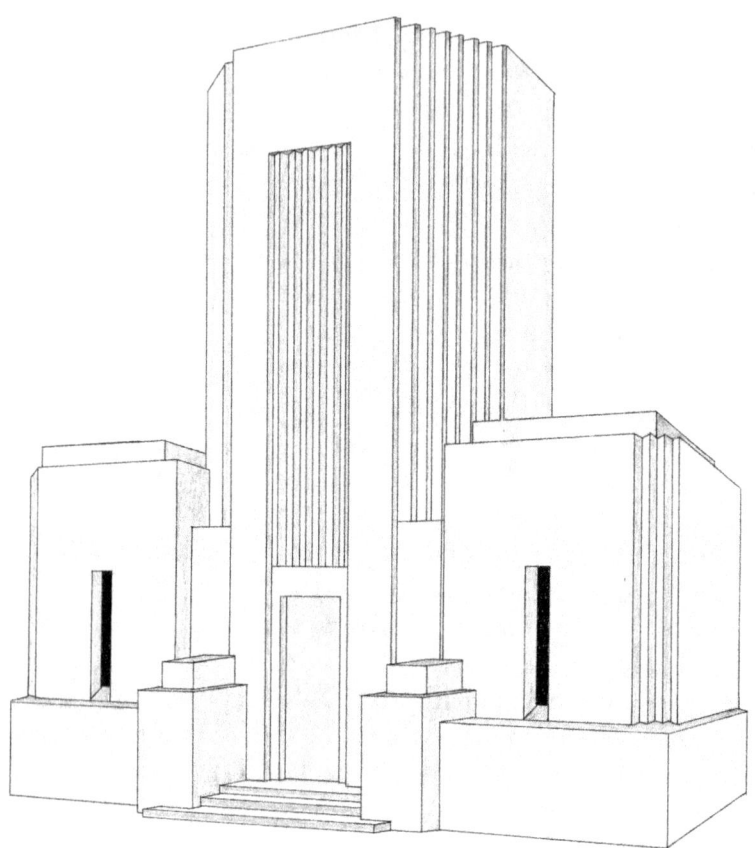

Mausoleum at Joensuu

his proposed designs for a Mausoleum at Joensuu. Here
we both agreed that form must represent something other
than the obvious, built out of brick or stone. Not quite
function following form, but rather, form following
function. It must reflect a *rationale* in it design to elicit a
response. In the case of Saarinen's design; he is seeking
to invoke regret and sadness at the loss of someone
through a process of nature. But at the same time a

celebration for those who continue, and the fact of their being able to respond readily to that invocation of feeling loss," said Mahler, in an confident manner.

The Daily Telegraph's man was quick to conjoin here, "Is that a fact Mr. Mahler, because we have it on good authority that your *protegé* Bruno Walter, the conductor, is reported to have said that when Rickard Strauss criticized your Sixth Symphony, you were depressed almost to tears? And, that he also remarked that the Sixth was 'over scored', a comment that worried you for a long time and ultimately caused you make extensive revisions including thinning out huge orchestral passages. It that your interpretation of the symphony embracing every-thing?"

"One can always improve upon a work," replied Gustav.

"You have already alluded to Goethe's dictum and that of canvassing ideas from friends, but can this then later justify extensive revision; how do you balance this apparent dichotomy?" asked *The Echo's* reporter.

"Simply as part of the creating process," Mahler answered incisively.

"Following on in your tragic vein Mr. Mahler, could you tell us about your Third Symphony, the one, in D minor, a doom-ridden key, would you not agree?" asked the gentleman from the *London Chronicle*.

"D minor?" repeated Gustav, but before he could answer it, the reporter from the *Morning Post* interjected.

"Just for the record Mr. Mahler, could you clarify the following, by answering, the questions raised in that symphony?"

Mahler looked perplexed, as indeed I was curious.

"In your symphony, you claimed that the inherent gaiety is not going to be understood or appreciated! It is that gaiety, that rises above your previous symphonies in the first and second – with their conflict and pain and can exist only as a product of the world.

You then go on to claim the name *symphony* would be inappropriate; as the work does not follow the traditional form. The term *symphony* means an ability to construct from existing resources and available techniques. In this respect, you say, that you must always first learn to re-create your medium of expression. Accordingly you introduced language in the form of the human voice into your Second Symphony to make yourself understood.

You regretted not applying that *technique* in the First Symphony, but applied it in the second and third by incorporating two poems from *Des Knaben Wunderhorn* and a poem by Nietzsche. The sound of military music is heard, in order to effect the arrival of the martial hero. A struggle ensues between the two adversaries; winter and summer, with summer ultimately vanquishing winter. Naturally, this movement will be kept humorous, even *grotesque*! I quote you Mr. Mahler:

"It then continues with:

'I.   Summer marching in.

II.   What the flowers in the meadow tell me!

III.   What the animals in the forest tell me!

IV.   What the night tells me!

V.   What the morning bells tell me!

VI.   What love tells me!

VII. What the child tells me!'

It is true, that about no other work are you so loquacious and communicative. You then decided to call this collection your 'Joyous Science', a title; I believe you have taken from Nietzsche?" asked the man from the *Morning Post*.

There was a profound silence as the enormity of what

the reporter from the *Morning Post* had asked of Mahler became apparent and its implications understood. Indeed the assemble journalist looked at my friend for some kind of explanation.

The silence was deafening.

It was the *Daily Chronicle* who got in first with the predictable follow-on question; or indeed a Mahlerian hammer blow.

"Persons who are well- known, famous even, are naturally reluctant to put their name to anything or indeed to promote an idea. Be it a matter of principle or of ambition to achieve one's goal in life, as you alluded to a few moments' ago. But, is it a matter of public record, that you personally endorse Dunlop's new improved vulcanized rubber tires for use on your *velocipede* when you enter Pan Moravian Bi-Cycling Championship to be held in Budapest?"

"What are we now discussing, Wagner's Ring Cycle? Is that a new type of improved Bi-Cycle or, is Wagner a bi-cyclist too?" asked the esteemed correspondent from *The Times*.

"People say you are full of doom and gloom Gustav and that your outlook on life is one of pessimism, given vivid expression in your favorite axiom; 'that every silver lining has a dark cloud!' Is this true?" asked *The Echo's* reporter. "And," he continued, "that this pessimism was given full reign during a String Quartet concert in 1907 when a fight broke out in the Dress Circle and you were only saved then by the intercession of the bigger lad, your friend, Carl Moll, the builder of your new house near Vienna?"

"Allow me to refute that slanderous remark once and for all," insisted my friend, Gustav Mahler, "I was invited to a performance of Schönberg's, String Quartet, the opus 7. During the undisturbed recital given by the Rosé Quartet, a critic suddenly shouted at the quartet to stop. That act let loose from the audience a *barrage* of discourteous noises and shouts. It was a fact that one individual positioned himself in front of Schönberg, who was sitting in a seat in the front row, and hissed loudly in his face. I went up to intervene but the man raised his fist to strike me a blow but was prevented from doing so by the timely arrival of Moll who separated us. Later the man, who hissed at Schönberg, confessed to hissing at performances of my work too."

"*Pall Mall Gazette* here Mr. Mahler; my fellow correspondents have just asked you about the sorrowful ideas expressed in your compositions, such as *Kindertotenlieder*, 4 a composition, where your wife, Alma was even moved to say to you, 'For God's sake you are tempting providence!'5 This was expressed by their keys, sometimes doom-ridden, like D major, the dominant key in your *Titan* Symphony?   But other works include *Das Trinklied von Jammer der Erde,* and, *Dunkel ist das leben, ist der Tod,* or *Der Einsame im Herbst.* Though, *Der trunkene in Frühling,* where the mood is predictably livelier, but still not happy!6   Incidentally, we note that the Titan Symphony was performed by the break-away London Symphony Orchestra, under the renowned conductor, Hans Richter, at no less than a promenade concert, at the Royal Albert Hall of Arts and Sciences recently."

"Yes my First Symphony, *The Titan,* was performed, as you say, at the Royal Albert Hall; and no I disagree, the key of D major is not doom-ridden!" said Mahler.

"Why do you call it *The Titan?*"

This question came not from the assembled esteemed journalists, the members of the Fourth Estate, but rather from a liveried hotel porter, who was leaning against a fluted green *Verde Acceglio* marble column. Mahler looked bemused, but answered him.

"Because the name, *The Titan,* derives from a book, of the same title, that I read by a fellow called Jean Paul Richter."

"Hang on there! Was not the First Symphony written by a chap called Hans Rott?" inquired *The Globe.*

"I think you are right," insisted the reporter from *The Echo,* "well let us ask Gustav."

"Let me quash these rumors once and for all...' insisted Mahler.

"Did Hans Rott write the First Symphony?" asked the journalist form the *Daily News.*

"But that was years ago," said Mahler "why do you drag up the past; is it because the English are obsessed with history and the yesterday?"

There was a stunned silence throughout the ornately decorated and expansive *foyer,* complete with various palm trees, and even the hotel liveried porter had abandoned his prime position next to the fluted green *Verde Acceglio* marble column.

"It is that ability that separates us English from the rest of the world, apart from our Empire!" said a lone voice emanating from the *St. James' Gazette.*

"Retrospective nostalgia is corrosive of the mind and lethal to the genesis of the creative process, surely you are better searching for the new than dragging up the old," replied Mahler, attempting to recover the initiative he had lost, due to his *faux pas,* and he may have succeeded, but the *Daily News* got there first.

"No, it is the old stories that are the best," retorted the correspondent for the *Daily News,* "because they simply go on and on!"

"If I can just pick up from my colleague there at the *Daily News*", said the journalist from *The Echo*, "about the old stories being the best because they keep going on and on; can you confirm the truth of Hans Rott and is there any basis of fact in the rumor?"

"That is a very interesting question," replied Mahler, "next question please!"

"What?" expressed *The Echo* member of the Fourth Estate, clearly unused to such flippant remarks.

"Am I not here to answer question about my *première?*" asked Mahler.

A silence again descended upon the room; the kind that is deafening in its intensity as journalists looked at each other with puzzled expressions. However, the Fourth Estate, used to such situations, was gathered to gain information not stand in respectful silence. After all, it was their job to know about such awkward things, though I knew at once that it would have been Mahler's old foe Pollini, who had alerted the gentlemen from the newspapers about the Hans Rott episode.

Notwithstanding this episode, the press conference was turning into another *débâcle*, so often associated with Mahler's public appearance. His temperament was not well suited to dealing with flippant members of the Fourth Estate, in any country. Mahler, by his demeanor, could come over very readily, as arrogant and antagonistic. Of course these characteristics are precisely what journalist focus on and, because of their constant practice in doing so, become adept and able to recognize and deal effectively with those innate characteristics, displayed. Witness the letter from Siegfried Lipiner [7] dated November, 1896 to the general management of the Imperial-Royal Court Theaters in Vienna regarding Mahler's application for the position of conductor at the Vienna

Court Opera. '…It has been pointed out to me that Mahler's temperament, his ways of dealing with opposition, is not always well spoken of…'

"Perhaps the *Maestro* would enlighten us on a profound subject, that must concern you, when composing deep and meaningful symphonies, as the ones we have been talking about here? The question is, where on earth do you find the time, with all your other commitments, including being head of the family, to train on your bi-cycle, and, is it your fervent dream to represent Bohemia in the forthcoming International Velocipede Championship and put your arch-rival Pierre Delacroix to shame?" asked the journalist from *The Daily Telegraph*.

"Would you agree with the notion that the German, being in search of a national identity, is a rather intense individual?" asked one frock-coated member of the Fourth Estate.

"No, I would not," replied Mahler.

"Which makes for German art, music, literature and philosophy, a conduit for this latent anxiety, and given expression in the condition of *angst*?" continued the frock-coated journalist.

"The Teutonic people have always maintained a serious approach to life, as we see it as something to be enjoyed and experienced fully. To be able to do this, one needs to understand the great and prevalent ideals which may equip one in achieving this eminent state of existence, no?" inquired Mahler.

"Other nations appear able to achieve this eminent state, as you call it," replied the frock-coated correspondent, "without recourse to anxiety as a natural condition of existence, which makes for an *angst*-ridden and introspective society; why even your language is petrified in defense, yes?"

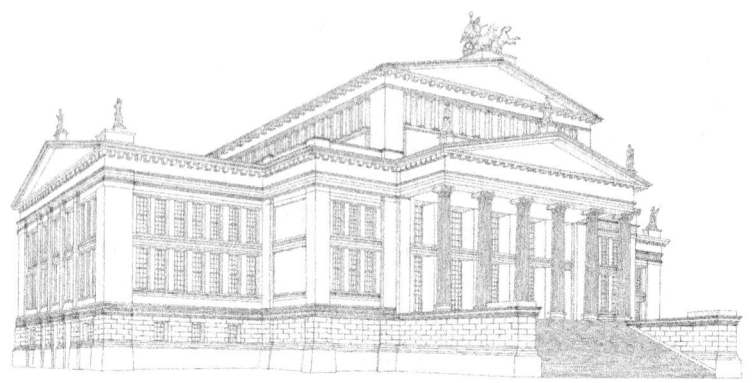

Schauspielhaus, Berlin

Looking at my friend, Mahler, he appeared to be somewhat perturbed by this inquisitive line of questioning and merely viewed the reporter with suspicion. The frock-coated journalist, on detecting Mahler's hesitation, seized the initiative and continued his line of inquiry, by answering his own question that my friend would not.

"For example," said the journalist, "in recognizing the awareness of, petrified in defense', being current throughout the Teutonic language; I am thinking of the fiasco in 1902, of your Third Symphony, that was not received well at its *première* in Berlin at the Schauspielhaus? In that Third Symphony you quote words taken from Nietzsche's '*Also Sprach Zarathustra*' [8] in the opening chorus of the fourth movement.

Oh man! Take heed!
What does the deep midnight say?
'I slept, I slept!
I have awakened from a deep dream,
The world is deep,
And deeper than the day remembers,

Deep is its suffering,
Joy is deeper yet than heartache!
Suffering speaks: Be gone!
All joys want eternity,
Want deep, deep eternity,

Irrespective of the fact that Nietzsche seems incapable of deploying synonyms for the word *deep*, would you say that these lines, which make up this *stanza* are profound and, that you yourself are subject to this conditioning, since you have incorporated this desired ideal into your Third Symphony composed in the doom-laden key of D minor?" inquired the frock-coated correspondent.

"As I said a few minutes ago, the Teutonic peoples have always approached life seriously, and see it as something to be enjoyed and experienced fully." replied Mahler, confidently.

This exchange itself was becoming all too intense and was turning rapidly into an *impromptu* debate and not quite what one expected at a press conference, called specifically to publicize the London *première* of the Eighth Symphony. Even Mahler was moved to terminate this rather tenacious and awkward development perpetrated by the very determined frock-coated correspondent.

"May I ask for which newspaper you write?" inquired Mahler.

"Yes, I write for *Sporting Life,*" replied the frock-coated gentleman.

---

1 Mahler was a keen, if inexperienced, bi-cyclist, as intimated to Natalie Bauer-Lechner and the critic Wilhelm Zinne in 1895
2 Alfred Roller's description of evening life at *Maiernigg am Wörthersee*, during which Mahler never touched spirits
3 The Symphony No. 6 in A minor

4 Songs on the death of children
5 Per Mahler's friend Alfred Roller
6 Drinking song of the sorrow of the earth;   Dark is life dark is death;
  The lonely one in Autumn;   The drunkard in Spring
7 Librarian of the Austrian Parliament
8 *Thus Spoke Zarathustra,* a philosophical work by Nietzsche

Chapter 6

The Green Baize Doors

We stepped smartly across a road called Langham Place, towards the Queen's Hall, in the hope the prevalent fog would afford us concealment and protection from the prying eyes of the Fourth Estate. In addition, I was aghast to realize that not one correspondent in the *foyer,* at that so-called press conference, had actually asked any question remotely to do with the *première* of the Eighth Symphony. I could not help thinking that we had created the fertile conditions for misfortune to thrive in. Hopefully the rehearsal would restore the very *rationale* that brought us to this fog-bound Metropolis. A few moments later we were standing on the footpath outside the Queen's Hall in Langham Place. It was in this august auditorium that the *première* was to take place and hopefully restore my friend's reputation, though privately my soul was filled with a nameless foreboding. Mahler, in contrast appeared to be in good spirits, despite the press conference, and was looking forward to carrying all before him in his inevitable triumph. I hoped so. His enthusiasm continued unbounded as he surveyed the *facade* of the Queen's Hall.

"It is not so much a concert hall," he said, as we both stood on the edge of the pavement, looking at this classical stone structure, as a huge pantechnicon lumbered by, "but rather a temple to music and this fact is reflected in its grandiose design. See the rich ornate detailing and the myriad busts of our great composers as Mozart, Gluck, and Handel!"

"The exposed balcony on the *piano-nobile* is festooned with various statues in the form of torsos of Greek gods that were fixed to the front in between several French windows that allowed access to the terrace and air during a concert interval. Look at that overhanging limestone frame triangular pediment supported by those fluted columns capped with Corinthian capitals." I said pointing to them with my cane. We then walked in to the hall past two stone statues of Olympian gods in the guise of *Atlas*, who appeared at that very moment to be bearing the entire weight of the building upon their broad shoulders.

Having introduced ourselves, we were escorted to the General Manager's office, through a *labyrinthine* set of corridors, the kind of which would have defeated *Theseus* in his quest. Eventually, we arrived at the green baize covered doors, and were ushered into a large airy room. A well-appointed comfortable chamber in fact, with of course, the compulsory ubiquitous palm tree growing out of an urn made of glazed stone. Hanging upon the wall was an extensive array of images of musicians, clutching their fragile instruments. Complementing these images were framed likenesses of artistes, in impossible poses and with banal expressions upon their faces. I looked around the impressive collection of images of immortalized composers or musicians, placed there in an attempt to lend verisimilitude to this room.

There was, for some reason, a photograph of Sarah Bernhardt, the name assumed by Rosine Bernard, in the improbable pose of the lawyer, Portia. And likewise, adjacent to her portrait was a sepia tinted *daguerreotype* of Lily Langtry, who was as famous for her on stage performances, as she was for her Blue Ribbon [1] activities off stage.

Mahler and I made ourselves comfortable on Chippendale chairs, the seats of which were covered in a pink *moiré* silk, to await our host. In front of us was a large ornately carved mahogany desk with inlaid red leather on its writing surface. On each of the two corners of the desk nearest to us, was a bronze lamp radiating a soft light through an *opaque* and patterned glass lamp shade. In between these lamps was an elaborate and pretentiously decorated red *Rosso Verona* marble inkwell and combined quill stand.

The General Manager's office was well appointed with expensive items of furniture ranged around a large airy room with a high ceiling, from which was suspended an intricate brass and crystal *chandelier*. On the walls, covered in red flock wallpaper with raised velvet decoration, were large gilt-framed paintings of sylvan scenes, including a Claude Loraine that I recognized. [2] Set into one wall, were three elongated, ceiling high french windows leading out onto a balcony fenced with iron railings. Pulled back and secured with gold coloured twisted cord were *brocade* curtains. In the middle of one of the walls, was an *alabaster* bust of some Victorian worthy [3] flanked by attendant palm trees in highly polished green urns

Against the opposite wall was constructed an extensive library filled with musical programs and bound orchestral scores. The floor of this office was uncarpeted and bare, made up of elm floorboards, which created a soft warm impression. In the corner of the room was a well-appointed bar, no doubt essential for easing contractual negotiations with the various artists and musicians that invariably present their skills or talent for performance in this august hall to the Muses.

More the office of a *dilettante* given the air of sumptuous and opulent indulgence, than a hardheaded concert hall manager, I concluded.

Voices were heard outside, becoming louder as they approached the closed door to the chamber. We both rose from our seats in anticipation. Moments later the door burst opened and in stepped two men, one of whom was wearing a black morning coat, striped trousers and spats covering a pair of highly polished patent leather black boots. His shirt was of white cotton and completed with a neck-tie of mauve silk fastened with a pin finished with a stone of *lapis-lazuli*, his only concession to fashion. As he approached Mahler he threw down onto a nearby *chaise longue* a shiny black silk coat with a collar of luxuriant Astrakhan fur.

"*Maestro, maestro!* You have arrived. Welcome to the Queen's Hall, I am Robert Newman and this is Mr. Henry Wood, our esteemed resident conductor and founder of our series of Promenade Concerts."

As he reached our position and shook our hands respectively, his gold rimmed monocle fell from his eye and in so doing revealed his unencumbered face. Newman was a jovial red-faced individual who then repaired to the bar located in the corner of the room and poured into four fluted glasses, chilled champagne. In addition, he poured himself an even healthier measure of whisky, to which he added a brown colored aërated beverage of sorts.

"Henry, one for you?" asked Newman. He motioned us to sit down and asked how my friend wished to proceed.

"What is that dark brown beverage you are pouring into your whisky?" inquired Mahler, out of curiosity.

"Oh this, the *Coca~Cola;* it is a dark, aërated beverage made with cocaine and sugar, and has more punch to it than your ordinary Schweppes aërated water, probably due to its being laced with cocaine!" replied the manager, whilst applying a lighted taper to his *trichinopoly* cigar, that had he taken out of his leather pocket cigar case, "I became addicted to the stuff when we were touring America."

Mahler, very experienced in such matters, spoke at length about the *première* and explained his requirements, both in terms of acoustics and other sundry matters. Newman accepted these without reservation. Henry Wood then went on to explain orchestral details to Mahler, after which we all stood up and shook hands. It was all very civilized; and that the talks were conciliatory and conducted with expediency and understanding was probably due to the three bottles of champagne we had consumed during that time.

Mahler then wandered over to a set of silver nitrate sepia-tinted *daguerreotype* images of composers in the far corner. I could not, from my position, determine who they were exactly, but assumed them to be of sufficient importance to attract my friend's attention. Indeed my supposing this to be the case was vindicated when Mahler produced his pocket book and wrote in it.

"Pray gentlemen, please let me take you into the auditorium and there introduce you to the Queen's Hall Orchestra, who await your arrival" suggested the Newman.

1 An abominable society committed to banning alcohol in drink.
2 *Landscape with Psyche and the Palace of Amor.*
3 The composer Henry Purcell.

Chapter 7

The Rehearsal

My friend, Gustav Mahler was about to begin rehearsals with the Queen's Hall orchestra and chorus, making up a total complement of just less than a thousand performers. Present were instruments not normally seen within a traditional orchestra, such as bass tuba, bass clarinet, contra-bassoon, and glockenspiel. Those instruments one normally sees within the orchestra were greatly increased in number for this occasion; twenty-four first violins and twenty second violins, sixteen violas, fourteen violoncellos, twelve double basses, four mandolins and four harps. The brass section fielded eight trumpets and seven trombones. The King of Instruments had also been coöpted to add its weight to this mighty assembly of orchestral forces needed to perform the Eighth Symphony. To complement the orchestra, there were scores of children further supported by an immense adult choir.

One of the criticisms leveled at the symphony, or at least by a low ranking critic, was that with the exception to the closing section of the end of the first movement, and of the *finale* to the symphony, and by that he meant, literally the closing bars, there was little to commend it. Despite the fact it marshals huge orchestral forces to give expression to its concepts, it succeeds, not in the *Veni Creator Spiritus;* but in only creating a loud sound. That criticism in itself is not helpful; but it does stress that, if one is not amenable or indeed receptive to the symphony as it is, then there is much that can be criticized. Nothing new in this or any innovative new work; the difference here is that the symphony is ambitious in lots of respects, not least in logistical problems in performing it. Would that it were a string symphony, but then one's ability to express concepts with such an orchestra would be severely compromised.

But in his so doing, Mahler abandoned the ideal of what could be called 'absolute music', and was therefore compelled to retreat to the concept of *sound* being the carrier of the idea. In this respect the symphony is programmatic – creating mystical images and feelings in the mind of the listener in order to address a voracious appetite of the imperishable soul.

"Right, we are going to take it from the first section," I heard Mahler command the orchestra.

I   Veni Creator Spiritus.

"And, ladies and gentlemen of the orchestra and chorus; let us attempt to do so with significance and meaning," said Mahler as he tapped his baton on the podium railing. I marked time and kept notation on my copy of the score. We had barely progressed into the fourth section from,

II   Scene from Faust
III   Pater Profundus
IV   Angels

when Mahler brought the proceedings to an abrupt halt. "You, the brass section are one beat behind and second strings constantly trailing on your picking up from fist violins.

Cannot you sight read?" asked Mahler, exasperated. "What elements of you down there, in the brass section are you attempting to perform, because it is beyond me?

Are you rehearsing my symphony, or perhaps someone else's work?"

V   More Perfect Angels
VI   Blessed Youth
VII   Doctor Marianus
VIII   Doctor Marianus and Choir
IX   Mater Gloriosa
X   Penitent Women

On numerous occasions I had lost my place chase reading, as though conducting, because Mahler would keep going back and re-visiting a section he felt still weak. I can only imagine the frustration coursing through his veins as he repeated passage after passage in the forlorn hope the performers might pick up what it was they were supposed to be doing at the appropriate time. It was for that reason that I nearly fell asleep during the orchestra's coördinated and precise transition to the sectional *finale*, where in creating the *crescendo*, the kettledrum failed to achieve the full strength of the *fortissimo* scored for the part. Mahler let that incident go and proceeded to tackle section XI with determination and gusto.

XI   Magna Peccatrix
XII   Mulier Samaritana
XIII   Maria Aegyptiaca
XIV   All Three
XV   Una Poenitentium
XVI   Blessed Youth

Mahler's determination was there; alas however, the gusto from the performers was not. My friend was much irritated at this failure, and he expressed it by a sustained octave in the form of an admonishment, screeched at all in general and the brass section, again, in particular. Nonetheless, he persevered in his attempt to galvanize them into a homogeneous whole.

XVII	Una Poenitentium
XVIII	Mater Gloriosa

The mistake seemed to be beyond rectifying, and indeed Mahler let this fact be known. He was not exaggerating in his intentions, and from the stall seats, where I was sitting, witnessed his frustration with that instrument. During this closing passage, Mahler jumped down from the podium and rushed through the orchestra to the kettledrum. Whereupon, on reaching it, he grabbed the sticks from the player's hands and began to beat the drum in a way that he wanted the passage to be played. He did this with such determination and force, as to cause the sticks to bounce off the skin of the drum and ascend into the air, landing some distance away behind the orchestra. So astonishing was this *impromptu* demonstration by Mahler, that members of the orchestra and some visitors spontaneously burst into rapturous applause.

"The final section ladies and gentlemen of the orchestra and chorus," said Mahler, "lets us do justice to my work with dignity and with an eye on the *tempo* as we proceed to the *finale*. Try to think of Heaven when you play and sing, or God help me, I shall dispatch you all to that place forthwith!"

XIX	Doctor Marianus
XX	Chorus Mysticus

We reached the *finale* and after a suitable pause to gather my wits, I made my way, against a tide of eagerly departing performers, up to the podium, upon which Mahler was leaning back against the railing looking exhausted and emotional.

"Despite repeated rehearsals, I cannot bring myself to praise the players in the orchestra for their standard of sight-reading the score, and remain unconvinced that the Queen's Hall orchestra is quite up to playing my Eighth

Symphony, The leader is passable but has little influence or leadership of the orchestra and does not understand that a work which takes nearly one and half hours to perform cannot be properly rehearsed in three hours," Mahler said. 1

"A little more practice in the weaker areas?" I ventured.

"However, we are here," continued Mahler, "but a *matinée* performance of the symphony is out of the question. Thus far they have succeeded only in making a travesty of the third movement, and of its *tempo*, which is clearly scored. Can they not differentiate between the long slow *adagissimo*, as indicated in the score and their relapsing into what can only be described as *adagio?* I deliberately wrote the *finale* to be played and sung at that lugubrious *adagissimo* speed in order to create those slow *langsam* sonorous chords – after all, we are supposed to be addressing Heaven!"

"I am fully aware that no orchestra that I have conducted has ever found my approbation easy to win. This is the price of perfection when under my baton. Several times I tapped my baton to stop them in continuing an interpretive error. Notwithstanding these reversals, we are managing to achieve some semblance of unity of purpose and homogeneity of form," offered Mahler.

"But Mahler, if rehearsal were not fraught and difficult, it is possible that one could have over-looked an intuitive element that may come back at a most inconvenient moment," I said.

After the rehearsal we made our way back to the office of the General Manager, Robert Newman, to thank him for the use of his hall and hospitality.

En-route, I dwelt upon the recurring challenge thrown up by the symphony; that of marshalling huge orchestral and choral forces. Almost a thousand performers are required to do justice to this monumental work. Its *sobriquet* of

Symphonie der Tausend is an apt one, and it could be that the work is just perhaps too big to be performed properly. The work has been dogged by misinterpretation and poor quality of performers since its inception in the villa at Meianigg am Wörthersee, when Mahler started to confirm his musical ideas in composing it.

A small chamber orchestra can be managed with ease and practice during a particular piece of music. A traditional orchestra, whether symphonic or philharmonic can be tamed with rehearsal. Add a chorus to an orchestra and immediately problems erupt. Irrespective of how good an orchestra is, its ability can be qualified by an inferior choir, or *vice versa*. It therefore becomes more difficult to get both halves to function as a whole with some degree of coördinated precision. The problem is greatly compounded when the performers number in their hundreds! This is essentially the weakness in the Eighth Symphony; it is more about *performing* the work and not its compositional integrity.

It was with these thoughts racing through my mind that we reëntered the manager's office. Immediately, Robert Newman sprang out of his red buttoned-leather seat and moved with surprising dexterity to the drinks cabinet.

"My pleasure gentlemen," he responded moments later to our salutation, while handing us a crystal fluted glass of champagne, "I am glad to be of service!"

It was whilst I was talking to Newman that Mahler drifted over again to look at the collection of some silver nitrate sepia-tinted *daguerreotypes* of images on the wall that had caught his attention when we were in Newman's office earlier. From where I stood, they appeared to be those of various musicians, but from their clothes and stance, suggested they were from the previous century.

Mahler then called Newman and me over to see for ourselves what had caught his attention. The reason for his close examination of these sepia-tinted likenesses was that they were of no less than four of our acclaimed composers; Weber, Dvořák, Liszt and Wagner, all of whom are heroes of Mahler.

"But of course," observed Newman, "you know all three lived within a few minutes of this Queen's Hall, including Antonín Dvořák who often stayed in the Langham Hotel, opposite us here in the Queen's Hall?"

On hearing this information, Mahler resolved, there and then, to make a pilgrimage to their places of residence and asked if I would guide us using my trusted *Bäedeker's* guide to London? Without further ceremony, we collected our coats and canes, whereupon Newman escorted us through the *labyrinth* of corridors and out through the back stage door of the Queen's Hall into a fog-laden Riding House Street, I think.

"*Auf Wiederhsehen*, Herr Newman, until the *première!*" said Mahler, whilst I thanked Newman for his generous hospitality.

The map I possessed in my *Bäedeker's* guide to London was not detailed, but did inform us of the location of our first shrine; that of composer, Carl Maria von Weber's. He had resided at No. 91 Portland Road, which was only a few minutes' walk from behind the Queen's Hall. We soon reached it and despite the pervasive fog, were able to just read an inscription carved into deep blue glass set in a square limestone frame that formed a *plaque* affixed to a red brick wall of a building. Mahler looked up at the commemorative *plaque* and remained motionless for quite some time. Pedestrians making their way along the footpath appeared in no way appeared puzzled by my friend's stationary vigil.

At length we retreated and made our way down the Portland Road in the direction of Oxford Street, I think. On reaching it we came across the St James' concert hall and noted the billing informed us that Antonín Dvořák's E minor Symphony - *Aus dem Neun Welt*, together with Tchaikowsky's F minor Symphony were to be directed by a conductor, Sir Charles Hallé, but yet to be confirmed.

We then arrived at Oxford Street, over which we crossed into a lane next to the Oxford Street Avenue *en-route* to our next shrine, that of the pianist and composer, Franz Liszt, who in 1841 lived at the end of Argyll Street. He lived in a building located just around the corner at No. 16 Great Marlborough Street. To Gustav Mahler, Franz Liszt was always the *Abbé* Liszt, preferring to refer to Liszt in his ecclesiastical designation. Mahler was very fond of the *piano forte* works by Liszt and often played them in times of crisis or unadulterated joy. Mahler was an accomplished pianist and could execute, with ease, the complex *arpeggios* and progressive scales, inherent in any of the *piano forte* works by Liszt. Mahler's playing of the transcriptions and paraphrases by Liszt, even on a domestic upright, were, without exception, always an experience of pure sublimity and sonority of chords, especially his interpretation of the *Harmonies, Poétique et Religieuses* and in particular, the beautiful *Invocation*.

Indeed I have much to be grateful for in listening to Mahler's playing and his particular ability in interpreting the works of Liszt. It never ceases to amaze me, how so effectively the music can arrest my attention and instill in my soul an appreciation of such rapturous *arpeggios* progression. I remember on one glorious occasion, in the villa at Maiernigg am Wörthersee, Mahler held us all in awe at his skill at the keyboard. During that memorable time the sublime music responsible for this ethereal sensation, was I remembered, the *'Tantum Ergo'* from the sacred *'Benediction'*.

Mahler fully appreciated that the *Abbé* represented an

innovative form of music in the middle nineteenth century, termed the '*Progressive*. It was later to be given powerful expression in the works of its great exponent, Rickard Wagner, who later became Liszt's son-in-law, in developing the *leitmotiv*.[2] Wagner was himself no stranger to the area, having lived in 1839 at 25 Old Compton Street, in the nearby *Bohemian* quarter of Soho. And so it was to that hallowed place that we now headed, after a suitable time for thought and reflection at Liszt's residence, immortalized by a limestone plaque with gilt lettering. Our next call was to this very place where the *Maestro* resided and who was held in awe and esteem by both Mahler and myself.

We carried out our mission with a zeal and determination one did not often observe in Mahler, who could, when motivated, be quite robust and full of energy that could carry him over great distances with the stamina of an athlete. Walking beside him, in the depths of the fog-bound huge Metropolis that London is, felt as though we were marching over some Alpine pasture in bright sunlight, such was his anticipation in seeing where Wagner lived.

On this occasion, our motivation was misplaced, for we had never seen such a street full of characters, most of whom did not give the impression of knowing who Rickard Wagner was, let alone of familiarity with his music or innovative *leitmotivs*. There was no recognizable sign, symbolic or otherwise, of the fact of Wagner's living there. Accordingly, we turned back and headed west to the Café Royal for well-earned refreshments, and possibly dinner, with gaiety and relaxation in opulent surroundings.

---

1 Also said to Franz Schalk on the final rehearsals in München.
2 A reference expressed in music of a recurring idea or character.

Chapter 8

The Café Royal - Polemic Part I

The rehearsals had been marginally successful but still needed attention in the Part III section: Pater Profundus, the Part X section: Penitent Women and the Part XV section Una Poenitentium. Mahler was painfully aware of these weaknesses and would deal with them. In the meantime we were now in the famous, or rather infamous, Café Royal; the last word in opulence and located conveniently between Soho and Mayfair. Here, it seems, the English were trying their best to be French, but the only thing French about the place was its architecture, which was that of French Second Empire.

We entered the main *salon* and looked around for a suitable table in an enclave in which to repose ourselves, and in so searching felt we stood on the threshold of eternity.

The place was a wild, eclectic mix of opulence and *bizarre*, *Bohemian* tastes, with drawings rooms in one area and a small hall for music in another. Accordingly, it attracted the rich and infamous, intent, at least so it seemed from my observation, on trying to imitate each other

My first impression of the *salon* at the Café Royal formed readily in my mind. The place resembled nothing more than an interesting combination of a scene depicted in Manet's reflections of the *brasserie* at the *Folies-Bergère*. And, the vision of ambience captured in Toulouse-Lautrec's *At the Moulin Rouge,* both complete in their expression of unbridled affluence and obvious ostentatious behavior. Except perhaps here in London; the atmosphere was altogether more of an English interpretation of European *café* society, and general indulgence in wild pleasures and verbal recklessness with *courtesans*. Members of the aristocracy were easily recognizable; not by their expensive sartorial arrangements, but rather by their arrogance and unbounded confidence. That they knew each other was beyond doubt, that they would come to know others amongst them, was equally so! The English, as it were, trying their best to be cosmopolitan. So I seem to remember some person once said!

The *salon*, is as fine an example of any opulently appointed interior one might expect to find in a Viennese *Konditorei* or a Parisian *Brasserie,* comprised walls covered in glazed panels with acid etched, intricate designs on those polished surfaces. They, in turn, reflected a myriad of light cascading down from numerous acetylene gas-fueled crystal *chandeliers* which were suspended from a cream-colored ceiling, extravagantly finished in an ornate Baroque design with raised, gilded filigree patterns. The dazzling effect of the chandeliers was to create a sumptuous, brilliant light that illuminated every aspect of this large spacious room, including reflecting off highly polished carved mahogany timber finishes. Occasionally, the light sparkled on ornate brass railings and fittings on various surfaces and augmented the extravagant *décor* which prevailed throughout the room.

The Café Royal was built in the late exuberant Victorian style of architecture that expresses opulence at every opportunity. Not one square inch of the *salon's* surface had escaped the architects' designs for the interior finishes. Very beautiful, but it was as though the Baroque and Victorian styles had collided to create a grandiose, though overpowering ambience, within the spaces afforded by this huge room.

Various marble columns, reaching up, terminated in arches supporting other ornate stucco ceilings complete with raised tracery designs. Some pilasters, flat columns set flush against the walls, were performing the same *rôle* in creating a vaulted ceiling decorated with figurines and gold leaf. Statues looked down upon to us as we walked through on a deep-pile red carpet. Heavy, red flocked silk wallpaper lined some of the walls, which intermittently gave way to mirrored panel and highly polished mahogany doors, set in wide door frames leading to other areas of the building, with promises of even more splendor within.

At last we threw open a massive double door clad in varnished walnut that gave us entry into a sumptuous *salon* proper, the tables in which were covered with purple *Fior Di Pesco Classico,* the only marble on which to place one's drink, in style. Ranged upon the marble bar were huge gasogenes dispensing aërated water on an almost industrial scale! Competing for space on the bar, were large, bronze *candelabra* with candles giving out myriad points of light. The whole effect was of dazzling opulence. The room itself had not, escaped the designer's attention. Suspended from the high, white, ornate stucco ceiling were acetylene-fuelled *chandeliers* radiating a powerfully brilliant light that illuminated the whole *salon.* Laid out on the floor was a purple broadloom carpet with gold stars woven into its pattern, and upon it were large sofas covered in a deep red *moiré* silk. Next to each sofa were palm trees very much in evidence. The whole place had an ambience of luxury where money was not a real option but imperial splendor was!

Various surfaces and walls were decorated with ornate carvings. There were statues, bronze and nickel metal fixtures, including window and doorframes, emblems and signage. Red, green and purple velvet curtains covered the various windows to the outside world that most patrons were eager to forget. All created a sense of magnificent Victorian red plush ambience of the vernacular type so beloved by the English, adding to the general ostentatious paraphernalia ranged around the room, all designed to create an impossible ideal of grandeur!

Huge panels of mirrors, the sides of which were supported by gilded *Caryatids,* adorned the walls; and it was from such looking glasses that patrons refined their reflected image, but also through such reflections persons espied one another.

Whilst Mahler, with keener eyesight, surveyed the spacious room for a vacant table, I took the opportunity to look around and absorb the opulent and luxuriant appointments. It was a fantasy of gilded ostentatious ornamentation and opulence filled with hopeful *femme fatales* in the making, mingling with actors of no great acclaim. They in turn were imitating aristocrats, and aristocrats who wished to be taken for jockeys. *Demi-mondaines* were dressed in bi-cycling costumes, sporting white and black vertically striped shirts. This new daredevil craze for bi-cycling appeared to have transfixed the minds of the English on this past-time. Perhaps this obsession explained the earlier confusion at the press conference of Mahler being an avid bi-cycling enthusiast, and why one correspondent termed him, a veritable '*Velocipedean!*'

Gliding amongst these characters, with the ease of

Proteus, were the seasoned blackmailers with their breast pockets bulging with compromising indiscretions. The Café Royal, though undoubtedly impressive, looked like an anaemic version of the *Folies-Bergeres* captured by Manet in his painting of the same name. There was also that pervasive noise of various glasses being continually replaced on white *Carrara* and *Fior Di Pesco Classic* marble tabletops, creating that distinctive *crescendo* 'clinking' sound, as though a cascade of diamonds was bouncing off these marble surfaces.

Several *Bohemian* painters and writers were sipping away at their absinthe in the hope of achieving oblivion just before penury set in.

We made our way gradually through the *salon,* looking for a table, whilst passing persons either introduced each other or received invitations.

It was one such invitation that my friend and I accepted from a character called Oscar Wilde, a renowned wit and *raconteur.*

Around the red *damask* covered oval table were assembled various artists, some of whom Mahler and I knew, or rather knew of, creating a vision of unrestrained enthusiastic self-indulgence. It was to this group that Oscar Wilde introduced us.

Oscar wore a royal blue morning coat, pearl grey trousers, silk and gold thread embroidered waistcoat, lavender gloves and a shirt finished with a neckerchief tie of mauve silk, secured with a gold clasp capped with a stone of *lapis lazuli,* and shirt cuffs that comprised wine yellow *topazes.* He rose to greet us, leaning on his gold-headed malacca cane for support. The fact of Wilde's being a sybarite was clearly self-evident.

"You have all the grace and mannerisms of Beau Brummel," I said, in an effort to be complimentary.

"Thank you, Friedrich, but I think the compliment premature, for I am not ready to engage a Brougham in order to cross the street. Nor lean on a friend's arm to gain the other side of a room to view a masterpiece upon the wall in front of which I might collapse due to exhaustion!" replied Wilde, "but the remark is elegant."

"You too, Oscar, look very elegant with your rather ostentatious tie," remarked Mahler.

"A well tied tie, my dear Gustav, is the first serious step in life!" replied Oscar, bidding us to sit down on to gilded Chippendale styled chairs.

"So is the ability to acquire the tie," responded Mahler.

"It is a pity Gustav you know, that you are not Chopin," continued Wilde, "as he is by far my favorite composer, for he surely is the master of the *Etude*!"

"I feel certain Oscar you would not say one thing and practice another," replied Gustav.

"May I introduce you to James Whistler, whom I think you may know but ought not to, and his compatriot Aubrey Beardsley; both were friends at one time, but now remain friendly enemies. The others, including Atkinson Grimshaw and Charles Rickett, I feel certain you know," said Oscar Wilde.

Quite an interesting group," replied Mahler.

"To get into society, one has either to feed people or shock them', asserted Oscar, "I prefer the latter."

"We were just remarking on the all-pervasive acrid fog shrouding your Metropolis!" I said in my second attempt to be cordial.

"If I may quote," said Oscar, "from my published essay, '*The Decay of Lying*', '...at present people see fogs, not because there are fogs, but because poets and painters have taught them the mysterious loveliness of such effects. There may have been fogs for centuries in

London; I dare say there were, but no one saw them, so we did not know anything about them. They did not exist until art invented them! Now it must be admitted, fogs are carried to excess. They have become the mere mannerism of a *clique* and the exaggerated realism of their method gives people bronchitis.'"

"Surely you do not advocate the continual presence of fog?" I continued.

"Where, if not from the Impressionists, do we get those wonderful yellow fogs that come creeping down our streets, blurring the gas-lamps and changing the houses into monstrous shadows? To whom, if not to them and their master, do we owe the lovely silver mists that brood over our river, and turn to faint forms of fading grace curved bridge and swaying barge?" replied Oscar.

"All the more reason," I continued, "to live in the sunlight and the fogless air of the country-side!" But looking at the surprise on Wilde's face, regretted saying it the moment that I had.

"I abhor the country-side," came Wilde's inevitable *riposte* at my expense, "and its apparent uselessness and resistance to change. In this respect, to me a field represents nothing more than ground that is yet to be turned into something more worthwhile."

"But change is the one thing that punctuates our lives; and in so doing, it makes them tolerable, surely," I said.

"I do not desire change in anything in England, except the weather," replied Wilde.

"Let me introduce you to John Singer Sargent, who had the misfortune to be born in Florence, of American parents, and was therefore compelled to study in Florence and Paris, but now has come to London to make his fortune!" announced Wilde.

"I am a great admirer of your painting entitled a *Portrait of Graham Robertson*. A fine work, brilliantly executed and so English!" said Mahler.

"Such an expression as English art is a meaningless expression, one might just as well speak of English mathematics," advised Wilde, "besides, our friend here is American and not remotely English."

We were introduced to a Mr. James Whistler, who was wearing a new white silk jacket with evident pride, as he on two occasions remarked upon the fine silk used in its tailoring.

"I am familiar with your painting Whistler, entitled *Sand Sea and Sky: A Summer Fantasy*,"[1] said Gustav.

"Did I paint that?" asked Whistler.

"I believe so, and, the interplay of light on your painting *Nocturnes* is reminiscent of an Atkinson Grimshaw," offered Mahler.

"Possibly!" replied Whistler.

"Ah I remember you now," said Mahler, "I seem to recollect that you were criticized for having charged too much for a canvas that took you all but two days to cover in paint."

"True," retorted Whistler, "but which is a result of a lifetime."

This was the same Whistler who had gained Mahler's admiration as a result of a successful lawsuit against John Ruskin. Ruskin was an arrogant neo-mediaevalist whose sworn aim was to drag modern society back into the medieval age complete with its concentrated ignorance and from which we have thankfully escaped. The case was reported widely in the Viennese papers, such is its relevance to the creation of art, especially that espoused by Mahler in applying Goethe's dictum. [2]

The Grosvenor gallery in London had exhibited a

series of paintings by Whistler, all of which departed from the previous style reflecting Pre-Raphaelite mundane medieval scenes so adored by Ruskin. In re-action Ruskin wrote a slanderous attack on Whistler in his unpopular newspaper, *Fors Clavigera,* which he edited, and in which he tried to promote the redundant and mundane cause of neo-mediaevalism to an uninterested public.

'I have seen and heard much of cockney impudence before now, but never expected to hear a coxcomb ask two hundred guineas for flinging a pot of paint in the public's face,' wrote Ruskin.

Whistler attacked Ruskin with the all the virulence and vehemence he could concentrate and beat him in a resounding victory in court. As a result of this lawsuit, and a bonus for all lovers of progressive art, Ruskin already ill, lost his reason, if any reason he had. This case brought to a timely end the influence of Ruskin, who was said to have once described the characters in a George Eliot novel, as being like, sweepings off the Pentonville omnibus.

"This can come as no surprise, since England is the home of lost ideas," said Wilde.

"It certainly was when Ruskin was influential," countered Whistler.

"Art's first appeal is neither to the intellect nor to the emotions, but purely to the artistic temperament," said Oscar.

"Do not be so sure; art and intellect are opposites as they are irrelevant!" said Mahler.

"Schopenhauer has analyzed the pessimism that characterizes modern thought, but Hamlet invented it

The world has become sad because a puppet was once melancholy," replied Wilde thoughtfully, as if examining the words as he spoke them.

"You know, of course, the Dublin born composer Sir Charles Villiers Stanford?" asked Wilde, in a change of mood.

"I do. Were you not up at Cambridge?" Mahler inquired.

"Cambridge? Do not speak to me of such horrors!" exclaimed Wilde, in mock re-action of despair.

"You have heard of me then I take it?" asked Sir Charles.

Yes I have, Sir Charles, because your *Enigma Variations* 3 have long since been a favorite of mine and indeed precede your reputation!" said Mahler, in a warm display of praise for another contemporaneous composer, and one older than himself.

"Gustav, if you should ever feel that being in the Café Royal is somewhat a daunting experience for your sensibilities, you might prefer Kettner's in the depths of Soho," advised Sir Charles, in a rare show of contempt for a comparative stranger.

"Why do you suggest Kettner's?" asked Mahler, with a confused expression upon his features.

"Because," answered Sir Charles Stanford, "Kettner's is a pale imitation of the Café Royal, a place of *lese majeste,* as it were. But-nonetheless comfortable, and would, I remain convinced, suit your sparkling personality, especially their *cabinet particuliers!*"

A person called Zemlinsky joined our group and without any introduction seated himself at our table. Mahler and I were very well acquainted with this composer. Previously he had taught music to Alma Schindler, now Mahler's wife. Zemlinsky had been a previous lover of Alma's, before she met Gustav. There existed between Zemlinsky and Mahler a tension that has intensified over the years.

"We attended your meeting with the gentlemen of the

press earlier today. I must say, it was all rather intense. How did you feel about it?" asked Zemlinsky.

"Ask Friedrich Löhr here; he was there and can give you an unbiased account of it," replied Mahler, whilst turning to field a question from Wilde.

Whilst I, as a courtesy, informed Zemlinsky of what I thought about the meeting with the Fourth Estate generally, and what I thought about him particularly, Mahler engaged Wilde in a discussion about his Ninth Symphony. A work of which of course, Mahler was in the process of composing.

"In answer to your polite inquiry Oscar, I am some-what exhausted, because I have been wrestling with the complexities of my Ninth Symphony; after all creativity must continue, irrespective of the occasional set back. '*Il faut lutter pour l'art* 4 as it were," replied Mahler.

"Occasional set back?" inquired Wilde, "it is always with the best intentions that the worst work is done."

"Yes, it involves the mysteries of artistic creation. Recently I went through the *scherzo* of the symphony again, since I first composed it, and it impressed me profoundly. It is a remarkable piece and I did not realize this when creating it! Creative activity and the genesis of a work are mystical from start to completion, since one acts sub-consciously, as if inspired from elsewhere," said Mahler.

It was at this point that a person, whom I recognized as being the Russian artist, Wassily Kandinsky, joined us at the table, though I suspect Mahler did not realize who he was.

"Do tell us, Gustav, whilst one is always grateful for a foreigner's efforts to master the intricacies of the English language, from whom or where did you acquire your peculiar accent and syntax?" Wilde asked.

Such was Mahler's poor comprehension of the English language I feared he might not understand Wilde's inquiry. I therefore leaned over and whispered the German translation into his ear.

"In answer to your question Oscar," replied Mahler, "the eminent Doctor Arnold Berliner instructed me in the use, pronunciation and understanding of English."

Oscar turned to another loquacious Irish dramatist and playwright in James Joyce, who, I think, resides in Zurich, but like Wilde, was born in Dublin, the state capital of Ireland. They conferred for a few moments, then Wilde, turning to my friend, retorted.

"Would that be the noted Doctor Arnold Berliner, who studied physics at the University of Breslau and subsequently worked for the General Electric Company in America? Then having quitted that august establishment to the applied arts, went to Hamburg, where I understand you held the appointment of director of the Opera House? However, our esteemed doctor held no such illuminating and illustrious post, other than being an *employé* at the electric light bulb factory of the *Allgemeine Elecktrizitäts-Gesellshaft*? 5

"So, Gustav you speak the English language as a mechanic! I trust *my* German diction and pronunciation is perfect?" asked Wilde.

"We all of us have our secrets of the soul, Oscar. Rather like your open secret, no?" inquired Mahler.

Wilde in a flash replied: "Secrets of the soul; what open secret?"

"Why of course on the occasion of your father's death in Merion Square in Dublin, in 1876, I believe. You recalled the event, some years later, when writing for some uplifting journal that I saw abandoned in a *Konditorei* in Vienna when I attended the University there. Permit me to quote from memory: '...before my father died he lay ill in bed for many days. Every morning a woman dressed in black and closely veiled, came to our house and unhindered by my mother would ascend the stairs to my dying father's bedchamber and sit at the end of the bed and stay there all day without ever speaking a word or raising her veil. She took no notice of anyone in the chamber and nobody paid any attention to her. My mother tolerated this veiled presence to enter our house unbidden, and sit by my dying father; not out of indifference to him, but because my father knew my mother loved him and would not deny him, before his supreme moment, the comfort afforded to him by the veiled woman.' Would you say that was am accurate description?" asked Gustav.

"You have quite a well-developed imagination and memory for fact," said Wilde.

"The irrelevantly sensational has always attracted my attention!" replied Mahler.

It was James Whistler who asked Mahler a question.

"You spoke earlier to Oscar, about the fact that you are in the process of composing your Ninth Symphony and about your ambivalent relation with your contemporary composer, Rickard Strauss, in his interpretation of concepts expressed in his symphonic tone poem, *Death and Transfiguration*. Yet you quoted your friend in Alban Berg's recognition of the death conscious music contained in the preliminary sketches for the first movement of your Ninth Symphony, as being powerful yet terrifying, as though a cataclysm were about to engulf one?"

"For some reason," responded Mahler, "people equate me with Strauss, erroneously in my opinion, since our musical styles are different. I used the symphony as an expressive form; Strauss, evidently prefers the looser

symphonic structure afforded by the *symphonic tone poem.*
I will compose *lieder,* whereas Rickard will revert to the
more formal song structure, as in his *Vier Letzte Lieder.*"

"I find that difficult to accept," continued Whistler.

"You mention your Nocturnes, Whistler, yet I always
thought of you as a painter. Do you compose nocturnes
in your spare time?" asked Mahler.

"I am a painter of course," said Whistler, whilst
rubbing down carefully the sleeves of his new and
expensive white silk jacket, "you are confusing my title
of my painting with music."

"Are you certain that you are not an amateur composer;
since I distinctly remember a work of yours entitled
Symphony in White, or was it, *Tone Poem in White?* Is this
not so?" inquired Mahler.[6]

"I think that I know what I am. I certainly do not need
to be informed as to whether I am a successful painter
or composer," said Whistler.

"To me you are neither!" interrupted Kandinsky.

"I particularly like," continued Mahler unabated, "the
inter-play of light shimmering off the surface of the water
producing a fascinating interpretation of Hull docks!"

"Really Mahler," said Whistler, "the painting you are
referring to is not my *Nocturne* but is another painting
called *Meditation* by my friend here Atkinson Grimshaw!"

"Your work precedes you in reputation, especially in
the way you capture the feeling of ethereal serenity and
helplessness in the stone," said Mahler, to John Atkinson
Grimshaw.

"Thank you," replied Grimshaw, "but what particularly
is it about the stone from which the structure is created
that is of interest to you?

"I was thinking about the juxtaposition of the various
limestone blocks, which together create the concept of

permanence – eternity almost," said Mahler.

"One would hardly describe a dwelling as reflecting permanence or eternity. Admittedly the place is built to last; but not for eternity!" replied Grimshaw.

"However, the fact remains that they are permanent, no?" asked Gustav.

"But when you refer to dwellings, by that do you mean the adjacent buildings; out houses and stables?" inquired Grimshaw.

"I was thinking more about the sheen on the limestone and the way the light plays on the surface of the stone. Such delicate use of shade and texture," said Gustav.

"Well the limestone is in the form of blocks which make up the dwelling," said Grimshaw, with a searching expression upon his face.

"Do you not mean dwellings?" inquired Mahler.

"If you include the out houses and stable, I suppose so" replied Grimshaw.

"Out houses and stables; I do not remember seeing outhouses or stables" said Mahler.

"You would not, as they were hidden in the background, by foliage and by the chestnut and copper beeches trees which surround the dwelling!" answered Grimshaw.

"Do you not mean cypress trees?" corrected Mahler,

"No I do not!" replied Atkinson Grimshaw, clearly put out by Mahler's inquisitorial manner, "after all I am the creator of the painting!"

"I am not disputing that, but rather questioning your use of the word dwelling," said Mahler.

"Well what else would one call a house?" inquired Grimshaw.

"A house; surely you cannot think the word *dwelling* is a suitable noun for describing a Mausoleum, because if you do then I somewhat am surprised, no?" inquired Gustav Mahler.

"Mausoleum, surprised?" stated Grimshaw, looking perplexed.

"Yes, I would hardly call a tomb cut into the living rock, containing a sarcophagus a dwelling. I would personally call it what it is – a Mausoleum! One of several that comprise the necropolis built on to that deserted island, no?" said Mahler.

"My painting contains no Mausoleum, crypt or sarcophagus – occupied or not, necropolis or deserted island anywhere on my canvas for that matter," said Grimshaw, indignantly, "it is a painting of a country house and I call it the *Deserted House,* not deserted island."

"Your painting then does not depict a deserted island complete with numerous cypress trees and huge limestone blocks in to which several Mausoleums and tombs have been excavated, containing a number of sarcophagi? And, where a woman, in a white shroud is guarding a corpse, which is being rowed across the water to this island necropolis, on which to intern the lifeless body? The dumb, as it were, rowing the dead?" asked Mahler.

"The dumb rowing the what; what can you be talking about? My painting depicts a late autumnal scene of an English garden that surrounds a forlorn and melancholic looking deserted house in Buckinghamshire in England!"

"It is not a Mausoleum then?" inquired Mahler.

Atkinson Grimshaw feigned an absorbing interest in the red tasseled menu card.

Mahler, in the meantime, had broadened his scope around the table and engaged in what I thought to be a rather intellectual discussion with some other artist.

"I know your work, now what is it called? Ah yes, '*The Nightmare'* by John Fitzgerald.

The Deserted House

"I think that you are confusing me with Fuseli's work called, *'The Nightmare'*, replied the artist.

"No, I consider the painting to be created by a nightmare," replied Mahler.

At that moment a highly unstable individual arrived with a woman. Clearly both had been drinking, heavily and this much was obvious to those gathered around the red *damask* covered oval table. The man kept repeating the phrase:

"Devil take that woman [7] and her loathsome Blue Ribbon Brigade. Beware, she is prowling the building Oscar!" That *Valkürian* woman is under the impression that I have taken too much champagne, or something. The devil take her!"

The woman with him looked as if she were in the latter stages of consumption, and coughed a lot. At length both sat, or rather collapsed, down onto two chairs that a waiter had conveniently commandeered for them. They were introduced to Mahler and me as Dante Gabriel Rossetti, the Pre-Raphaelite painter and his companion, an Elizabeth Siddal, an artists' model, or so I gathered.

"Have I not heard that name before?" asked Rossetti, looking very concerned and trying to think. "Ah! Yes, do you run a tailor's shop in the Whitechapel Road?"

Mahler was remarkably restrained and I think he put this down to Rossetti's inebriated state.

"No, I am a composer," Mahler retorted.

"Oh with the *Daily News* I suppose," countered Rossetti.[8]

"I am familiar with your work Rossetti; in particular the painting called '*Astarte*'. And, if I may say so, quite a magnificent painting, a real *tour de force* in the expression of powerful and vibrant images; and very *Klimtesque!*"

Rossetti looked at Mahler through red rimmed eyes and said:

"The painting you are referring to called is *Astarte,* and it was painted by John Singer Sargent, sitting there."

"Yes I know that," retorted Mahler, "yours is that '*Beata Beatrix*', the very scratchy effort, yes?"

Just watching this Rossetti character, I had difficulty in taking him seriously as the creator of *Beata Beatrix* and *Astarta Syriaca*, and I could well understand Mahler's feelings towards him being similar, and had as much as told him so.

Rossetti, on this occasion, let these slights pass, either because he was too drunk to realize them, or he was incapable of formulating a response, irrespective of re-acting.

The Pre-Raphaelites, of whom he was a founding member, had revolted against the archaic authoritarianism of the Royal Academy, and were inspired partially by the revolutionary zeal of the Chartist movement, when they, challenged the political *status quo*. Though I remained uncertain quite what it was they were seeking or indeed what it was they had achieved.

Nevertheless, Rossetti continued to amaze us with his next statement that was as sudden as it was unexpected, as though a desperate attempt to lend credibility to his presence and any subsequent statement.

"We are building our new house, the *Red House* at considerable expense!" announced Rossetti.

"No we are not, we are trying to save by not spending money; the only thing we spend is most of my time, knocking up fake medieval costumes and wall coverings," replied Rossetti's woman, Elizabeth Siddal, "and besides, it is William Morris who is paying for it."

"No Elizabeth, we are re-creating the splendors of the medieval past and an exercise in communal living, and by making our own handcrafted '*real*' furniture and furnishings to benefit us all," said Rossetti, clearly embarrassed by this unexpected justification of his domestic arrangements being aired in public, especially in a busy Café Royal.

"Yes, tell us about this new concept of communal living Rossetti." demanded Rickett, in a particularly loud voice, clearly intended to alert nearby interested third parties, or indeed anyone merely passing our table.

Rossetti then went on to describe with hesitant pride, that no less than three families all lived in this one house.

"There are William Morris and his wife Jane; the Ruskins; Algernon Swinburne and of course, Elizabeth and me," explained Rossetti.

"I could never bring myself to live under such conditions," offered Wilde, "as I cannot help detesting my relations. I suppose it comes from the fact that none of us can stand other people having the same faults as ourselves."

For myself, I was aghast on recognizing the implication of this admission of an actual variation on this *de facto* extant *ménage à trois*. As for my friend Mahler, I could not even imagine his re-action to this appalling domestic situation, but he did ask a rather pertinent question.

"Is there a critical shortage of houses in England, yes?"

"No we want to go back to the glorious days of the Middle Ages where people fabricated everything for themselves. There was no mass production, no factories, but a new Romantic art, am I not right here, Whistler?" asked Rossetti.

"Romantic art begins with its apotheosis," remarked Wilde.

However, Whistler did not get an opportunity to answer this question; instead it was Siddal who replied, and vehemently:

"That Red House; the color of which is neither here nor there, it should be called Bleak House. Whose idea was it to paint those stupid cupboards in the hall-way in that amazingly dull and *naïve* style, depicting impossible mock medieval so-called idyllic scenes straight out of Mallory's Arthurian legends, if you believe in that rubbish? We are living in the twentieth century Rossetti, not in some God-forsaken, medieval, plague-ridden, rat infested village surrounded by the despairing and the idiotic."

"Morality was an intolerable affectation of style,' countered Wilde.

"You do not have to spend hour upon hour on that wooden loom locked away in that damp outhouse that leaks every time it rains because that thatched roof simply cannot hold back the rainwater, and..." said Siddal

"It needs to be damp in the outhouse, Elizabeth," interrupted Rossetti, somewhat put out by Siddal's outburst," otherwise the weft would break if it were dry and you would not be able to weave that natural cloth we need to make our clothes from."

"Cloth to make our clothes from; you call these rags we are compelled to wear clothes? Well Rossetti, I am not impressed. And," said Elizabeth Siddal, whilst drinking deeply from her cut crystal glass, "being in that damp shed all day has got me not a case of fine loom-woven material, but a severe case of consumption."

"You were afflicted with your condition of consumption well before you met me and wanted to join my progressive march back to medievalism," retaliated Rossetti.

"Absolutely right, but as my physician said to me in the consumption ward, at Stansfield House in Hampstead, if I could get myself off to Switzerland, I could overcome my condition and improve my health. Perhaps I should have kept house for James Joyce here, he lives in Switzerland. Why do you really think, Rossetti, that I took up modeling for you artists? Because I like remaining still for hours or even days on end; because, it takes you, Rossetti, forever to create a likeness of me? I was talking to Alexa Wilding, and she said that when she models for Holman Hunt, even he could knock up a painting of a morning, easily by lunchtime, and then go out to the bars and drink for the Empire during the afternoon.

The whole reason I came to model for you artists was to earn money to be able to go to Switzerland and breathe and be cured. What was a girl supposed to do to earn money? Go and work in that Bryant & May's matchstick factory in the Mile End Road making phosphorus matches? With all that sulphur and phosphorus about the place how long did you think I would last, with my consumption, in that death factory?

No I came to model for you so-called Pre-Raphaelite Brotherhood, to earn some money and all I have earned is consumption. Even that Millais had me lying in a bathtub of tepid water, in his large house in the Glouces- ter Road, for days on end, and when I asked why the water had to be miserably tepid, all he could say was *'he wanted to capture the cool sparkle of the cold water in a brook'.*[9] He was too mean to heat up the water in the bath tub for my comfort, even though he knows I suffer from consumption.

And, when I asked him why is it taking you days to create that painting with me soaked to the skin and my long luxuriant hair all damp and matted, he replied to me that he wanted to *'capture the translucent sheen of the wet skin of the dying Ophelia as she drifted down the river!'* My mother would have fits if she knew what I got up to for you artists. And why is it that Jane Morris, William's other half never gets to be soaked or incommoded? All she does is pose, looking like a little daisy all sweetness and light – with that enigmatic look on her face, whilst I get drenched, contract pneumonia and consumption. More- over, Millais still has not paid me for modeling for him. And why is it Rossetti, you got her to pose for you as *'Proserpine'* clutching her half eaten pomegranate, which I bet she finished off afterwards? You never ask me to pose in comfortable expensive dresses eating free fruit, do you Rossetti; anyway none of you would care if I dropped dead of pneumonia right now at this table, would you?" asked Siddal.

Immediately after slurring this pronouncement, Siddal slumped forward and in so doing knocked over a full glass of red *Volnay Beaune* Burgundy over the table and Whistler's new white silk jacket. I knew from bitter experience, that a red wine stain is impossible to remove. Alas, Whistler's pride and joy was no more than an expensive piece of tailoring prematurely relegated to the status of red wine-drenched rag.

I could detect in Mahler's eye a repressed euphoria at Siddal's clumsiness. The Germans have a beautiful phrase for it, and only they could have thought it up.

Siddal's clumsiness had in no way however, deflected her from her verbal task in hand.

"No," she continued, trying to galvanize her thoughts, "it is not, it is to save money, to save money, to save money. Why do we not simply go to Liberty's Emporium, up the Regent's Street and avail ourselves of our necessaries there, as other nice middle class families do? That is what I want to know Rossetti, that is what I want to know?"

"Young people these days imagine money is everything," said Wilde, "and when they grow older they know it is!"

"No Elizabeth," soothed Rossetti, "we are certainly not middle class, and we have no pretentions or aspirations to be so. We are neo medievalists enjoying a spiritual existence, as *artisan-artists*, and therefore we rise above such mundane considerations as to which class we belong."

"We are born in an age where only the dull are taken seriously, and I live in terror of not being misunderstood," said Wilde.

"No we are not," countered Siddal, "we are poor, our so-called Red House is like the old curiosity shop; full of redundant broken items of furniture that have long since passed their usefulness. The place is the last word in discomfort, with all that handmade wooden furniture and rickety squeaking chairs without padding but with nails sticking out, and timber so rough as to give you splinters even looking at it. Do you know there is not one comfortable armchair or sofa in the whole of the house?

That is why Rossetti, friends never come to visit us; who could blame them? Why make the effort to organize a full-scale expedition out to Bexleyheath, in the middle of nowhere in Kent, miles from the civilization that you have here in London? And then when they do arrive to stay for a day or two, they take one look around the broken down hovel we exist in, and make their excuses, remembering, all of a sudden, a previous engagement. It is all too depressing and we live as though we were but one pace from the workhouse. It is as though, living in that Red House, we are living in a place that is falling apart in slow motion.

I tried to cook some vegetables for dinner a few days ago and it took me four hours in our kitchen that would be put to shame by a kitchen in a medieval hovel. The smoke bellowing out of the wood burning fires meant I had to leave the kitchen for the garden, every ten minutes in order to breathe, and what with me and my consumption! And the worst thing was, when I had finally cooked the vegetables, they were burnt to a cinder due to the ferocious flames upon which I had to cook them, and where is my red wine I had, my *Volnay Beaune*?" Siddal demanded to know.

A silence fell upon the table.

"Those who know are confident; those who do not remain intolerant!" remarked Siddal whilst looking deliberately at Wilde.

"Do not be ridiculous, Siddal; I was at Oxford!" countered Wilde.

"I do so admire your painting of *Ophelia*," offered Mahler, in an attempt to turn the discussion on to more sober concerns," in which your friend here, Elizabeth Siddal sat as model."

"What!" Rossetti exploded, bringing his wine glass down with such force that we feared it may have shattered in his clenched hand. It had broken, releasing through his fingers sparkling champagne now *rosé* colored onto the red *damask* table cloth. Realizing what he had done, he merely removed the paisley *bandana* from around his neck and wrapped it around his hand.

"How dare you! That monstrosity, was painted by that John fellow 10 and should be consigned to the furnace to provide heating for the work house." spluttered an apoplectic Rossetti, "it was that fiasco that gave Elizabeth her consumption, aside of which, what would a foreigner as you are, know about art, since you are a tailor?"

"I do not claim to be English, but with a name such as Rossetti you sound the foreigner, possible Sicilian, yes?" replied Gustav. "But more informatively I recall from my literary studies that it was *Ophelia* who went mad? The reason I mention this is because of the lifelike characteristics of the painting, in that one can almost feel the mental torment emanating from *Ophelia* in her despair, giving the distinct impression that your companion was not acting out her *rôle* as *Ophelia*. I might also add that it is also probable she exacerbated her consumption when she posed with floating robes in a bathtub of water, when Millais painted his *Ophelia* floating down a river."

Oscar was watching this encounter with bemusement. Indeed, we all were, but Oscar did say,

"I am jealous of everything whose beauty does not die!"

At this juncture, a glass of wine was knocked over and

Rossetti attempted to reach for it, either to set it up straight, or more probably, to use it to establish an *a priori* to conclude his proposition. However, at this point, fate intervened in the form of Charles Villiers Stanford's restraining hand on Rossetti's arm.

It was an inescapable fact that Rossetti was mentally unstable, which was evident to anybody observing him. What was not immediately observable, but becoming rapidly so, was the fact of his displaying pronounced symptoms of having incipient psychotic leanings. And that Rossetti was born Charles Dante Rossetti, but dropped the Charles as a result of his obsession with the poet Dante Alighieri, could only confirm this prognosis.

The first of Rossetti's several mental breakdowns was in June 1872. According to his own volition, he 'spent his days in a haze of chloral hydrate and whisky.' For me, his drinking habit was not a valid reason to adopt the mannerisms or behavior of a psychotic. Irrespective of my personal thoughts about Rossetti's state of mental health —or deterioration, what then transpired during the conversation indicated that Rossetti was irredeemably ill.

The conversation turned on to another of Rossetti's monomaniac conditions manifest in his fascination for, and obsession with, wombats:

"Absolutely," Rossetti confirmed with evident pride, "no family should be without wombats. I get mine eventually to climb up onto the Dining Room table and go for a nap in the basket placed in the middle of it. It amuses my dinner guests!"

"When does it form part of the menu?" asked Zemlin-sky, with a facial expression the very definition of seriousness.

Rossetti continued without answering, but by his demeanor was upset that such a destiny could befall one of his precious wombats, to say nothing of the implicit disrespect shown for it.

"When my guests have got bored with my slumbering wombat, I get a large toucan bird, dressed in a cowboy hat, which I have trained to ride a llama round the dining table for the further amusement of my guests!"

Rossetti narrated this *bizarre* story as if he were describing an everyday normal occurrence, with no self-deprecatory feeling or embarrassment, but in fact thought it highly humorous. It could be that this activity in the domestic Dining Rooms is quite normal in London. Mahler, with absolute incredulity, looked aghast at Rossetti.

"Do tell me Rossetti," asked Mahler, "where on earth do you find time to scratch out those *naïve* paintings of yours, immortalizing a particular woman, especially in that effort called, '*A Portrait of Ellen Terry*' [11] you painted recently?"

Rossetti was clearly working himself up to commence an all out onslaught on my friend. However, the eruption came not from Rossetti but from an unexpected origin. It came from the woman seated next to him.

"Who is this *Helen* Terry? You been painting her? When, come on tell me, tell me now this instant, how long have you being seeing her, tell me, now?"

The woman in question, Elizabeth Siddal, I later learned, was Rossetti's mistress. It was difficult to imagine her being the inspiration for such works by Rossetti as *Beata Beatrix* or *Ophelia* in her present state. The woman then ceased squawking but now looked intently at Rossetti. She was dressed in cheap tawdry clothes ill fitting and dirty, possibly home made on a wooden loom at the Red House. Her hair was light brown and long but greasy and she wore what looked like the remains of a bonnet that had clearly seen better times. Indeed it was difficult to determine whether it was the lining of a hat or hat in its own right. On her thin neck were quite easily observable bruises she had attempted to cover with the aid of a greyish neckerchief. Her dress may have been linen at one stage in its life but was now covered by a matted woollen shawl that she draped upon her shoulders. The scuffed boots she wore on her feet did not match and were neither of the same style or color.

She looked even worse for wear than Rossetti, and indeed, acted as though she were an automaton and kept repeating herself *ad nauseam.*

"Tell me now, I demand you tell me you snake, is that why you have been covered in the deep red paint recently? Painting her auburn hair? Is that what she got? Auburn hair, is that what she wears on her head? As Siddal spoke these words, she became more emotional and hysterical by the minute.

At last we reached the inevitable approach to the apotheosis, though quite how it would manifest itself was left in the lap of the gods.

What then followed defies belief, and even more so the fact it happened so quickly.

Siddal was, by her erratic behaviour, without doubt, the instigator. Exasperated with Rossetti's feeble replies to her intense inquiries, she over reacted in a melodramatic fashion. And in a show of irritation and impatience with Rossetti, flung her arms back behind her head straight into a passing waiter's face who, at the time, was delivering Rossetti's favourite dish; a tureen of warmed *bouillabaisse.* The inevitable happened and Rossetti got his *bouillabaisse,* though not in quite the manner he was used to. Things might have taken a turn for the worse, had it not been for the fact that Siddal, oblivious to the fact that

Rossetti, resembled not so much the arbiter of taste and aestheticism, than a steaming mass of fish lumps and thick reddish-brown soup, staggered off to the powder room, or to another bar.

"I do not like scenes," said Wilde nonchalantly," except on the stage."

It was Stanford who attempted to ameliorate Rossetti's fury, for obvious reasons he was incensed at being baptized with *bouillabaisse* fish soup. Despite the efforts of two waiters dabbing his clothes down with flannel towels, his anger would not quite dissipate.

"Rossetti," Stanford said, proffering him a full glass of champagne, "since we were discussing Mahler's unfinished death conscious Ninth Symphony, do regale us with your remarkable story about that *bizarre* episode in your life."

"Which one?" asked Rossetti.

"The one where you were thought to have died, but had in fact not done so, but where your relations insisted on the funeral arrangements going ahead anyway, if only out of respect. And, that not a moment should be lost in your being interred into a vault at Highgate Cemetery!"

1 Mahler is confusing Whistler's *Nocturne* waterscape with Atkinson Grimshaw's *Sand Sea and Sky: A Summer Fantasy*!
2 'The artist must create what the public ought to like, not what it does like,' per Goethe.
3 Composed by Edward Elgar.
4 'Art must be struggled for'
5 AEG Building designed by Walter Gropius
6 Painting of a girl
7 Lilly Langtry
8 A *compositor* assembles the print layout for a newspaper
9 *Ophelia* by John Everett Millais in which Siddal posed with floating robes in a bathtub
10 Sir John Everett Millais
11 By George Frederick Watts

Chapter 9

The Fiasco in the Necropolis

In order to maintain some semblance of peace, the state of which was at best precarious due to Elizabeth Siddal's inadvertent accident, causing Rossetti to receive the better part of a tureen of warmed *bouillabaisse* fish soup, an invitation was offered. The invitation, given by no less a composer than Charles Villiers Stanford, was to the deranged and still furious Rossetti. It invited him to relate to us a particular *bizarre* episode in his life, and in so doing, filled Rossetti's face with a subdued delight. He wiped the last vestige of soup from his face and commenced the most *outré* of narratives.

"Yes, after I had ingested some chloral hydrate and passed out," commenced Rossetti, "I was taken for dead by my relatives, who themselves were in no fit state to assess whether life was extinct in me or not. My brother William, I later learned, insisted that I be treated with dignity and that not a moment should be lost in my being interred in the vault at Highgate Cemetery. The funeral arrangements were put in place there and then, in what could only be described as being with, 'indecent haste'.

"Naturally enough, at the time, I was unaware neither of my being dead nor of the funeral arrangements being put into place. However, having regained consciousness, I made my way out of the Red House in Kent, and staggered off back to London, to Tite Street in Chelsea. A day or so later, whilst taking my usual absinthe at the Cadogan Hotel in Sloane Street, at Knightsbridge, I read with horror of my own demise. I tried to make sense of the obituary, which was, I might add, riddled with inaccuracies, exaggerations and mistakes about events in my '...*short and tragic life*'. That they had, on no less than three occasions in the obituary, spelled my surname incorrectly, came as no surprise to me. In life I am always subject to this carelessness; and so it seems too in death. I remembered at the time feeling more outraged at their misspelling my name than the fact that I should be dead.

Then it occurred to me; I had, in a fit of *pique* and carelessness, made adequate provision for my funeral, an elaborate funeral, including a lavishly constructed Mausoleum of polished limestone. It might be of interest, I reasoned, to see what could happen to my inert body? I therefore resolved there and then to attend my own funeral *incognito* of course, at Highgate Cemetery.

At length, I arrived, at the somber stone entrance to Highgate Cemetery. In particular, the Western Cemetery, wherein lies the Egyptian Avenue, with its series of catacombs and Mausoleums, including mine, and leading to the Circle of Lebanon, dominated by a huge cedar tree. For some hitherto unexplained reason, I expected to see a mass of black-garbed mourners; instead, I witnessed a sea of colour and gaiety. I also certainly saw that the fashionable clothes from my wardrobe were well represented on the shoulders of various mourners. Why one of the mourners in particular, felt the need to wear a rather ostentatious striped blazer with such gay abandon, at my funeral, was beyond me. I supposed people to have their own way of dealing with grief. Then it struck me;

maybe the mourners simply could not contain themselves and perhaps were even happy at my demise!

My so-called mourners," Rossetti continued, "who comprised apparent friends and well-wishers, the majority of whom though I knew not, alighted from the various *char à bancs* in a festive mood, as if they had indeed arrived at some coastal resort on a day's excursion. A jollier group of individuals, intent on unadulterated pure enjoyment and making merry, would have been hard to envisage. I got the distinct impression that had the mourners thought the sun might have been shining on Highgate Cemetery, instead of being shrouded in fog; they would have supplied themselves with an assorted collection of Fortnum & Mason hampers, complete with cotton parasols and striped blazers with caps.

Despite this, these so-called acquaintances, none of whom I really knew, formed a *cortège* as such. It seemed at variance with their clearly determined intention to have fun between here and the crematorium chapel of the necropolis, in which the *Requiem* mass, in accordance with Roman Catholic rite, was to be held. Later, the interment service was to be conducted at the Mausoleum and there, elaborate funereal ritual *exequies* [1] were to take place upon my coffin, as it was inducted into the sarcophagus located within the stone burial vault. Then, it was to be bricked up for eternity.

Whilst standing at the back of the *cortège*, waiting for the coffin to be retrieved from the hearse carriage, I read the printed card containing the Order of Service. I was gratified to see in the Introduction, what looked like an attempt at bringing dignity to the proceedings.

Our thoughts and prayers go out to Gabriella Dante and his family and fiends at this time of sadness and reflection.

"That is, until I then realised, with horror, they had, yet again, spelled my Christian name incorrectly, and had attributed the *feminine* to it, and that my second name had been assigned to that of surname! I can only imagine the word *fiends,* was a printer's error and should have in fact read *friends.*

I was just getting over this shock, when another more formidable one was about to assault my sensibilities. There appeared to be a commotion of some kind involving shouting in the vicinity of the hearse carriage. I could not from my position determine immediately the reason for it. It seemed that a liveried *employé* of the London Cemetery Company, the owners and operators of the Highgate Cemetery, was advising verbally, a carriage driver from the local funeral undertaker. He was suggesting in no uncertain terms and in language becoming crystal clear, as it was audible to all, precisely what the hearse driver could do with his *'gaudy funeral cart'*. And, I heard further, the London Cemetery Company *employé* even ventured a permanent place where the rival carriage driver might like to put his hearse. Further mutual advice was offered which resulted in blows being freely exchanged between each *employé* from the two rival undertakers, which escalated as others joined in the *mêlée.* After much shouting and cursing, other officials from the Highgate Cemetery arrived to bring this outburst of tempers to an abrupt halt. Without success as it happened, and during the *fracas* the *catafalque,* bearing my coffin draped in purple velvet cloth, had been wheeled out of the hearse, and pushed, unceremoniously through this commotion.

Immediately, and with very little dignity, an official ripped away the purple velvet cloth covering my coffin. In so doing, he revealed in one fell swoop, there in the fog-bound necropolis for all to see, my coffin! On observing it, even from a distance, I nearly fainted to the ground. I only prevented myself from so doing, by gripping a nearby monument, to some Victorian worthy, in the form of a fluted sandstone column leaning at a precarious angle. I could not quite believe the spectacle that presented itself to my eyes and sensibilities. There, resplendent in the dull muted light of the fog-bound cemetery, was my coffin. I remembered quite well the design of my casket. It was to be of black ebony wood with bronze handles, hinges, *plaque* and other ostentatious paraphernalia constructed in accordance to my very detailed aesthetic and artistic specification.

Instead far removed from my detailed wishes, which I had paid for months ago, was a cheap coffin of pressed wood, an almost imperceptible grade above card-board! This was the cheapest coffin it would be possible to purchase, and place a corpse in, within the provisions of the law. Anything less than this, then the coffin would have been relegated to the status of an outsized soapbox. I was appalled by it, being light grey in colour with hinges of string and with no metal work used in its construction. What was happening? Had I arrived at the wrong funeral? Clearly not so, for I recognised some of the mourners, still wearing my clothes and whom, I noted, more alarmingly, did not exhibited any surprise on observing the apology for a casket.

Then four men in long black coats and wearing black top hats of the 'stove-pipe' variety, approached the coffin – or soapbox, and without ceremony, man-handled it as though it were a crate of assorted vegetables. They then marched off in the direction of the crematorium chapel, at a pace, I might add, not normally associated with a funeral march, but rather more indicative of a funeral gallop.

Naturally enough, somewhat out of breath, we reached the crematorium chapel in double quick time, in indecent haste, as it were, to dispose of my person.

Even as I arrived, there was an undignified pushing and shoving as mourners fought amongst themselves for prime position in the pews. Quite what they were expecting to witness from the front rows was beyond me. Or, was there something arranged that I, again, was not privy to?

The funeral chapel was a stone built structure devoid of any architectural detail. It resembled more a place of functionality than of prayer and reflection. Indeed the presence at the back of a coal-fired oven indicated its more fundamental use. If the architecture of the chapel was bland, the congregation of mourners was not. *En masse*, they resembled not so much a gathering of mourners as a group of day excursion trippers to nearby Hampstead heath for a picnic, who had lost their way in the fog, and found themselves here in the Highgate Cemetery instead.

Here was an opportunity to observe those who had come to my funeral. There in his rather loud checked suit, was Oscar, looking not in the least bit distraught, but with his roving eye on the main chance for future literary work from the congregation, or any other wealthy person, for that matter.

I confess to being horrified at not knowing more than a handful of mourners, though I recognised my wardrobe on the shoulders of some. It was the only thing I could with certainly claim to recognise.

However, it was the front row that focused my attention. Looking like the *Dame aux Camellias* in full distress, racked with consumption, and all the more valetudinarian, acting as if she were about to endure her *supreme moment*, there and then, or at any rate pass-out, was my so-called distraught lover Elizabeth Siddal. She was dressed from head to foot in deep black *crepe*, and wearing a hat that in its own right merited some kind of architectural recognition, such was its construction.

"Seated in the second row were the creditors I instantly recognised. Scattered throughout the chapel were a few relatives and friends, some wearing my clothes. The rest looked as if they had been supplied by a theatrical agency. Irrespective of the various types of mourner gathered to pay their last respects to me, all had one thing in common. Seated, as they were in this sanctified chapel, most looked thoroughly bored, but some expectant, as though waiting for something to happen.

Something did happen, a woman overcome with grief, so I would like to think, passed-out and fell crashing onto a mourner standing next to her. She in turn fell, and both unconscious and conscious mourners tumbled out into the chapel aisle. Apart from a piled mass of black *crepe* material, and language quite not concordant with being in a sanctified place, they managed to carry the unconscious woman out. As they did, I distinctly overheard a few people remark that it was an amazing feat that she had even got anywhere near to the crematorium chapel. Most did not rate her chances highly of even being able to get off the *char à banc*, let alone gain the confines of the chapel.

Eventually a peace descended upon the congregation as the organ started bellowing out some unrecognisable harmony. However, this truce was short lived as another woman, ostentatiously dressed in deep black, overcome with grief, and with the back of her hand pressed against her forehead, collapsed onto the floor of the chapel. Quite why she did so in such an exaggerated manner, I could not imagine for I certainly did not know the woman, nor I suspect, did she me.

We were assembled to celebrate the *Requiem* mass with emotion and tears and little room for anything else, nor indeed, time for reflection. Except time for yet another distraught woman to collapse, being unable to contain her emotional outburst, she fell to the ground sobbing and moaning, 'a great loss, a great loss'. It may have been directed at my demise, or more probably the fact she had lost her purse.

Whether people simply accepted this kind of behavior in keeping with attending a *Requiem*, I could not say. Mourners were falling down to the chapel floor all around, and at one stage there must have been more persons having collapsed and lying crumpled on the floor, than those of us left standing. It was all very distressing, and I felt that at any moment I too might just as well collapse to the floor and have my inert body man handled, legs first, out of the funeral chapel.

However, upon closer examination of the Order of Service, I saw that we were to listen to a recital on the organ, of the '*Lost Chord*', a dear and favourite anthem of mine - the only semblance and adherence to my specific funereal instructions. But what was this music now emanating from the organ? It was not the '*Lost Chord*' but a substitute in the form of the exhortation '*Abide with me*' a hymn I have always detested, as it is absolute anathema to me for its nonsensical and ludicrous senti-ments contained therein. It was presumably substituted, I imagined, as being an easier option for the mourners to attempt to sing without the possibility of inducing mass apoplexy amongst them. My blood instantly ran cold as the service began.

A priest came in duly wearing a regulation black *cope*

and swinging an ornate brass perforated thurible containing burning frankincense, the aroma from which wafted about the chapel. At the same time he chanted the antiphon *De Profundis &c.* followed by the, *Et lux perpetua luceat eis.*

My specific request for the beautifully sonorous and harmonious *Tantum Ergo,* as a prelude to the *Requiem Aeternam dona eis, Domine* proper, too was dispensed with, no doubt due to time constraints and other considerations. Never in my life have I witnessed a funeral being conducted at such a furious pace. We had barely completed the *Introitus Ad Altare Dei* and *Kyrie eleison* before lurching into the *Offertorium* with such indecent haste as to make the customary reflection somewhat redundant. Quite where the powerful statement expressed in the *Dies Irae* and the harmonious *Lacrimosa* had got to, confounded me, for I do not recall witnessing either.

Even though I was technically dead, I was beginning to experience feelings of depression and sadness, as the disrespect manifested itself with a sickening emphasis. It was as though my deepest wishes had been expressed within a vacuüm, devoid of caring persons. Unfortunately I had not about my person any chloral hydrate and whisky, to make tolerating this indignity bearable.

Such was the express speed of the *Requiem* that we were already at the *Agnus Dei* and from that without a pause we entered the *Sanctus.* The *Sanctus et Benedictus with Oblation of the Victim to God – 'Unde et memores',* lost its relevance and meaning to me in this service. From the *Sanctus* we progressed, or rather rushed, into the *Libera Me.* I dared not bring myself to witness the preparatory *In Paradisum deducant te Angeli* and so I left the confines of the funeral chapel and sought refuge outside from this travesty.

When I did so I could not believe how many so-called mourners had elected not to enter the chapel and attend the *Requiem*. Most were chatting amiably with one another and some were even smoking! One fellow was sitting on a stone sarcophagus with a large cigar in his mouth, whilst holding a conversation with another gentleman who himself was standing against a tombstone that was leaning at a precarious angle.

A few minutes later, he pointed with his cigar, to a plume of black smoke rising from the back of the crematorium chapel, into the fog-laden sky!

"Good God that cannot be me!" I screamed in my mind to myself.

It became abundantly apparent by the general conversation now being carried on in the cemetery, that indeed it was me who had just been burned up, disposed of, cremated. Again I railed against the indignity of my being set on fire!

Not surprisingly, within a few minutes the mourners came pouring out of the chapel as though they were leaving the theater after a *matinée* performance. They in turn were followed shortly by the four ubiquitous stove-pipe hatted pallbearers, who again manhandled my coffin with such disrespect that at one stage I really thought that they would dispense with the inconvenience of carrying it, and resort instead to dragging it behind them. The pressed wood coffin now only carried a few ounces of ash, my ashes! Without being prompted, mourners began to assemble behind the coffin resembling now, nothing more than a substantial elongated cardboard box.

I joined the queue of mourners at the back of the *cortège* as it began its march to the crypt through the fog bound necropolis to my lavish limestone built Mausoleum. My interest in seeing it was not great, but somehow looked forward to reëxamining it and the stone features I had elected to incorporate into the overall design. I might, at least once today, be pleasantly surprised by the results of something I had planned some time ago. There was one especial feature that I particularly liked as a heart-rending touch! It was the detached *alabaster* statue of the angel, looking forlorn and desolate, at the bronze crypt door entrance to my Mausoleum!

Looking at some of the names, familiar and famous, inscribed on various tombs, stone sarcophagus, columbaria and other monuments to the dead, I could not help thinking that I should repose in good company in this *Pantheon* of eminent Victorians.

Walking through this garden of Temples to the Dead, we passed several ornate sealed tombs the size of houses. Some were of Gothic design, most though, were of the Classical style with colonnades of masculine Doric columns. Interspersed among the columns, were monstrously large stone urns set upon pedestals, some of which were draped in black cloth, indicating that corpses had been recently interred within them. One Mausoleum, surrounded by an iron fence, resembled nothing more than a series of upright columns and pilasters positioned to receive a roof, but here, no roof had been constructed. For whatever reason, clearly the builders had abandoned this forlorn monument to house the dead. The only beneficiary of this half-built Mausoleum was the pervasive creeping ivy.

To my right, I noticed a large, red, granite, monumental tomb, upon which had been fixed a highly polished limestone carving of a relief. Alas, that figure placed upon the tomb was in the form of an angel in repose, with her wings still extended, as in readiness for her ascension into Heaven!

Then we saw it, gradually coming into vision, in the swirling fog, the stone arched portal, complete with overhanging foliage, which leads in to the Egyptian Avenue. The spectacle of this monumental entrance guarded on either side by two ancient Egyptian columns with their capitals based on the lotus bud, was truly a sight to behold! Gradually, our funeral *cortège* made its way through this portal and entered the Egyptian Avenue, the Avenue of the Dead. It was a late autumnal day and therefore there was a dampness, as well as the fog hanging in the aëther; in addition to a smell of rotting leaves and vegetation. However, those sensations somewhat increased in the avenue, perhaps concentrated due to its construction.

The Egyptian Avenue is a broad thoroughfare about twenty feet wide and is constructed of stone walls to either side, eighteen feet in height. Into these stone walls were carved or fixed, masonry funereal decoration and stone symbols, representing concepts of eternity, and bereavement and its attendant loss. On some of the more elaborate Mausoleums, the symbol of the ancient Egyptian deity, *Nephthys,* with outstretched wings, was emblazoned in the stone fronted vault, guarding the entrance to the Mausoleum.

Cut into the wall were several openings to vaults, surrounded by elaborate stone frames of varying designs. Some were designed in the classical Greek style; that of a protruding stone triangular shaped pediments. Others represented the massive Egyptian hollow and roll in place of a pediment above the entrance to the opening in the wall leading to a vault within the Mausoleum wherein the deceased is laid to rest in a sarcophagus. These structures, of course, housed the various Mausoleums with which the avenue is lined.

As our funeral *cortège* progressed along this dank avenue, I noticed that some of these mortuary temples were covered, not only in pervasive ivy and foliage, but also with elaborate stone symbols of funereal paraphernalia, including martial helmets set upon shields or urns. The word 'Eternity' was prolific and carved on many of the more ostentatious monuments. Other symbols were represented in stone, including carvings of shoulders and heads of persons, but with their faces hidden from view by the overhanging folds falling from a veil. Such was the masonry fronting these Mausoleums in the avenue of the dead.

Another funereal structure we came across was an extended columbarium in the form of a colonnade in the ancient Egyptian style, complete with columns supporting splayed-out lotus leaf shaped capitals. The stone wall of the colonnade had angled door openings cut into it, creating burial vaults located in the dark recesses of the columbarium's open tombs, with their exposed stone sarcophagus. There were several impressive tomb structures located in the Egyptian Avenue, and in one such edifice we saw a faint, dull, yellow glow emanating from deep with the interior of the Mausoleum, even though it was partially shrouded in the fog.

As we progressed through the necropolis, and rising up into the fog, that for some reason now felt even danker, was a structure I could not quite believe capable of being built and occupied a raised island site. Immediately in front of us set in isolation and unreachable, was a huge Mausoleum built in the ancient classical style and constructed of massive limestone blocks set upon each other to form a sealed tomb.

The Mausoleum comprised four massive walls forming a square structure of at least twenty feet in height on top of which were a series of stepped backed terraces culminating in a recessed tower rising a further fifteen feet. Into this inner tower *façade*, at the top of a series of steps, was an elongated and dark recessed door aperture from which no light emanated, making the Mausoleum as menacing as it was monolithic.

I stood there transfixed by this monumental edifice and the feeling of stillness it radiated from the depths of its tomb. As my eyes became accustomed to the fog surrounding it I also noticed yet another structure rising even further into the fog but sufficiently obscured as to make ascertaining its structural details difficult. Then, my heart nearly failed, as I became aware of what this tower was supporting. As the fog swirled around the tower it caused vortices, making the fog thin out in places, and in so doing created a brief vision that I observed with my eyes wide open.

The *vista* came into my sight, and then as quickly, disappeared from view the enshrouding fog reclaimed the structure, again making it invisible. Then, again, then fog receded and coming back into vision, was a gigantic monumental sculpture, in bronze at least forty-five feet or so in height, of four interlocking wings, creating a cross at its base.

What was this Mausoleum, the limestone structure of which, had metamorphosized into an upper elaborate and ornate bronze sculpture of wings, were they a symbolic profile of the Wings of Eternity?

That the wings were supported on four connected piers creating a cruciform added yet more significance to the whole structure and its sculpture. Consistent with the orthodox concept of a Mausoleum it comprised a *sombre* fortress-like limestone structure to protect the sarcophagus within and a recessed door aperture.

Wings of Eternity

The exuberant monument of wings might easily be interpreted as addressing eternity and the symbolic preparation of the journey of flight to the hereinafter. I continued to stare at the upper section to this remarkable structure, focusing on the layout of the limestone blocks, forming the structure thrown high into the fog-laden aëther, in the absence of which, it would no doubt dominates the locality. I also began to wander if whether I had in fact, ingested some chloral hydrate? I could not be certain.

Farther down the avenue, our attention was arrested by the presence, just visible in the fog, of another Mausoleum built in the style of an ancient Egyptian tomb, with its wall slanting inwards and addressing the avenue, in which we were standing. The inner two of those columns were tapered to a capital in the style of splayed leaves of a papyrus plant, but in contrast the two adjacent outer columns were square and undecorated. The external walls and columns of the tomb supported a monstrously overhanging curved Egyptian architrave, in the form of a hollow and roll that supported the stone slab roof.

On the front *facade* of this vault, was a door architrave in the shape of a metal Masonic winged image, above the recessed doorframe cut into the wall of the tomb, into which two large, burnished, copper doors had been positioned. However, apparent even to us, were signs that these copper doors had been forced, because they were both hanging off their hinges!

I then remembered reading a learned treatise [2] where the writer reasons, that we as a society today are more overt in our expression of funereal concepts, as confirmed typically, in the construction of this elaborate Egyptian avenue of Mausoleums, here in the Highgate Cemetery. This *rationale*, he goes on to propound, is based partly on the reaction to a perceived weakening of religious authority and its inability to guarantee peaceful repose after death, that compels us to seek consolation in fantasy concepts. Such concepts are complete with crocheted towers, pinnacles, turrets and spires, and the elaborate Mausoleum. Neo-Gothic architecture is now the natural choice in expressing fantasy to fulfil this consoling need and is the preferred style of architecture for important buildings, including typically, the St. Pancras Hotel, in London.

It was with these profound thoughts tearing through my mind that we eventually arrived at the end of the Egyptian Avenue, which leads in to the Circle of Lebanon. In this circular avenue are more Mausoleums but it continues until coming back on itself, rejoins the Egyptian Avenue. Dominating this Circle of Lebanon, just barely visible in the swirling fog, was a huge over grown cedar tree. The clear unequivocal symbolism represented in this cedar tree was not lost, even on me.[3]

On approaching my Mausoleum," Rossetti continued unabated, "the *cortège* paused. I think it only stopped to enable mourners to catch their breath, such was the speed of the forced funeral march to the crypt. To my consternation, I noticed too that a decorative feature on my Mausoleum, that of the detached *alabaster* statue of an angel looking forlorn and desolate at the bronze door to my Mausoleum, was nowhere to be seen. The angel had either been stolen or removed to some other corpse's dwelling! However, before I could marshal my thoughts to deal with this outrage, the *cortège* was on the move again, marching at a maniac's pace as our feet crunched the wet gravel of the avenue.

As we continued toward my Mausoleum the *cortège* suddenly veered right into another gravelled avenue and continued past my mortuary temple. No! I thought, they are in error, they have passed my Mausoleum that I have caused to be constructed and in which to inter my corpse, but alas, to no avail. Instead the funeral procession, marched out of the Egyptian Avenue of the Dead, with some of the members of *cortège* were still laughing, continued to an outer part of the necropolis, to the cheaper areas. We made our way through rough cut grass and almost scrubland to a rather desolate part of the cemetery that had not been attended to or looked after and was in a state of extreme dilapidation.

Of the three classes of funeral offered by the under-takers, I had obviously elected First Class, culminating in the interment of my remains into the Mausoleum the design and erection of which I was justly proud. It was apparent to me that the *cortège* was now progressing into an area of the necropolis that was clearly reserved for graves of paupers of the parish. I could not believe it. My ashes were to be dumped in a pauper's grave, a hole in the ground without a gravestone or even a marker to indicate my presence!

As we approached the graveside, the four pallbearers moved with a coördinated precision, obviously dab hands in executing the *manoeuvre* about to take place. Without verbal instruction or prompting, they approached an elongated hole in the ground and stopped. There they positioned themselves, two pallbearers on either side supporting the coffin over the hole in the earth. One of the pallbearers even had a lit cigarette in his mouth! Then they lowered the casket down to ground level over the opening in the ground that was the grave. I distinctly heard one of the stovepipe hatted pallbearers say some-thing like...now! Whereupon, they simply dropped the box - coffin, unceremoniously, into the grave and then simply walked off leaving two gravediggers to fill in the hole with rubble from an adjacent pile!

I stood there filled with bewilderment and incredulity. What was happening? Could I complain bitterly or even vicariously? The inevitable answer came resoundingly to my mind as I railed mentally at my inability to do so. Then a feeling of horror gripped my heart and I turned away aghast at what I had witnessed concerning the treatment meted out to my body, or rather warm ashes. Had it really been me! I could scarcely believe this ignominious action of the mourners, some of who had benefited from my will. Is this how they wished to remember me – in a pauper's grave, burned up, incinerated and, what was to become of my precious Mausoleum, *requiescat in pace*?"⁴ That Elizabeth Siddal had some explaining to do, I resolved."

Both Mahler and I had listened to Rossetti's remarkable story with incredulity and could scarcely take in what we had just heard. That Rossetti and these other persons represented the breakaway group from the Royal Academy was too incongruous to believe. Was that how leaders in English aesthetics, definers of standards, indeed, the *Arbiter Elegantiarum* behaved rationally; irrespective of attending their own funerals in order that they might see what happens to their corpse?

Was this how one tested potential bereavement arrangements in England whilst influencing artistic direction and development? The more I thought about these Pre-Raphaelites, the more convinced I became that Rossetti's monomania was not an isolated case, and indeed I thought the condition was widespread among the Pre-Raphaelite Brethren. I remembered reading only recently, that one of their brethren, a John Millais in his painting *Speak Speak,* depicts a dead wife in her bridal gown at the foot of the bed, exhorting her very much alive husband, to come and join her in death!

One got the impression that the mental intensity of these Pre-Raphaelites would equip them adequately for any activity, including being committed revolutionaries, perhaps even nothing less than by way of being covert Nihilists.

I previously thought the Pre-Raphaelites, in general, were concerned in conveying realism in nature. The realism was typically expressed as romanticized depiction of chivalrous scenes based on legends, similar in style, which Wagner adapted for his operatic scenes in his sacred music dramas such as *Parsifal* or *Lohengrin*. Instead, sitting in the Café Royal, the ideas and behavior exhibited by the Pre-Raphaelites reflected those expressed by Wagner in '*Götterdämmerung*'; another opera concerned with fantasy, doom and redemption. In other instances, both Mahler and I witnessed, the Pre-Raphaelites' real obsession, a fated embrace with an unrealistic fantasy, that continues to dominate their thinking; in the art studio, in the Café Royal and in Rossetti's case, in Highgate Cemetery.

But, the *malaise* was all pervasive, and not merely confined to Rossetti, who was of course an extreme example. It was as though the Pre-Raphaelites were frozen in action and attitude from which they could not devise an escape. Everything was repetitive to the extent the concept became all-consuming to the detriment of new ideas. Both Mahler and I had on numerous occasions discussed the fact that *any* art must evolve to accept the new. Were it to fail to do so; it would die. In this respect the Pre-Raphaelites had buried themselves alive in a Mausoleum more suited to keep ideas out; not retain them. The Pre-Raphaelites' artistic spectrum ranges from the classically motivated ethereal and symmetrical Elysian dreamscapes typical of Laurence Alma-Tadema and Albert Moore's. To the implausibility represented in John Anster Fitzgerald's inspiration to create his series of '*Nightmare*' paintings. In these paintings, he depicts dreamers during nightmares being beset by demons bearing bowls of laudanum and other toxic liquids. The Pre-Raphaelite style now seemed to have transmuted into the unremittingly *grotesque*, and was reminiscent of the drawings of Beardsley which are characteristic of this later period.

Rather than embracing changes, however inconvenient, wrought about by the remorseless and irreversible industrialization of society, the Pre-Raphaelites had rejected this reality in favor of a make-believe fantasy. This had culminated in the ridiculous concepts that attended the Red House, from which the lunatic Rossetti occasionally escaped. Elizabeth Siddal, albeit a drunken consumptive wreck, at least had the intelligence to define the Red House for what it really was. Not the revolutionary innovative center of progress and experiment; but rather a retreat from reality, in which they made their own clothes, on a loom, and where mediaevalism was dominant.

One need only look at the subject matter beloved of the Pre-Raphaelites. An over indulgent obsession with females, represented as lost damsels, that somehow had wandered from the twelfth century and into the nineteenth century together with their cloned sisters, who pervaded the paintings of the Pre-Raphaelites. It was especially so in those of Burne-Jones', including his 'Golden Stairs' and 'Pygmalion: The Godhead Fires' complete with their dreamy or dozy facial expressions, reflecting an impossibly romanticized past.

1 Funeral Rites
2 A book called 'Visions of Architecture'
3 Symbolic representation of Eternity
4 Rest in Peace.

Postscript:

Sadly, we learned sometime later that Elizabeth Siddal died of an overdose of laudanum. Predictably Rossetti's reaction was as *bizarre* as ever; in full grief he could not quite bring himself to accept Siddal's death, insisting that her corpse be left exposed for seven days on the kitchen table at the Red House in the vain hope she might recover. She did not, but was instead eventually buried in the Western Cemetery at Highgate -where they tried to bury Rossetti! However, before her coffin was lowered into the grave Rossetti had placed in it the only copy of his collected poems. Seven years later he had second thoughts and exhumed Elizabeth's coffin in order to recover the lost poems!

Chapter 10

The Titan Symphony – Polemic Part II

Our being invited to join Oscar Wilde's table in the Café Royal in the company of his guests who included Atkinson Grimshaw, Zemlinsky, Rickett, Joyce, Stanford, Beardsley, Whistler, the deranged Rossetti and his woman Siddal and others, was in itself quite revealing. Not only in terms of meeting members of the Pre-Raphaelites Brotherhood, but rather experiencing in close proximity the manic intensity that propelled them. I thought that Rossetti was but a pace away from having his freedom severely curtailed and that his days as a free, sane person were numbered. However, an even bigger shock for us was imminent in the person of an even more deranged individual, George Antheil who had just joined our table.

"George! Where have you been keeping yourself?" asked Oscar Wilde, "we have not seen you for weeks"

"Where have I been keeping myself? Well you should know Oscar. I have been a prisoner, yes a prisoner of my purse, unable to move but one yard without recourse to its empty silk lining," replied George Antheil.

"Gustav and Friedrich, please allow me to introduce you to George Antheil, an American no less, but a leading exponent of what they call the *Music of the future*! Indeed George has met with great acclaim for his revolutionary and innovatory *'Ballet Mecanique'*, complete with electric bells, automobile horns and sixteen Aëolian player pianos!" said Wilde.

"I would be delighted meet any person not shrouded in the damp material of dead music, for which Mr. Mahler is as notorious as he is an accomplished practitioner," replied Antheil.

"George, George," said Wilde, "we were just discussing Gustav's First Symphony – *The Titan*, and in particular implication of the sub-mediant."

"The sub-what?" queried Antheil.

"You heard Wilde!" informed Mahler.

"Please explain to him Gustav," invited Wilde,

Surprisingly, Mahler rose to the occasion to lecture Antheil, as clearly Wilde had hoped he would.

"I feel confident," Mahler began "that George knows precisely what the *sub-mediant* is, being of course, the sixth degree of a minor or major scale, to denote a lesser importance. Here the mediant occupies a position between the *tonic* and *dominant,* whereas the sub-mediant exists in equidistance from both the *sub-dominant* and *tonic.* The one dominant is five degrees above the tonic whilst the other is five degrees below. This of course remains a cardinal tenet of serious music and is accepted by all commentators."

"What, you mean that retrospective look back in its attempt to address outmoded romantic gestures and the antics of tedious hero-types?" said Antheil, in response to Mahler's definition.

"George that is not the way to address a famous conductor," advised Wilde.

"I suspect that electricity is about the only thing Mahler could conduct successfully!" retorted Antheil, "other than composing retrospective music concerned with death."

"Perhaps I could one day conduct your *Ballet Mecanique*, complete, as Oscar has kindly informed us, with electric bells, automobile horns and sixteen Aëolian player-pianos!" offered Mahler.

"My *Ballet Mecanique* is not yet ready to die at your hands Mahler," said Antheil, "unlike you at your recent address to the gentlemen of the press, where we understand you got an intense reception, especially from *The Pall Mall Gazette* to say nothing about what the correspondent for the *Sporting Life* put you through?"

"Only the usual run of polite inquiries about all my symphonies," answered Mahler.

"The *Pall Mall Gazette* does not think so; and thought you to be obsessed with death, especially of children. Is this so?" inquired Antheil, whilst accepting a flute of champagne from Wilde.

"George will be more amenable when he has drunk a bottle or two of champagne; please be tolerant and give him a few minutes in which to do so," said Wilde. "However, Gustav, George's remarks do, as it were, elicit the question; do you thrive on writing songs on the death of children?"

"Are you indirectly referring to my *Kindertotenlieder?*" inquired Mahler.

"*Kindertotenlieder,* that dreary collection of poems drenched in death?" asked Wilde,

"Well, yes, rather like your *De Profundis* representing nothing more than the ramblings of an incarcerated and deranged mind," remarked Mahler.

"*Kindertotenlieder!* Whatever possessed you to tempt fate by concocting such a dirge in composing music to them?" inquired Wilde.

"Why, Oscar, the same fate that compelled you to confirm in writing your *Requiescat* as an ode for the death of your nine year old sister Isola, no?" replied Mahler, "how does the first *stanza* go:"

Tread lightly; she is near under the snow,
Speak gently; she can hear the daisies grow,
All her bright golden hair, tarnished with rust
She that was young and fair, Fallen to dust.

"Ironically," replied Mahler, "I had considered that at one stage I might even set the verses of which your *Requiescat* is comprised, to *lieder*. But on reflection, I felt my skill should be deployed for the enrichment of mankind. So instead, I elected to complete Carl Maria von Weber's unfinished draft to his opera '*The Three Pintos*' he had started in 1824 based on a drama by Theodor Hell!"

"Perhaps," said Wilde, "you should avail yourself of Hugo von Hofmannsthal's drafting skills in constructing interesting and workable *libretti*, as he clearly does with his successful collaboration with Rickard Strauss, especially in that unassailable magnum opus in *Die Frau Ohne Schatten* [1] or indeed *Der Rosenkavalier*. [2] You may then find the music-loving public will accept your efforts, especially if you can transcend beyond that failed attempt at serious pantomime you call *Die Drei Pintos*! [3] What! Had you lost your reason when you constructed that, that ridiculous comic operetta set to what can only be described as *divertimenti* music? But do tell me, were you having one of your intense episodes of monomaniac depression?"

"Well I might say the same about you my dear Oscar," said Mahler, "in that being, I believe, a consummate writer, dramatist and in particular *playwright*, can you write a play right?"

"Of course I can, I went to Oxford, but nonetheless,

I remain honored that you know and can quote *verbatim*, my prose and verse. In order to return your compliment, I too, of course, am *not* familiar with your First Symphony. And, if I may venture to say so, it exceeds all expectation in its peculiarity!" said Wilde.

"Oh, that is a rather an unsubstantiated remark," I said to Wilde, whilst intervening, "please, allow me to enlighten you."

"Oh very well," said Oscar.

"The Symphony No. 1 in D major, *Der Titan,* originally had five movements, the *andante* was in between the first and third movements, but was removed upon a subsequent revision. The symphony is now set in the usual four movements, *allegro comodo, scherzo, lento moderato* and *finale* in the form of *allegro furioso.* The program structure for the symphony is based freely on that of the literature of Jean Paul Richter, especially his novel *'The Titan'* from whence the symphony gets its name. The symphony was completed in 1888 at Leipzig in Germany, and *premièred* to great acclaim is Budapest in 1889," I announced.

"There is, though, a rumor that you Mahler may have been influenced by one of your compatriot students who claims to have created the symphony too?" asked Zemlinsky.

"Rather like you and your so-called plagiarize *'Lyrische Symphonie',*" answered Gustav.

"Whatever possessed you to call it *The Titan*; is it worthy of being so called?" asked Wilde.

"The name *Titan* is taken from the novel written by Jean Paul Richter called, *Der Titan,* and his work influenced me when drafting the symphonic structure," said Mahler.

"Really," replied Wilde.

"The Titans," continued Mahler, "as you probably

know, were a race of demi-gods who were defeated by Zeus, and a new order of gods, based in Olympia, introduced a new *régime*.

The Titans, who themselves were descendant from Uranus, Gaia and Chaos, were, Rhea and Cronos – whose sons, Zeus, Poseidon and Pluto, ended the Titans' long reign. It was Zeus who persuaded Pluto to create a living entity, in avarice, so powerful it could defeat their parents.

Subsequently, Zeus became ruler of the heavens, Poseidon, of the oceans and, Pluto that of the under-world of Hades. Zeus created man, in order that humans might feast on adoration of the gods, and in so doing, the Olympian divinities might derive perpetual life.

The term *Titan* has come to mean powerful and gigantic. In terms of philosophy it has been applied in the sense of unassailable propositional truth, as in a Titan of intellectual prowess."

"Do you not mean Olympia next to Earl's Court here in London?" asked Whistler, in all earnestness, provoking general laughter around the table.

If Mahler understood this witticism he displayed little sign of appreciating it.

"Would this Jean Paul Richter be in any way, related to the Johanne Richter; the woman in the midst of your earlier failed relationship?" asked Zemlinsky, with a glint in his eye.

"It is better Zemlinsky, to have loved than not loved," remarked Mahler.

"The symphony," I continued in my description, "is unusual in that the beginning of the first movement is one of the most beautiful openings in the symphonic *repertoire*. The sustained high octave A major chord gradually unfolds a sequence of descending *fourths*. The First Symphony remains my friend, Gustav Mahler's, enduring contribution to the symphonic *repertoire*. The work is divided into two symphonic sections; Part I, *Days of Youth,* concerns itself with concepts from nature as, *Frühlings,* dawn of nature, flowers, and progression.

Part II, *Commedia umana,* reflects on disaster, resulting in a funeral march in the manner of a woodcut by the Weimar printer, Jacques Callot. In that woodcut, used by Mahler for inspiration, Callot's depiction forms the basis of the symphony's third movement; essentially a funeral march, devoted to a dead hunter. His *cortège* is made up of creatures of the forest, which include hares carrying pennons in front of the hearse, followed by deer, cats, foxes, bears and other animals, all of whom are playing musical instruments! The originally inspired music of the funeral march contains within its sounds of stepping *Fourths,* as the beat for the *trauer marsch,* albeit conveyed as a cynical parody of the music, which is given further expression in the song *Frère Jacques.*

These sub titles in the symphony were an afterthought, reflecting *motif symbolism* of Heaven and hell expressed by Wagner as redemption in his sacred music drama *Parsifal* and the *Abbé* Liszt in his *Dante Symphony* - in defining the Cross. In the *finale* to the First Symphony, Mahler begins the movement addressing '*Inferno et Parsdiso*' from the *Dante Symphony,* with a piercing dissonance, as *allegro furioso* depicting a shrieking hell. This opening section further addresses the concept of a living hell conveyed as a '*wound to the heart*' and attendant re-action after emotional crisis. Here Mahler's Symphony reflects ideas first explored in his *lieder* cycle, *Lieder eines fahrenden Gesellen* [4] aspects of which are re-incorporated in the final movement, but given eventual triumphant interpretation." I explained.

"We know you were working on your song cycle, *Songs of the Wayfarer,* whilst composing your First Symphony.

But, during that hectic and creative period, were you not influenced by personal tragedy, failure, rebuff, and rejection; by at least two women to whom you were attracted? One of these women we know to be the actress Johanne Richter, but the other, well Gustav, perhaps you could enlighten us, no? Oh well, perhaps later then?" asked Zemlinsky, with the same smoldering glint in his eye and with an obvious ulterior motive.

"Your symphony has taught you to love it for its own right; will it teach you though to loathe your own soul?" This question came from Wilde.

Imperceptibly at first but gradually becoming noticeable, was the fact that other patrons in the Café Royal were attracted to the vicinity of our table by this *Titanic* struggle being played out to great amusement and for the instruction of others.

"Animals," said Antheil, "all of whom are playing musical instruments; can one believe in such nonsense? You ask the intelligentsia to accept your symphonies Mahler; and yet you drench them in this rubbish, involving instrument playing animals. And no Mahler, the fact of their being string or percussion instruments is not relevant here. What is; are those who are playing."

"George, sit down before yo..." advised Wilde.

"And this is the man," continued Antheil, "who attacks me for my music, my *Music of the Future!* At least in composing it, I avail myself of what humanity has to offer in responding to the needs of the soul. How can man raise himself from the barbarity of animal instinct if we continually refer back to those creature the God gave us the ability to escape from, and recognise a greater intelligence in evidence around us? Hares carrying pennons straight out of a medieval woodcut by Callot; what imagination!

But it could be said that there may be something plausible in a hare carrying a pennant, in that one might possibly be able to train one to do so. What certainly cannot be achieved, even with the *bizarre* imagination of Rossetti there, is the ridiculous notion expressed in your Fifth Symphony. That particular work commences, or at least so I believe, with yet another funeral march, the effects of which pervade the symphonic structure throughout. However, it is in your *rondo finale* movement to the symphony where your imagination exceeds that of even Rossetti's. I understand," said Antheil, "in the score, horn calls receive a reply from the bassoons, which themselves quote from, '*Lob des hohen Verstandes,*' taken from your *Des Knaben Wunderhorn. A s*eries of songs, in which an animal, an ass no less, is judging a singing contest, presumably to the standards set in *Wagner's 'Die Meistersingers von Nürnburg'!*"

Clearly, even Wilde's prediction of Antheil being more amenable was woefully under-estimated. The champagne, rather than making him more conciliatory, appeared to have released that latent resentment which had defined this individual, who of course was known to both Mahler and me. Antheil's mannerism and general demeanor represented nothing more than a premonition of worse to follow.

"With such idiotic retrospect Mahler," continued Antheil, "is it any wonder that you fail to understand why the Futurists have little tolerance of your so-called music, and consider *you* a danger to the progress of humanity? Cannot you see that your promotion of retrospective introspection can only earn you the scorn of your detractors? You prohibit the progress of humanity and you sit with these Pre-Raphaelites, who themselves are like you, fatally obsessed with the past, and an impossibly romanticized past, filled with disease, hunger, violence and ignorance.

How many of you sitting around this table, acting as automatons on your day off, have read the inspiring works of Verne, Huxley, Ezra Pound or even Thomas Carlyle? These writers address a brave new world in which we form a part. They do not hide behind retrospective religious idiocy in music, or the redundancy of mock medievalism. Unlike the Pre-Raphaelites in their abject terror, they perceive the present to be, and given cogent expression by that living fossil called Burne-Jones.

I still have difficulty in trying to understand how that prolific Pre-Raphaelite painter, Burne-Jones, when asked just what the hell he thought he was doing in painting the death scene of some medieval despot in Avalon [5] - that had taken him eighteen years to complete – replied, 'I am in Avalon'. How can you take such a person seriously? The establishment even bestowed a knight-hood upon him for his retrospective efforts. His anaemic acolyte, Ruskin, even had the temerity to announce that the noise created by anvils and machines was deafening. It ought to be; they were trying to wake him up, and to this day still continue to do so.

These outmoded concepts and ideals would all be consigned to oblivion, were it not for the re-actionary influences of the Pre-Raphaelites in general, and you, Gustav Mahler in particular, yes, you!. You both prolong a calcified aversion to reality and therefore progress. You Mahler, with your religious concepts in music and the Pre-Raphaelites and their neurotically propelled obses-sion with a mediaeval fantasy of knights and damsels, are far removed from science and the creation of our industrial machine age. The machine and all it represents shall usher in a new age in which society will be rid of neurotically propelled escapism and fantasy propounded by neo mediaevalists such as yourselves.

Who was it that said, '*I shall lead a call to arms against Victorian values – to wage a crusade and holy war against the machine age. The more materialist science becomes; the more angels I shall paint*'? Sir Edward Burne-Jones of course, the leading exponent in the regress of aesthetics! One wonders; did he say these words after he was committed to an asylum or before? But examine his words, *crusade, holy war* or *angels,* said by a so-called arbiter of taste, the *Arbiter Elegantiarum* This is a person who is suppose to define aesthetic or artistic direction and purpose.

The Pre-Raphaelites, in not leading society in to accepting the machine age, have instead by their innate aversion to change, created a nightmare set to music by Mahler. This apocalyptic syndrome, given frightening reign, now let loose by that moribund state of mind, is given credence and practised in the Red House, by Rossetti, Morris and other fossils living in a doomed Avalon," concluded Antheil.

"George, George, you have delighted us long enough with your passing whims on this matter. Now do have more champagne! Ah, but I see that you have drunk all our champagne!" noted Wilde.

"Smile if you will Mahler," continued Antheil, "but an electric bell or automobile horns and sixteen Aëolian player-pianos have more significance today, than stray cats playing trombones in a *cortège* in the forest or asses judging vocal range competitions!"

1 '*The Woman Without a Shadow*' opera premièred in 1918
2 *The Rose Cavalier* opera *premièred* in 1911
3 *The Three Pintos* opera
4 Songs of the Wayfarer
5 '*The Sleep of King Arthur in Avalon*'

Chapter 11

The Ballet Mecanique – Polemic
Part III

Our joining Wilde's table at the Café Royal had become incongruous, rather like our meeting with the Fourth Estate, the gentlemen of the press at the Langham Hotel, Mahler was not at his best at such times, in that his diplomatic skills left much to be desired. Both Mahler and I, of course knew George Antheil to be unbalanced and certainly deranged. A confrontation with this gentleman normally spiraled upward, very rarely settling down to compromise, since due to his innate intensity, he could neither forget nor forgive. In some aspects though, I retained a grudging respect and indeed, slight admiration for Antheil. Much of what he propounded, when considered in the cool light of retrospection, could add up to a cogent argument. What was, however, of over-riding concern to me, was the fact of Antheil's inextricable links with the Futurists movement, lead by the fanatical Menotti with his overtures to the Nihilists. Naturally enough, Antheil lent them his support and approved of their nefarious activities, if only because they cited his music and promoted it enthusiastically. This lethal mixture was likely to ignite at any time, with predictable combustive results. Certainly this combination, ought not to be applauded, but rather in fact avoided. In comparison, Antheil's intensity and behavior put the thoughts and actions of the lunatic Rossetti and his woman Siddal into the shade.

"Are you saying Gustav," asked Villiers Stanford, "that clearly no person imagines for a moment that the animals of the forest had clubbed together to bury, with honors, the very person who had spent his life hunting them down, irrespective of the fact that the stray cats are dab paws at playing trombones at funerals?"

"Certainly not; the listener to my First Symphony is deliberately invited to consider this proposition, after Callot's woodcut," answered Mahler.

"But surely you are being serious by alluding to aspects of the symphony taken out of their harmonic or allegorical context?" rejoined the renowned composer Sir Charles Villiers Stanford.

"Of course he is being serious Sir Charles," said George Antheil, "you do not know this person. I do. He would have you believe in even more preposterous nonsense. We are here now talking about his first collection of noise, sounds and religious incongruity; he has seven more to unleash on an unsuspecting audience. A bit like deranged Rossetti here and that woman of his, being released from the medieval hovel called the Red Barn or some such name!"

"When you say collection of noise, sounds and religious incongruity, Antheil, are you referring to that infernal *Ballet Mecanique* again?" asked Mahler.

"I agree with Mahler," said Rossetti, commencing his attack on Antheil for his remarks about him, his medieval hovel at the Red House and his woman, Siddal.

"What I said Rossetti, I meant, and am prepared to repeat it again to you if you have a hearing problem or are too drunk to understand me now. I shall say what I want and with impunity, Rossetti. But do not panic, I should like to help you in your appallingly overcrowded domestic predicament. Perhaps if we gather a few Futurists together, and avail ourselves of a *char à banc,* we could mount an expedition to that mediaeval encampment you call the Red House. Once there, we could rebuild it for you, in a non-vernacular style and perhaps even lay on central heat for your comfort and ease! Speaking of which, where is that woman of yours, still weaving woollen clothes on her loom?" inquired Antheil.

"If you really wish to upset your enemies – forgive them!" whispered Wilde audibly into Rossetti's ear.

"You talk incessantly about this so-called age of the machine that we live in and your *Ballet,* that resembles nothing more than a preposterous collection of sounds scored for anvils, electric bells, automobile horns and sixteen Aëolian player-pianos. Yet what kind of cacophony is that, where is the beauty, and how are we to perceive it?" asked Stanford.

"Who said anything about beauty, real or apparent? Such aesthetic concerns I leave to the moribund Mahler and his dead acolytes as Rossetti. My music, my *Music of the Future,* reflects the noises and sounds we hear daily as part of our existence. Were I to be one of those instrument-playing animals portrayed in that *cortège* in the forest; then I would expect to experience sounds prevalent in such a place."

"You would advocate the noise of a clanking steam engine as being representative of the *Music of the Future?*" inquired Stanford.

"Yes and I would include a fully operating steam engine into my score, if I knew that it could be got onto the concert platform," replied Antheil.

"What about the noise generated by a telegraph apparatus?" asked Mahler.

"Good idea, I had not thought of that, but I shall now include it into my next work without delay! Thank you Mahler, you have actually proved yourself useful for once," acknowledged Antheil.

"Despite this," asked Stanford, "where is the harmony, or something for the listener to relate too? If this is not the case, then one may as well go and stand in a railroad station and concentrate on the sounds made by various machine in action"

"You would attract no criticism from the Futurists; for that is precisely what they advocate. There is harmony in such sound that is created by machine. What is a piano? Nothing more than an Aëolian harp set into a horizontal timber reverberating frame, capable of creating sound when the chords are struck. What then becomes of that piano when it is mechanically driven in producing the very same sounds one experienced when being played by a pianist?

Where persons as Mahler fail is that they will not accept innovation. He will tell you that he accepts the player- piano, the Aëolian pianola, only because it makes a recognizable sound, however contrived, that conforms to his strictures of music construction,. The Futurists are not mad, nor are they fanatical, they are however, observant and wish to enjoy and explore a world teeming with musical possibilities. Each sound, however created, whether from discordant cacophony or melodic harmony is a sound to be appreciated. Open up your ears, as the Pre-Raphaelites have closed their eyes to the world around them!" thus spoke George Antheil.

"You argue with passion George," said Stanford, "but you do not convince."

"Convince? I am not trying to convince, for it is not I who is endeavoring to defend a moribund and redundant style of harmonic progression; as my music takes me to the future, precisely my intention. Whereas your music can only take you backwards, to a now dead dream," said Antheil. "And, as I have remarked before, I hold with Goethe's dictum; 'that the artist must create what the public ought to like, not what it does like'."

"The Futurists and their compatriots, the Nihilists, at best appear to be confused in what they really believe. They are strange martyrs who have no faith, who go to the stake without enthusiasm and die for what they do not believe in!" said Oscar Wilde.

"Speaking of Nihilists," I interjected, "we experienced a *concentration* of them only yesterday at the Royal Albert Hall of Art and Sciences, during a performance of my friend, Gustav Mahler's First Symphony. Though they were too few in number to be considered a real threat and disruption, and it is possible they just sat back in their cheap stall seats, and enjoyed the concert!"

"I did not know my play *Vera and the Nihilist* was being performed there! I thought it had been withdrawn due to the assassination of Alexander II, whose daughter, as you all know, is the Duchess of Edinburgh and sister-in-law to the Prince of Wales," said Wilde in mock outrage at this revelation.

"You are really incorrigible Wilde," said Mahler, "and I doubt you could not even wrestle with your conscience!"

"No more than you may have to wrestle with the drinks bill at the end of this session!" retorted Wilde. "And, by the way Gustav, the whole point of having a waiter wait upon us is to confuse him when giving our orders from the menu!"

This remark by Wilde was in response to Mahler's ordering more champagne and food from an over elaborate menu, and giving specific instructions to the waiter.

"Do tell us Mahler, How is it that you have this undoubted skill of dispatching forthwith colleagues and friends of yours to the madhouse?" asked Alexander Zemlinsky.

"What can you possibly mean Zemlinsky?" inquired Mahler.

"Well I mean," continued Zemlinsky "the incident of your having an affair with the actress Johanne Richter, is one thing; but with the wife of a certain Captain Weber of Leipzig, grandson of the great composer Carl Maria von Weber, whom you so admire, is another matter, no? Am I correct in believing the captain tolerated his wife's infidelity as you continued to a *liaison* with her? Of course any man will re-act to this deceitful behavior as the captain did eventually and with tragic consequences. Your affair became critical and reached a climax whilst Weber was travelling with other passengers on a train to Dresden.

The story goes that Weber burst out laughing manically for no apparent reason, but then produced a revolver from inside his coat and started shooting the *antimacassar* covered cotton head-rests of the train seats! Eventually, he was overpowered and the train brought to a halt and Weber taken to a police station raving mad and thence committed to an institution for the criminally insane! Did you not feel any remorse, shame or even compassion?" asked Zemlinsky.

"Wrecked marriages Mahler; do tell? pressed Wilde.

"Wrecked marriages, I should have thought was your province Wilde," retorted Mahler.

"It most certainly is, on the stage," replied Wilde,

"But what about Hans Rott," continued Zemlinsky,

"Anton Bruckner's favorite pupil at the Vienna Conservatory and his First Symphony in E major of 1878? Though the symphony was ungraded by his professors, Rott took it to Brahms to seek his advice on the work, but was ignored unceremoniously. However, later the symphony found its way into your possession after his tragic death in 1884. That your first symphony, I believe you call *Der Titan* and composed in 1888 at Leipzig bears a more than a passing resemblance to Rott's symphony, or is that just coincidence? Perhaps Rott suspected that you might have plagiarized his musical ideas and style, now self –evident in your first and subsequent symphonies!

But, it is what happened to Rott, as a result of your borrowing Rott's *genre* of harmonic development. Was he too not on a train, *en route* to Mühlhousen, when he suffered a mental breakdown? Yes, he was on a train and with his revolver, Rott threatened a fellow traveler, telling him to desist from lighting his *trichinopoly* cigar, on the premise it would be too dangerous to do so because Brahms had packed the train with dynamite! Naturally enough, he too was apprehended and committed to the psychiatric clinic of the General Hospital in Vienna, diagnosed with hallucinatory insanity and persecution mania! Clearly the revolver, brandished about on a train, appears to be your preferred choice of dispatching friends forthwith, no?" concluded Zemlinsky.

"You should have attended your composition classes, for had you done so, it would have been apparent even to you, that a general style of symphonic structure was not only being taught, it was recommended. Several symphonies were of a similar style, as one would expect, if the professor had promoted such a method of composition and counterpoint. Rott was no exception in receiving this tuition and his, as with any other person's, mental collapse, is of course to be regretted," said Gustav.

"Should there be anything salvageable one at least can be certain that it was created by our dear lost friend in Hans Rott," said Wilde, whilst standing up and raising his glass into the air. Where upon the assembled group followed *suit* raising their glasses too, with mock solemnity to their dead hero.

"Oh dear, here comes that dreadful woman," hissed Oscar to Whistler.

A few moments later a rather self-possessed and confident woman, with an all too obvious over-bearing nature approached our red *damask* covered table, littered with glasses and bottles.

"Good day Mr. Wilde, are you sober?" asked the woman.

"As much as I ever shall be, since I have experimented with absinthe but achieved no result," replied Wilde, cordially.

"You do not appear to be so."

"A little bit too much is just enough for me," said Wilde, "and of course I drink; but let me assure you, only to excess."

"That much is insuperably evident," replied the woman.

"You may be right; perhaps I ought to *race* myself!"

"Do you not mean, *pace* yourself?" offered the woman.

"I know precisely what I mean!" replied Wilde.

"Clearly not your *début* in this matter is it?" she inquired.

"To get drunk deliberately is as foolish as to get sober by accident," suggested Wilde.

"Would you then prefer that I call you a carriage?"

"I would rather you simply called me, Oscar!"

"…to have you conveyed to a place of confinement to allow you a reasonable chance of recovering what wit you still retain," continued the woman.

"...And perhaps entertain myself making knots out of redundant blue ribbon? [1] Good day madam, you have delighted us long enough with your kindly concern!"

That woman, she is fading like a silver nitrate *daguerreotype*" commented Wilde, in her absence.

"Rather like the painting of Dorian Gray!" riposted Mahler.

"The simile is an apt one," said Wilde, "but apart from that woman Gustav, what brings you to the Café Royal?"

"To relax after rehearsals for the *première* of my Eighth Symphony," replied my friend, nervously.

"You are too serious Gustav," said Wilde whilst resorting to his gold-latten matchbox, "regarding *première* nights. I remember saying to Robert Ross of the *St. James' Gazette,* that I am not nervous on the night I am producing a new play. I am exquisitely indifferent. My nervousness ends at the last dress rehearsal. I know then what effect my play, as presented on the stage, has produced upon me. My interest in the play ends there, and I feel curiously envious of the public – they have such wonderfully fresh emotions in store for them. It is the public, not the play, which I desire to make a success. The public makes a success when it realizes that a play is a work of art. Had the dimensions of the stage admitted for it, I would have called the public before the curtain!"

"None the less, it remains my fervent hope, Oscar, to launch successfully the Eighth Symphony into the orchestral *repertoire*. In this respect, at least, wish me success," asked Mahler of Wilde.

"Anybody can sympathize with the sufferings of a friend," replied Wilde, "but it requires a very fine nature

– it requires, in fact, the nature of a true individualist – to sympathize with a friend's success!"

"Oscar, you remain too kind," responded Gustav.

"Just before my recent first night, I was asked by Robert Ross of the *St. James' Gazette*:

'Do you think the critics will understand your play? asked Ross.

'I hope not,'" I replied.

'What sort of play are we to expect?' inquired Ross.

'It is exquisitely trivial, a delicate bubble of fancy, and it has its philosophy,' I replied.

'It is philosophy?' asked Ross.

"That we should treat all the trivial things of life seriously, and all the serious things of life with sincere and studied triviality," said Wilde.

"You might have found this encounter instructive Gustav!" said Charles Stanford, to general approval.

Wilde was evidently pleased with his homily, and accordingly caused more champagne to be poured into waiting and expectant glasses. Despite the general cheerful disposition of Wilde's guests sitting around the table, it was the somewhat furtive-looking Zemkinsky who asked the following question:

"I wonder, from what obscure publication you got those ideas for the Eighth Symphony in E flat major?" continued Zemlinsky, as he referred to a concert program, that I recognized was from the München *première*. He started quoting sections from it:

'Part I of the Symphony, *Section I - Veni Creator Spiritus* - with significance and meaning set on empyrean heights.

Part II of the Symphony. Final scene from *'Faust'*
Section I   Choir and Echo

Section II	Pater Ecstaticus ecstasy
Section III	Pater profoundus intellectual insight
Section IV	Angels criptic
Section V	More Perfect Angels
Section VIII	Doctor Marianus and Choir Marian devotion
Section IX	Mater Gloriosa penitence forgiveness redemption
Section X	Penitent Women
Section XVII	Una Poenitentium
Section XIX	Doctor Marianus Marian devotion
Section XX	Chorus Mysticus'

I found it hard to realize and almost incomprehensible to watch Zemlinsky, once a friend of Mahler's, act in such a facile and shallow manner in mocking the content of the Eighth Symphony.

I resolved to take over the description rather than let Zemlinsky traduce it further. I began accordingly.

"Part II ends with music refined into melodies of truly ethereal beauty. The *finale* to the symphony commences with a sonorous theme played on violin, which transcends an E major chord emanating from harmonium and harp combined and continuing into the *Chorus Mysticus* with re-iteration of the *Veni Creator Spiritus,* concludes the symphony triumphantly.

The symphony, sometimes known as *der Symphonie des Tausend,* calls for huge orchestral and choral forces to give full expression of Gustav's confirmation of the Christian experience of faith and Devine redemption of the soul, by incorporating the ancient serene and beautiful Latin hymn of *Veni Creator Spiritus* in its vision of the Creator.

In certain parts of this complex symphony, especially in the first movement, there are aspects of inner turmoil in Mahler, and personal hurt as a result of loss, indicating a possible spiritual collapse or at least a defined diminution in the whole concept of faith against intellectual reality. With such pervasive pessimism; can there be a place for religion, which seems at time powerless to prevent hurt and loss? This can be expressed in terms of Gustav's Jewish ancestry and background and of his becoming a Roman Catholic with the dichotomy and paradox that entails.

On the one hand one has the basic and strict Augustinian Catholic doctrine which involves us being on this earth as a prelude to eternal existence in Heaven. This life is not important; rather it is the hereinafter that should concern our every conscious moment. And, our consciousness should be devoted to recognizing symbolism in nature. That is to say typically, a red rose represents not a flower colored red, but rather the blood of Christ. The green grass, or leaves, represents green for envy, water for the tears of the Virgin Mary and wood for the Cross upon which our Lord was crucified. It was upon such doctrines that the early Catholic Church was founded.

The rather *naïve* Latin hymn of *Veni Creator Spiritus* was not designed to address the intellectualism of the late nineteenth century, that Mahler was experiencing, nor the inherent dilemma of unconditional faith he was feeling.

"The second movement is given over to a consideration of Goethe's scenes from a regenerated *Faust* and the true nature of redemption. This of course is a symbolic interpretation by Goethe, and Mahler has difficulties combining two very different approached to redemption. On the one hand spiritual belief in faith and unconditional belief, through the application of Catholic dogma, not being a democratic process, and the libertarian intellectual symbolism of *Faust* albeit expressed as Love, in the *Mater Gloriosa*. There are difficulties inherent in the symphony, which account for its awkwardness or unintelligibility in Mahler trying to fuse two radically opposing concepts. Christian mysticism and current psychological thought, both in terms of the *psyche* clash; one must choose, as it were.

This can often be the case where one has come late to a belief without the organic construction of that faith as an integral part of the growing up process. In the main most people at fifty years of age do not question their religious beliefs; in that they are part of our thought process. Only after a cataclysmic event that could destroy such a basis of belief, might one revise one's religious priorities.

This was an important consideration for my friend Gustav, as it is basic to the symphony's *rationale*. Mahler treated Catholicism as synthetic because he embraced it late in his life as opposed to being organic that come from someone who was brought up in Catholicism, from say childhood. The faith and its myriad of meanings and interpretation, has been a constant as person grows up. But, as all who embrace any alternative to that which they grew up with find, a greater intensity and respect is generated resulting in a profound love and appreciation of it - because one has embraced it from an alternative *rationale*. Perhaps such a convert is able to see in Catholicism more than say the organic Catholic, who may be disposed to take his faith for granted without question.

Mahler in this respect was addressing this essential conflict, which was evident throughout the symphony. However, this dichotomy, as it were, did not detract from Mahler's typical approach in trying to resolve the irreconcilable with sonorous and truly beautiful and harmonic music. Alas, to no avail, since the real message never materializes as an acceptable answer. Should one want sonorous melodies and a truly powerful and confident *finale*, then that is provided; the significance of thought was not. With the exception of the *finale*, and by that I mean, literally the closing bars, there is also much to commend the symphony. Despite the fact it marshals huge orchestral forces to give expression to its music, the inherent concepts can be a challenge to express. In so doing it succeeds, to an extent in the *Veni Creator Spiritus*, in creating a powerful testament and recognition of sublimity, not easy to convey even with a large orchestra and chorus, it does however, conclude with optimistic chords," I concluded.

"I have the greatest contempt for optimism," responded Wilde.

---

1 Blue Ribbon Brigade a society dedicated to abolishing alcohol and was led by Lilli Langtry

Chapter 12

The Pantheon of the Gods – Polemic Part IV

Certain facts were beginning to dawn on me, chief amongst which was the in depth level and apparent current understanding that some of the persons around the table, exhibited about Mahler's music and his concerns. Seated around a large red *damask* covered oval table in the renowned Café Royal were various distinguished artists and musicians. However, the group was being lead by the loquacious Irish writer and dramatist, Oscar Wilde, who considered it amusing to traduce the reputation of my good friend Gustav Mahler, in a concerted effort to ridicule him and his music. Joining Wilde in his antagonism toward Mahler were others, including the composers George Antheil and Alexander Zemlinsky, both of whom clearly relished endeavoring to puncture Mahler's ego-centricity. Mahler may have been indiscreet in attacking Antheil's musical work, *Ballet Mecanique,* with potential devastating consequences that had yet to manifest themselves. In the mean time the conversation had now moved onto a broader discussion of music.

"Your symphonies appear to reflect deep religious concerns Mahler," said Wilde.

"They reflect, I should like to think, concepts of Heaven and religion," replied Mahler.

"Speaking of Heaven," Wilde remarked to Mahler, "*je trouve la terra aussi belle que le ciel, et le corps aussi beau que l'âme.*[1] And speaking of religion? What is that but the fashionable substitute for belief."

"You are a skeptic?" inquired Mahler.

"Never! Skepticism is the beginning of faith; but do tell us, where do you see yourself in the future, with your religion-fuelled music to address the God-head?" asked Wilde, in tones of sincerity.

"Certainly not in the hallowed, but pagan, *Pantheon of Heroes*, worthy of immortality at Regenburg," [2] said Mahler, decisively.

"Immortality," stated Wilde, "I should not know what to do with it; as for eternity; I have no time for it."

"But come to think of it; does not your mentor and teacher now reside there. I forget his name B...?" asked Wilde.

"Beethoven?" interrupted Mahler, with a flourish, "though I hardly think so. He was neither my mentor nor my teacher, for he died thirty-three years before I was born!"

"I did not mean Beethoven," said Wilde, "before you rudely interrupted me; I was about to say Bruckner. Should I wish to refer to Beethoven, that monumental ego-centric, I should be able to do so, and with ease."

"You cannot be serious in your statement about Beethoven?" asked Mahler.

"I am never serious unless I am being frivolous," remarked Wilde.

"You do not appreciate Beethoven's music?" continued Mahler.

"My dear Mahler, I detest Beethoven, wrapped up as he was, in his own ego-centric fuelled anxiety leading to *angst*, very much as the intense, tortured bore in the garret.

Everything to him was problematic in a relentlessly unforgiving world that misunderstood him and his obsession with his own monomania. His music reflects his inherent indifference to society for failing to appreciate his style of music, the interpretation of which is a penance in the extreme!" stated Wilde.

"You are referring to the composer of *the* Ninth Symphony are you not?" responded my friend.

"Do you mean Bruckner, Schubert or Dvořák's?" inquired Wilde.

"I am of course, referring to Beethoven," answered Mahler.

"I know you are; but his music, including his dreary Fantasia in C major for clavier, chorus and orchestra, you know the one, the Opus 80, can only be a collapsed proto-type for an even more boring composition, that of the D minor symphony?" said Wilde, whilst addressing the entire table with a turn of his head.

Heads then turned in Mahler's direction for his considered reply.

"You dare to mock Beethoven? I wonder what he would have to say about that?" riposted Mahler.

"I imagine very little, since he was not so much *tone* deaf as *stone* deaf!" insisted Wilde to great acclaim and back slapping from his friends.

Having neatly delivered his *coup de grâce*, Wilde continued in his remorseless attack on Beethoven. This was designed to provoke Mahler into an ill-prepared re-action from which he might not recover his poise or argument. Wilde was taking the heights of hostility to Mahler's preferred choice of arena, that of music, even though Wilde was a dramatist and not a musician of even low stature.

"Can you really credit a person," Wilde began, addressing himself more to the assembled audience rather that just Mahler, "who claimed pretentiously, that his Ninth Symphony in D minor was going to change the world, in making mankind behave more respectfully to each other, merely because he quoted, an obscure poem by Schiller? In particular, the rather *naïve* reference to, *'Alle Menschen werden Brüder'?* [3] A laudable sentiment, but somewhat impractical given the preferred option of the nation states of Europe; as defined by Hegel's interpretation as indulging in their favorite past-time, leading unequivocally to the *'Slaughter bench of humanity'* and generally being beastly to one another!

Beethoven, with this one work was going to change that and in so doing, civilise society? What temerity, what arrogance and what misguided display of confidence inordinate to his abilities! Except, perhaps the one where he unsuccessfully contemplated taking his own life! He was not the only composer to be aware or recognise the political changes then sweeping Europe. Other composers equally recognised compelled social changes including Mozart. Even Chopin gave the *sobriquet, Revolutionary* to one of his *etudes.*[4] Whilst the much vaunted Wagner was forced to flee Dresden and seek asylum in Switzerland, as a result of his revolutionary activities. His father-in-law, the *Abbé* Liszt, did much to promote the sanctity of his homeland, Hungary, from imperial ambition by others," said Wilde.

"Speaking of Wagner," interjected Mahler to register the fact that he was not a spent force and had something to say in this respect, "there was a person who changed the world, especially through his operas, including the sacred music dramas of *'Parsifal'* and *'Lohengrin'.* In those operas, Wagner explores the concept that mankind is vulnerable and will disappoint, but has the ability to achieve redemption, and despite these weaknesses, sometimes transcend to noble thought."

"Consider Mozart, his music is appreciated and adored by all, because not only is it innovative but also elevating and thus fulfils those sublime and noble virtues that our souls cry out for. By comparison, the *angst*-ridden Beethoven tortures mercilessly the soul and consequently his music remains esoteric and superseded only by that of the repetitive and sanctimonious JS Bach's, and of course one knew what Bach could do with his fugues!" said Wilde, much to the sound of laughter by those around the table at Wilde's observation of Bach.

"Even Georg Telemann," Wilde continued, "a contemporary of Bach's, was moved to remark that, 'If nothing new is to be found in harmony, then search for it in melody'. The mere fact these two giants of ego-centricity and banality existed, in the persons of Beethoven and Bach, cannot in itself compel us to accord them deference. In this respect I am inclined to agree with the great German composer, the one whom you adore Mahler, Carl Maria von Weber's accurate, if generous, remark about Beethoven's Seventh Symphony; in that it should be consigned to the mad house!" 5

Mahler raised his chest almost as though in indignation at Wilde's remarks, refilled his glass, thought for a moment and then prepared to retaliate in his decisive and unequivocal manner. We all, around the red *damask* covered table, mentally braced ourselves for an onslaught, not of indifference to Wilde's statements, but rather for a series of invectives and a dogmatic attitude to support Mahler's fervent objections.

Irrespective of this potential and frozen indecision, again Wilde seized the initiative.

"The point here Gustav, is that no one person, such as Beethoven or any other tortured soul existing in an attic, has a monopoly on expression, whether *angst*-ridden with intensity or not. Ideals and concepts can be conveyed with equal effectiveness in both a positive and acceptable form, other than one of negative inclination. Indeed, were one to introduce a radical idea or observation, it would be as well to promote it, in terms of music or word, in a more conciliatory form, humorous even, to achieve the required acceptance. We all of us recognise our hero-types as they march through literature or music. But, their definition is made more appealing to us by their ability to raise our souls and aspirations to greater heights, than to lower or consign them to the depths of despair!" Thus Wilde delivered his soul upon the matter.

"But Mahler, you have still not answered the question!"

The question was asked not by Wilde, but by the painter Kandinsky. Mahler thought for a moment to recollect what the question was, during a deathly silence that followed Kandinsky's interjection.

"I came into contact with the ageing Bruckner," replied Mahler, eventually, "whom you mentioned Wilde, but of course deny being his pupil."

"But did you not receive composition classes from the great master?" continued Kandinsky.

"I was never a pupil of Bruckner's," continued Mahler, "and this rumor must have arisen from the fact that we were continually seen together in my early days in Vienna, but not as his pupil."

"Is that so," Charles Stanford asked, "but then where then did you acquire your skills in composing symphonies?

"Why of course from Hans Rott!" replied the whole group in unified chorus, worthy of a well-rehearsed choir.

Undaunted, Mahler continued, but showed signs of faltering.

"I was certainly one of his enthusiastic admirers and promoter of his symphonic works," replied my friend, Gustav Mahler.

"I know," I interposed coming to Mahler's aid, "for I have it on good authority from Bruckner's publisher, Theodor Rättig, that Bruckner spoke highly of you Gustav. And, you were one of the first to transcribe, for piano duet, a Bruckner symphony, in particular the Symphony No. 3 in D minor, the one dedicated to '...the master Rickard Wagner, in deepest respect.'"

"Bruckner always maintained a fondness for my friend here, Mahler," I said, addressing the whole group seated around the table, but focusing on no one in particular, "especially when you reciprocated that affection by writing to him about your conducting his glorious and powerful *Te Deum* in 1892 on Good Friday, I believe, at Hamburg. And, I seemed to recall after you had conducted the work, members of the orchestra, chorus and audience were affected profoundly by Bruckner's truly sublime conception of the work, and remained sitting without a sound. It was only when you led the performers off the stage, did a storm of applause erupt from the audience!"

A waiter appeared in our midst, wearing a red and black waistcoat, a white apron and sporting a large moustache, and inquired of no one in particular, did we wish for more refreshment?

"Rather, more champagne!" came an instant and resounding unified response from the assembled guests seated around the table.

"A *trichinopoly* cigar and a large whisky, with a dash of the *Coca~Cola,* for me if you serve it," said Mahler, decisively.

"Would that be the whisky or the *Coca~Cola,* that you are referring to, sir?" inquired the waiter, with an air of expectancy in his features.

"The *Coca~Cola,*" said Mahler, emphasizing the beverage.

"I have it on good authority that you never drink sprits and abhor drunkenness" stated Wilde, much to the consternation and *chagrin* of the people gathered around the table, all of whom put down their glasses and looked sternly at Mahler.

"I cannot imagine who would say such a thing!" [6] remarked Mahler, with a confident degree of aplomb.

It was the writer James Joyce who posed the question uppermost in the minds of the assembled company.

"What in the name of God is that dark stuff you are pouring into your single malt whisky with such a sacrilegious disregard?"

"Oh this, the *Coca~Cola,* it is a dark, aërated beverage, laced up with cocaine and sugar, to give it more punch than your ordinary Schweppes's aërated water can deliver!" replied Mahler, whilst applying a lighted taper to his *trichinopoly* cigar, the brand of which he had become fond.

At this juncture, people turned to one another to discuss the critical issues, such as the merits of the freshly delivered champagne.

"Would you say Mahler, that Rickard Strauss was the acceptable face of modern music, rooted in Wagnerian Romanticism?" inquired Wilde.

"It is true that Strauss exhibits much in his music that can be traced back to Wagner; in particular his adept and skillful use of the *leitmotiv*. Indeed he could be said to be Wagner born fifty years later!" replied Mahler.

"Do you consider Rickard Strauss to be your musical rival, possibly your better in that you purchase his scores as they are published by Johannes Aibl in München, possibly for inspiration?" asked Wilde, with a discernible glint in his eyes.

"The notion is preposterous," replied Mahler "and it would be unlikely, even though we are composers, our style and mannerisms are entirely different. My preference is for the symphony and *lieder;* whereas Strauss' preferred mode is in opera and the symphonic tone poem, as one would hear in *Ein Heldenleben, Tod und Verklärung* or *Panathenäenzug.* And although Hans Hanslick, the critic, who does not particularly like Rickard Strauss, accused him of sliding down that 'slippery slope to tone poems' I myself am fond of them. It would be like saying Wagner copied Meyerbeer's style because he appreciated his music, anymore than my emulating Carl Maria von Weber's because I too appreciate his music."

"Would you say Mahler, that your appreciation and expression of tonal values arose from the pioneering work of Wagner, in his ability to balance concepts and thus exact more from the music? Typically expressed in the operatic spectrum using *Tristan und Isolde*, to explore philosophical ideas, *Parsifal* for mystical revelation and *Der Ring des Nibelungen* for symbolic meaning?" asked Stanford.

"I have intimated before of my willingness to explore areas to seek a truth. In this respect, the first part of your question I could agree with. As for Wagner examining philosophical tenets through, typically, his opera *Tristan und Isolde*, then my answer should be no. Opera is not the vehicle, as it were, that I would deploy to investigate philosophical truths or meaning. As for *Der Ring des Nibelungen* being used for symbolic meaning, again opera is not my preferred option to explore for intellectual expression. Other composers can do so, Strauss, Schreker, Korngold and of course Wagner," said Mahler.

"I take it you are familiar with the compositions of Rickard Strauss?" countered Wilde.

"I am indeed, and know the person and count him amongst my friends!" replied Mahler.

"Really," retorted Wilde, "then you will remember the occasion when you invited your good friend Strauss to a concert in Hamburg, a concert when your First Symphony, *Der Titan,* the symphony where forest animals make up the *cortège,* was to be performed, together with songs from your *Des Knaben Wunderhorn,* your series of songs, in which an animal, an ass no less, is judging a singing contest!

However, on receiving your generous invitation Strauss, whilst wintering at Weimar, pleaded a pressing engagement in his rehearsing *Lohengrin,* the sacred music drama by Wagner. And I think he also went on to say, 'that it simply is not true that the only living conductor interested in your compositions is yourself; when Strauss asked you some time ago to send him some of your symphonic writings, you refused to do so did you not?" inquired Wilde.

The silence was deafening and all looked at Mahler for a suitable riposte.

"Even Ernst Otto Nodnagel, felt moved to utter the prophecy; 'The present belongs to Strauss and the future to Mahler', when attending the *première* of my friend's Fourth Symphony, in November 1901 at München," I said clearly and loudly, in Mahler's defense.

Wilde was not impressed and clearly wanted more.

"Well Mahler, did you refuse Strauss?" demanded Wilde.

Another deathly silence followed Wilde's interjection; but at least more champagne was poured during the lull in the exchanges.

"I understand that you maintain a house, a villa no less a three storey villa at Maiernigg am Wörthersee in Lower Austria. It must be very beautiful, pleasant even?" inquired Kandinsky.

"I do, and it is very restful and permits me that peace I require when composing. As I am sure you too will appreciate, as an accomplished painter, the need for solitude and quietude!" replied my friend.

"Indeed," said Kandinsky, "I believe you had in 1901 just completed your Fourth Symphony in those idyllic surrounds. Why was it then that you denied your friend Rickard Strauss the opportunity to *première* it in Berlin for you, as he wished to do? What were you reported to have written in your letter to him? '...Please do not include my Fourth in your own plans for the present...'."

"Berlin audiences to date have never been receptive to my innovative musical works; as witnessed by what happened to my Third at the Schauspielhaus in that city," responded Gustav Mahler, without inflexion in his voice.

"Well that is interesting," continued Kandinsky, "because a friend of mine, the critic, Theodor Kroyer, reviewed the Fourth after its *première* in München, in November, 1901. And, he was of the opinion that your Fourth Symphony in G major, failed to rise to expectation, for the following reasons, and I paraphrase:

'The form of the symphony surprised him; if anybody had hoped for a sign of progress towards something healthier, a return to the fountain-spring of all art, which is naturalness, was doomed to disappointment. No trace of spontaneity, not a single autonomous idea, no original feeling, indeed not even pure colors for the impure images; nothing but technical skill, calculation and inner deceit, a sickly ill-sounding '*super-music*'. The weeds that germinated in the Third Symphony have grown in this Fourth Symphony into a thorny mass of noxious vegetation. Here the compositional talent seems to be dissipating energy for its own sake. Everywhere a display of the most extraordinary orchestral fireworks to dress up an amorphous stylistic monstrosity collapsing under the weight of its own surfeit of clever detail...the symphony's impression on one was highly disquieting."' 7

"That arbitrary condemnation," I intervened, from my own recollection, in order to lay the record straight, "remains a personal opinion. The Fourth Symphony may well have its detractors, any art does; but the acclaimed critic in Julius Korngold8 felt obliged to write in the *Neue Freie Presse* on 22 December, 1901 to the effect that my friend here, Gustav, achieved, in Vienna, his first success as a composer with his Third being performed by the *Musicvereinssaal* at the Krefeld Music Festival, and preceded, not entirely smoothly, by three other symphonies in the First, Second and Fourth.

The Third," I continued, "may have fallen on more receptive ears and is stronger, certainly more powerful and more immediate in its impact. The Third Symphony survived the ordeal of a baptism of fire when performed in our home city of Vienna. The audience applauded after every section of the symphony. At the end, there were endless ovations in which the public and players took part in with equal enthusiasm. The Third Symphony displays sublime ideas in both its musical and poetic structure, so that it once again bears witness to my friend's extraordinary technique and tonal imagination."

It is possible Kandinsky was himself displaying signs of annoyance and frustration at having to listen to what I had just said, but continued his hostility expressed in his fervent antagonism to my friend.

"But going back to the infamous Third; you demanded of Strauss that all your requirements regarding its performance must be complied with, including …'the six cow bells are not at all the most important thing - there is no need to insist on them; perhaps four would be available – that would be enough!' But you then finish with the words, '…please do not be upset by the fact that my initial response to your friendly sympathy consists of nothing but difficulties'," said Kandinsky.

"It is the prerogative of any artist to specify how he wishes the work to be performed, as much as you insisting on a certain minimum light in which to hang your paintings, no?" answered Mahler.

Kandinsky did not reply, but simply got up from the table and walked off out of the *salon*.

"I never trust a man who would indulge in the preposterous notion of carrying his own parcel of any size, even if it is a box of chocolates from Fortnum & Mason!" said Wilde, in anguished tones of disgust at Kandinsky's burden.

My friend, however, was left facing the remaining persons to deliver his response.

"In that same letter, I mentioned Strauss's *Feuersnot* and the fact that the censors would not pass the work for public performance. Accordingly, I promised Strauss that I would call upon the censor himself and represent his case; in any event I should not give up," countered Mahler.

"The one true observation ascribable to Rickard is that he possesses real inspiration in music and refuses to

intimidate by convention or *régime*. Unlike some composers we might know, who believe that one has not
arrived until one has been banned by the censors at least
twice!" remarked Wilde.[9]

"It really is a matter of getting it right to avoid being
censored," responded Mahler, whose words initiated
immediately a hushed silence in the group.

"What was that you said earlier, about Goethe's
dictum, which you uphold; the artist must create what
the public ought to like, not what it does like?" said Wilde

"Well that is certainly true if one has the strength and
conviction to carry it through," riposted Mahler, "but
one does need that conviction and unflinching belief in
one's own ability to create!"

"So, applying Goethe's dictum, of which you are fond;
are you able to reconcile your approach to that of
Goethe's?" inquired Wilde.

"In what respect?" asked Gustav.

"Well, in the respect that you ceaselessly revise your
musical scores. Your so-called *Titan* Symphony was
substantially revised, I believe, the *andante* - in between
the first and third movements was removed altogether
upon a subsequent revision. Having completed your,
Symphony No 4 in G major in 1901, we understand that
you are still revising it – eight years later! And, that you
gave it the *sobriquet* in the name '*Humoresque*', intriguingly
enough also, the poor Fifth, born in 1902 has not escaped
your constant revisions during the period 1907 through
to 1909. I read in the *St James' Gazette* only a few weeks
ago that you actually have changed the position of where
the slow movement will now appear in relation to that
of the *scherzo*! The Sixth of 1905 was spared no lesser
treatment only emerging in 1906 after extensive rework-
ing of the whole work," said Wilde.

"Revising for the sake of getting it perfect," said Mahler.

"Perhaps, like your teacher and mentor Bruckner, this urge to revise could be put down to his equally infectious desire to revise those symphonies he composed? Or, would you put this impulse to indulge in endless revision of your works down to your lack of confidence in yourself to create? Or to your inherent anxiety and introverted intense temperament and the constant adverse criticism that seems to attend your music, which could, I suppose, cause a deep feeling of insecurity, irrespective of Goethe's dictum?" inquired Wilde.

Before Mahler could formulate a response to any of the three questions raised, Wilde afforded him no opportunity, but instead delivered with unerring accuracy his *coup de grâce*.

"Why did you violently oppose Rickard Strauss' fervent wish to use my play *Salomé*, as the *libretto* for his opera of the same name?"

"Because I knew it would be banned by the imperial censors in Vienna, as indeed your play was in England!" retaliated Mahler.

"Believe you me Gustav, the censor would be doing me an inestimable favor, if he but knew it, were he to ban forthwith some of my earlier masterpieces!" retorted Oscar.

"It is not too late," replied Mahler. "But the differences between Strauss and myself are not confined to style or restricted to mannerism; they can reflect a more personal approach to concepts of heroism, life, death and religion. My Second Symphony is a case in point."

"One can perceive an inherent rivalry between you and Strauss," said Wilde, "but what do the French say when faced with this awkward situation? Ah yes I have it, ...*there is something not unpleasant about witnessing the misfortune of a close friend!*"

"My Second Symphony in C minor, *Die Auferstehung,* [10] composed in 1894, is a choral work concerned with aspects of the state of death and eventual splendid release in the form of resurrection into the sight of Christ. It commences with the funeral rites of a hero, expressed in the exploding *tremolo.* In my Second Symphony, the Titan, who is the subject of the First Symphony is reëxamined here, in terms of justification; *'to what purpose have you lived?'* This was a recurring theme, that occupied various composers and writers around the period 1890, including my friend Rickard Strauss, whose own interpretation found form in his *Tod und Verklärung,* composed, I believe in 1889.

The following two movements reflect the wisdom imparted by the orchestral transcription of the song of the sermon of St. Anthony and the Fishes. This section is expressed as part orchestral interlude with *ländler* and, generally accepted as being very beautiful and serene when addressing the approaching *scherzo,* after which, the *contralto* makes her entrance with the song, *'Urlicht'.* This reference to the *Red Rose, 'O Roschen Rot'* by the *contralto* is with specific allegorical meaning concerning the Rose of Sharon and its Christian symbolism.

Toward the closing section, I quote the march from the first movement as the vehicle to convey thoughts of eternity and redemption expressed in Klopstock's hymnal *'Auferstehen' - O Glaube, mein Herz, O glaube* [11] preparing the listener for the next orchestral passage based on the *Dies Irae.* The Arch-angel Gabriel's summoning the dead from repose is intimated by the brass and percussion section of the orchestra, which leads into the symphony's conclusion with a triumphant *finale.*

The eventual decay of Romanticism is reflected in the idiom of my music. Romanticism intensified the concepts and depths of emotion in various forms, either religious or neurotic, or even spiritual. '*For when the ideal is realized, it is robbed of its mystery, and becomes simply a new starting-point for an ideal that is other than itself.*' Especially, when treating such concepts as the tragic and an awareness of death; which as we know is an all too present facet of life. In addition, some commentators have alluded to the symphony as reflecting the philosopher Hegel's concept of the '*Slaughter Bench of Humanity*'. I however, see my symphony as an unequivocal celebration of overcoming unreasoned fear and instead, transition into an eternity and, into the sight of the Christ!" said Gustav Mahler.

It was Wilde who broke what was a stunned silence that greeted his description of the symphony.

"In this respect Mahler," said Wilde, "were you ever heavily influenced by Strauss' *Tod und Verklärung* which was composed in 1889? I merely ask this question, because of course, your Second Symphony came out five years later in 1894."

"As I have just said, but will reiterate for your benefit Oscar. Several writers, artists and composers, Brahms in *Ein Deutsches Requiem* and others including Strauss, were thinking in terms of intellectual thoughts, involving the concept of '*death and transfiguration*', that may, as some commentators state, have originated from Hegel's philosophical observations".

"If you are so preoccupied with mortality and death, does that not make you presumptive of the intervention of a God-head you have accepted upon your recent baptism into the Catholic Church? Catholics know that they have a finite time here on earth, but do not torture themselves with the when, why or wherefore? Rather, they live and enjoy that God-given grace without recourse to demanding an explanation of God's *rationale* you have alluded to in the final section of the fifth movement of your Second Symphony in C minor, the *'Resurrection'*. There you invoke the re-assuring chant '*O glaube, mein Herz, o glaube*', as though you know this is a prerequisite of faith," said Wilde.

"No," answered Mahler, "I did mention this fact earlier. My embracing the Catholic faith has made me develop a profound love and appreciation of Catholicism, because I came to it later in my life. But in so doing I can see the attractive aspects of the faith perhaps more clearly than those who have been immersed in it from childhood."

1 If I do live again I would like to be as a flower - no soul but perfectly beautiful!")
2 The Pantheonic Temple of Valhalla built by Schinkel to house dead heroes.
3 'All men shall be brothers'
4 Etude No. 12 in C minor Opus 10.
5 Said in 1826 whilst living in the Portland Road.
6 Per Alfred Roller on describing evenings in the villa at Meianigg am Wörthersee
7 Quoted by Theodor Kroyer, in *Die Music*, 22 December, 1901
8 Father of the composer Erich Korngold, who later dedicated his violin concerto to Alma Mahler.
9 Rickard Strauss' operas *Feuersnot* and *Salomé* were both initially banned.
10 The *Resurrection*
11 *'Believe my heart, believe!'*

Chapter 13

The Secessionists – Polemic
Part V

It was becoming all too evident that Mahler and Wilde upon their meeting for the first time, despised each other, and with a detestation that was increasing almost exponentially by the minute, as we sat around the large oval table. The more champagne consumed, the more vitriolic and intense the exchanges between them became. Seated around this table were Wilde, Mahler, Rickett, Whistler, Beardsley, Rossetti, Antheil, Zemlinsky, James Joyce, Sargent and Elizabeth Siddal, who had returned from her *sojourn* in an even worse state. In the meantime, Kandinsky had left. However, also emerging from this discussion was an awkward significance that must have been searing through Mahler's mind, as it was through mine, as that of an observer. It concerned Mahler's wife, Alma Maria Schindler, whom he married in 1902. She was the daughter of the notable Viennese painter, Emil Schindler and had been Gustav Klimt, the Byzantine style painter's close friend. Later she received musical tuition from Zemlinsky, with whom she was also close. Through Alma, Mahler came into contact with the artists of the Viennese Secession movement, including Klimt, Carl Moll and others involved in the so-called *Fusion of the Arts*. Klimt, in fact, was elected as the Vienna Secessionists first president. For the time being this encounter, exchange of ideas or discussion was moving inextricably into the realm of *Fusion of the Arts* and with what that entailed in terms of Mahler's involvement. I decided to question Wilde on this European *vogue* for a *Fusion of the Arts*, in an attempt to deflect intensifying criticism away from my friend.

"What do you know about the Vienna Secessionists, Oscar?" I asked.

"The Vienna what?" replied Wilde, whilst reaching for a bottle containing chilled champagne precariously nearly full.

"The movement that attempts to fuse the arts," I informed him.

"Oh that; only that 'music is the most expensive of noises' and Hugo von Hofmannsthal, after Baudelaire, wished for a fusion amongst the arts - including, music," said Wilde in a remarkable dexterity of reply I would not have thought possible from him.

"Oh, perhaps then you are unfamiliar with developments in Europe, in which both Mahler and I are involved and I think would have elicited your interests, if not approval," I ventured.

"They may well do dear Friedrich; but do continue your most interesting narrative!" said Wilde, with some degree of sincerity.

"Our '*Vereinigung Bildender Künstler Österreichs*' [1] was formed in 1897, I continued, "as a re-action to the more conservative Association of Austrian Artists who maintain, even today, an outmoded historicism towards the arts. Rather like your Pre-Raphaelites seceding from the Royal Academy. The founding members of our new group are the architect, Carl Moll, whom Mahler knows, Rudolf von Alt, Koloman Moser, Max Kurtzweil, a fellow Moravian and scene designer, Josef Hoffmann and hopefully, other persons involved in the creation of the arts and who wish to be a part of our Secessionist Movement too!"

"I am trying to work out in my mind," said Wilde, "whether this *Josef* Hoffmann, the architect and co-founder of the Secessionist Movement based in Vienna, is in any way related to the painter *Joseph* Hoffmann, who, I recall was retained by Rickard Wagner and to whom he entrusted the creation of the scenery for his operas *Der Ring des Nibelungen?*"

"No Oscar, he is not the same person; their Christian names are spelled differently," I told him.

"It might be of interest to note at this point that my friend here, Gustav," I said, gesticulating in the direction of Mahler, "is in fact related to the architect and another co-founder of Vienna Secessionist Movement, Carl Moll, as a result of Carl's marriage to Alma Mahler's widowed mother.

The Secessionist, of course fused all the arts together, making it difficult to determine just who was what, irrespective of their origin; artists creating buildings and architects involving themselves with interior art finishes!

The Secessionist Movement," I continued, "is centered on a specific structure, an exhibition hall we call the Secession Building in the Karlplatz, in Vienna. You might have seen the building; it is near the Karlplatz Stadtbahn. It has a very distinctive gilded dome and was designed by Joseph Maria Olbrich, another co-founder. The building, with its dome has become an icon for the Secessionist Movement that is dedicated to what we call *'Fusion of the Arts'*. Indeed above the main entrance is our commitment, *'Der Zeit ihre Kunst. Der Kunst ihre Freiheit'*, and immortalized in stone. [2]

In this respect, the development of Secessionist

Movement ideals could have a direct bearing on composers such as Mahler, especially in his music and that of Schönberg's. Music, the Secessionist suggests, should play a significant *rôle* in exploring unconventional ideas and form in endeavoring to understand the human condition. Mahler here, has espoused the virtues of design, especially in addressing space. Space is an important consideration in my friend's day-to-day existence; since he spends time trying to find an acceptable equilibrium in which music can be amplified, as one might expect in a concert hall. This search for understanding spatial concepts and consideration is what interests Mahler, and not as our critics have erroneously described as being... *'an obsession given his propensity for depression and pessimism, captured in that axiom: 'every silver lining has a dark cloud'.*

That Vienna and Berlin are lively cosmopolitan centers of intellectual debate, where artists, philosophers and creative individuals can mix in society with ease allowing ideas to propagate, is beyond doubt. Both Mahler and I are prominent members of Viennese society and meet with other leading figures on a regular basis; at the opera, Musicverein or in the *Konditorei*. The crossover of ideas has resulted in some innovative and fascinating ideas emerging from this *Fusion of the Arts*.

In June 1905 Gustav Klimt and other artists, including Hoffmann, seceded from the Vienna Secession due to differences of opinion over artistic concepts. These artistic concepts included designs by the architect Otto Wagner, and his preference for applying the emerging *Art Nouveau* style. He applied this style, typically to his designs for buildings which included the Karlplatz Stadtbahn [3] and Österreichische Postsparkasse [4] both of which are in Vienna.

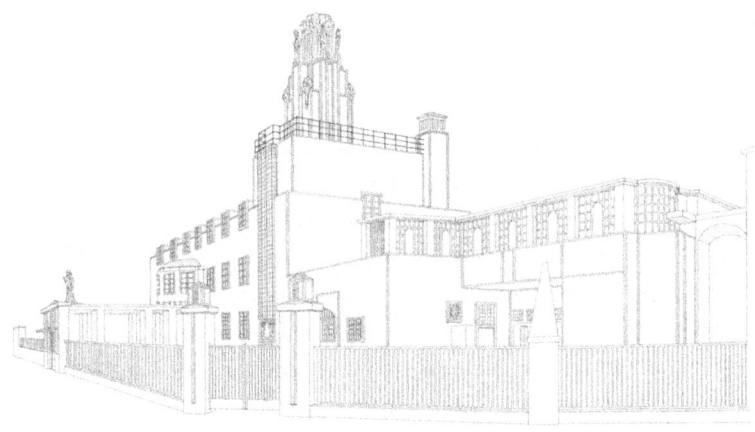

Stoclet Palace

Neither buildings found favor with some of his Secessionist pupils, including *Josef* Hoffmann and Koloman Moser who then seceded from the Secessionist to form their own group in 1903, called the *Wiener Werkstatte Gruppe* - an art society committed to defining further the *Fusion of the Arts* – to include all the applied arts. They exhibited works by guest artists including Arnold Böcklin, Charles Rennie Mackintosh and Max Klinger. The *Wiener Werkstatte Gruppe*, became the arts and crafts arm of the Klimt group and went on to design and construct the Stoclet Palace completing this landmark structure to the *Fusion of the Arts.*

For example," I said, to Wilde's guests seated around the oval table "Josef Hoffmann has just created this masterpiece in the Stoclet Palace, a structure that indicates a final return to Classicism in style. However, he has used, in its construction, reënforced masonry that comprises *ferro-concrete*, in order to span great distances within the building. This method of construction allows light to flow, unimpeded, along the ideals propounded by Aalto Alvar. The project involved the *Wiener Werk-statte Gruppe,* in contributing to the design of the Stoclet Palace, with large metal-framed glazed areas to facilitate light and internal decorative finishes by another Secessionist artist in Gustav Klimt.

This newly constructed palace represents a successful prototype of the *Fusion of the Arts,* and the *Wiener Werkstatte Gruppe's* avowed intention to fuse all the arts together. In so doing, they address innovative concepts expressed in music, sculpture, architecture, design, drama and the humanities, including even the new science of psycho-analysis and the implications of hysteria propounded by Freud! Women, including Alma Schindler were encouraged to be involved in a variety of ways!" I said.

"Alma Schindler, who is this Alma Schindler?" asked Beardsley.

"Surely you know her; she was a musical student under our composer friend here Zemlinsky who in addition to teaching her, also taught Schönberg and Korngold," said Stanford.

"Never heard of her," replied Beardsley.

"People will someday however," enjoined Stanford, "for she is Gustav's wife!"

"She remains quite a formidable person, humorous even, in her own right," offered Whistler.

"Humor, that is a rather commonplace *début?*" said Beardsley.

"She is a genius," said Whistler.

"That may well be the case here," said Siddal.

"I know," offered Wilde, "Women represent the triumph of matter over mind, just as we represent the triumph of matter over morals!"

"How do you conclude so?" asked Stanford.

"Whenever a man does a thoroughly stupid thing, it is always from the noblest motives!" responded Wilde.

"As usual Wilde, your pomposity clouds your thinking" remarked Siddal.

"Do go on, Oscar," said Stanford.

"Where is my drink?" demanded Siddal.

"But, we interrupt Friedrich Löhr's narrative," insisted Beardsley.

So, in response to Beardsley's request, I continued my description of the exciting developments taking place in Vienna regarding the *Fusion of the Arts*, and, my attempt to move the conversation on to less contentious issues.

"Within society," I continued, hesitantly, "new intellectual ideas are being discussed and improved, especially those relating to the psyche. It is a time when ideas about human behaviour and condition are being propounded by Freud, and acted upon by the architect Alvar Aalto in sanatorium construction and by Walter Gropius in his designs addressing spatial concepts and light. As my friend Mahler will agree, his development and that of other people's, coincide with the emergence of *German Expressionism* and Fraudian psychology and where Romanticism intensifies the concepts and depths of emotion in various forms; either religious or neurotic, or even spiritual!

For example, Freud has remarked that when dealing with my friend Mahler, in Leiden, *'no light fell at the time on the symptomatic façade of his obsessive neurosis. It was, as if you would dig a single shaft through a mysterious building.* [5] You can imagine gentlemen," I said, "the reason for Freud's departure from medical terminology into construction analogy, was because intellectuals considered disciplines of interests other than their own, imitating the Renaissance ideal. This is what the *Fusion of the Arts* is all about;

and is of course an interesting and exciting time!

Previously, as we know, Mahler was involved in the construction of the München Exhibition Hall, *Die Ausstellungs Halle,* 1906. There we had our rather disappointing *première* of the Eighth Symphony. However, the hall was built using new ideas such as reënforced concrete, iron columns and fabricated metal framed glazed panels. They were used in order to 'create adequate daylight and space, the building supported large areas of glass and is based on simplicity and restraint', as described in 1908.

Because of the free movement of artist, designers and intellectuals, the arts are fusing together to address innovative concepts expressed in architecture and the humanities including the new concepts by Schönberg and his music, *'Guerellieder',* sonorous and sublime and in no way the precursor of his Twelve Tone regime. Von Zemlinsky and Mahler played a significant *rôle* in exploring with other artists, unconventional ideas and forms in endeavoring to comprehend the human condition. Mahler was acquainted, as I have stated earlier, with the architect Carl Moll, who was in the process of designing a house for Mahler near Vienna," I concluded.

"But do tell us Gustav, you are quoted as saying 'all this talk about the arts being sisters is nonsense. Rather than being equal, they are infinitely different in rank! First by far is music – the art of the inner space, next comes poetry followed by a long gap. Only then the creativity of painting and sculpture come – which take their subjects from the outside world, with architecture, having to with scale measurements and ratios, coming right at the far end. But the great true work of art consists in the combination of all the arts!'" remarked Wilde.

"I think you will find that it was not I who uttered

those words; but rather they were spoken by the great Rickard Wagner himself!" retorted Mahler.

"How can that be," interrupted James Joyce, "did not Rickard Wagner entrust, to the late Joseph Hoffmann, the Viennese painter and scene designer and whose widow Nina Anna Hoffmann, is a friend of Mahler, the designs of the scenery for his *Der Ring des Nibulungen* [6] at the first Bayreuth Festival in 1877?"

"Do not utter the name of Wagner in civilized society; for it reminds one of all those *Völsunga* saga-fuelled legends of those gods, mortals, female warriors and heroes plotting in the depths of the *Nibelung*, on how to get their grubby hands on an ill-fated golden band, in addition to a demented woman, who throws herself onto a flaming funeral pyre, in order to be re-united with her dead hero lover for eternity. And, all singing interminable nonsense set to music that sounds like a tradesman ringing one's door bell repeatedly clutching a handful of unpaid bills!" said Wilde, in a surprising, if accurate, *précis* of Wagner's operatic masterpiece.

"Believe me Oscar, I can well understand your loathing of Wagner, especially the opera *Götterdämmerung;* for who would want to see a reënaction of the immolation scene, in which Brünhilde throws her person onto a flaming funeral pyre to join the corpse of her lover," responded Mahler.

"Are you referring to when my two half-sisters went up in flames?" inquired Wilde.

"Rather," replied Mahler, looking into his now empty flute of champagne, "the news, though tragic, was in its own way, I suppose, quite absurd. Imagine, two sisters going to an evening ball, when the crinoline dress of the elder sister caught fire, and the younger sister embraced her elder sister in an attempt to save her, with predictable consequences."

"Well," recanted Wilde, ignoring Mahler's recollection, "that is not quite true, Wagner does have his uses. I like his music better than anybody's. It is so loud that one can talk the whole time during his opera, without other people hearing what one says. And, musical people are so absurdly unreasonable; they always want one to be perfectly dumb at the very moment when one is longing to be absolutely deaf."

"Your *Penny Dreadful*, or whatever you call them including, '*The Drawing of Dorian Gray*', is more reminiscent of Zola's '*Nana*' or indeed, Daudet's '*L'Immortel*'! Do tell me Oscar; were you heavily influenced by either novel?" asked Mahler, in defense of Wagner.

"Neither," retorted Wilde, with a glint in his eye," I remain only influenced by my own works, since no modern literary work of any worth has been produced in the English language by an English author, except of course Bradshaw's Railway Guide....in that I would sooner lose a train by the A.B.C. than catch it by Bradshaw!"

"I can well understand that, because *Dorian Gray* would ostensibly reflect you and your involvement with the aristocracy, would it not?" inquired Mahler.

"My acclaimed novel charts the decline of many concepts and beliefs, including the horse aristocracy *en-route* to Gentlemen's Clubs, now superseded by the Ritz Hotel and the automobile Why even Thomas Mann likened my *Dorian Gray* to his recent work addressing the same idealism? '*Der Tod in Venedig*'[7] about the final days of writer Gustav von Aschenbach in his futile Nietzsche-propelled search for truth. Rather like yours Mahler, between the god of restraint in the form of the god *Apollo;* and excess in all things, represented by the god *Dionysus*. All in distinct contrast to erotic love and philosophical wisdom propounded by Plato and addressed in his *Symposium* and *Phaedrus.*" said Wilde, to great mumblings of approval of those sitting around the table in the Café Royal.

"You say that your book, *The Picture of Dorian Gray,* is meant to be both poignant and disturbing?" inquired Mahler, perceiving a weakness in Wilde's book *Dorian Gray.*

"Absolutely; I designed it to be precisely that. I must say Mahler, I remain surprised at your recognizing such genius in one so young as I!" said Wilde.

"Would you not say Oscar that Dorian is a series of caricatures based freely on works like Edgar Allen Poe's *William Wilson,* - doppelganger or, RL Stevenson's *Doctor Jekyll and Mr. Hyde* or, Balzac's *Le Peau de Chagrin, Splendours et Miseries,* or even from Gautier's *Mademoiselle de Maupin* or *Manfred* by Byron?"

"No I would not," answered Wilde decisively and chortling in the process.

"From what Mahler is saying Oscar,," said Siddal, "it would be quite feasible for Dorian to meet Sherlock Holmes in the fog; one searching for crime, the other for unadulterated pleasures afforded by such a combination of circumstances!" This remark by Siddal, elicited a round of unrestrained laughter and a rapid refilling of glasses as compliments flowed readily to the initiator of this witticism.

"Well Siddal you are not entirely inventive," responded Wilde, "alas I did meet Conan Doyle, the creator of Sherlock Holmes on the occasion of a luncheon given by Lippincott's Magazine. We were there and then invited to submit, for publication in the magazine, a mystery or suspense. I submitted Dorian and a fellow author, Conan Doyle, his *Penny-Dreadful,*[8] called, I think, the *Sign of Four*, featuring a fictitious character named Sherlock Holmes."

I was not convinced that Mahler understood this verbal paradox, and so whispered to him, "*Eine spaß!*" [9]

Unlike you dear Oscar," Mahler stated "I have no urgent need to undertake forays into the depth of the East end for inspiration or be obvious in the vicinity of the St. George's Brewery in the Commercial Road. But then I forget you were inspired by such a place in your apocryphal pseudo memoirs recounted in '*A Picture of Dorian Gray*, no?"

"Your knowledge of me, I am pleased to say, is at least up to date!" replied Oscar.

"As is the attractiveness of Catholicism being recognized in *Dorian Gray*," responded Mahler

"As it was in your convenient conversion – for religious reasons of course!" retorted Wilde.

"I said *inspired*," continued Mahler, "but then you were an avid reader as a precocious child, were you not and, heavily influenced by the fictitious writing of Disraeli; his fictitious writings, as a novelist, not as the First Lord of the Treasury [10]?"

My innovative novel *A Picture of Dorian Gray'* still has the capacity to move people," replied Oscar

Really, do tell me, what was the name of the first novel by Disraeli that you read?" inquired Mahler.

There was a stunned silence as the seated guests all directed their attention onto Oscar Wilde for an answer to a question nobody knew existed.

"'*Vivian Gray*'," replied Wilde.

"Disraeli's novel *Vivian Gray*," Mahler said to the group seated around the red *damask* covered table, "charts the rise through adulthood of an ambitious individual and his venal endeavors to succeed in the corrupting world of politics. Accordingly, Vivian deteriorates into a self-possessed arrogant person who, is ruthless in his pursuit of power and concerned only with his personal advancement in his despising of the rigidly restrictive social structure of England. Whilst at the same time he was unable to resist glorifying the aristocracy for its ridiculous affectations and its vices. Indeed your interpretation of *Vivian Gray* expressed in your *Dorian Gray* would make the latter compelling reading – for the gentlemen at Scotland Yard!" said Gustav Mahler.

But at that moment Wilde countered with an unwarranted comment motivated by alcohol.

"You talk Mahler, about the humanities with a glib ego-centric definition based upon your own perception of the world. And yet you completed no recognized course at the University of Vienna, leaving before you achieved a qualification," said Wilde

"Not quite, Oscar, I obtained my diploma from the Vienna Conservatory; a University degree was useless to me. My wish to become a conductor was frustrated as conducting was not taught at any of the conservatories. Practical experience in conducting, usually at provincial theaters was thought the best way to learn this art; which is precisely what I did. This included conducting the operas of Verdi, Bizet and the music dramas of Wagner in London at Covent Garden, and Puccini's *Madame Butterfly* in 1904 with the Vienna Court Opera. But then I am gratified to learn that you read Classics and Humanities at Trinity College, Dublin, for which you won the gold medal; a gold medal that subsequently was to be well known to pawnbrokers of Dublin, no?" countered Mahler.

"The trouble Gustav, with the *bourgeoisie*, is the only means to escape their condition, is through the hallowed halls of Academia. Their impetuosity to arrive at the class immediately above is their undoing. They can never change to become that which is beyond them. What they do instead is to subjugate aspects of the upper classes' domain, the Promenade Concerts or Wimbledon; Henley or Goodwood. Rather than adapting, which they cannot, they try to impose their values. In so doing they destroy the very thing they desire! The only thing they achieve is to shunt upwards that class above them, who perforce will find alternative interests and venues. Your *bourgeois* class, yet again finds itself with a *Pyrrhic* victory resounding in hollowness as they survey the deserted *rationale* of their effort. Rather than dwell on the importance of music, they concentrate on the pianist; rather than consider the depths of the painting, they will applaud the painter. All in their inordinate adoration of the cult of the personality, irrespective of profound talent," declaimed Wilde.

Those acerbic words spoken by Wilde, were meant as a veiled reference to my friend, Gustav Mahler's *bourgeois* background; and his wish to scale polite Viennese society in order to attain conducting appointments with various orchestras. In so propounding this sentiment, was it possible that Wilde had now laid himself open to the same social failings he imputed in Mahler? If I were able to recognize this *faux pas,* and others around the table had, then Mahler would almost certainly have done so, and accordingly, was not long in responding by delivering his devastating *coup de grace.*

"It seems to me Wilde," said Mahler, "because of your failed desire to originate from an Irish aristocratic background, like Disraeli's *Vivian Gray,* upon whom you have clearly based *Dorian Gray,* and your own aspirations too, are obsessed about the English aristocracy. You remain captivated by them and their obsequious recognition of title rather than merit!

In your endeavor to describe me in your previous remarks, '...*rather than dwell on the importance of music, they concentrate on the pianist; rather than consider the depths of the painting, they will applaud the painter. All in their inordinate adoration of the cult of the personality, irrespective of profound talent,*' you have described yourself and failures!" responded Mahler.

"At least," insisted Wilde, "I possess an ability to aspire as well as inspire with my clever observations, which have not deserted me yet, unlike yours!" countered Wilde, though haltingly.

"It is almost certainly probable that in your clever observations you are indeed a wit, Oscar; I could not judge; but in not being able to do so I am prepared to compromise!"

"You are, as usual, none too generous in doing so, Mahler," replied Wilde.

"Allow me then to be generous; I am prepared to compromise as to your being a wit," continued Mahler, "perhaps we can agree on that?"

"Regarding my wit, I am always prepared to compromise!" stated Oscar Wilde, for all to hear.

"Good, said Mahler, "I am pleased that you agree to compromise and in so doing admit you can only be a half wit!"

Wilde looked at Mahler through his now bulging eyes. He then scraped back his gold-painted Chippendale-styled chair, as he raised himself up. He stood there momentarily swaying gently from side to side, leaning on his gold headed Malacca cane for support. He was about to utter a remark, but thought better of it. Instead he then turned on his heels and walked out of the *salon* bumping into another chair as he did so.

Both Mahler and I immediately got up and followed in the direction of Wilde's departure. Not to catch him up; but rather to leave his stunned guests with a not inconsiderable bill for the afternoon's entertainment and drinks!

1 The Vienna Secession
2 To every age its art. To art its freedom.
3 Karlplatz Urban Railroad Station
4 Austrian Postal Savings Bank
5 Stated in a letter to Theodor Reik
6 *Der Ring des Nibulungen* is a cycle of four operas comprising, *Das Rheingold, Die Valküre, Siegfried* and *Götterdämmerung'.*
7 Death in Venice, published in 1912)
8 A disparaging term implying the book is a cheap sensational novel costing one penny to purchase
9 A joke.
10 British Prime Minister.

Chapter 14

The Premiére

Mahler had held his own against an *impromptu* and concerted attack in the Café Royal, and acquitted himself successfully against that antagonism. However, despite his inherent tenacity, I could not feel confident in his ability to marshal those orchestral and choral forces needed to give expression to the Eighth Symphony. His re-action to attack was liable to manifest itself at the most inconvenient of times. I wondered, therefore, whether Henry Wood could be prevailed upon to conduct the *première* instead of Mahler. And despite our *Pyrrhic* victory at the Café Royal over Wilde and his retinue of syco-phants, our primary purpose for being in this fog-bound Metropolis was imminent. We were to have the *première* of Mahler's Eighth Symphony in E flat major in the Queen's Hall, in the hope of salvaging some vestige from the remnants of the disappointment that attended its *première* in München earlier in September.

Whilst preparing for this momentous occasion, we were drinking in the parlor at the Queen's Hall with the manager, an amiable fellow called Robert Newman. Mahler was resting on a *chaise-longue* covered in green watermarked silk and reading the concert program that had just been handed to him.

"You have nothing to worry about Friedrich; I have

seen more *premières* than I care to mention," said Newman, whilst handing to me yet another glass of *Veuve Clicquot* champagne.

"Possibly, I said, "but that is not what happened in München; hence our being here drinking your champagne!" I replied.

"It has been my experience," said Newman, "that the London audience is a fickle one, but do not under-estimate them. They have a proud tradition of welcoming new works of music; for they know, quite rightly, that every work was once a new work, even a novelty – innovative or traditional."

"Let us hope so," I responded.

"You did mention earlier Friedrich, that there may have been malicious forces at play during the *première* in München and, that they were possibly responsible for the chaos and disparaging press reviews that ensued?" inquired Newman.

"There is no possibility about it, the severity of the disruption was vicious as it was coördinated by people who are not well disposed to Mahler," I continued.

"But," enjoined Newman, "this is his Eighth Symphony, and the previous symphonies have more or less been accepted into the standard *repertoire* of all the major orchestras of America and Europe. His Second and Fifth Symphonies feature on a regular basis in all the concert halls, certainly here in London."

"True," I said, "but critics will have their way for a myriad of reasons; fair, indifferent, vicious or simply based on ignorance."

Then it happened. It was whilst I was replenishing our glasses with more champagne that Mahler uttered a groan of such profundity as to make Newman and me think instantly that he was suffering a heart attack or some other such calamity.

"What is it Gustav, what can the matter be?" I asked.

Whilst finishing my champagne I approached his reclining person, still on the *chaise-longue.*

"Look! Look at what those imbeciles have done, look!" Mahler cried, as he handed me the concert program with one hand as he clapped the back of his other hand to his forehead, in a dramatic gesture of futility.

I took the program and started to read it. In the meantime Mahler had abandoned the *chaise-longue* in favor of an armchair, covered in green leather, into which he lapsed.

Reverting my gaze back to the program, it appeared to be yet another program made of thick gilt edged card with a highly polished ceramic surface, upon which were printed the usual descriptive words, and was gratified to read the aim of the Queen's Hall Orchestra, as printed at the top of the card. It declared, in the following distinct and bold words; I checked the accreditations regarding the concert. Then I noticed an error in the printing; the key of the symphony was shown incorrectly as being in the key of D flat minor, and not correctly in E flat major.

I then realized, to my horror, that more than half of the front cover to the program was taken up with the most appalling and outrageous gaudy advertisement. It was placed, without Mahler's knowledge, by the sponsor of the concert; an artificial prosthetic limb manufacturer, promoting the benefits to those who wished to be informed, of the availability of improved wooden or refined aluminum limbs, appendages and other prosthetic protuberances for the limbless person!

I looked at Mahler, who by now was beside himself in an apoplexy of despair. I could well imagine the thoughts racing through his mind, at the prospect of his symphony, his pride and joy, being irretrievably linked to a manufacturer of artificial prosthetic limbs. The fact of their being fabricated out of wood or refined aluminum, or the fact of the rubber foot or hand, even possessing the most natural appearance, was neither here or there.

What was of monumental significance, was the fact that the sponsor of the concert was a manufacturer of these rubberized protuberances. And, that we were trying to salvage what vestige of reputation was left of the Eighth Symphony, to say nothing of its dignity. Given the adverse criticism meted out of the symphony earlier in München, its triumphant acclamation and acceptance into the established symphonic *repertoire* from this point now looked to be even more doubtful. Mahler knew this to be not so much a possibility, but almost certainly a probability.

A drink to settle his taut nerves would clearly be out of the question, for alas he was to conduct the symphony in less than an hour. At least so I thought as I replenished my empty, heavy lead crystal, fluted glass with chilled *Brut Veuve Clicqhot.*

Presently a knock upon the parlor door was heard and moments later in stepped a person sporting a large moustache; he then introduced himself.

"Good evening gentlemen, I do hope that I am not disturbing you during the final preparations to your concert, but I wanted to convey to you my best wishes for your *première,* and that I am looking forward to experiencing your Eighth Symphony."

Mahler turned his head toward him and asked:

"I did not catch the name."

"Elgar, Edward Elgar."

"I understand that you are an aspiring conductor..." said Mahler.

"Rather!" interrupted Elgar, "and an accomplished composer too.

"… of brass bands," re-continued Mahler, put out by Elgar's interruption, "which comprise the inmates of the local institution for the insane"

"I beg your pardon," responded a confused Elgar

"Oh very well then, the local institution for the *criminally* insane," continued Mahler whilst turning on his heels and promptly marching out of the parlor, denouncing Elgar in the process.

I felt the need to intervene.

"You must forgive my friend's re-action to you. All *premières*, as you yourself probably know, are fraught with anxieties and uncertainties. My friend means no real disrespect. He does have a tendency to return a remark without thinking, especially if his mind is pre-occupied, as it is at this moment."

"I understand," said Elgar, "and hope my bursting into your parlor has not upset Mahler"

I have heard some of your works and they show immense promise; in particular your *Enigma Variations*. [1] Your First Symphony in A flat, I know was *premièred* in December 1908 by a good friend of Mahler's in Hans Richter. At the time he spoke very highly of your abilities when Mahler and I met him some time after that concert performed by the Hallé Orchestra."

Whilst I was still speaking, Mahler reëntered the parlor smoking a *trichinopoly* cigar. He looked at Elgar.

"My friend is quite correct," said Mahler, "as always, Richter thinks highly of your symphony, as indeed we do. I can only hope the *première* of my symphony meets with the same success and acclaim as yours enjoys today. Personally I like your five *Pomp and Circumstance Marches* – they are constructed beautifully and very evocative. I feel certain that Wagner would have enjoyed listening to them, because of their consistent compositional integrity that remains evident throughout the series of marches!"

This is the Gustav Mahler I know and respect. On occasions he could be very accommodating and generous with his feelings and encouragement. He could also by just a few words instil an unbounded confidence in the person he was addressing, even though that person was in awe of him, as Elgar had shown himself to be.

I was reminded of our mutual friend Bruno Walter's description on first meeting Mahler in the office of the director Pollini ... 'when he talked to someone, the most amazing changes of expression! Never before had I encountered such an intense personality or dreamed how a sharp, pointed word, an imperious gesture, a concentration of will-power, could throw others into anxiety and terror and force them to blind obedience.'

Despite his terrifying presence, the recipient, one could imagine, would treasure a kind word of encouragement, recognition of latent talent from Mahler!

As Elgar, beaming gratitude to Mahler, opened the door to leave the parlor, a commotion was heard in the hallway. Suddenly as Elgar left through the open door, a person burst into the room and slammed the door closed behind him. His face was familiar, and unfortunately I could wish for no other person to be in Mahler's presence at this crucial moment, especially when I was trying to prepare him for his *début* with the Queen's Hall Orchestra conducting his Eighth Symphony.

"Do you know who I am?" the stranger said, addressing Mahler directly.

"Of course I do; you are George Antheil. I remember you from the Café Royal in Oscar Wilde's retinue of sycophants!" said Mahler.

I understand that you consider my *Ballet Mecanique* - the *Music of the Future*, to be a work of nonsense. I have come to ask you to justify your remarks to me face to face," demanded Antheil, who clearly had been drinking.

It was Newman who intervened.

"How dare you, how dare you barge in here. This is a private part of the Queen's Hall and the public are not allowed here. So kindly remove your person now."

"No," said Mahler, "Mr. Antheil has a right to know why I concluded so, and ..."

"You cannot abide the new *Music of the Future*," interrupted Antheil, "and the *régime* it induces, simply because it rejects unequivocally, that which is *passé*, redundant and sterile. You spoke at length in the Café Royal about your Second Symphony and the fact of its quoting *verbatim* long since dead concepts and beliefs, including Klopstock's *Resurrection Ode*. How are we to take seriously a series of songs and symphonies that when they are added up produce nothing more than an extended *Trauer Marsch* into pessimism!

We live in the Twentieth Century, or at least some of us do, and have no wish, desire or need to indulge in romanticized retrospection, dwelling on medieval fears contained in chants and responses. You quote selectively from the works of Nietzsche; but have you really read him – have you considered the tenets he propounds in his philosophy? How can you reconcile what he propound in '*Also Sprach Zarathustra*' and '*Man und Uber Mensche*' and the implied dismissal of a God with your Second and this Eighth Symphony? It is all nonsense," said Antheil.

By now Antheil was working himself into a hysterical state of mind, the beginning of which we were nearly compelled to witness in that Café Royal, and for which he is renowned. This can often be the precursor to his preferred method of conclusion.

"You spoke of your much-vaunted *Der Titan Symphonie,* yet the origin of its name goes further back than Jean Paul Richter's application of it for the title of a nondescript novel; the name addresses a much more frightening concept of struggle of the new against the re-action of the old - which you represent.

I have quoted you as having plagiarized Nietzsche without fully understanding why or what you have done. You talked incessantly about the sanctity of your symphonies and what they in turn represent. Yet, you quote from a dead poet. Nietzsche, who himself lost his reason in the very year you launched the symphony called *The Titan* Nietzsche, had you composed the symphony, could have availed you of a more appropriate title in his last book *Ecce Homo.* For that is the godless *Titan* Nietzsche is addressing. Not Richter's and certainly not the defeated pre-ancient Greek gods, who perished at the hand of Zeus, because of their inability to accept the new. I know this to be the case, simply because you reveal yourself to indicate you are either totally confused or just ignorant. This is expressed by your promotion of yet a new set of ideals that you have adopted conveniently in your Second Symphony.

However, putting aside your inability to understand fully, you attack my work because of my skilful use of the percussion. Yet the press think of your use of percussion as being outmoded, almost comical. Why there is even a caricature of you, headed *'Tragische Sinfonie'* on the occasion of the performance of the Sixth Symphony. The caption to the cartoon –which shows an array of instruments including sledge-hammer, cow-bell, a wrench, timpani and automobile horn - informs the reader that you had omitted the automobile horn, but will include it in the next symphony!

Even Robert Hirschfeld's review in the *Wiener Abenpost* of your Sixth Symphony, the one in A Minor, a psychotically revealing choice of key, stated that if you were capable of expressing tragic feeling through the power of musical sound, you could readily dispense with the hammer and fateful blows. He also said you lack genuine creative strength. And so in your *Tragic Symphony,* at the highest peak of excitement, you reach for the hammer. You cannot help it. Where music fails – a blow falls. This is quite natural; where speakers, whose words fail them at the decisive moment, beat the table with their fists!" said George Antheil.

"I express a range of sounds found in nature, even if this means the real representation of..." began Mahler.

"At least Ezra Pound," interrupted Antheil again, "considers my *'Ballet Mecanique'* as the music of the new Machine Age. *The* new Machine Age, Mahler, the age of electricity and steam turbine, not ox carts and medieval myths perpetuated in your so-called music – with or without the delicate use of sledge-hammers and errant automobile horns.

I cannot believe that any contemporary composer with a basic wish to create for the future could resort to block-clappers and bits of timber to be used in the percussion section of a modern day philharmonic orchestra. And as for the use of those cow bells, why? Perhaps to entertain the milkmaids when milking cows or to soothe the cows when being milked by the milkmaids, which?

Well Mahler, what have you to say, tell me if you dare?" demanded Antheil.

"I think my contribution to your diatribe would be somewhat redundant as you seem to be doing very well without it," responded Mahler, whilst drawing deeply upon his *trichinopoly* cigar.

This response by Mahler could only inflame Antheil, who was, I could detect, pitching to land his *coup de grâce*. His argument if followed closely, despite his being laced up with alcohol, was cogent and possibly did represent the new.

"How can you ascribe the term music to such rubbish that comprises cowbells and sledge-hammers, so ridiculous and pretentious you..."

Antheil spluttered out these words out, whilst trying to steady himself against a nearby fluted *Breccia Pernice Rossa* marble *gardenier* that supported the ubiquitous palm tree. He wavered, whilst swaying gently from side to side, clearly expecting a massive response from Mahler, who just looked at him impassively.

"We are not finished here Mahler," continued Antheil, "and it is my intention to continue this at my convenience and..."

"We are finished here sir," interrupted the Robert Newman, who had walked over to Antheil and was now delivering him into the hands of two ushers in their morning coats, with red piping, summoned from the auditorium downstairs.

At his departure we all burst out laughing.

"Does he give good advice?" asked Newman, "people are very fond of giving away what they need most themselves!"

"At least if nothing else," said Gustav, "it takes the edge of the anticipatory nerves before an important launch of a symphony..."

And before he could complete his sentence, Newman had thrust a fluted glass of champagne into his hand and together touching our glasses, we made a toast to the, 'inevitable success of the *première* of the Eighth!'

I was not as sure as I gulped down my champagne.

What Antheil had said was not totally the ravings of a deranged personality - which he clearly had. Though in keeping with the general behaviour of the psychotic, Antheil had isolated, and applied cogent argument in Mahler's own perceived area of knowledge. And whilst Antheil's intellect was there, his contribution to music could also be measured as the equivalent of dousing flames with gasoline. Such was his intense and explosive nature that I suspected he meant what he said about revisiting us at his convenience.

The one thing that I was certain of was that Antheil had upset Mahler profoundly by his remarks. I therefore felt very concerned about my friend's ability to marshal his own thoughts, let alone marshal the huge orchestral and choral forces now assembled below us in the auditorium, ready to breathe life into his symphony. I could only hope against hope, as it were, that Mahler did not experience a psychotic re-action to this unpleasant encounter with Antheil. Such concerns, though in my mind, were somewhat demoted in their rank of priority as Newman took my arm and nodded, intimating that we should find our seats. Accordingly, we left Mahler in the capable hands of the resident conductor, Henry Wood to escort my friend to the podium.

Both Newman and I made our way to the Dress Circle of the Queen's Hall. In trying to get to our seats we had to negotiate our way past some rather unsavoury individuals who were intent on acting in a confident manner and displaying very determined behaviour in our presence, such as I had not experienced before in a concert hall, at least not in Vienna. This was ominous I thought. Eventually, we found and took our seats. The hall was filled not only with people but expectation too.

I looked around the concert hall and took in the

beautiful appointment of this highly decorated and lavish interior with its ornate plasterwork panels on the walls with gold *filigree* detailing. The ceiling was a feast of art, depicting classical cherubs cavorting in a sylvan landscape where ribbons were very much in evidence. In the middle of the ceiling was a series of ornate raised circular patterns, forming a lavishly detailed rose, culminating in a massive gas fuelled *chandelier*. This sumptuous assembly of light globes looked as though it was defying gravity in all its arrogance. A massive gilt organ with side balconies facing the audience completed the whole opulent effect of the hall.

A hush descended whilst the lights were being dimmed. Then, a thunderous applause commenced, heralding the arrival on to the podium of the great *maestro*, Gustav Mahler in his black tailcoat and white gloves. A few moments elapsed, and then on bringing his baton down with a sweep of his arm, he launched the orchestra into his opening section of the Symphony No. 8 in E flat major the *Symphony of a Thousand*. In so doing, he called to life his mighty Symphony.

The orchestra opened followed by the chorus with a powerful rendition of the Part I *Veni Creator Spiritus*.

We had arrived and our *première* was now being performed. I sat back in my red velvet seat and began to drift with the music, which I knew intimately. From my seat in the Dress Circle I was able to view the entire hall and the beauty of its interior design and *décor*, which complemented the soaring and sonorous chords from Mahler's first movement of the symphony.

I could detect the echoes of the main theme of the grand *finale* as we approached the closing bars of this first section of the symphony. It was a fore taste of the quite glorious sonority of chords, which together in dominant

E flat, bring the symphony, in my opinion, to a triumphant and resounding *finale*.

Though clapping is appreciated at the *end* of a musical work, it is discouraged during the work because it can be a distraction. However, this did not stop a determined group of bearded persons, with deep black eyes, from clapping well beyond a reasonable period, at the end of the first movement, however unwelcome.

However, after this delay that accompanied the end of Part I, we progressed smoothly through Part II Scene from Faust, onto Part III Pater Profundus, and then onto Part IV Angels

The symphony was being performed well in my opinion and I knew this could only galvanize Mahler's confidence and provide peace of mind.

We proceeded through Part V More Perfect Angels, Part VI Blessed Youth, Part VII Doctor Marianus Part VIII Doctor Marianus and Choir Part IX Mater Gloriosa and into Part X Penitent Women.

The first part had been a success and I felt even more relaxed. Once again my mind drifted in unison with the sensuous music and the architecture of the hall. My eyes followed the fluted grooves of a *Rosa Atlantide* marble pilaster set flush against the wall that terminated in the area of the floor beneath the balcony, dedicated to the seats which comprised the stalls. I did not realize at first but gradually became aware of movement, as if someone was trying to barge their way into or out of those stall seats.

Then it happened. The chorus and orchestra developed a *dissonance* that Mahler frantically tried to correct. Mahler's gestures to the orchestra looked for anyone to see that he was spiritually and intensely absorbed in the music, but this was certainly not the case. He was desperately trying to restore order and keep some vestige of control of the musicians, that he was barely able to do. This was exactly what had happened during rehearsal. I felt like going off to the crush bar and abandoning my friend to his fate.

All of a sudden there was a lot of shouting, notably in Italian accents, coming from the cheap seats. Those very same seats, in the stalls, that my gaze had been drawn to and from which pandäemonium was erupting and breaking out elsewhere.

It then dawned upon me. We were of course victims of the Italian Futurists Movement and, from what I could determine by their smouldering dark eyes and furtive expressions, the Nihilists too. 2

"Robert," I said, turning to Newman the general manager of the Queen's Hall, "we are victims of what is known as the Futurists, an extreme organization, that wishes to redefine music in terms of 'noise-sounds' and is led by a deranged composer with the implausible name of Marinetti . Chaos in sound, as in cacophony, is allowed; indeed it is to be encouraged. Chaos is also applauded in double booking concert hall seats to, 'engender chaos' in the aisle, as people argue over who has the right to occupy a particular seat!

In Europe, we are aware of the activities of this movement and their reaction to what they perceived as inferior performances by artistes. It would, for example, not be beneath them to throw large vegetables or hurl fruit at the performers on stage, of whom they vehemently disapproved. This could be for any number of reasons, and not necessarily connected with the quality of music being played; personal dislike would be sufficient cause!"

"Really Friedrich," answered Newman, "well, that might be the case in Europe, but I think this episode is more of the English type; for is that not our friend George Antheil down there leading what looks like a charge by Nihilists from the cheap seats into the more expensive ones?"

Before I could reply Newman had leapt over the rear balcony parapet wall of the Dress Circle, and had disappeared into the back to attempt to bring order into the stalls.

Needless to say, chaos reigned for several minutes as an unholy alliance of Futurists lead by Antheil and a *concentration* of Nihilists fought it out with the ushers in their morning-coats led by Newman. The *mêlée* spilled out over into the central section of the auditorium, attracting the attention of members of the orchestra and choir, especially the children, most of whom had stopped singing. Against all odds Mahler continued to conduct, even with some Nihilists chanting loudly their blood curdling slogan, '*be it now or never*'. What surprised me was the speed in which Antheil's threat of retaliation had taken place.

As for the reflective and somewhat melancholic aspects of Parts XI Magna Peccatrix through to Part XVI Blessed Youth; they were a total fiasco and their sonorous impact wasted on an audience more interested in the organized commotion in the stalls than having their spirits uplifted to the glorious reaches of Heaven.

Eventually Newman and his morning-coated ushers ejected the Nihilists and it was only during Part XV Una Poenitentium, that they succeeded in finally establishing order, of a kind. Though the symphony had not been stopped, partly due to Mahler's tenacity in this respect, whole sections had to compete with the pandäemonium that had broken out. Just when we thought things had settled down, another disruption would occur in a different part of the hall, again, notably in the cheap seats.

It was against this background that the work was performed. As we approached the final movement of the symphony I could not help but think about the words which comprise the chorus of the last section that of Part XX, the very beautiful and sonorous, Chorus Mysticus:

'All things transitory,
are but parable.'

Under Mahler's expert conducting, even more evident given the circumstances, the symphony progressed seamlessly to its glorious conclusion, represented by the powerful force of the orchestral affirmation contained in the closing bars pounded out by the percussion section. On this occasion, they did not miss a beat. In so doing, they ushered in the graceful transitional sustained chords, which yielded to the final descending chords. These establish unequivocally, a resigned, but triumphant conclusion to the symphony; and its exploration of spiritual understanding, creating a real confidence where doubts have been banished from a renewed sustainable faith.

---

1 Variations on an Original Theme – Enigma. Op 36 premièred in 1898
2 Nihilists – those who are by way of being revolutionaries and sometime in league with the Futurists when their sworn aims co-incide

Chapter 15

The Solace and Despair

Between the manager of the Queen's Hall, Robert New-man, and Henry Wood, the resident conductor, we had managed to get Mahler from the podium in the auditorium and up to Newman's office. There we had laid a despairing Mahler on a red *damask* covered *chaise-longue*, in an attempt to console him after the *débâcle* that had attended the *première* of his Eighth Symphony. A wet flannel had been placed on his fevered brow. In addition, it looked as if he were slipping into one of his recurrent migraines, an affliction usually brought on by over mental exertion or stress. Tonight's catastrophe could hardly have helped. A doctor had been called for and we feared not only for his health but his very sanity too.

"Is it possible," I ventured to suggest, "that a concentration of Nihilists and Futurists may have attended the *première* in München under the auspices of your deadliest foe Pollini? I mention this fact because in order to ascertain any weakness in the symphony, or ways by which they could disrupt it, they would need a detailed outline of the work, so as to know when to clap deliberately out of synchrony or indeed know when to cough during the quieter passages!"

"Nihilists in the auditorium; I detect the hand of Pollini behind this. He is determinedly against me, of that I am certain," said Mahler, "ever since we fell out over my dismissal as conductor at the Hamburg Opera."

"I agree that the disruption had all the hall-marks of a well planned and sustained malicious campaign. I suspected Mahler may have been the Futurists' prime target on this occasion, and it seems that he was! There is concerted effort being applied here, and I suspect, as you do Newman, Pollini's guiding influence in the background; he does after all have the contacts with which to organize such an event. In addition to this is the fact Polline loathes and despises Mahler because of his embarrassment at the hands of his supportive public when at the Hamburg Opera. And Antheil, that miserable creature; it was he who organized the Nihilists' invasion of this *première* when they attended *en-masse* causing unmitigated pandäemonium at the performance we have just witnessed," I said, addressing my remarks to Newman.

"I feel his ridiculous music, including that *Ballet Mecanique*, played by its *bizarre* range of instruments, would make him a favourite son of the Futurists Movement. His so-called *Music of the Future* is based on a cacophony of sounds, including those made by 'Thunder-clappers', 'Screamers', 'Cracklers' and other assorted mechanical devices, each capable of creating a distinct noise. So at least Antheil claims and in my opinion is best appreciated in the mad house from which he has clearly escaped!" replied Mahler, whilst looking pensively into the middle distance.

He might, of course, have been correct, or was this Mahler's paranoia inventing a scenario to define a *rationale* to replace what could be simply a failure? Not every art creation succeeds for a myriad of reasons, I thought, trying to maintain a grip on reality.

It was as much as we could do to get Mahler into an open Landau carriage to convey us back to the St. Pancras Hotel. Having arrived, we headed straight to the Grand Drawing Room on the *piano-nobile* for a restorative brandy and seltzer. Gradually Mahler recovered his composure, or the alcohol was taking effect, and the despair he was experiencing by degrees dissipated into anger.

We drank until our anger had abated. At length, we were able to take a less passionate view on the *débâcle*, and instead adopt a more philosophical stance. At one stage we both confirmed that Mahler's music was so revolutionary in its style and form that it would, perforce, upset the conservative elements in the musical establishment, including Antheil and the Futurists!

Swearing an oath to each other we agreed that my friend should continue to compose music in his particular idiom, irrespective of the critics!

"My music is for the people; not for a rabble of failed composers turned critic," said Mahler, as we staggered off to our respective Hotel rooms for the night.

The next morning when I came down to the Grand Dining Room to take break-fast, Mahler's facial expression bore testimony to the news he was absorbing from the various newspapers ranged around on the table.

Before I could even drink my much needed *Santiago noir* coffee, Mahler threw over one of the broadsheets.

"I have been reading the concert reviews in the London papers," he said, with a look of distain upon his features.

I responded by picking up the newspaper, the '*Morning Post*', no less, and located the offending article, which had caused such consternation in Mahler. I could well understand his re-action to the review and, even with my innate gullibility, found difficulty in believing what was printed regarding our experience yesterday at the Queen's Hall.

The *'Morning Post'*, stated quite authoritatively, 'It is reported that a group of militants, sitting in the cheap seats, attempted to interrupt a concert last evening. The militants, commonly known as Nihilists, are sworn to disrupt the music played at any philharmonic concert which does not conform to what they consider is *proper* music. It was only due to the vigilance of the observant management of the Queen's Hall that a semblance of order was brought to bear. Eventually, the trouble makers were escorted from the auditorium, and thus was prevented a possible repeat of this outrage by these belligerent individuals later during the evening!'

The *'London Post'*, was, as usual, quite vitriolic in it's reporting of the event. 'Disaffected parties have again imposed forcefully their grievances and impossible claims upon the unwarranted attention of ordinary decent members of the concert-going public. They achieved this deplorable state of affairs by behaving in an un-gentlemanly manner and, in public too! It is time the government acted against these over confident malcon-tents and introduced legislation in Parliament to severely curtail their activities. It was reported that the mob had assembled inside the Queen's Hall *foyer*, before repairing to the crush bar where several had been seen drinking heavily. Then, reëmerging from the bar they immediately went to take their seats in the cheaper areas of the stalls. During the concert, they proceeded to disrupt and generally behave in a thoroughly outrageous manner offering threats and insults to all and sundry. A full thirty minutes of this rampage had elapsed before order was imposed. Having satiated their thirst and intent to cause havoc, they dispersed into Langham Place and disseminating into the broader fog-bound Metropolis and thus escaping detection.'

'*The Globe*', was even more virulent in its condemnation, if also inaccurate. 'Yet again we have witnessed disorderly conduct on the very streets of the London with renegades rampaging, this time through a concert hall in the very center of our Metropolis and acting in a confident manner, dispensing insults at members of the public. We know this outrage to be the result of the activities of an extreme sect called the Nihilists - who are by way of being revolutionaries. We at '*The Globe*' campaigned vigorously against their being allowed to form into *concentrations*, from which they are able to wreak havoc, at most inconvenient moments, typically during concerts. It is reported that a *concentration* of these Nihilists arrived at the Queen's Hall in London in a disorderly manner, and tried to set the concert hall on fire. Some even repaired to the lower depths of the Queen's Hall to spread the blaze there, and no doubt, whilst there, all manner of oaths and nefarious deeds were indulged in. Thereafter some of them, no doubt satiated with emotion and drink, emerged from the depths of the hall, hoping to wreak their havoc upon audience and repeat their rampage, and instill fear into members of the public, by uttering the blood-curdling slogan, '*be it now or never!*' The day was saved only by the intervention of fire engineers, who were *en-route* to another fire in nearby Seymour Place.'

Opening another newspaper, it appeared that, true to form, the well vaunted Fourth Estate had quoted differing versions of a non-existent incident.

'*The Daily Telegraph*', informed its readers that 'A *concentration* of Nihilists, intent on causing maximum disruption, acted in a confident and provocative manner in the very Dress Circle of Queen's Hall, yesterday evening during a piano recital. Some time had elapsed before order was eventually restored and then only after *employé*s of the Queen's Hall intervened against the Nihilists often at risk to their persons. It is to be commended that such gallant *employé*s as they, were prepared to deal effectively with these persons, whose only wish is to disrupt our democratically based society. On contacting Scotland Yard for a response to this commotion, *The Daily Telegraph* was advised that they knew absolutely nothing about it. This brings to the fore the whole question of the effectiveness of our police force, charged with the duty of protecting the public and ensuring that law and order are maintained throughout London, including in our concert halls ranged across the Metropolis.'

'The Times', normally reticent in such matters, lambasted the management of the Queen's Hall. 'There are reports that a major incidence of civil disobedience erupted at the Queen's Hall last night as the audience, dissatisfied with the indifferent service offered to them by the management of the Queen's Hall, vented their feelings freely and with confidence and, we might add, in a public hall. In some cases, it was reported, that members of the audience acted with determination and intolerance toward any *employé*, easily identifiable in their velveteen morning-coats with red piping. In isolated areas of the concert hall, Queen's Hall *employé*s were heard having heated discourse with members of the audience. A representative of the management of the Queen's Hall informed 'The Times', that the incident had been wildly exaggerated and involved only one or two individuals, who were escorted out of the auditorium, for failing to have about their persons a valid concert ticket.'

Whereas *'The Echo'*, if less reticent, seemed to be at a loss as to what it was supposedly informing its readers about. 'Concert goers reported hearing a noise from the depths of the Queen's Hall during a concert of chamber music that sounded like a boiler exploding, followed by a major commotion. Minutes later, they saw people emerging in to the concert hall bearing minor cuts and bruises to their persons. We also understand that servants of the Queen's Hall were at great pains to deny that any such incident had occurred during a wonderful concert of Hungarian Rhapsodies and Elegies for violin and orchestra. And, any noise would have come from the percussion section of the orchestra -as very much part of the music.'

The *'Daily News'*, always contemporaneous with news of any description, merely reported in its banner article, '... the spiralling costs of maintaining the Palace of Westminster and exhorted the government to sell off the building to the highest bidder!'

It occurred to me that there was not one review of the symphony, instead the papers restricted themselves to describing the real or imaginary activities of the Nihilists rather than the reason we were assembled in the concert hall – presumably to listen to the *première* of Mahler's Eighth Symphony!

Chapter 16

The Visit to Devonshire Place

What was of over-riding concern to me was Mahler's persecution complex taking on substance in the form of focusing on Pollini, in particular, as the cause of all his problems. It is true, Pollini was no friend of Mahler, and could in fact be considered an implacable enemy, but neither, I think, could Pollini be blamed for all the misfortune Mahler attributed to him. For this reason it was important to maintain a balanced perspective on events as they unfolded. The reason I mention this, was not that one condoned Pollini's actions, whether real or apparent, but because there could be other reasons with equal validity and application. I refer to Count Géze Zichy, who as the Arts Commissioner in 1891 forced Mahler from of the position of director of the Pesh Opera. Even in later years, Zichy still had the occasional vitriolic remark to make about Mahler. In that instance that antagonism was based on the fact of Mahler being forced to leave the opera. There were, not for the first time, concerted public demonstrations of support for him. That support erupted, on one occasion, into a riot breaking out in the Dress Circle during a performance of Wagner's sacred music drama *Lohengrin*. A memorable performance, for obvious reasons, with Schröder-Hanfstängl in the *rôle* of Elsa, and who was not in the least bit perturbed by the commotion. She sang flawlessly. Order was restored only when police detectives appeared on the scene!

Pollini, as director of the Hamburg Opera House was without doubt, the sworn enemy of Mahler, and, irredeemably set in his attitude of spiteful hostility towards my friend, who himself reciprocated a detestation and antagonism which were given increasing distressing expression over the coming years. Naturally enough, in the public mind, Pollini was cast in the *rôle* of villain.

The critic Heinrich Chevalley, once confided in me the deep rooted reasons for these vitriolic relations on his taking up his duties in Hamburg in 1896, as critic. Up until then, battles between Mahler and Pollini had largely been fought in private, literally behind the stage scenes. Now their differences had erupted into the public domain and were followed with interest by the musical establishment, some of whom did not consider this to be appropriate behavior by representatives of the Opera House.

Mahler had somewhat irritated Hamburg's conservative musical circles by his choice of concert material to be played, which included modern works and also Mahler's own symphonic works. His style and approach to conducting was remarked upon, especially his arbitrary treatment of another composer's score by the removal of bars from a particular *scherzo,* or the positioning of the orchestra, all designed to give emphasis – or not - according to Mahler's ideas on the music.

Of course the irritated musical establishment emboldened Pollini, who began to act against Mahler with inordinate confidence by making his position as conductor, particularly untenable by reducing his privileges and authority. This situation was made worse when Pollini invited the less experienced conductor, Krzyzanowsky to the post of deputy conductor. The implication of this was not lost on anyone, not least Mahler, who viewed the appointment as nothing, less than an encroachment upon his authority and position.

Pollini, as director, held the right to apportion work to both conductors, and he did this in a typically arbitrary manner, designed to further humiliate and annoy Mahler. For example, Pollini awarded the conducting of Rickard Wagner's operas *Die Meistersingers von Nürnburg* and *Tristan und Isolde* to Krzyzanowsky to annoy Mahler whom he knew to be fond of these operas. However, in one attempt to relegate Mahler to oblivion, he gave him Verde's *Norma* to conduct, an opera he thought Mahler despised. Mahler did not, and went on to conduct the opera to great critical acclaim! In this respect there was more drama *off* the opera stage than on it!

Clearly irreconcilable differences were being built up between them and became acrimonious as Pollini submitted musical works on Mahler to conduct that had not been vetted as suitable by the latter in his *rôle* as chief conductor of the Hamburg Opera House.

Other critics, such as Victor von Herzfeld, music critic of the *Neues Pestor Journal,* and Hans Kössler commented on Mahler's music on an all too regular basis, sometime harshly; other time indifferently. But all criticism, whether leveled fairly or with malice is the re-action to any creativity. Mahler, on numerous occasion had failed to understand this inevitable, if irritating, principle.

As for a *concentration* of Nihilists disrupting the performance in the auditorium, I could not bring myself to think that Pollini would stoop to such disgraceful and outrageous measures. However, I did detect the hand of Antheil and his loose association with the Futurists, whose sworn aim was to '...*disrupt any established and defunct performance of dead music in whatever arena it is dying...*' were behind this *outré* and extremely confident behavior

It was becoming obvious, to me at any rate that Mahler was beginning to display those symptoms, so easily recognizable in him, of nervous exhaustion. This was precisely what I feared in tacitly agreeing to Mahler making the journey to London. His visit, was to say the very least, premature and the consequences of this action might well be with us for some time to come.

"He has it in for me, of that I am certain!" Mahler said continually in his delirium, as if the needle in one of those new fangled *gramophone* sound repeating contraptions had become irretrievably stuck in its *Shellac* [1] groove.

Despite these misgivings, fortunately there was perhaps a solution to hand. I had taken the precaution of making discreet inquiries about Sigmund Freud, by cablegram, before we left Maiernigg am Wörthersee for our journey to London. Mahler, so I believed, had seen Freud in Leiden some time ago. But it was Freud and his pioneering work in psycho-analysis and the treatment of the new fashionable condition of hysteria that was of particular interest to me at the moment.

By co-incidence, an acquaintance of mine, Doctor Kraff-Ebing, himself an eminent Viennese psychologist, had suggested I contact Freud if necessary whilst in London. I had also learned that Freud maintained a clinic there. I was therefore pleasantly surprised, when Freud, by reply cablegram, agreed to see Mahler, '*should the occasion call for it.*' The occasion had now called for it. And, because there was, in my mind, a real fear that Mahler might succumb and relapse into a chronic condition, only intensified my resolve to call upon Freud at the earliest opportunity. Not a moment should be lost in bringing Mahler to Freud's clinic for a consultation.

I had also been informed in Freud's cablegram that his clinic at Devonshire Place was in fact located in what he referred to as the Doctors' Quarters, in a district called Harley Street. Accordingly, we availed ourselves of a Barouche four wheeler carriage and instructed the liveried coachman as to our destination in the Doctors' Quarters of London.

He responded by looking at us as though we had broken out of some secure institution and were trying to make good our escape. Our German accents did not make for an easier discourse with him. Nonetheless, he turned his chestnut horses' heads around and trotted along a street the name of which I did not notice.

We were in the carriage for all of six minutes when the coachman announced, pointing with his whip to a front door, that we had arrived. We could have walked as quickly, I pondered whilst paying the fare plus tip.

The house in Devonshire Place was typical of those Georgian town houses of which the majority of the streets in that quarter of London were made. Flat-fronted and often with a metal-railed balcony addressing the *piano-nobile* of the first floor, they represented the epitome of respectability and solidity in all the matters one associates with stability and affluence. I suppose these visible characteristics of the buildings would be an essential requirement for a practitioner, such as Freud, in establishing his credentials, when he is confronted with all manner of persons with nervous diseases of the mind. Especially so, when he might have to deal, on an all too regular basis, with the hysterical, the confirmed hypo-chondriac and indeed the generally mentally deranged!

Undeterred by these personality traits, possibly appli-cable to Mahler, we approached Freud's black-painted,

The House in Devonshire Place

cruciform-paneled, double-leaf front door, which was completed by a highly polished brass knocker and matching handle. I pulled at the adjacent bell wire and a faint tinkle announced our presence. Presently the hall light shone through the semi-circular glass window above the door, upon which was inscribed the number of the house, as being 221 b. Suddenly, the door was opened and a button pageboy beckoned us into the hallway and then led the way up a broad red-carpeted staircase to the *piano-nobile* in which Professor Freud held his clinic.

We were shown into the study of the great psycho-analyst and commentator on the new fashionable disease of hysteria.

"Lie down on that *chaise-longue* and make yourself comfortable," he instructed Mahler, whilst referring to a sheaf of papers with his back to us.

"Well I am not long risen from my own bed and do not really feel tired," Mahler replied.

I sat down on a *chintz* covered Chippendale chair in the far corner of the room and kept myself out of the consultation process.

"Please do as I have advised, it is part of your way forward. Please now, how bad are you feeling?"

Even I was somewhat taken aback by this over-familiarity and intrusive line of inquiry into Mahler's personal life. Mahler too seemed at a loss as to how to reply, but presumably could only conclude that this was perhaps how one greeted a person in London.

"Not bad actually," Mahler eventually spluttered out, with some degree of aspersion in his reply.

"Really, when did you begin to realize you were being ignored by your father?" continued Freud.

"I am not certain as to the correct form of answer," said Mahler, "or from whence my being ignored came, but my father passed away some twenty-one years ago."

"Interesting; when did you begin to harbor subsequent feelings of disappointment towards your mother?"

"I beg your pardon, whom do you think you are addressing?" Mahler replied, with all the feelings of outrage he could summon at his command, whilst rising reluctantly from the comfortable *chaise-longue*. "My mother passed away in the same year as my father, in 1889, making it somewhat difficult to harbor feelings of disappointment or anything else towards her."

"You really must learn to control your emotional outbursts and consider the situation from the perspective of other persons and not your own selfish ego-centric view," replied Freud.

"Now look here, I came here to perhaps elicit your help and have a meaningful and reasonable consultation with you, not to be insulted!" replied Mahler.

"People who come here invariably wish me to help them; otherwise their journey would be futile. Is your journey futile, or are you willing to be positive? Professor Freud inquired.

"Well,"Mahler replied, "feelings of inadequacy often attend my thoughts, but inevitably I rise above them".

"You do surprise me, for I thought you were a manic-depressive with what I term a Bi-polar Syndrome, causing you to experience extreme mood swings, ranging from the respectful and attentive to the downright rude and aggressive."

Bi-polar? This could very well have described Mahler's condition: mood swings, rude and aggressive sometimes, I thought.

"I am not perfect, but would hardly describe myself in that way…"

"I am describing you in that way, it is what I am paid

to do," interrupted Freud, finally turning around to face Mahler.

"You, who are you?"

It was I who answered.

"My name is Friedrich Löhr and this is *Maestro* Mahler," I replied, "we communicated by cablegram some days ago about the possibility, of our coming to see you should the occasion warrant it."

Freud waved us into comfortable armchairs facing his desk, into which we both sank quite literally, as I could barely see over the top of his desk.

"Herr *Lowe*, I think you have made a mistake. I was expecting a psychotic patient of mine, a new patient, a woman who suffers increasingly from Bi-polar Syndrome," said Freud.

I noted, but resisted the urge to re-act to the incorrect pronunciation of my surname, and also disregarded Freud's blatant attempt to impute failure to me for *his* mistake. Were we not shown into his study by the button pageboy and had not Mahler merely complied with Freud's request to make himself comfortable on the *chaise-longue* whilst answering his inquiries, I asked myself? I now began to harbor thoughts that, probably like Mahler, Freud too suffered from monomania, given his propensity for denial, total denial, for his failure – or was I confusing this personality trait with Bi-polar Syndrome?

"If the patient you are expecting is a psychotic woman, then why did you fail to detect in my voice that I am clearly a man?" Mahler demanded

"Because the neurotic woman, Rayment, in her feeble endeavors to dominate, acts and speaks like a man, which is symptomatic of her chronic state of Bi-polar Syndrome.

Not allowing Freud any more opportunities for insults at Mahler's expense, I too began.

"Now look here, as I have said before, my name is Friedrich *Lowe*, sorry I mean Löhr, and I am a close friend of Gustav Mahler, the famous composer. You must have heard of him, he consulted you some months past in Leiden?"

"I see countless people every day and cannot be expected to remember every one of them now, can I? You say composer, composer of what?" Freud asked.

"He is a composer of *lieder* and symphonies, which explore the human condition and frailties, but invariably rise to greatness and nobility, in that my friend's works may offer a solution to those who are in desperate search of an answer," I said.

Freud looked at me with his eyebrows raised up.

I knew this definition to be meaningless even whilst speaking it; therefore I reverted to an old stand-by.

"Does the name Gustav Mahler really mean nothing to you?" I demanded.

"No, *Lowe*, it does not. Now as I have intimated before, a psychotic patient of mine, a woman called Rayment, is expected and takes priority over your friend's immediate need, since you have not booked an appointment with me. Good day gentlemen."

And with that *Parthian* shot, Freud returned to his sheaf of papers, whilst pulling at the bell rope for the pageboy to escort us off the premises!

"The arrogance of that man knows no limit," I remarked to Mahler on gaining the footpath outside.

"I suppose it is to be expected from a person who deals exclusively with the mentally wrecked, and he is alas bound to have a somewhat warped view of humanity in general!" replied Gustav, smiling.

1 Early *gramophone* disc.

Chapter 17

The Curious Individual

Having been unceremoniously ejected from Freud's consulting rooms, there was nothing for it except to make our way back to the St. Pancras Hotel and attempt to derive solace and comfort there. Whilst waiting in Devonshire Place for a carriage, of some sort to convey us back to the Hotel we became aware of a singular activity unfolding on the door step of a neighboring house. Neither Mahler nor I would claim to be cognizant or indeed, over familiar with English traditions and customs, as was evident by what we were witnessing.

From where we were standing, there appeared to be a commotion on the steps leading up to the rather respectable-looking town house, very similar to the one from which we had just been ignominiously ejected.

Almost immediately, one person in particular, who had positioned himself on the doorsteps leading up to the building, caught my attention. In fact it would have been difficult not to notice him. He was dressed in an ill-fitting black frock-coat made of robust broadcloth that matched his tight fitting, black trousers which were made of a similar material. His boots, though originally black, were scuffed in several places, which indicated to me a lack of care and of self-esteem. I noticed too, that the socks he wore comprised bands of colour, forming garish ring patterns, as it were. This may well be an English trait, but I could not be certain.

The shirt he wore had clearly started life possibly white, but had become grey as the years had taken their toll upon its fabric. Nonetheless, the frayed collar was closed with a rather flamboyant black silk necktie secured with a stud in which was set a polished purple stone. Capping this sartorial assemblage was a rather absurd tall top hat of the stovepipe type, often worn in England, slightly crumpled but in keeping with the rest of his tired apparel. Upon closer examination, I noticed that the top hat was not so much crumpled, but rather had wrapped around it a kind of black *crepe* material, giving the impression of a ribbed textured fabric of the hat. Two black ribbons hung from the back, completing the arrangement.

His face was pock marked and of a blank pallor, as though he had applied a white powder to it, as if it had been rendered in *staff*. [1] Accordingly, his facial condition complemented the white gloves he wore on his hands, which twitched as though he were in a state of extreme agitation. It was either that, or he was afflicted severely by St. Vitus' Dance. Indeed his whole manner appeared to be one of agitation and his black eyes rolled aimlessly around in their sockets, set in his white powdered face.

I then realised why this individual was dressed the way he was and, did so with confidence. He was, of course, what they call a *Dumb-Mute*! I had read about these persons in some uplifting journal or guide, [2] and seemed to remember, that these characters are an optional funereal feature and very popular in England, and especially London I believe. His sole function, on an occasion as this, I recalled, is to re-live the agonies of dying for the benefit of those members of the family and friends who were most unfortunate enough to miss the actual recent death of the master of the household! And, whilst we were rather surprised, it was intriguing, therefore, to witness one of them actually performing for the benefit of mourners come to take their farewell of the person having died but these few days past.

Mahler found the whole of the proceedings to be of great fascination. He even began to look animated at the event that he was witnessing in this fog-laden street in London

Bäedeker's guide to London, I recalled at the time, went on to explain this rather curious ritual of the English when dealing with their deceased.

I tried to explain to Mahler from my recollection of reading the information in *Bäedeker's* guide to London:

"It is customary in London," I explained, "as an optional extra to any funereal proceedings, to hire the services of a professional *Dumb-Mute* at six *pfennigs* an hour. His sole function," I said, pointing to the *Dumb-Mute*, who by now was anything but, "is to locate himself outside on the doorstep of the house where death has occurred and imitate the death scene, including painting his face white. This is so, for the benefit of those who were unfortunate to miss the actual death!"

Humorous as this scene was to me, of course it represented a deeper significance for my friend, who stood there transfixed in his endeavours to absorb the enormity of the situation and the ludicrous state of affairs that had enveloped us. For me, it was shocking and *grotesque*, an experience that I had never endured in all my life and certainly transcended even the pathos of a Greek melodrama!

I looked at Mahler at the conclusion of our mutual experience undecided as to whether to laugh or cry, at this *impromptu* performance we had just witnessed in stunned disbelief.

"You must bear in mind Löhr, the reason for this morbid requirement, based as it is on a growing disillusionment with religion. We know that the teachings of scripture are being discredited as irrefutable advances being made in science, not least those in evolution. It makes some people question their beliefs. The attractiveness of the supernatural, including ghosts and fairies are all too apparent in funereal ritual and paraphernalia."

"But Mahler you cannot be serious, for you have become Catholic. Think of the Christ."

"I do Löhr, believe me, I do. And, in so doing, derive strength in my private conviction!

It may be easy," continued Gustav, "to comprehend why the cult of mourning is seen as the last remnant of a religious age. No longer certain of what may lay beyond the grave, we hold on to life for as long as possible in delaying the inevitable. When that inevitability happens, it is dreadful for some. You have just witnessed how this dread is given elaborate expression in the funeral ritual of the *Dumb-Mute* that will no doubt culminate at some monumental tomb; thereafter- nothingness. As the ancient Egyptians did, so we are compelled to construct extravagant mortuary temples to our dead. Often, it might be said, in more superior buildings to those we inhabited when alive, certainly judging at the state of this forlorn looking town house, outside of which we are standing.

It is precisely these concepts and beliefs, or in some cases, the lack of them, that I am addressing in the Eighth Symphony. There has to be meaning after life; otherwise what is the purpose of experiencing it? To live, only to have one's life culminating into a glorious funeral, with or without the assistance of a *Dumb-Mute*? Then what? To be bricked up in an elaborately designed Mausoleum, in the manner of Rossetti?"

On returning to the St. Pancras Hotel, we were informed by the red tail-coated *concièrge* at the reception desk that a telegram had been delivered for our attention, moments after we had left the Hotel earlier in the day. On receiving it, I tore open the buff colored envelope, across which the word 'Urgent' had been scrawled.

The telegram was from Robert Newman, inviting Gustav and me to join him in his club in Soho for an afternoon's quiet relaxation and erudite discourse. Mahler and I decided we would accept his kind invitation, and accordingly agreed to meet in the *foyer* in thirty minutes.

Within a lesser period of time we were clattering along streets that made up that quarter of London Mahler thought was called Bloomsbury. After negotiating our way, in the fog, through a myriad of streets, we then turned sharply into Covent Garden. Here, despite the fog, tradesmen were plying their wares and busy at stalls laden with vegetables and fruit.

"Is not Covent Garden the home of English opera?" I asked Mahler, rather surprised to see the level of street trading around the famous Opera House.

"You are quite correct Friedrich; it is also a large vegetable market!" replied Gustav.

Eventually having traversed a series of back streets illuminated only by the lamps of our Barouche carriage we turned into Dean Street and then arrived at the famous Colony Room Club embedded in the depths of Soho. As we entered the street door of the building, I overheard our coachman hiss something under his breath, and with a look of abject horror upon his face

Colony Room Club, Soho.

disappeared into the swirling fog, where I thought, he would prefer to be. What was this place I wondered, that horrified the carriage driver?

Though the fog had not depressed my spirits, it seemed to have almost the opposite effect on Mahler. Nonetheless, he led the way along a dingy corridor with a *terrazzo* stone floor and walls covered in what was at one time a greenish paint, now grimy with age and abuse. At the end of this corridor was a door above which was a motto I believed to be a quotation from Dante's *Devine Comedy*, in particular *Ill Inferno*. [3] Mahler opened the door and ascended a rickety staircase. I followed, grasping the banister that nearly came away from the wall when I pulled against it for support.

Presently we entered a room, a rather peculiar room, and the talking ceased immediately. I then became aware of glowering faces staring at us. Then as suddenly as the talking stopped it continued again, after a voice in the depths of the room shouted out and addressed Mahler. It was Robert Newman, and he greeted us as long lost friends.

It was however, our experiences in the remarkable Colony Room Club, embedded in the depths of Soho, which provided fuel to our conversation. The personalities meeting there, the faces that came into focus only to recede into the smoked filled recesses of the room, were all subjected to the acidic wit or sarcasm of the proprietor, for whom Newman obviously held a deep fondness and affection.

We spent an enjoyable afternoon and evening there, meeting various artists and musicians as well as other persons engaged in the arts. The Colony Room Club had a soothing effect on Mahler, and he relished discussing various concepts and ideas with anyone there willing to engage with him. The place, though without doubt peculiar, exuded a reality that agreed with Mahler's own preference. Ideas were exchanged freely and people there were prepared to listen as well as to argue vehemently for what they believed in. Prodigious amounts of alcohol were consumed which invariably fuelled most of the conversation being carried on in the room. I could well understand Gustav's reluctance to leave the establishment, but leave we had to for a variety of reasons.

After much conversation and heavy drinking with Newman, we took our leave of the Colony Room Club. Outside I hailed a passing open Landau carriage from the depths of the merciless and oppressive fog that was still evident.   After giving the coachman an appropriate instruction, Gustav and I sat back on the red-buttoned leather seats and headed back to the St. Pancras Hotel.

The hooves of our two horses pounded the wet cobblestones as they pulled our carriage through the almost empty and ghostly streets of the Metropolis. Mahler then explained to me during our journey that an idea had occurred to him regarding the *Dumb-Mute* and a character he had met in the Colony Room!

Sometime later we learned that the club now alas is no more, its remarkable members being scattered to the four winds, including those souls that ride the gales to Heaven.

1 Plaster
2 Mentioned in *Bäedeker's* guide to London.
3 'Abandon hope all that enter here'

Chapter 18

The Re-action

It was only a matter of time before I knew the inevitable re-action to recent events would present itself and reduce Mahler to a nervous wreck. The *première* had been an unmitigated disaster and the repercussions of that calamity had yet to manifest themselves. The experience of seeing the *Dumb-Mute* did not help matters but rather sent Mahler into a soul-searching frenzy from which he might not emerge for some considerable period. Rather than helping Mahler's recovery, our visit to London had, in my opinion, made more chronic the depression already affecting his vulnerable state of mind. The near mauling at the hands of Wilde in that infamous Café Royal was severe as it was cruel. However, notwithstanding Mahler's treatment at the hands of Wilde, it was the planned disruption and pandäemonium organised by the mentally deranged Antheil that finally wrecked any chances of success. The chance of the *première* of the symphony being even remotely considered successful in London, and therefore possibly elsewhere was severely in doubt. Its future was now doubtful and might possibly be consigned to oblivion, for such is the will of posterity. It was therefore with some degree of surprise that I entered the Grand Dining Room to take break-fast, only to see Gustav looking fresh and rather pleased with himself.

"Good morning Friedrich," he said rising to shake my hand, "I trust you slept well?"

"Yes I did rather," I replied, whilst attempting to catch a waiter's eye, "what about yourself?"

"Fine, considering the bed they have given me," said Mahler as he poured out hot steaming *Santiago* coffee into my cup.

I looked at my friend expectantly, and he responded.

"This morning I arose early, unable to sleep properly, and made my way down to the *salon* on the *piano-nobile*. There I glanced at the books lining the shelves of a small library. I was intrigued by one book called *Visions of Architecture* 1 in which the author propounds some rather innovative and interesting interpretations and observations.

He argues, for example, the *rationale* for this actual building that we are presently sitting in – the St. Pancras Hotel. It was built as the prototype for the English Foreign Office here in London. The government rejected the designs of the building and so in 1867 it became instead the terminus for the London Midland Railway. The style of the building reflects the High Victorian secular Gothic style current at the time, allowing the Victorians the facility of constructing their Neo-Gothic structures inexpensively and quickly, using the new iron frame technology throughout England and their Empire," concluded Mahler.

"Very interesting Gustav, but I do not see a connection that could remotely be of interest to you," I offered.

"Please, indulge me," continued Mahler, "the author actually answers questions succinctly that have alluded me; and their origins are from a position not immediately obvious, For example, the author argues, the railroad train is perhaps the most potent symbol of the Victorian era, a result of advances made in technology representing progress and domination over nature. It was the prime mover needed to sustain the unstoppable momentum of Victorian progress in creating the modern industrialised nation England was becoming. As the needs of a rapidly growing population increased so did their requirement for more buildings. The Victorians searched for a style that would satisfy this need. They chose the Gothic style. However, the Victorians for all their progress and success were deeply troubled by the concept of the improbability of life after death!"

"I understand your position now, my friend, but how does this involve George Antheil?" I said.

"An astonishing fact emerged from this anxiety about the improbability of life after death, a fear based on the consequence of the scientific advances being made especially those in evolution proposing the improbability of the existence of a God. It questioned the relevance of scripture that subsequently led to an erosion of the church's authority and ability to guarantee peaceful repose after death. It made the Victorians seek refuge and consolation in fantastic concepts, including relating eagerly to the emerging artistic period of Pre-Raphaelite Romanticism, especially fairy scenes immortalised in their paintings. Most of the members of the Pre-Raphaelite movement including Rossetti, Millais and Burne-Jones concerned themselves with scenes of chivalry and romantic themes based on medieval legend," said Gustav.

"Yes I know; their obsession with a dead romanticized past, as Antheil has gone to great pains to impress upon us, rather forcefully, on no less than two occasions," I replied.

"However within this Pre-Raphaelite Movement were elements of psychotic concern that found expression in a variety of ways not necessarily in medieval legend.

Rossetti's paintings are not untypical nor those of Millais and other artists who painted in a distracted manner. Rossetti was, before one of his numerous mental collapses, an acclaimed artist at the forefront of art expression and interpretation that profoundly influenced the Victorian mind in its dealings with the perceived life in the hereafter.

Other less dramatic artists, especially those of the New Olympian trend, depicted scenes of classical buildings and temples in which classical gods disported themselves in this newly perceived godless world. Others like Atkinson Grimshaw restricted himself to painting melancholic autumnal scenes, whereas Charles Doyle, a renowned painter of scenes depicting pre-occupied fairies was also the father of the creator of the *vogue* Sherlock Holmes stories –as Wilde pointed out to us in the Café Royal, who himself believed in spirits. This Victorian yearning for a romantic escape from reality to oblivion and fantasy was also represented in music. The young Elgar was a notable exponent of this music, where he freely describes fairies appearing prominently and especially in his Wand of Youth Suite Op.1 and Starlight Express Op. 78. This combined artistic output from artists, writers and musicians, so the author of the book continues, was not only designed to satisfy a deep public appetite for fantasy and escapism, but rather to perpetuate it!"

"I see, the point you are making from the book '*Visions of Architecture*' can be seen as an alternative description to what you propounded in your Eighth Symphony – a coming to terms, a re-affirmation, a realization," I ventured.

"It may at first seem incongruous," Mahler continued, "to conceive the idea that perhaps fairies may have been the motivating inspiration and powerful force behind the designs of huge railroad stations, but they were. The idea of fairies expressed in fantasy was no joke or cause for levity, rather the concern was taken very seriously, especially when wealth and architecture combined as it did with the wealthy marquis of Bute's and William Burges' designs.

Together they produced a monumental fantasy by 1885 at Cardiff Castle, confirming further the proposition that the Victorians, for all their industrial and scientific progress, were spiritually terrified. Bute evidently endorsed William Beckford's approach to building fantasies, and was only copying his approach at a place called Fonthill Abbey. Here Beckford and his architect Wyatt, did not allow money to be an obstacle in the creation of *his* fantasy at Fonthill Abbey," said Mahler.

"Do you remember Gustav when we attended a concert of Rickard Wagner's *Wesondonk lieder* recital at Neuschwanstein Castle? Notwithstanding the combination of impractical functionality, the concept of Romanticism was taken to its ultimate conclusion in the castle built by the temperamental Ludwig II, King of Bavaria. He commissioned castles, the designs of which were clearly based on scenes straight out of Wagnerian opera. They included *'Parsifal'* Op. 98, *'Tristan und Isolda'* Op. 67, *'Lohengrin'* Op. 135 and *'Götterdämmerung'*[2] Op. 84. Admittedly, the most infamous structure to emerge from this super-Romantic fantasy was not least the castle itself at Neuschwanstein, in which we heard Wagner. Built in Bavaria in 1880 and reminiscent of a theatrical fairyland castle complete with stretched pinnacles and towers, it was bolted on to the top of a mountain, so that the team of horses had difficulty pulling our carriages up the steep road!" I said.

Mahler thought for a moment before replying.

Fonthill Abbey

"The Gothic style of architecture with its spires, crocheted towers, turrets, crenellated gable ends and pinnacles, was the natural choice to make in fulfilling that spiritual need. The Victorians adopted this style enthusiastically, applying iron frame technology to construct, quickly and cheaply, decorative pseudo-Gothic buildings throughout England, including this St. Pancras Hotel. This yearning for religious exoneration may inspire me to write a series of *lieder* reflecting this concern.

That book has reminded me exactly what I used to strive for. The answers, as usual, are not embedded in esoteric convoluted concepts, but rather obvious if one knows what one is searching for. You and I witnessed earlier how this dread is given elaborate expression in the funereal ritual of the *Dumb-Mute* that will no doubt culminate at some monumental tomb; thereafter nothingness," said Mahler, in a concerned way.

"Does the book lend credibility or give credence to your symphony?" I asked.

"No, the book merely reminds me that there are different ways to the same goal in understanding. Some retreat into fantasy; others into spiritual ecstasy, others into intense devotion in order to achieve an equilibrium of consolation for the soul," replied Mahler.

1 Published by Bloomsbury Publishers.
2 *'Twilight of the Gods'*

Chapter 19

The Triumph at the Bechstein Hall

Mahler, talking in philosophical terms, something he often did, alerted me, as a friend of several years standing, that he was moving into an introspective mental state. He would reëxamine himself from the centre of his spiritual core outward. His confidence would, I knew, be severely shaken and tested. It was his way of dealing with failure, whether self defined or imposed by critics. Either way, he would be harsh on himself and sometime on those upon whom he had come to rely in times of crisis. However, despite our tribulations, there was some welcome news that came our way. Looking through the newspapers for any review or positive report of the *première*, my eyes caught an article, or rather a notice, stating that there was to be a concert at a place called the Bechstein Hall, [1] in Wigmore Street.

The concert is to feature a new work, conducted by someone called Russolo, and then *lieder* by Mahler to be sung by Lilli Lehmann, a dear friend of ours.

"I had no idea my good friend Lehmann was even in London," said Mahler, "the last I knew, she was warbling like a nightingale in New York at the Metropolitan Opera House!"

"Still, it must good to have a friend in her, especially at this rather low moment and in this fog-laden Metropolis.

Anyone who is capable of reminding us of Vienna and can speak German without an accent is welcome as a long lost friend," I offered up jestingly.

This new work to be played before my *lieder*; let us hope that it meets with acclaim and that the composer of the work receives better treatment for his *première!*" wished Mahler.

"Well, at least we know that she is more than capable of doing justice to my *Rückert lieder* and *Kindertotenlieder* even at the Bechstein Hall. But it does make me think about the chance meeting I had with Friedrich Rückert, and consequently, of my setting his poems to music in creating the *lieder*. An unusual source of inspiration, but an interesting one I thought at the time," said Mahler.

"Not a moment should be lost in our acquiring tickets for the best seats in the Bechstein Hall and I shall arrange that immediately after break-fast." I responded.

We spent the day relaxing in the various *salons* the St. Pancras Hotel had to offer. At one stage we found ourselves ensconced on red button-down leather Chesterfields, reminiscing about Mahler's conducting *début* at the Metropolitan Opera, New York in the January of 1908.

"I particularly remember," said Mahler, "the time I heard played in New York, Antonín Dvořák's Ninth Symphony in E Minor, the one he calls, '*Aus dem Neun Welt.*'" [2]

"What do you think of it?" I asked.

"Interesting symphony," said Mahler, who I know always liked Dvořák's style of composition, using basic dance rhythms and folk melodies from his native Bohemia.

"This symphony," continued Mahler, "is composed with America in mind and he borrows native tunes from that country woven into a European styled symphonic structure. It was composed to celebrate the World's

Columbian Exposition, Chicago in 1893. The symphony opens with a slow, but rising *crescendo*, inviting the listener on a journey through various musical landscapes. The power of the music portrayed in the minor idiom is immediately obvious to any trained musical ear. It promises to be the precursor of a monumental harmonic journey of discovery. As it plays on, the ideas encapsulated within the symphony, I felt, express very succinctly the hopes, aspirations, dreams and optimism of that nation. Among the musical abilities radiating from Dvořák is a characteristic, yet unexpected, harmonic development, together with the fresh and vital application of orchestral forces in expressing a coherent melodic progression which, in so doing, achieves a rich intensity of feeling."

"I too am fond of his E Minor Symphony!" I said.

"Such were the hopes of Dvořák expressed very succinctly in his Ninth; shall we see if we can emulate him?" said my friend, as he produced his red leather *valise* out of which he pulled the notation for the score of his partially completed Ninth Symphony.

"Any ideas Friedrich?" he asked.

"Absolutely, "I responded, "life after all goes on!"

Later, refreshed and having taken a late lunch, we climbed into a London Four Wheeler carriage for our journey to the Bechstein Hall in Wigmore Street for our concert. As we made our way inside the hall, we could not quite believe the pandäemonium, yet again, which could be heard coming from in the Dress Circle. In trying to get to our seats we had to negotiate our way past some unsavoury individuals who were intent on acting in a confident manner and, displaying very determined behaviour in our presence, the like of which I had experienced before in the Queen's Hall.

I was all for abandoning our venture and instead going elsewhere, but Gustav insisted that we must support our Lilli Lehmann. That last remark had the effect of emboldening me. For my experience of Lilli would suggest that any Nihilists, intent on causing an outrage in her presence, whilst she was singing on the stage, would themselves be at risk from the retribution she would exact upon their person. We took our seats and waited nervously and expectantly for the concert to begin.

All of a sudden there was a lot of shouting, again notably in Italian accents, coming again, from the cheap seats. Then, thunderous applause commenced during which, onto the *podium* stepped a diminutive man, wearing, with inordinate confidence, a white tail-coat, white trousers and more alarmingly, white shoes! I heard people remark that he was the great Russolo, whoever he might be. Then with a sweep of his arm, he launched the small orchestra into quite what, I do not know. The so-called music was based on a cacophony of sounds, including those made by 'Thunderclappers', 'Screamers', 'Cracklers' and other assorted mechanical devices, each capable of creating a distinct noise. Antheil would applaud this music, I thought to myself.

Suddenly an angry woman, of Italian appearance, came up to Mahler, and demanded that he vacate her seat, the very seat that he was occupying!

"Look here madam," Mahler started in, "we have purchased these tickets an..."

Before he could complete his statement, she had launched into tirade of abusive language, of the type certainly neither Mahler nor I were accustomed to hearing in a public hall; well at least not in Vienna. It was only by my intervention, by waving our tickets in her face, that this encounter was brought to an abrupt end. But,

I had noticed, during this outburst, that other patrons were too being subject to a similar type of treatment, and that Mahler's experience was not an isolated one.

I looked at Mahler in total bewilderment. In the meantime the white-suited conductor was engaged, not so much in conducting the small orchestra, but rather in conducting various arguments with several members of the audience. Also, I noticed, that the orchestra had ceased taking directions from the conductor, Russolo, and were instead playing more or less what they fancied, whilst chatting to each other over the cacophony.

"The concert," said Mahler, rather irritated and flushed by his encounter, "we are expecting to enjoy, is billed as comprising Mozart's overture to the opera 'Die Entführung aus dem Serail'. [3] Followed by his Serenade in E flat, and finally, a performance of my songs with Lehmann as *mezzo-soprano*. Just what are we experiencing Friedrich?" inquired a rather bemused Mahler.

"My dear friend," I remarked to Mahler, "we are victims of what is known as the Italian Futurist Movement, an extreme organization, that wishes to re-define music in terms of 'noise-sounds' and is led by a composer called Marinetti. Chaos in sound, as in cacophony, is allowed; indeed it is to be encouraged. Chaos is also applauded in double booking concert hall seats to, 'engender chaos' in the aisle, as people argue over who has the right to occupy a particular seat, as we have just experienced!

When I was in Italy last year I was aware of the activities of this Movement and their reaction to what they perceived as inferior performances by artistes. It would, for example, not be beneath them to start a riot in the concert hall, often spilling out into the surrounding streets, over someone they vehemently disapproved of, or for any number of reasons, and not necessarily connected with the quality of music being played, but indeed, personal dislike would be sufficient cause!

Indeed I tried to explain this phenomenon to Robert Newman in the Queen's Hall during your *première*, when they acted in a confident manner there. Including their usual trick of clapping too early or too late and usually in syncopation to disrupt a concert deliberately," I informed Mahler, who immediately burst out laughing.

Somewhat taken aback by Mahler's behavior, I looked at him earnestly.

I felt ridiculous enduring this disruptive *coup de théâtre* and suggested we abandoned the place, as our presence here was becoming untenable. Whilst attempting to do precisely that, I considered asking for a refund at the ticket office, but the risk of inviting a full scale riot, similar to the one that was now in progress in the Dress Circle, was all too likely.

I could scarcely believe the situation we found ourselves in. The concert was one of series, to be conducted by a fellow called Toscanini and organized by the Philharmonic Society of London. The society's aim, I distinctly recall was, '*to promote the performance, in the most perfect manner possible of the best and most approved instrumental music*'. What we had just endured seemed to defeat this laudable, if noble intention.

We left the Bechstein Hall and repaired to a nearby hotel until the second half of the concert commenced an hour and fifteen minutes later. Then we hoped to see and hear our Lilli Lehmann perform Mahler's *Lieder*.

Whilst waiting for a carriage I felt somewhat redundant and about as much use as the absurd information contained in an advertisement poster we were standing adjacent to headed;

I was trying to determine if there was, any significance in this advertisement and the *fiasco* we had just endured, or indeed, their choice of business address, opposite the Palace of Westminster; presumably another Music Hall, and perhaps lend verisimilitude to their rubberized garments.

Having relaxed at the bar in the nearby Langham Hotel, of which of course we were familiar, we returned to the Bechstein Hall. There were remnants of the futurists and the odd Nihilists in attendance; but their numbers were much diminished and the groups' general confidence and ability to affect, muted.

Later we went back stage to meet our dear and

long-standing friend, Lilli Lehmann, who, upon seeing us standing in the doorway of her dressing room, expressed surprise at our being in London.

"My dearest Gustav," she said, whilst pouring champagne into his glass, "I thought you were locked away composing your Eighth Symphony at Maiernigg am Wörthersee?"

1 Now called the Wigmore Hall.
2 *From the New World*
3 *'The Abduction from the Seraglio'*

Chapter 20

The Invitation

The fiasco at the Queen's Hall was still fresh in our memory and causing concern to me about my friend's ability to deal with this challenge thrown up to him. I feared he was not mentally strong and that caused me further consternation. It was therefore with trepidation that I entered the elegantly appointed Dining Room to take break-fast with Mahler. He was sitting there looking forlorn and I supposed depressed. Who would not be, I thought, given his emotional oscillations over the previous few hours?

"Good morning Gustav, how are we this morning?" I asked hesitantly.

"Ah, Friedrich, good morning to you too," replied Mahler, "I have ordered some cheese and ham and some warm Vienna rolls. But, here let me pour coffee for you."

"I have been giving some thought to those Nihilists and remain convinced that they are in the pay of Pollini. Why would they isolate you as the focus of their rage, as they did when we witnessed a performance of Schönberg's String Quartet?" I asked.

"My good friend, the Nihilists, in conjunction with their compatriots, the Futurists, consider my music to be dead, comprising nothing more than moribund ideals and a retrospective look at the dead hand of Classicism punctuated with Romantic metaphors," replied Mahler.

"Their actions, though regrettable and an inconvenience to say the least, are not entirely to be met without a cautious welcome," I offered to Mahler, who viewed me over the top of his gold *pince-nez* with a skeptical look. "Consider the fact of their actions. All we have to contend with are in effect, the actions of a disaffected minority of extremists. Yes? Those whose main focus is primarily political, on the one hand, and an absurd development of musical tonality on the other; then their disruption is perforce qualified, is it not?"

"What exactly do you mean Friedrich?"

"I mean that the concert-going public has not rejected your work; rather *concentrations* of Nihilists, together with the Futurists, have done so. In addition, they have combined, with the express intention, of exporting their chaos and probably motivated by financial reward by any number of your enemies!"

"Go on please Friedrich," said Mahler.

"Your music can be difficult, even disconcerting at times, because it explores regions of the psyche not yet fully understood. We all of us search for the eternal in our souls; but in so doing, learn about things integral to us, good or bad, but from which we are formed. In this respect, Gustav, your music combines conflicting aspects of harmony especially with intellectual precognition through thought – and development. But, so doing can exact great demands from the listener. Yours is a music that is not immediately accessible; in order to derive ultimately that sonority and beauty of construction of counterpoint and its reflection of idealism. In this respect your music is an acquired taste. Do not forget Gustav, your First Symphony was *premièred* in 1889, twenty-one years ago and that with the *Wunderhorn Symphonies*, are now established works in the musical *repertoire* of all the great philharmonic orchestras!" I said, so delivering my soul upon the matter, whilst looking at Mahler, who appeared moved by my statement.

"It seems that we have someone who too, would endorse your sentiments," he said, whilst pushing across the breakfast table, an envelope bearing a red seal, "this letter was delivered to my room earlier, and apparently is of the utmost moment," said Mahler.

Laying down my cup of *noir*, caffeine-enriched, *Santiago* coffee; I opened the envelope and extracted a large folded sheet of heavy cream-laid quarter sheet paper, very heavy with a ribbed texture and a faint watermark. The sender had caused to be printed on the foolscap sheet, a coat of arm of immediate dubious report in a feeble attempt to lend, as it were, verisimilitude to the origin of the letter. Curious, I read the letter out aloud:

My Dear Gustav,

'I was very pleased to be able to attend the premiere of your wonderful symphony at the Queen's Hall the other evening. I liked very much the tunes in it - especially at the end, the Auferstehung bit, very moving.

It is a pity those rowdy persons got into the hall and tried to spoil your concert. But, that is democracy for you - the right of anyone to purchase a ticket and enter a concert hall irrespective of whether they appreciate a good tune or song. I know this because I am a bit of an impresario myself!

However, we can discuss this later, because I should deem it a great honor if you would care to dine at my town house this evening. I will send a carriage for you to arrive at your hotel at 7pm. Your hotel concierge can confirm this arrangement by the 5/- reply paid cablegram to the address below.

I look forward to meeting you this evening, &c. &c.'

"Will you accept this invitation Gustav?" I inquired.

"Yes, we will accept it. One never knows what might come of such an encounter; after all he calls himself an *impresario* – he might even commission me to write a symphony!"

"That much may be true, but I am uncertain which *première* he attended, because he refers to the *Auferstehung* for chorus which features in your Second Symphony, and not in your Eighth Symphony?" I said.

"Oh, he may have just been excited at the prospect of meeting me and confused his knowledge of my symphonies. He is an *impresario* is he not; and as you have pointed out earlier, my symphonies are now standard works in the *repertoire* of all the great orchestras and therefore he must have heard my music. By the way what is the name of this *impresario*, do we know him?" Mahler inquired.

"I do not think so, I replied, "but his signature, though rather elaborate in that obvious and practiced way, would indicates that it is from a Michael William Lodge, whoever he may be.

"Oh," said Mahler, in a nonchalant manner, and handing me a copy of the *London Chronicle*, "you might be interested in this review."

Accordingly, I searched impatiently, with my heart racing, for the offending review that had annoyed Mahler, and only now had made him suggest that I read it. I found it and began reading it whilst at the same time formulating in my mind words of commiseration. *Kindertotenlieder* as a cycle of songs were very dear to Mahler and reflected his still intense loss of his precious love, based on poems by Friedrich Rückert composed in, as Mahler himself described, '...in an agony of fear lest this should happen.'

Mahler's worst fears were ultimately given substance

when in 1907, his eldest daughter Anna Maria died. This did more to confirm Mahler's obsession with mortality and attendant expectation of *Fate* manifest as the opposite to joy. For joy will be followed by pain, happiness tinged with misery and elation by despair. The hammer blows of the Sixth Symphony reveal this inner turmoil and doubt. It is also to be remembered that Mahler was one of fourteen children, of whom eight died in infancy and both his parents died when he was twenty-nine in addition to an elder brother taking his own life.

This has always been my fear, not only with Mahler's contemplation, but his acceptance of such an inevitability, to make his resisting it only nominal. This chronic state of mind, was reflected in his profound feelings expressed in *Kindertotenlieder,* which had occupied my friend over the last few months. They had been further acerbated in his psyche, now given further fears upon which to feed, and creating a *rationale* to justify this morbid fear. The fear was of in his all too real premonition of his own impending demise reflected clearly even in the only partially completed *'death conscious music of the'* Ninth Symphony. [1] A most unfortunate number, but this fear could be explained and, given credence by the fact that other composers, such as Beethoven, Schubert, Bruckner and Antonín Dvořák, had all died soon after writing their ninth symphony.

It was with trepidation that I continued to read further the *London Chronicle's* review:

> 'Despite the fiasco by the Nihilists at the Queen's Hall recently, we were on this occasion, yesterday evening, pleased to be able to hear, uninterrupted, a *lieder* recital composed by Gustav Mahler and sung by the very

accomplished and versatile *mezzo-soprano* Lilli Lehmann. The concert comprised a recital of *lieder,* the first set, of Rückert *lieder* based on poems by Friedrich Rückert. Next we heard Lehmann sing in a very passionate, but controlled manner the heart-felt tragedy that comprises the *Kindertotenlieder.* Lehmann completed her recital with a beautiful rendition of Mahler's *Lieder eines fahrenden Gesellen* in the Bechstein Hall. It is always an unadulterated pleasure to listen to Lehmann's fine and powerful voice, and she continues to delight audiences with her singing to great acclaim.

Such were the calls of *bravo,* which greeted her recital that Miss Lehmann was called repeatedly, and in the end she relented with an *encore* taken from Mahler's last setting of the Rückert lieder –'*Ich bin der Welt abhanden gekommen,*' [2] and sung with a sensitive appreciation of the lyrics, together with an innate feeling and great control of the expression of emotional turmoil that the song invariably generates in the heart of the listener.'

I could barely conceal my absolute joy at reading this review, a review that would mean very little to most readers; to Mahler however, it was a testament of his ability. The one weakness in his compositions might be ascribed to the *Kindertotenlieder* cycle of songs. A blow to these could be a lethal blow to his self-esteem and ability to respond positively. I was grateful that the review was in his favor.

I remember well when the *Kindertotenlieder,* to verses by the poet Friedrich Rückert and the Rückert *lieder,* were *premièred* in 1905, and in particular what Anton Webern, who attended the concert had to say about them. *The Kindertotenlieder* he found less satisfying and in some parts sentimental as a result of outpourings of emotion, which in places have become tainted with sentimentality. However, in the [later] Rückert *lieder; 'Ich bin der Welt abhanden gekommen'* he admired the tremendous expressiveness of the vocal line, in possessing an inner truth.

When they were *premièred* in New York in January 1910 the reaction in the press was not so favorable; and this was the basis of my fear for the recital of the previous night.

The *New York Times* thought: 'They are mournful, gloomy in tone, and do not make any immediate appeal; but there is much beauty in them, and much poignant expressiveness in them.'

'Mahler feels but does not create,' advised the New York Sun.

'They are weighted with grief of such poignant sincerity that one must conclude that they have an autobiographical significance. We have not heard any music by Mr. Mahler which has so individual a note, or which is so calculated to stir up the imaginations and the emotions,' claimed the *New York Daily Tribune*.

For the first time I felt as if our visit to London might not be the calamity into which it had seemed to be developing. Our souls had only been rejuvenated with hope not to be confused with redemption. However, with the prospect of the evening before us, we continued our break-fast with our spirits elevated and a belief in the immediate future.

1 Quoted by Alban Berg

2 *I have lost my way in the world*
   I have lost track of the world,
   With which I used to waste much time;

It has heard nothing of me for so long,
It may well think that I am dead!
And for me it is of no concern at all,
If it treats me as being dead.
Nor can I say anything at all against it,
For in truth I am dead to the world.
I am dead to the chaos of the world,
And repose in a place of quietness!
I live alone in my heaven,
In my loving, in my song.

Chapter 21

The House in Bergen Avenue

Whilst the name Lodge meant nothing to either Mahler or me, we were none the less grateful, that someone should wish to extend good will to my friend in making his acquaintance. Though the invitation was to Mahler by name, we responded by indicating that both Mahler and I had accepted the invitation to dine with Mr. Lodge in his town house. His undoubted connections in the London musical world, could, we reasoned, only be helpful help and provide potential opportunities for the future, including the *première* of the Ninth Symphony.

The day went by in an agony of suspense as we waited for the appointed hour when a carriage would arrive in front of the St. Pancras Hotel, and then convey us to our *rendezvous*. Our host, one Michael William Lodge, had unfortunately witnessed Mahler's disastrous *première* at the Queen's Hall, including a disruption caused by a *concentration* of Nihilists together with the Futurists, both groups were, of course, contemptuous of privilege and sworn to committing outrages, especially at public concerts.

We were waiting in the ground floor coffee *salon* when a message was delivered to us on a silver salver. It was as we expected; a note to advise that a carriage awaited us inside the western *Port Cochere*. Mahler bounded out of his silk covered armchair and moved almost with the swiftness of a gazelle, swerving past items of furniture with the maneuverability of a seasoned waiter.

At length, we stepped down into the stone built *Port Cochere* and toward our liveried carriage driver, who was waiting outside the Hotel in the fog-laden aëther, which seemed to have become thicker since last we were in its acrid embrace. The driver beckoned us to climb into a highly varnished Barouche carriage that was hitched up to a four-in-hand comprising magnificent chestnut horses. We duly obliged and made ourselves comfortable on the red, buttoned down leather seat and covered our knees with a tartan blanket. Whatever else Lodge was, he was obviously a man of substance and it was to be hoped that his apparent wealth would be expressed generously at the dinner table.

Our liveried coachman then gently flicked his whip and led his team of four horses along the front of the phäntasmagoric *façade* that was the St Pancras Hotel. At the eastern end of the Hotel, he turned his horses around and down a slight incline in to the Euston Road. There he waited momentarily, allowing a ghostly procession of green lanterns to approach us, only to become red as they receded away. . At length he reined his horses left into this vicissitude of carriages, and we too joined the silent procession.

I was pre-occupied listening to Mahler express his hopes and aspirations about our host and the positive aspects that might emanate from our being introduced to this *impresario*.

"Do not build up your hopes too highly, Gustav," I warned him, "as often you do; only to collapse back into disappointment. This fellow Lodge might just be an ordinary businessman of the theater, with an eye to the main chance."

We talked about the possibility of perhaps launching the Ninth Symphony, when completed, at the Royal Albert Hall of Arts and Sciences, using the good offices of Lodge. Maybe, under his expert guidance, we could really make a success of that *première,* and set the musical establishment reeling with astonishment at our audacity in innovation!

Accordingly, it came as a surprise to be informed that we had arrived at 536 Bergen Avenue, the home of Michael William Lodge. I had no idea where we had travelled to in the fog-bound Metropolis, but Bergen Avenue appeared to have all the attributes of a well to do affluent district. Our driver had jumped down from his high bench and was now holding the carriage door open, proffering his own arm as a banister to assist our decent to the footpath. This was achieved with some difficulty, as immediately in front of our carriage door was a narrow fluted cast iron gas lamp post culminating in a set of double globe lanterns. It occurred to me, that this was why our driver had deliberately stopped at this point, to take advantage of the bright illumination afforded by these lamps. He then mounted his bench and clattered off into the shrouds of fog leaving us alone on the footpath.

The town house at 536 Bergen Avenue turned out to be one of those four storey buildings, the *façade* of which resembled an eclectic representation of design details under the general style of Italianate Renaissance. Though partially obscured in the fog, one could make out some interesting architectural details in the design of the house, reflecting the prosperous district in which it was constructed.

The building at 536 Bergen Avenue formed part of a terrace of town houses, the *façades* of which were clad in

The House in Bergen Avenue

reddish brown *terra-cotta* slabs. This design feature was deliberate, in that it conveyed the impression that each house was constructed of substantial masonry blocks. The house we were about to enter comprised three bay windows, each containing three window reveals, which addressed the front of each of the floors, from the basement up to the *piano-nobile*. The three-sided bay window structure was crowned with a substantial over-hanging decorated architrave, comprising ornate recessed alternate deep consoles used for corbelling, supporting a lesser detailed stepped cornice, typical of the Renaissance style. These designs were repeated, in the arrangement addressing the roofline above the flat fronted top floor attic, defined by an unadorned deeper cornice fronting a parapet wall with coping slabs.

The building was remarkable, not least for its front door, at the top of a set of steep steps, in between ornate metal handrails rising from the footpath to the first floor. We ascended the steps leading from the pavement to the front door threshold. The front door was adjacent to the first floor bay window, the reveals and sills of which were immediately above a series of half balusters impressed into the masonry transom wall and forming a false balustrade for decorative effect only. Mahler in his impatience to meet the *impresario* Lodge immediately pulled vigorously at the bell rod.

We stood there for quite some time, waiting for the door to open. Mahler pulled repeatedly at the bell rod to alert the household as to our presence. In the mean time my attention was taken up with the front door, or rather its over ostentatious decoration. Two over-ornate double doors were set into an arched timber door-frame which formed the reveal surrounded by masonry. The doors themselves were of timber and painted gunmetal blue. Each door comprised an opaque glazed panel, at the base of which was an *acroterion*, set in front of a metal grill reflecting ornate tracery in the form of curved and flamboyant floral designs, more reminiscent of the *Parisian* style than the Renaissance.

With the exception of the lock plate, that had no integral barrel-lock, surprisingly, there was no other brass decoration or paraphernalia, in the form of door handles, letterbox knocker or nameplate one would expect to see on a town house front door. What was even stranger, I noticed, was the absence of a letterbox. And a protuberance which seemed as though it might have formed the letter box, positioned just below the glazed panels of each of the doors, had been made inoperable and indeed painted over to blend in with the doors as though forming part of their integral timber fabrication.

Eventually the door opened. It was opened very slowly and to the accompanying sound of creaking. A head then materialized and scrutinized us, as indeed, we looked upon his face that seemed to register surprise at our being there.

"Gustav Mahler and Friedrich Löhr, we are guests of Mr. Michael Lodge," I said to the retainer," perhaps you could inform him that we have arrived."

"Certainly sir, if you would just wait a moment," he mumbled, and then promptly closed the door upon us.

At least five minutes elapsed before the door re-opened and a person we took to be the butler, beckoned us in to a dimly lit hallway. He them promptly marched off leaving us standing there. The hallway was long and uncarpeted and devoid of any decoration or fittings to the grey-tinted walls. Except that is, an incongruous architectural feature in the form of an inordinately decorated lathe-turned newel post at the foot of the uncarpeted timber staircase. The pier comprised a dado in the form of a pedestal that was octagonal in shape and formed by eight surfaces each with an elongated rebated central panel. This design feature was repeated on the inclined column rising from the pedestal and which progressed to a capital in the form of a wooden handrail terminal. From this terminal, I noticed, protruded a threaded metal bar to which an ornate metal lantern should have been screwed, or possible a gilded cherub, as a feature of architectural fashion.

Indeed the hallway was devoid of any furniture, and the only observable structure was a staircase to our left addressing the upper and lower domains of the house. Several minutes later the person we took to be the butler re-appeared and looked at us as though we should have followed him earlier. With a curved sweep of his arm he motioned us to follow him down the dimly lit corridor to what terminated into a reception room. When we handed our top-hats and canes to him, he appeared even more uncertain as to what to do with them. At length he merely just threw them down on to what looked like a Queen Ann vanity table.

The butler was attired in a rather over ornate extravagant outfit, that made him look as if he had just returned from a Louis XIV[th.] pageant held at the Palace of Versailles. He wore a red tailcoat with gold braid emblazoned on the front and epaulettes to match. His trousers were baggy and black, and his boots were brown and scuffed.

"Make yourselves comfortable in this Drawing Room," he commanded, whilst opening a door for us. Having done so and looked into the room, he then immediately closed it.

"Wrong room!" he said and led us back up the corridor along which we had just walked.

He approached another door, which he opened cautiously; put his head round it, but then, to our surprise closed it again. He made no comment but merely continued through the corridor. The butler seemed more lost in this house than we were, but eventually, his exploration paid off and we were ushered into a Drawing Room, which I think was at the front of the house.

The uncarpeted Drawing Room we found ourselves in, comprised walls that were covered in a dull greenish yellow paint, complemented by a white oiled based finish applied to all the timber surfaces, including skirting, window and door frames. Two sets of arched double doors, one of which had half acid-etched glazing and a chimneypiece set into the wall, were also finished in white and reflected an evident arch *motif,* that may have been *Romanesque.* The white *décor* continued on the ceiling, where it was applied over raised beading details, which formed square patterns, and to a stepped cornice, connecting the ceiling to the walls. Suspended from the ceiling were two elaborate brass *chandeliers,* giving out a surprisingly weak light, including one illuminating an alcove formed by the bay window. The windows were undressed in terms of the usual velvet drapes, of which there were none. Nor, I noticed, were there any paintings or decorative objects on the walls.

These observations did not make the Drawing Room in itself peculiar; but rather the furniture of which it was comprised. What furniture there was resembled an eclectic combination assembled without any systematic coördination or thought. It was as though Lodge had acquired the furniture, as a job lot, from possibly a forced sale of various items at an auction. Typical of this collection was an oversized *Salon Français* styled red velveteen covered *chaise-longue* that had possibly once adorned a large *salon* in France, but remained totally unsuited for the room because of its huge size.

Other items of furniture were of a gaudy aspect and most were finished with a gold colored paint. There were two *Biedermeier* styled sideboards that clearly had seen better days. Upon one of the sideboards was a gold painted cherub that in one hand was holding forth a lantern in the shape of a firebrand; and in the other a bunch of grapes, some of which were missing. Indeed several fingers from the cherub's hands were also missing, possibly from a fall the statue had clearly experienced at some stage in its existence. Most of the furniture was in the late Victorian style, and all had been heavily varnished by an inexpert hand.

I pulled back several folds of a dusty purple heavy velvet material that clearly had once been drapes to a window, and in doing so, revealed a large ornately decorated gilt frame they were covering. Once the dust has settled, both Mahler and I examined the art work contained within the substantial gilt frame. It was a drawing, a very beautiful and detailed drawing entitled, '*Visions of Architecture*'. The drawing combined an exquisite elegance with serenity interpreted as a perspective of an ethereal vision of buildings from antiquity. Alas, it was unsigned lending even more of an air of mystery to its skilful creator.

Mahler and I were just discussing the finer points of the drawing, when a commotion of sorts was heard in the passage on the other side of the door. Within moments a footman dressed in an even more flamboyant uniform, complete with a grey horsehair powdered wig, flung the door open. Without any form of ceremony he merely beckoned my friend and me to stand up. He then moved sideways from the open door and in stepped

Visions of Architecture

another person wearing a frock-coat. The trousers he wore were striped and his ensemble completed with black, patent leather boots. His mauve necktie was of the vulgar ostentatious variety, but which at that time were popular.

"Gustav, Gustav, how very pleased I am to make your acquaintance," he said, holding out his hand to me!

We both assumed this fellow to be our host in the person of Michael Lodge.

"I am Friedrich Löhr; this is Gustav Mahler," I responded, pointing to Mahler.

Lodge immediately withdrew his outstretched hand, and instead swerved with a practiced and seasoned skill, almost seamless in its action, as he diverted his amended, but increased enthusiastic sign of welcome to Mahler.

"My friend, Friedrich Löhr, and I are honored to meet you Mr. Lodge," offered Mahler.

"Please, please, no formality here; my friends called me 'Loge'. Apparently friends do so in honor of the only noble character in the opera *Das Rheingold*, that I believe is from Wagner's *Ring Cycle of the Nebulous*. Quite where my friends ever got the idea to give me that name remains an absolute mystery to me!" [1] said our host, and gave a little suppressed chortle, whilst rubbing his hands together.

Mahler, I noticed, desisted from calling our host 'Loge'; more out of respect for the fictional operatic character, I suspect, than for Lodge himself.

"Well Loge, we are pleased to be your guests," I said, feeling distinctly uncomfortable using his *sobriquet* in addressing him. It was for us Viennese, too informal a way of addressing someone, especially at a first meeting.

"Gustav, Fred," he said, devoid of any such reservation, "please do sit down, and wine for our guests," he clicked his fingers at the footman, who accordingly responded into life and left the room, presumably to fetch a bottle of wine from the cellar.

"Well Gustav, how are you enjoying our fair city, or at least what you can see of it during this accursed fog?" inquired Loge.

"It is a far cry from the elegance for which our Vienna is renowned," replied Mahler, "but the public buildings are monumental and impressive. I particularly like the St. Pancras Hotel in which we are staying and the Royal Albert Hall of Arts and Sciences, I believe?"

"The disruption at the *première* was a disgrace I thought," said Lodge, "it should never have been allowed to happen."

"It is unlikely the management at the Queen's Hall knew anything about the *sabotage*, surely? I asked.

"Do you get much disruption of this kind on the continent?" asked Lodge.

"The only disruption is that which is organized by the critics, though not normally during the concert but rather later in the newspapers," replied Mahler.

"Ah what do critics know?" cut in Loge obliquely.

"Well an awful lot!" replied Mahler.

An age seemed to pass before the surly footman returned, not bearing a dusty bottle of wine from the cellar, but rather a wooden elm tray with three small glasses of wine upon it. This rather surprised Mahler and me because we had been brought up to believe one poured wine, or any drink, from the container into the glass in front of the recipient. Also, we had neither been asked which wine we would prefer.

At last our host did as we expected, and invited us to follow him upstairs to the Dining Room for dinner. I was glad to comply in the hope that there might be more drink on the table, with a greater choice of wine.

On entering the Dining Room one was immediately struck again by the *bizarre* assortment of furniture ranged around the place, including three servants, all of whom were wearing different uniforms, and simply stood there, with apparently nothing to do. Nonetheless, we took our seats at the table, unassisted by the servants.

The Dining Room was a replica of the Drawing Room we had just left, except an effort had been made to make it more hospitable, though by no means to the level one might hope. Again, there was no systematic or aforethought of any description with regard to the furniture or its dispersal around the room. Set against the windows in the alcove were long heavy green velvet drapes, faded at the folds, and the kind that block out all daylight. Again, the room was sparsely furnished; and the items of furniture present, were of a heavy varnished over-embellished type, the origins of which, resembled more Queen Anne in style than Victorian. The walls may have been painted blue at one time, but now gave off a gunmetal hue, adding to the general gloominess of the room, augmented by the dim light emanating from a brass *chandelier* suspended from the center of the ceiling immediately above the dining table.

In a corner of the Dining Room, occupying an inordinate amount of space stood a huge mahogany sideboard partially covered in a red *brocade* material. Upon it rested a bust of some worthy or other, and probably made out of fired-clay, but painted to give the effect of being green *Verde Patrizia* veined marble.

On one wall, and built of timber, were gaudily blue painted shelves that had at one time carried an enormous and extensive library. Now, most of the shelves contained only layers of dust in place of books and a few china figurines in impossible poses. What few books there were on the shelves appeared to comprise legal tomes as well as a number of what might be judiciously termed, books of a sensational nature?[2] There were however, some *gramophone* discs propped up on one shelf that proclaimed that the composer Franz Lehár had got his waltzes immortalized in *Shellac*. Could it be possible that Lodge was possibly a *devoté* of the *divertimenti* music of Lehár? I thought, or most probable, the person from whom Lodge acquired the collection was.

In one corner I saw a tall chest of drawers partially painted in yellow, with a fold-down writing shelf, that was made of a honey colored wood inlaid with intricately shaped colored glass and red veneers impressed into its various surfaces. Ranged around the room was a *Biedermeier* sofa covered in robust striped silk, and a torn *moiré* watermarked silk covered *chaise-longue*. Four gold painted Cathedral straight-backed chairs were placed around the dining table.

Against the other long wall was a piece of furniture

that may have been at one stage quite an exquisite object. Now it looked as if its ability to please had long deserted it. This elaborate Victorian sideboard was made of heavily varnished, dark mahogany but with distinctive fluted Corinthian columns made of black ebony and gilded ornate capitals attached to its four corners. How did they, I wondered, get this large item of furniture from the street up those stairs which we had just climbed, and into this room? I then noticed that the heavy sideboard was on polished brass casters shaped as lion paws.

In the Dining Room, between some wall-mounted *appliqués,* were some works of art on the walls, albeit of a rather *bizarre* style. However, Lodge's choice was *naïve* as it was disappointing. The paintings, set in inordinately large gilt frames, were obviously a set, painted by the same artist. On the canvas were depicted exotically beautiful native women, wearing the remnants of straw hats and beads, sitting on logs outside simple huts, next to a blue lagoon on some tropical desert island paradise playing ukuleles.

"Please gentlemen," requested Lodge, "please do sit down."

We did so at a table that was above normal height. Upon it was a threadbare creamed colored linen table-cloth. Neither the plates nor crockery matched, nor did the dining utensils and were clearly from different sets of cutlery. The absence of coördination applied to the glasses which were placed haphazardly on the table cloth.

I got the distinct impression, looking around this Dining Room, that all the furniture was of an ostentatious and gaudy kind, as if it had been used for quite another purpose. It also occurred to me, that the reason for this eclectic range of furniture, almost certainly stemmed from Lodge's connection with the theater. Clearly, somehow he had acquired the contents of some forlorn theater, with which he has furnished this house.

It was as though the furniture was nothing more than an eccentric collection of gilt painted theater stage sets, comprising broken cherubs with missing fingers, gaudy paintings in large frames, and all as if acquired from the forced auction of some hapless individual's possession. Clearly no thought had been applied as to how to disperse the furniture throughout the house.

"I hope you do not mind Gustav and Friedrich, but it is a little fad of mine. I am partial to having high class music played whilst I enjoy my evening repast; I find the music aids the digestion!" Loge announced with a flourish.

Both Mahler and I exchanged glances, expecting to see secreted somewhere a string quartet or small chamber orchestra. We were to be disappointed, and with a click of his fingers, Lodge instructed one of the liveried footmen to go to the dark mahogany sideboard at the far end of the room. The footman duly obliged and upon reaching it, retrieved from its interior a large substantial *gramophone* apparatus complete with an oversized brass horn upon which an intricately ornate pattern had been engraved, including the letters, *'Electrical Musical Industries'* etched into the design. Lodge then produced from a drawer in the base of the *gramophone*, a *Shellac* disc that he proceeded to place on the turntable. Having wound up the apparatus, Loge carefully dropped the needle on to the record saying:

"I do so like the female voice; especially *adagio* and *tenor.*"

Both Mahler and I prided ourselves in having some knowledge of music, but what was screeching out of that infernal repeating device was such that I had never heard the like of before. The songs were being sung quite badly and by a not very well-trained *soprano*. What was more, they were of a suggestive nature and seemed more suitable for enjoyment by the lower orders, perhaps in a Music Hall.

Besides the quality and contents of the songs being played out through the brass horn, the noise blaring out, almost screeching, made conversation difficult, as we could neither hear properly, nor be bothered to construct sentences that one knew would not be heard over the music. The footmen and servants standing by, listened to the music and considered it a treat for them, judging by the expressions upon their faces.

"Let us see what my French cook has decided to treat us to," said Lodge as the Dining Room door opened and a trolley wheeled in by the oddest-looking waiter I hope ever to see in my life. Our host introduced him, hesitantly as if not too sure, as Aloysius, as he shuffled by pushing the trolley containing a vast, tarnished, silver plated soup tureen. In the meantime Lodge was pouring the wine that one of the footmen had brought to the table.

Eagerly I accepted a glass and took a sip. To say the wine was poor would be a gross understatement. The wine was without doubt inferior and definitely corked, but Lodge claimed it had come from the Emperor Franz Joseph's esteemed wine cellars at the Schönbrunn Palace. Had it done so, then our Emperor retained no palate for wine.

The waiter, Aloysius, I think, had been fussing around with the soup tureen and at length plunged a ladle into it. He then looked around furtively to see whom he should attempt to serve first. Apart from his gait, he was quite peculiar in other respects too. He had a pro-nounced defect in one eye, that kept twitching, almost in general syncopation with the rest of his general physical demeanor. He seemed to be suffering from Parkinson's disease, that, or to be in the final stages of St. Vitus' Dance. It was difficult to determine between the two. However, on one occasion, his shuffling attempt to bring the soup tureen round to me filled my heart with such alarm and dread that I declined the soup emphatically.

When Lodge and Mahler had finished their soup, one of the footmen marched over and gathered up the bowls and placed them on the trolley. To my utter surprise, the waiter then produced three plates from inside the trolley cabinet, which he then proceeded to place in front of each of us. The plates were cold and had upon them an item of food that was indescribable, to the extent that I could not discern whether it was meat, fish or possibly vegetable. Also on the plate was a whole tomato sitting on a bed of limp lettuce.

Despite being encrusted in truffle-impressed salt, to mask the flavor of whatever the dish was, it had that distinct aroma and taste of being off and possibly rotted in the center. When I put a morsel into my mouth, my worst suspicions were confirmed.

Lodge, who seemed oblivious to the decaying food set before us, kept reminding us:

"These delicate cuisines," said Lodge, "prepared by my French chef, have yet to be unleashed on an ignorant public who know nothing of good *specialité* food. But they shall learn, you will see! They shall learn." He kept repeating this claim throughout the meal.

At one stage during dinner, I asked one of the nearby bored waiters, for some ground black pepper to be brought to me.

"Why?" asked Aloysius.

"Because I wish to alter the flavor of my food to suit my palate," I replied, with asperity.

"Oh the chef will not like that; he has spent a very long time preparing this food," he announced, and then promptly left the room.

Astounded at the servant's impudence I tried to attract my host's attention, but the noise from the *gramophone* was such as to make this impossible. In addition, Loge was engrossed in a deep conversation with Mahler about the price per song he was thinking of commissioning Mahler to compose, and might there be, for several songs, a discount available, I heard him ask.

A few minutes later Aloysius did return, without black pepper, but reeking of alcohol. After dinner, if it could be called that, Lodge ordered brandy and *trichinopoly* cigars.

"I like to live well," said Lodge, "and spare nothing in enjoying a luxurious life. What with attending concerts, going to picture galleries, eating delicacies from French cuisine and enjoying a good *trichinopoly* cigar with fine cognac, I am well content!"

The cigars he handed out with his fingers were neither *trichinopoly* nor even a decent cigar, but rather a cheap brand of the cheroot type, which can burn the throat. As to the so-called fine cognac, it resembled more a cheap, dry sherry of the kind one would use in cooking, possibly the French cooking that we had experienced over dinner.

1 Name misspelled by a newspaper.
2 Penny Dreadful, is a cheap sensational novel costing one penny and popular with the lower orders.

Chapter 22

The Royal Aquarium Building

Whilst an amiable host, the evening was punctuated with peculiarity superseded only in intensity by the actions of his servants, who themselves comprised a *bizarre* assembly of characters. Lodge himself was not above this extra-ordinary situation made more singular by his insisting on Mahler and me calling him by his *sobriquet*, a certain *'Loge'*, based on a character from Wagner's opera *Das Rheingold*.

"My friends, Gustav, Fred," continued Lodge, "let us get down to business; I am, as stated in my letter, an *impresario*. I am always on the lookout for new talent, especially in the musical world. You will be pleased to know that I was quite, quite impressed with your music Gustav and would like to be of assistance to you!"

My friend, gave a shallow bow in appreciation of this unexpected accolade from Loge.

"I have connections in both the theater and the musical worlds at Victoria," he continued, "and would, as I said earlier, like to commission you to write some songs for me. Nothing too complex, but with good tunes, that is what my audience pay for; and that is what I give them."

"What themes do you want my songs to reflect; the tragedy of life, the beauty of nature, the inevitability of...," said Mahler.

"No, no, no!" interrupted Lodge, "something very

topical, something current that my audience can understand and relate to instantly to bring the house down."

"To bring the house down, what you meant to destroy, yes?" inquired Mahler.

Lodge then proceeded to lay out his elaborate, if defective plans, which he had in mind, during which he spent most of the time trying to inveigle Mahler into writing songs of an *outré* nature.

And when Mahler on numerous occasions asked him did he mean as in his, "'*Das Lied von der Erde*' or '*Das Klagende Lied*' or indeed something more jaunty, like the '*Lieder eines fahrenden Gesellen*,' no? And sung by Lili Lehmann?"

Lodge would nod his head enthusiastically and say:

"Well not quite like those ditties but more in the line of songs that could be sung by say, who do we have, ah yes, I am thinking in terms of your unsurpassable Marie Lloyd, even the renowned and delectable Katie Lawrence or better still, the incomparable and indomitable Dot Hetherington! All three can sing beautifully, with or without a barrel organ, but are particularly good when accompanied by a wind-up brass plated Aëolian pianola. What say you to that Gustav?" asked Lodge.

The mere fact that Mahler and I retain views on these matters appears not to affect Lodge's opinion, or indeed attitude, in the slightest.

"Perhaps we could have in the Royal Albert Hall of Arts and Sciences, the *première* of the songs or even better my Ninth Symphony both of which I can expedite and have completed if you can offer me a date?" responded Gustav.

"The Royal Albert Hall?" inquired Lodge, "I was thinking about a hall I can get quite cheaply at Victoria. I know the management there and they will help if asked," said Lodge, who then tapped the side of his nose. I assumed he thought that he was about to sneeze.

Lodge kept rubbing his hands, in a disquieting manner, as though a *presentiment* of a surprise was imminent. Though a pleasant enough fellow, there was something not quite right with him; but difficult to quite put one's finger on. He had the most disconcerting habit of continually looking over his shoulder and for no apparent reason or re-acting to a premonition.

"Yes I like to get out and about and be seen in the right places. That is how I make my contacts you know. You have to be seen to be everywhere almost at once," said Lodge, pretentiously, "I have to be omnipotent."

He said this last word slowly as though not quite convinced it was the correct word to use. I think the word he was looking for was omnipresent, unless of course he was referring to something entirely different; which, knowing Loge, might well have been the case.

"It is always a treat for me to go and experience fine music. Why only the other evening John," said Lodge pointing vaguely to one of the three liveried footmen, "drove me to St George's Hall [1] at Oxford Circus, where you can listen, in peace and quiet, to great piano concerto symphonies or overtures to symphonies. John knows a few overtures to symphonies do not John?"

John did not deign to answer, but looked instead at his fingernails, presumably unaware that Loge was addressing him.

"You say that with your great connections you could get a concert hall, in which we could *première* the songs that you wish me to compose and possibly the Ninth Symphony. What *Musicvereinssaal* did you have in mind?" asked Mahler still pursuing his original inquiry.

Lodge temporarily stalled at this question, but then recovered his wits.

"The *musicver*...., the hall I have in mind," said Lodge, decisively and laying down his empty wine glass, "is a very well known hall and has seen famous, and I mean famous, *artistes* come and go. Very centrally located at Victoria is this hall and very red plush inside, very comfortable."

Again, Lodge indulged in his habit of tapping the side of his nose with his index finger when offering up this fact.

Loge continued his extravagant descriptions, invoking all manner of corroborative testimonials to support his exaggerated and pretentious claims about what he could, given enough notice, lay his hands on. He then walked towards a purple painted cupboard in the corner of the room, opened the door and then closed it again. He thought for a few moments, and then retraced his footsteps and moved towards the over large ornately carved but inexpertly varnished, gaudy sideboard. After pulling open several drawers in turn, he retrieved with the flourish a pamphlet he was searching for, and returned to the table. It was now becoming obvious to Gustav and me, that this *impresario* had no idea where things were, least in this house. Every act he undertook was one of a major exploration, and his footmen too, were equally lost.

"Fred, this is what I have in mind for my friend here Gustav Mahler," said Loge.

It was I to whom Lodge handed the pamphlet. I took it in my hands. It was a program, quite worn and battered and covered with stains and ring marks. On the front, was a picture of an *artiste* in rather peculiar dress, resembling a layered petticoat above exposed horizontally striped knickerbockers and standing next to a military cannon. Above this picture was a drawing, a very fine

Royal Aquarium Building

drawing, of what a banner proclaimed to be the Royal Aquarium Building.

Lodge sat back in his creaking, gaudily painted Cathedral chair and with a smile of expectancy upon his face, looked at me for my response. His impatience compelled him to pre-empt this.

"I know, I know," said Lodge, "words fail you, do they not? You had not expected something as grand as the Royal Aquarium had you? It is certainly more impressive than that Ausstellungs Halle, that tin shed in München you hired out and had to make do with for your *première* there. I see great things for us Gustav - I am thinking big here; together we are invincible, what with my contacts and your music!"

Mahler had by now, assumed a look of absolute

incredulity upon his facial features, the likes of which, in the many years I have known him, I had never born witness to. He raised his glass to his lips only to realize it was empty and replaced it on to the threadbare cream-colored linen tablecloth.

Even the servants had a looks of disbelief on their faces at Lodge's outrageous boast. But, it was Aloysius's response that suggested there was more to the Royal Aquarium's past than our host had informed us about.

"Would your involvement in that place be confined to that of the Imperial Theater? And, its remarkable disregard for scantily dressed females that go through acrobatic performances for the delectation of the audience, whilst some their erstwhile companions are shot out of the mouth of a cannon?" asked Aloysius.

"Thank you," said Loge, "please make yourself useful in the cellar and fetch more wine."

Lodge was obviously perceptive, but had misunderstood the reasons, at the sight of five remaining faces looking at him in disbelief.

"As I say, words fail you, I know!"

He was right; both Gustav and I were frozen in a paroxysm of disbelief, unable to speak.

"The Royal Aquarium Building," he continued, "or the 'Royal Aq', as we in theater circles call it, is *the* renowned palace of entertainment in Victoria, and houses within its ornate iron and glass structure fully grown palm trees and pieces of sculpture. Very artistic!

The 'Royal Aq' is not like your other palaces, such as your, Palladiums, Hippodromes, Alhambra, Coliseums, Pavilions or Heaven forbid, the Hungerford, all of which I will have nothing to do with and I shun all connection with them. Those places, with their gaudy *décor* and cheap furnishings and their attendants dressed in uniforms more fit for one of Napoleon's field marshals, are built to entertain the undeserving poor.

The '*Royal Aq*' is like no other building you will see in London; it is hailed as the '*Emporium of Taste*' There is an orchestra that plays popular waltzes, overtures and a selection of *intermezzi* from various operas, lending verisimilitude to the place. So you can imagine Gustav, Fred, the '*Royal Aq*' is the *crème de la crème*! And, accordingly, has in addition, furnished rooms for dining, smoking, debating and reading as well as a skating-rink for those of a more athletic bias.

It even has a picture gallery for those wishing to enjoy the visual arts. The idea of the Royal Aquarium and Winter Garden, opened in 1876, was as a *Place of Improvement of the Mind*, in every respect. These high-minded ideals are promulgated with art exhibitions under the auspices of the renowned painter, Sir John Millais. Classical music concerts under the composer, Sir Arthur Sullivan are a frequent event, including the recent *première* of his Festival Te Deum played to great acclaim. And, even that woman, Lilley Langtry, manages to give thespian renditions on stage, when she is not up to her neck in promoting enthusiastically the ideals of her abhorrent society. [2] So it is, Gustav and Fred, a great place of learning and to educate the mind in the various arts —as I was talking about before.

Incongruous as it may be, we do not have those 'Assault at Arms' tournaments [3] which are often featured at the Royal Albert Hall of Arts and Sciences. No Gustav, the Royal Aq is *the* emporium of tastes and improvement of the mind, not its denigration!

There are sundry other activities that go on there; but they do not concern us or our high minded intentions or ideals! [4]

And Gustav, let me set your mind at rest about those Nihilists and their timid companions, the lunatic Futurists. They may have disrupted your *première* at that snobbish Queen's Hall, but we have our ways of dealing with that mob. If you think we are going to let a set of cowards and bullies try to intimidate ordinary members of the public, just out for a night's entertainment and fun at the '*Royal Aq*', then they have not reckoned with Michael William Lodge!

From my sources, most people attending concerts and the theater are not interested in the Nihilists or the demented and nonsensical Futurists. What with their ridiculous notions on how music should not evolve, but rather be forced into reality of the day – even the future. They may be dab hands at causing trouble, riots even, but we will be ready for them and by the time we have finished with them, their own *future* may not be that certain," thus delivered Loge on his thoughts about the Nihilists' threat to Mahler.

In the mean time, our so-called waiter, Aloysius, was beginning to show signs of impatience in having to stand there waiting on us, and kept coughing loudly to remind us of his presence. At one stage I was aghast to see that he put a cigarette to his lips and lit it by striking the match on the sole of his boots! Often he would look at Lodge as if he ought to know him. But clearly Alzheimer's would prevent him from making that mental leap of judgment in recognizing the person for whom he was a *de facto employé*. His physical condition however, did not in any way diminish his ability from returning abrasive and sarcastic comments whenever the urge took him; irrespective of being asked on numerous occasions by Lodge to desist from so doing.

Indeed I began to postulate that all the servants had

been hired from the local institution for the mentally impaired, and, that they had been decked out in ill-fitting, if extravagantly designed uniforms, as though hired from theatrical costumiers, and possibly at discount prices.

Lodge continued to chat with Gustav over the blaring *gramophone*. However, the full implication of what Loge had proposed was so preposterous, that I tried to eradicate it from my mind. Indeed, everything about this Lodge fellow was odd, what he thought and said, what he did, his servants, what he ate and his gastronomic preferences, the music he listened to and from what questionable origins he derived his singular pleasures.

My friend though, continued to chat away with Lodge about compositional details and they seemed to have a rapport with one another. I was convinced that Mahler thought this was just a story over dinner and could not possibly involve his *première* being ever performed there. Whether there was a language barrier, I could not say, but time and time again, I would witness a basic flaw or misunderstanding that indicated to me a mistake not of comprehension, but a fundamental mistake of principle.

To the polite inquiry by Mahler of Lodge, about what his thoughts were on our great Austrian composer Bruckner, Lodge thought for moment and then replied:

"Would he be a concert hall manager or an *impresario* like me; and if so I will have a word with him about using his hall as well, at other times, if the '*Royal Aq*' is booked out solid" he said, again whilst tapping his nose with his index finger, as though , again, trying to suppress a sneeze.

Lodge uttered these words in all honesty whilst still indulging in his habit of looking over his shoulder, which I found unnerving.

What I found even more disquieting was the certain probability that Lodge was living proof that a little knowledge was dangerous. Somehow, he managed, to inveigle Mahler into a discussion about the essential altruistic *rôle* of the Music Hall in society. In particular, Loge argued, there were educative aspects of the Music Hall and its ability to lend dignity and imbue the soul with nobility of purpose. For example, he proposed, emanating from these eminent establishments, were such noble ideals as hope, aspiration, courage and even fortitude in the face of adversity.

"And indeed," continued Lodge, unabated, "such magnanimous intent should be conveyed in the idiom of music and song for the whole of humanity, in its diverse forms, to endure, and not just for clever people like we.

Might not the Music Hall," Loge suggested, "be used to convey such ideals as perfection in harmony, and indeed thought? I am thinking of Schubert's *lieder*, the one sung during his Clarinet Concerto for Klavier. And of Mozart's aria from his ballet, *Dan Giovanni*, where the piano player sings a lovely song written for *soprano*! In those day composers wrote songs for people, not for entertainment you understand, but to educate. Now take that Frenchman, Ravel, and his '*Pavane pour une infante défunte*' 5 and that dreary song about a dead child, or whatever, we do not want any songs about dead children now do we. Nor do we want death-laden symbolism creeping into music, like that Roman composer Delius and his so-called *Mass of life*. Sounds more like a *Requiem* if you ask me, even though it is based on that Nietzsche fellow who was inspired by ideas in his work *Also Sprach Zarathustra*. Songs are supposed to cheer us up, and get the audience going, not consign us to misery or into Freud-induced manic depression and prolonged introspection of amaranthine proportion.

My motto in life Gustav, Friedrich," said Lodge, in all

sincerity, whilst moving his arm in a wide sweep to indicate possession, "has always been, 'if you cannot raise the pulse; then you might as well stop it!'"

That Loge's proposition was fatally flawed was never in doubt; I just could not see the mistake because of being swamped with the *avalanche* of unsubstantiated fact being propounded in the process. Neither Mahler nor I interrupted or corrected him; not out of courtesy, but more out of expediency. For where does one begin to correct, faced with such monumental and insuperable senseless information? We continued to let him lecture us; after all, he was our host, or rather, we were his guests. [6]

I could also detect in Mahler's 'facial expressions the reflection of that very basic feeling enveloping his heart that any possible opportunities with this so-called *impresario* were rapidly evaporating at a frightening rate. It is possible that Mahler, may have retained a glimmer of hope that Lodge may still be an *impresario*, albeit one who was not blessed with musical knowledge. However, even this extravagant, if futile hope was inextricably slowly but remorselessly being extinguished, as Lodge continued, unchecked, his appalling diatribe on the ethics of music.

As the evening wore on it became patently evident that Lodge knew even less about music than his so-called butler John. And what he did know as an *'impresario'* was confined to the more dubious establishments, which in England are called Music Halls, especially the one he mentioned to be at Victoria.

Either way, it would most unlikely that this Lodge could organize a riot in any concert hall, including the Royal Aquarium or the Royal Albert Hall of Arts and Sciences, even with either hall stacked and filled to the rafters with the massed ranks of disaffected Nihilists or Futurists at his disposal. Let alone could he put on a concert involving the symphonies by Mahler or indeed any other composer!

It was blatantly obvious to me, at any rate, that what Lodge purported to be was in itself highly suspect. That he had made money to buy this town house was not in doubt here; but rather quite how he had done so, certainly was.

"Being an *impresario*, you must entertain frequently and have had quite a few famous composers and musicians here at one time or other, yes?" Mahler asked more out of politeness than a desire for an answer.

"You can be sure," said Loge, "you can certainly be sure, for I have had royalty here."

On this occasion his words were not accompanied by his looking over his shoulder, though, for some fathomable reason, Mahler and I suspected the royalty he was referring to did not have blue blood coursing through their veins.

Most of the so-called servants seemed to have disappeared one by one, or at least abandoned us at our table, rather emulating Haydn's hint in his '*Abschieds Symphonie*'.[7] No matter how many times our host rang the bell, no servant, including Aloysius, appeared to attend to our needs.

Not being attended to, nor receiving any responses to his constant ringing the table bell to summon a waiter, even the surly Aloysius, was beginning to grate on our host's nerves. Accordingly, his habit of looking over his shoulder increased exponentially. At length, either because his neck was now aching, or to find out why his servants had deserted him, he got up to investigate.

"I cannot understand this lapse," said Lodge, mildly perturbed, "perhaps they are in the kitchens merry making, I will be bound, and have forgotten us. They shall though, pay dearly for their neglect of our comfort!" And with that *Parthian* shot, he strolled out of the Dining Room, though, through a door that did not lead to the hallway or staircase; abandoning us to our fate, and the *gramophone* record still blaring out the most appalling collection of songs.

1 St James' Hall.
2 Blue Ribbon Brigade a society dedicated to abolishing alcohol in drink and lead by Lilli Langtry
3 19th Century Victorian description of displays of close-quarter martial skill deploying horses, sword and lance.
4 It was the notorious activities of the Imperial Theater, located within the confines of the Royal Aquarium Building, which brought the whole establishment into disrepute, having systematically, deteriorated into a raucous and tawdry Music Hall. This infamous theatre, with its reputation, was often in peril of having its license revoked, because of the dangerous acts performed on the stage. This included women being shot out from the mouth of a military cannon, while no less than knives being thrown in an arbitrary manner around the stage, to the accompaniment of fire being played with during an act.
5 A Death-dance for a noble child.
6 Lodge's mistakes are too numerous to correct
7 Called the *Farewell Symphony* in which the players one by one leave the concert platform, until none are left.

Chapter 23

The Mid Hour at Night

It was difficult to grasp just what kind of *bizarre* household Lodge was running at 536 Bergen Avenue. The household seemed to comprise the singular and extraordinary at every turn, reflecting Lodge's predilection with the absurd, unbounded. As to his servants, they appeared indifferent to him or his instructions. Even the loquacious Aloysius, never lost for a word or an unbidden *impromptu* remark at someone's expense appeared unsure in his *rôle* as Lodge's manservant. On several occasions both Mahler and I observed him thinking deeply before commencing any form of action, and when he did it resembled an exploration of the unknown.

"Something not quite right about this Lodge fellow," said Mahler, as he poured out some warm, indifferent, slightly corked, white wine into our glasses.

After about thirty minutes or so there was still no sign of Lodge and it looked as though he too had disappeared. Eventually, we decided to leave the Dining Room in an effort to find Lodge, or even a servant. Opening the correct door of the Dining Room, that we knew gave egress into the hallway of the *piano-nobile*, we abandoned the room. We then found ourselves in a dimly lit passageway, illuminated only by the weak blue gas light emanating from the two wall-mounted bronze *appliqués*, in the form of angels holding forth fire brands. After our eyes had adjusted to the low light, we made our way along the gloom of the hallway, in our search to find a servant in order to complete our so-called dinner and replenish our drink.

At length we came to the staircase addressing the *piano-nobile* and looked over the balustrade. We looked up into the upper floors of the house and then down into the depths of the building. Both were in darkness and in silence, with not a trace of activity or noise. But then, just at that moment, we did hear a sound, a distant sound, made by a clock tower in the vicinity of Bergen Avenue, striking out the hour. We instinctively stopped and counted the chords as the bell struck out its toll. We counted twelve chimes indicating that the time was indeed, the mid hour at night!

"Where do we go to find someone?" Mahler asked.

"Presumably look in the basement; as I understand servants normally exist in that part of any household," I offered.

We both gripped the wooded staircase banister to steady ourselves whilst descending in the dark, to the lower regions of the house. We had only walked down four or five bare timber risers when we heard a sound. It stopped us instantly in our descent. It was the sound of weeping, very soft at first, but clearly somebody was crying. It sounded like a girl in tears, possibly a maidservant or perhaps another nervous domestic *employé*.

"Well, at least we know someone is around this place, even though tearful," said Mahler.

Accordingly, we retraced our footsteps in the darkened hall and climbed the stairs leading to the upper floors of the house and in the direction from whence the sound of the crying seemed to be coming.

We continued through various corridors making our way to into the upper reaches of the house following the sound of weeping, eventually ascended those stairs that led to the top of the house. At the top of this flight of steps we came to a landing that gave out into the beginning of a corridor that was lined with a strip of coconut matting along its length. At the far end of the corridor was a small, solid-looking, elm door that led to even further recesses of the house. We continued towards this closed door and upon reaching the threshold, attempted to open it. We had difficulty pushing it open, but when Mahler and I applied our shoulders to it we found the door's resistance too great and it would not therefore yield.

By that time the crying had now ceased and had replaced by an even more singular sound. It was coming from a room in an adjacent short corridor. This peculiar sound, very faint at first, but increasing in loudness as we approached the door, was the sound of a piano. We made our way, in the dim light, towards what we thought was the origin of the music, as much as hoping to intercept a servant or even Lodge. Both Mahler and I expected to see Lodge at the piano, or perhaps even loquacious Aloysius playing for his own amusement.

"Personally Löhr, I have my doubts as to Lodge's playing ability; for some reason he did not seem the type to caress ivory keys in any kind of order," said Gustav.

Eventually, we actually located the room from whence the sound of the piano was coming. The heavy, highly varnished, mahogany door was slightly ajar and so with some hesitation, for I neither wished to disturb Lodge at the keyboard, or be an over inquisitive guest in someone else's house, I pushed the door open.

What we found was neither Michael Lodge in rapture

over the keyboard, nor Aloysius, but rather an expensive Aëolian pianola playing quite contentedly to itself. It also appeared that the mechanism operating the keys was being powered by electricity.

The room was more in keeping with the rest of the house, in that it had its allocation of *bizarre* furniture and matching paintings on the wall. In one corner was a stack of black painted and highly varnished balls made of *papier-mâché*.

I was examining the piano-roll on the Aëolian pianola and was gratified to note that it was a piano work by Edward Plesse called '*Echoes of Valhalla*' with which both Mahler and myself are familiar and fond of. Perhaps this Lodge did have a decent musical streak in him after all if he had the piano works composed by Plesse in his collection.

It was not Plesse's elegant and sonorous music emanating out from the Aëolian pianola that had arrested Mahler's attention, who when I looked at him, seemed petrified in a paroxysm of abject fear; it was rather, what he was holding in his hands. I walked over to him and looked over his shoulder and on examining the parchment, took a sharp intake of breath. Mahler was still gripping the manuscript tightly between his fingers and thumbs. We both of us were looking at an original score of what looked like symphonic sketches, written in the key of E major! [1]

The manuscript was faded but undoubtedly original and the notation proved that it had been the first draft of the work. From my cursory examination, the manuscript was almost perfect in terms of symphonic structure and counterpoint with very few mistakes. Someone though, had attempted to obliterate the original signature on the manuscript upon which the score for the symphony had been written, and another name substituted. This attempt had resulted in virtually destroying that part of the manuscript upon which the composer had originally written his name!

By now Mahler had left the room and was walking down the staircase slowly, as though in deep thought. I followed a few moments later and having gathered our coats, canes and what wits we had left, we walked to the front door of the house that opens on to Bergen Avenue. There in the street, hopefully, intercept a passing carriage, to convey us back to the St. Pancras Hotel for badly needed drink and then, possibly food.

Having got to the front door however, and tried to open it, we were confronted by a vast array of locks. We concluded this was not going to be an easy task to open the door and gain the outside. We did however, persevere and eventually with some difficulty managed to release a series of catches and locks, more appropriate to a bank vault than a house, but, I supposed, typically in keeping with the general peculiarities of Lodge's house.

Eventually, having opened the door and stepped outside, we paused for a moment at the top of the steps. There was no sound at all, not even a solitary carriage plying the streets for a late fare. We possessed our souls in patience and descended the steps leading down to the street. In so doing we both noticed, with a degree of not totally unexpected amazement, a red tail coat with gold braid emblazoned on the front and epaulettes to match, abandoned on the metal handrail of the stone steps. We continued walking down the steps and into Bergen Avenue and in search of a carriage back to the St. Pancras Hotel.

It was only when we were some distance away, walking along the wet York flagstones of the pavement in search of a carriage, that I realized who *'Loge'* was. Yes, he appears in Wagner's operatic *Ring Cycle,* in particular *Das Rheingold* and was course that venal and mercurial character intent on concocting defective strategies to Wotan amongst others. Perhaps Lodge's friends had in fact chosen an apt *sobriquet* in the name *'Loge'* for him. I am not sure quite what we had gained from our excursion to Loge's town house in Bergen Avenue for dinner; except in my case, a raging thirst and rapidly worsening stomach ache.

1 Possibly Hans Rott's original draft for this Symphony in E major

Chapter 24

The Criterion Bar

On our eventual return to our Hotel, we were informed by the *concièrge* that a telegram had been received addressed to Gustav Mahler, and was of the utmost moment. On reading it we learned it was from a Mr. Walter Sickert, who wished to make Mahler's acquaintance and had suggested luncheon at the Café Royal. Mahler, fearing a repeat of the previous *débâcle,* there, was, quite naturally reluctant to patronize that august establishment again, at least not while Wilde was in town, possibly looking for revenge. Accordingly, Sickert had responded to our reply telegram later that morning, with the suggestion that we might meet at Kettner's in Soho or the Criterion Bar at Regent's Circus, Piccadilly, both of which were renowned. We agreed on the Criterion Bar, as Mahler seemed to recall that the composer, Charles Villiers Stanford had something to say about our using Kettner's.

Accordingly, the next day when we were more recovered and with subdued excitement, clambered into a highly varnished Landau carriage outside the St. Pancras Hotel. On leaving the Hotel's precincts we entered the busy Euston Road complete with lumbering wagons, pantechnicons and omnibuses all making their way to their various destinations. We traversed this busy thor-

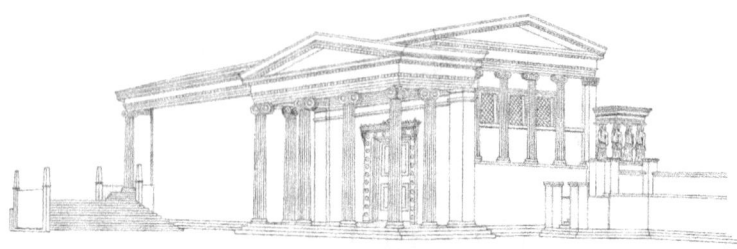

Temple of Erechtheion

oughfare until we reached the St. Pancras Church, complete with its replication of the Temple of Erechtheion, at the Acropolis in Athens. Here our coach driver turned the horses left into Upper Woburn Place and southwards to our *rendezvous* with Sickert at the Criterion Bar. The hooves of our two horses clattered on the cobbled stone road as they negotiated their way through the fog.

After what seemed an interminable drive, we entered the Regent's Circus at Piccadilly and arrived in front of the Criterion Bar.

If we had thought that our troubles were over; then a major shock was in store for us. Our appearance at the Criterion Bar to meet with Sickert proved to be greatly mistaken. A substantial *concentration* of Nihilists, furtive and sporting full beards, and augmented by their compatriots in arms, the fanatical Futurists, viewed us with their dark venal eyes as they chanted their contempt at us.

They had reconvened at the Regent's Circus at Piccadilly, particularly around Alfred Gilbert's newly erected sculpture of the Angel of Christian Charity.[1] This aluminum-sculptured statue had attracted their attention, because they regarded it as an arrogant and provocative symbol of the abandoned and reckless affluence of the upper classes. On this occasion however, their *concentration* was considerable and they were clearly agitating in a confident manner, for a final reckoning. A reckoning with whom or what, it seemed, was neither apparent to them, or indeed to us. However, that uncertainty did not in any way deter them from shouting their dreadful chant; *'be it now or never'* or *'dispatch forthwith the upper classes to their oblivion'*. They chanted whilst clenching their fists at all and sundry, including ordinary members of the public passing by and on one occasion, a horse, pulling a Phäeton carriage.

Notwithstanding this potential inconvenience to our persons, we threw open the main double doors of the place and stepped into a brilliance of incandescent light emanating from large lanterns of glass and *chandeliers* suspended from the ceiling which illuminated the plush red carpet below. The whole effect was to create a *crescendo* of light, a euphoric sensation of ecstasy and warmth, all of which we needed so desperately having travelled through the acrid all-enveloping fog. The light filled our senses as though experiencing the final closing chords of a Wagnerian opera, music so close to our hearts!

Presently we found ourselves inside what I took to be the *salon*, which was large, noisy and decorated extravagantly and exuberantly It combined Queen Anne and Baroque styles built of highly polished mahogany woodwork with brass fittings, handrails, marble surfaces and ostentatious acetylene gas-fuelled globe lanterns. Complementing this style was incorporated the generous neo-Byzantine opulence of mirrors and mosaics on various walls and surfaces. There were rich, red velvet drapes framing engraved windows and decorative glazed panel openings in the internal timber partition walls.

The ceilings were of painted and gilded molded plaster looking down on elaborately patterned carpets with *fleur de lys,* upon which were positioned several indoor palm trees. The back bar, set in front of a mirrored wall, displayed decorated bronze stands on which were fixed curved glass globes containing various liquors. In between them, and dominating the whole, was an enormous brass till of such intricate and ornate raised design as to be almost a work of art, rather than a cash depository. The effect was one of an opulent sumptuous, if meretricious establishment clearly patronized by a wealthy *cliéntele.*

We pushed past a variety of patrons and at length we managed to gain the pale green *Emperador Chiaro* marble covered bar, whereupon Mahler said, to a passing bar tender, "Two large whiskies, one neat, the other with the *Coca~Cola,* if you serve it."

"We do indeed sir," said a jovial red-faced bar tender, wearing a white apron and sporting a large handlebar moustache, "some of our customers drink nothing else. They drench their drinks with the stuff. Why only yesterday a group had the *Coca~Cola* in their Napoleon brandy, a bit excessive, so you would think, and if you were to ask me, a waste of good the *Coca~Cola* and all those ingredients it is laced up with!"

Looking around the Criterion Bar, I noticed several sepia tinted photographs that I could barely make out, ranged on various walls, but the artistes' names and faces meant little to me and certainly nothing to Mahler, who spent most of his time trying to extract some foreign body from his glass of whisky and the *Coca~Cola.*

Whilst contemplating my drink and admiring the interior *décor* of the establishment, I became aware that a young man was staring at Mahler intently. There he was standing, with all the dumb aloofness of a Greek god. As to whether he recognized Mahler, I could not be certain. Then our host arrived, and walked straight up to Gustav and held out his hand.

"*Maestro,* my name is Sickert, Walter Sickert, I believe we are to have luncheon together?"

"I am Gustav Mahler and this is my friend Friedrich Löhr."

"I am delighted to make your acquaintance," he responded, whilst banging his fist on the bar to attract an idle bar tender, "champagne, for my friends, *Veuve Clicquot Parsardin.*"

"You do not," asked Mahler, "have a *sobriquet,* a name based on a character from the opera by any chance?"

"I am sure, Gustav, perhaps people refer to me by names which they would not address to my face: but no, to my friends, I prefer to be called Walter!"

We made ourselves comfortable on blue *damask* covered sofas at the bar that had the usual indoor palm trees ranged around.

After several drinks we left the noisy *salon* and repaired upstairs to the Dining Room for luncheon.

We ascended the broad grand staircase on to the *piano-nobile* and into the expansive Dining Room, resplendent in all their opulence and luxuriant fittings. We were greeted by two carved white *Carrara* marble *nymphs* on the stair's head plinths. Each held in their hands a white, *opaque*-glazed, illuminated globe lantern. The most striking aspect of this extravagant luxury were two smooth, gold-painted columns tapering to lavish Corinthian capitals, seemingly holding up the ornate stucco ceiling with its intricate raised and gilded tracery designs.

Echoing these pillars was a pair of grooved mahogany pilasters set flush against the wall. In between them, the walls were lined with red silk-flocked wallpaper ornamented with gold filigree. Set into the architrave were highly varnished panels depicting even more complex designs. Some of the recesses were sufficiently deep as to take highly decorated porcelain vases. With the exception of four ceiling-mounted lights, ostentatious wall-mounted acetylene gas fuelled globe lanterns and *candelabra* provided most of the illumination.

The Dining Room continued the combination of Queen Anne and Baroque styles with brass fittings and ornaments ranged around the room, with the walls paneled in highly polished elm; one of which supported a counter of white *Perlino Bianco* marble. Complementing the general style throughout, were incorporated rich drapes of red velvet, framing engraved windows and decorative glazed panel openings in the internal timber partition walls. The ceilings again were painted white with raised gilded filigree detailing looking down on to a deep red silk carpet with intricate *fleurs de lys* elaborate patterning. Ranged around the room, in between the tables, which were covered in crisp white linen cloths, were several sofas, upholstered in red *damask* with white cotton *antimacassar* headrests and of course, being in England, numerous ubiquitous indoor palm trees.

"Sickert," said Mahler, "that is a very English name, whereabouts in England are you from?"

"Where am I from? Bavaria, München actually, I was born there and Sickert is a Danish name!" replied our host.

My heart sank at the prospect that this meeting was going to deteriorate from the outset into a Titanic battle of wills reminiscent of our experience at the Café Royal. However, my fears were soon dispersed as both Mahler and Sickert searched around for subjects of mutual interest. Within minutes they were addressing each other in terms of intimacy, as though long lost friends having found each other again.

"I should be interested to learn of your thoughts Gustav, regarding the inevitability of the European vogue for the *Fusion of the Arts*. I am aware of your association with the Secessionists in Vienna and would consider it an honor to share your ideas in this respect.

For myself I paint scenes, scenes of social reality, ordinary people, attending a Music Hall of an evening, for admittedly popular, sometimes raucous entertainment, but still noble for its application and purpose. They will never reach the ethereal heights of Covent Garden; but then they have no aspiration to do so!"

"I have seen some of your work. Realistic it is and I particularly admire the way you capture the interior *décor* of some theaters. Without such gaudy interiors, I doubt the places could function as *rendezvous* for entertainment," said Mahler, much to Sickert's *chagrin*.

"You are very perceptive Gustav, if I may say so," responded Sickert, "I have made this *genre* my own, and have a series of paintings set inside various Music Halls. My paintings of Gatti's Hungerford Palace of Varieties, the Old Bedford Music Hall and the great Metropolitan Music Hall, I number among my most successful in capturing the naturalism of this period. I have evolved this technique from Degas, of whom I remain a disciple. Others artists are involved in this group. We call ourselves the *Camden Town Group*, and live in or near Mornington Crescent."

"Forgive me," I said, "does your group, the *Camden Town Group*, in any way resemble the aims of the Pre-Raphaelites?"

"I appreciate your question Friedrich, but to us, the Pre-Raphaelites represent nothing more than bankrupt, defunct ideals and wrecked dreams. That they are destined for oblivion from whence they originated is a surety," answered Sickert.

"In these paintings," he continued, "we try to capture

the essence of the theater including the ostentatious and shabby *décor* prevalent in such establishments; but which is, for me, essential to the overall desired effect of the hall. As you have mentioned, Gustav, this ostentatious *décor* is an essential aspect of a successful Music Hall."

"You should paint the interior of Michael Lodge's town house in Bergen Avenue - if you want a real challenge in capturing the essence of shabby and gaudy *décor,*" I suggested.

"One could hardly," went on Sickert, "put on a *burlesque* show, complete with attendant *risqué* or *outré* mannerisms in a classically designed temple. Complete with fluted white *Carrara* marble columns with purple cloth pennons hanging down from the architrave and swaying in the breeze, reminiscent of imperial Rome, could one? Such reckless dignity would invariably defeat the essential *rationale* of the Music Hall - and the drama on the stage, and off it.

Whilst I understand the Viennese Secessionists are more about a *pan* unification of the arts, I am more interested in how one might express art in terms of music. In particular, I was struck by a work I heard only recently by a Tsarist Russian composer called Rachmaninov. His work, a symphonic tone poem, is called, *'The Isle of the Dead'*. This symphonic fantasy is itself based upon a canvas by a Swiss painter by the name of Arnold Böcklin. What struck me was how the deep texture of the oil of the painting reflected the rich tonal passages of Rachmaninov's music," said Sickert.

"You would have done well had you joined us at The Café Royal recently," responded Mahler, "your inquiries could have been answered there and then by such august persons as Wilde, Whistler, Rossetti, Villiers Stanford and even Antheil!"

"What, that pretentious group of heroes who represent

nothing more than the facile and futile? When they are not locked into a death struggle with their consciences, then they are with reality," rejoined Sickert.

"I often think that the music in some respect is deliberately composed to suit the hall in which it will be played. I know some of Mozart's music was composed, almost as *divertimenti*, but also with some theaters in mind, irrespective of the actual seriousness or joviality of the music in question," Sickert concluded.

"The concept of *'programmatic'* music, where the music is descriptive of something, has never really made an impact on me," said Mahler; "Rather, I prefer to create an experience in which the listener can form their own appreciation of ideas submitted to them. In this respect a great exponent of *'programmatic'* music is Rickard Strauss. There, one can find an extensive *repertoire* that comprises several tone poems reflecting various ideas set to a musical interpretation. Others who explore this *genre* are Tschaikovsky and perhaps Mussorgsky, especially in his celebrated musical depiction called *Pictures from an Exhibition.*"

"Of course, the master exponent in this respect is Rickard Wagner and his development of the *leitmotiv*, a musical mechanism for expressing a distinct and clear concept. The *Ring Cycle* abounds with them and they are to be found in the sacred music dramas of *Parsifal* and *Lohengrin,*" I said, to support Mahler's sentiments.

"Despite the fact that both Friedrich and I support, and are involved, with the *Fusion of the Arts*, in Vienna at least, endorsement should not be confused with subjecting every art form to another art form. We all know that various writers have had their plays become the basis of a *libretto*, and thus an opera. Wagner's *Ring Cycle*, is itself based upon the *Völsunga Saga* of Hildebrand. Or Verdi's

Merchant of Venice based on Shakespeare's play. One has to be careful that one does not interfere or compromise the integrity of the original form of expression, because of an inferior later representation."

"Are you saying," asked Sickert, "that for example, if one did not like Verdi's music, integral to his opera, the *Merchant of Venice*, that one might be deterred from exploring other works by Shakespeare? And, that one might not simply appreciate the original play, because of one's experience of Verdi's interpretation in operatic form?

"Yes," replied Gustav, "another aspect of this fusion to be considered is the re-interpretation of the original, often written, composed or acted with nuances in the expression of thought or ideas. Let us say one reads a book, Jean Paul Richter's The Titan, since he has been in our minds these two days past. Here Richter invites the reader to play with the concepts or ideas he has introduced, within the parameters of the novel.

He leaves the reader, as all good novelists do, with the ability to exercise their imagination in dealing with certain concepts introduced by the author. Notwithstanding the use of adjectives by the author, the reader, in effect, is able to direct the course of the book within a set of circumstances. The important aspect here is that the reader of a play, novel or *libretto* of an opera can imagine the style and feeling of the book. The reader is given free rein to experience the book and its nuances at a rate set by himself without the arbitrary interpretation by a third party, such as a director of a play or opera. To the reader, the hero or anti-hero, as the interpretation may demand, might have dark hair and wear a black frock-coat. But in an interpretation by another person, set to opera or a play the hero might now have blond hair and wear a white suit!" concluded Mahler.

We continued into the afternoon drinking and talking about the aesthetics of art and music. If nothing else Sickert, turned out to be a prodigious drinker, but showed no signs of it affecting him, and continued discussing various concepts with Mahler.

Sickert's ideas about music reflecting a *programmatic* idea, as we know the term, were of interest to me. Indeed I remember discussing this very concept with Alban Berg in Vienna when attending an *impromptu* meeting of the Secessionists some years previously. Then, during the intense debates and discussions that took place at that formative time, when ideas for inclusion into our *manifesto* were accepted or rejected, I endorsed this point promoted by Berg. I was therefore pleased to hear Mahler and Sickert's views on this all important and truly fundamental aspect regarding the *Fusion of the Arts*.

Sickert consulted his gold Hunter on two occasions, indicating that he would have to leave soon. But, before doing so, he asked Mahler to sit still for just a few moments. With a questioning expression upon his face peering over his gold-rimmed *pince-nez*, Mahler obliged. A few moments later Sickert had got his sketching pad out and with a few well-placed lines and curves had produced a likeness of Mahler! Even from my view I could see that Sickert had caught clearly Mahler in a pose, with a look that one rarely sees, even with my experience of him. I knew from the expression of delight upon Mahler's face that he was greatly moved by this gesture, which he responded to with words of such gratitude and fond affection.

After a considerable period had elapsed we all eventually abandoned the ornate Dining Room and made our way down stairs to the more opulent *salon* whereupon

Gustav Mahler

Sickert shook our hands warmly and making his farewells staggered off towards the main entrance leading out into the Regent's Circus. We repaired back to the pale green *Emperador Chiaro* marble covered bar from whence we had first started.

We were just congratulating ourselves on having enjoyed a reasoned and intelligent discussion, when in walked three individuals who had been present at the Café Royal during Mahler's discourse with Wilde and others. My blood froze as the realization of what this meant to Mahler became all too apparent. I suggested that we abandon our drinks, which we had just paid for, and instead search for an alternative *salon* in order to avail ourselves of refreshment. Mahler resisted my offer and intimated that it was his intention to remain precisely where he was.

1 Statue of *Eros*.

Chapter 25

The Final Reckoning – Polemic Part VI

The *concentration* of Nihilists, which we had witnessed outside, had not, after all been able to cause disruption. We were congratulating ourselves on having enjoyed an informative and intelligent conversation, when Aubrey Beardsley and two other person of dubious report arrived at the bar, intoxicated, but their inebriation did not prevent them from recognizing us. The prospect of another encounter filled me with a foreboding apprehension.

We had by then settled ourselves on a mauve colored *moiré* silk covered sofa when Beardsley and two others that I recognised as being Charles Villiers Stanford, the composer and the painter John Singer Sargent, walked over to us. They stood there, or rather swayed momentarily, and then collapsed in unison on to the only vacant sofa, immediately opposite us in this busy bar.

Beardsley looked at my friend intently, that, or he was trying to focus on him though his dim eyes. At length he consulted with his companions and then hailed a nearby waiter and shouted out his order.

"Waiter a bottle of bottle of *Perrier-Jouët* champagne and three large glasses of absinthe and..., no make that... two glasses of absinthe and a glass of vermouth and orange-bitters with a few drops of concentrate of lime with a dash of the aërated for my reckless friend here,

Stanford," ordered Beardsley, "and my other good friend, Gustav Mahler, sitting there, will pay!"

The waiter looked at Mahler for a nod of approval. None was forthcoming.

"I am afraid Mr Beardsley, that I should have to charge it to your account, if this gentleman that you pointed to will not indulge you sir," said the waiter.

"Oh, very well," agreed Beardsley.

The waiter continued to progress through the crowded bar to fulfil Beardsley's order and in so doing confirmed the fact that we would have to tolerate their behavior. I looked at Mahler to register my concern and desire to leave, but Mahler remained steadfast in his resolution.

"Do you not think that you might a least offer a drink to those who funded your insatiable habit these two days past; I refer to the bill in the Café Royal you abandoned us with?" said Beardsley, looking hard at Mahler.

It was I who replied.

"I think that you must be mistaken sir; we abandoned no such responsibility for the bill. If I recall, we were invited to join at his table, as guests, your friend and mentor, Oscar Wilde. It is with him that you should take up this matter if you are unable to meet your obligations at the Café Royal. Now sir, if you do not mind, I wish to continue my conversation with my friend here and therefore will be grateful if you would cease interrupting us."

"This is a public bar," responded the painter John Singer Sargent.

"I am aware of that fact. But if you must sit on that silk covered sofa, please do so without interrupting us. Thank you," I replied.

"Waiter," said John Singer Sargent, to another passing waiter, "a bottle of champagne any will do, so long as it is French!"

The waiter, without stopping, simply ignored him. Hopefully our encounter with these acolytes of Wilde's would soon be at an end so at least we could enjoy the rest of the afternoon in that lively cosmopolitan establishment. That hope was premature for just as Beardsley was about to launch into a tirade, he was invited to stay by Mahler!

"I am intrigued Beardsley," I began, "by your interpretations of the characters from Wagner's *Ring Cycle*, in particular your drawing of *Merlin* and *Nimue* looks like a cartoon of that pre-Raphaelite painter Edward Burne-Jones' painting of the same name, no?"

"I restored Wagner and made him now what he was with my drawings. I put the man on a pedestal for the whole world to see," said Beardsley, with his usual modesty.

"I think that you will find that Wagner was an acclaimed force in his own right before he got to even thinking about composing the *Der Ring des Nibelungen*," I countered.

"I have immortalized Wagner's *Siegfried*, depicting him in his heroic stance in my drawing of him, which was published in 1893 in the first issue of '*The Studio*', stated Beardsley.

Ironically, this one drawing of *Siegfried*, the alleged hero of Wagner's *Ring Cycle*, was drawn, not to portray the heroic aspects of *Siegfried*, but rather to emphasize the intricate drawing abilities of Beardsley. He had, in this drawing, depicted *Siegfried*, not as a fearless hero, but as an anaemic effeminate individual. The drawing, represented more a testament to Beardsley's ability in draughtsmanship in drawing intricate ornamentation and a concern for decoration comprising curved lines, with little regard for the real expression of the operatic scene in which *Siegfried* exists.

It occurred to me as I spoke, that Beardsley's interpretation of *Siegfried* was precisely what we were discussing with Sickert. The drawing of *Siegfried,* can be set irredeemably into the mind of the person looking at it, an impression very much opposite the one the Wagner had striven to create. None the less I continued to engage Beardsley.

"And from what I understand of Wagner's *Ring Cycle,* most of the illustrations of the numerous scenes are by an artist by the name of Arthur Rackham," I stated.

"Rackham," said Beardsley, "that imbecile could not draw a straight line without getting it wrong! I urge you to consider my interpretation of Wagner's *Das Rheingold,* from my Third Tableau and see how I have impressed the viewer with the juxtaposition of venality and innocence. Then compare Rackham's drawing, the one he calls, *The Rheinmaidens Teasing Alberich.* The drawing is an exercise in sterility, devoid of passion, mundane and fit only for the faint-hearted. His drawings are riddled with doubt and inherent *ennui* from a dead soul."

This remarkable statement by the modest Beardsley surprised me, since Beardsley and Rackham interpreted scenes respectively, from Wagnerian opera *Das Rheingold* – after Wagner's death, twenty-three years and twenty-seven years before.

"I have seen some of Rackmans drawings in an illustrated version of the *Völsunga Saga,*" I said.

"Quite possibly, but they could not detract from his general style, and therefore, perforce remain within the category of the mundane," said Beardsley. "If art has a function, a *rôle,* if you will, it must be to inform and attract the sensual in the observer. It cannot be about the reproduction of mindless *patina* on canvas - it must do more, much more to one's soul.

Consider my drawing of *Salome.* This is no romanticized interpretation of an evil woman; the drawing reeks of the result of her machinations regarding her reward in the form of a severed head. *Salome* holds her prize, uncertain what to do with the head that is metamorphosing into a nest of vipers. Worthy even, of Medusa as she hunts in her condemned domain on that death-laden island of *Seraphos*. What can one do with a severed head; glorify it?" asked Beardsley.

"I am sure the good Doctor Kraff-Ebbing of Vienna, would know what to do with it!" mused Mahler.

"The nearest," continued Beardsley, ignoring Mahler's interjection, "one might come to experiencing a similarly powerful interpretation on the theme of *Salome,* might possibly be in Jean Delville's, painting *The End of Reign.* As he does there, I too capture not the *femme fatale,* as desirable - Pre-Raphaelite obsession, but rather in the portrayal of the ruthlessness in women when deprived of their intentions."

"I agree with you Beardsley. I remember that Rickard Wagner was impressed with Delville's interpretation of *Parsifal.* In that work he depicts the errant knight *Parsifal,* almost as though dead beneath a transparent shroud undergoing a spiritual transmogrification into a state of grace," I said.

Beardsley gave me a searching look, without replying, as though the nearest he could give to an acknowledgement.

"As you will no doubt appreciate," responded Beardsley, "art and the ability to express it, is a rare ability and not all possess this skill, and certainly not Rackham or Walter Crane, from whom he takes his inspiration; art must to succeed, shock the senses!"

"Yes, but we have seen some of your drawings; they not only shock, they remain *grotesque,* no? And, given the

Pre-Raphaelite spectrum at the time ranging from the classically motivated ethereal and symmetrical Elysian dreamscapes of Albert Moore to the unremittingly *grotesque* and nightmarish attributes of the later period, characteristic of your work, as you say, to shock, why?" I ventured, knowing this remark could invite retaliation.

He did not do so, but continued instead to talk to the assembled group in the Criterion Bar, on the basis that he would prefer to lecture us than argue, and thus lose control of the discussion.

"Rackham's drawings are pedestrian with no feeling and he invariably tries too hard to emulate Walter Crane," said Beardsley.

"Ah, then you recognized Crane as being an artist?" I queried,

"I most certainly do not! Besides he is a socialist and I suspect is a covert Nihilist. He should like to dispatch us all into an artistic and social oblivion," remarked Beardsley, emphatically.

"But surely his art..." I said,

"If you like the impoverished," interrupted Beardsley, who by now was growing impatient with talk about Crane.

"Charles Ricketts, whom we met at the Café Royal; surely his illustrated interpretation of Wilde's poem *The Sphinx* is of critical acclaim, no? And did he also not illustrate Wilde's other work, *A Picture of Dorian Gray*?" I inquired.

"Possibly, but it was I, yes me, who set the stamp of the *fin de siècle* with my distinctive and unique draughts-manship and graphic brilliance!" retorted Beardsley.

"Perhaps, but do tell me; why do you call your drawing of '*Isolde*', a '*Chopin Nocturne*'?" I asked.

Whether there was an interpretation of language

difficulty I could not say, save only that Beardsley looked at me as though I had lost my reason, eventually however, he did reply:

"Why of course, in the event of the drawing attaining a higher meaning or use!"

"You mean an eventual buyer willing to pay more?" I said.

"Yes!" replied Beardsley decisively.

Thinking to puncture the pride of this supercilious and arrogant Beardsley, I remarked casually:

"I supposed you have made famous the names of various persons across the artistic spectrum from music to literature to painting?"

"And the stage, let us not forget the stage," said Beardsley, "I illustrated the stage sets for Wilde's play *Salome* with Ada Leverson in the title *rôle*. And, I made Wilde's reputation, at least in this respect, with my creation of *Salome*. Who would have heard of such a dread-filled story had it not been for my drawings - I breathed life into the moribund that the play represented."

"As it happens I retain a fondness for your *The Wagnerites* from your *Tristan und Isolde* series. I remain fascinated by the seemingly amorphous mass of humanity, in the theater seats, but given individual expression by their shoulders and head. The drawing, finely executed, is one of sternness!" I propounded.

"Are you an expert in art too?" inquired Beardsley.

"No," I replied, "but remain familiar with those works which represent simplicity at best and *naïveté* at worst, and believe that your work rises above the mundane, in this respect at least."

Beardsley merely replied whilst looking at his fingernails:

"It is the destiny of a creator; that he is condemned to be lectured on his own idea!"

"Ah, then you endorse the concept propounded in Schopenhauer's philosophical work *The World as Will and Representation,* as further interpreted by Thomas Mann. Here Schopenhauer proposes that we, as human beings are continually dissatisfied with the *status quo*, and that this condition in itself, via the ego, propels us on to greater, or at least, alternative things. Could this be why the arts are continually in turmoil, as one concept inescapably replaces another in rapid succession?" I asked.

"I could not possibly comment on that aspect, "replied Beardsley, "my understanding of Schopenhauer, is that he talks about the preservation of reality, of a yet known, but undetermined truth. In this respect we are disposed to delaying the event, especially a positive pleasurable event. We are always preparing for tomorrow, rather than dealing with today. That fact alone propels us forward, at least in accepting what tomorrow might bring. With our focus clearly on the near future; we delay the immediacy of the moment. This idea can be is explained by our not reading a letter from an important source, or denying ourselves the contents of a present, until later. We delay the perceived positive aspects of the event, and so doing derive greater pleasure by that delay, and that..."

That reply to my question by Beardsley, and indeed our discourse was relegated to oblivion by the activity and commotion emanating for the main entrance into the *salon.*

From what I could make out there seemed to be a number of gentlemen, in the entrance way, all wearing wide brimmed hats and beards. Some were throwing their arms about in an abandoned manner, whilst others talked loudly with the *concièrge* and other members of staff including waiters.

The argument generated by these persons appeared to revolve around their being allowed *entré* into what was a public establishment.

"I have every right to avail myself of your hospitality," said one of the bearded persons, "as I have ready money here in my hand with which to do so!"

"No you do not have such a right sir," replied the *concièrge.*

"Are you saying this establishment is only for the privileged few?" asked one of the bearded persons.

"Well of course sir, this is the Criterion Bar!" replied the *concièrge.*

"Why do you think that I am not privileged?" inquired the bearded gentleman wearing a black frock-coat and wide brimmed hat dark sunken eyes, which smouldered like burning coal.

"That you are dressed solely in black and sporting a full beard sir," continued the *concièrge*, "the fact of your looking furtive, has no bearing on the matter of privilege."

"The fact of my wearing black is in marked respect for my mourning a dead aunt," insisted the grief-stricken bearded fellow.

"Really," replied the unconvinced *concièrge*, "are you perhaps a radical by way of being a confirmed sub-urban revolutionary, albeit a grieving revolutionary?"

"How dare you! How dare you be confident with me; in assuming my being middle class," responded an outraged, grieving, classless revolutionist.

A moment or two elapsed, and then the sound of a whistle was heard. At that instant it seemed as if all pandäemonium was let loose in the main reception as swarms of dark clothed Nihilists invaded the privileged sanctuary of the Criterion Bar. In so doing, easily over powering hard-pressed waiters, who with one hand were bearing various drinks upon trays, from which the Nihilists helped themselves readily, whilst shouting that dreaded chant; *'be it now or never'* and *'inconvenience the rich now; our failing to do so shall be at our peril'* to the assembled patrons of the establishment.

The Nihilists, encouraged by their compatriots, the Futurists, had made to go for it, in their concerted attempt to incommode and consign us all to oblivion.

Members of the staff tried but in vain to contain their adventure into the Criterion Bar, and were encouraged verbally by several patrons to take a firmer line with those persons.

One Nihilist, approached the sofas that we and Beardsley and his companions were sitting on, and had the audacity to actually deposit on our low cream colored *Serpeggiante Silvabella Classico* marble table, a black painted *papier-mâché* globe with a piece of string protruding from it and then tried to disappear into the *mêlée*.

"You have forgotten your *infernal device!*"[1] said Aubrey Beardsley, as he threw the black painted highly varnished ball, fabricated to replicate a bomb, at the fleeing Nihilist and in so doing made contact with his head. I noticed that by now quite a large *concentration* of Nihilists had congregated at the pale green *Emperador Chiaro* marble covered bar and were clamoring for free drinks, beyond those they had appropriated from various patrons and waiters' trays.

Beardsley was simply enjoying the spectacle that the Criterion Bar had become, while the Nihilists were indulging in determined behavior, whilst shouting various decrees. They ranged from, *'inconvenience the rich now; our failing to do so shall be at our peril'*, to the more simple and direct, *'be it now or never'*, whilst throwing black painted hollow *papier-mâché* globes about.

One of the more determined of the Nihilists decided to make an example of any person he thought suitable. He decided on Beardsley as his object, and moved toward him in a fashion that indicated his resolve to incommode Beardsley at a most inconvenient moment. Beardsley was oblivious to this *manoeuvre*, perpetrated by the Nihilist. However, Mahler was not and it was he who instinctively acted; and in so doing, averted an inconvenience on Beardsley's person.

The Nihilists in question had secreted about his person a not insubstantial drinks tray made of sturdy elm, and was about to bring it down on Beardsley's head. Mahler leapt up and pulled Beardsley to one side. This caused the blow to dissipate into mid air, and thus making the Nihilist lose his footing. In so doing, the Nihilist fell headlong onto our low cream colored *Serpeggiante Silvabella Classico* marble table, along which he slid, taking our glasses and drinks with him down on to the elaborately patterned deep red silk carpet with *fleur de lys* integral designs.

Both Beardsley and his friends looked at Mahler in total amazement.

"But, but that fellow has wrecked your drinks," Beardsley said, with profound concern in his voice.

"We can soon remedy that," said Mahler, stopping a passing waiter with a tray in one hand and a disaffected, but defeated Nihilist in the other.

"A magnum of your *Perrier-Jouët* champagne and five large glasses, "asked Mahler.

"Vintage or *cuvée* sir?" inquired the waiter.

"Waiter this *is* the Criterion!" said Mahler.

"Vintage it is sir!" replied the waiter, disappearing back into the *mêlée* and taking his captive Nihilist with him.

By now the Criterion Bar had got the Nihilists'

expedition in hand and a line of waiters and patrons were moving in a broad front and sweeping all before them. Despite their call of '*be it now or never*' being drowned out by the repeated volley of '*more champagne for all*' and their failed attacks upon the privileged, it did not deter some of the more reckless and determined Nihilists from still drinking from abandoned glasses.

The Nihilists were being rounded up, pushed back into the reception. And, eventually ejected out into the Regent's Circus at Piccadilly, from whence they came, fanning out into the fog, and the broader Metropolis. Then the whole bar, comprising jubilant patrons spontaneously ignited into a *crescendo* of clapping and congratulations being freely bandied about in recognizing that a great victory had been achieved with the minimum loss of drink and inconvenience.

"This is how we deal with revolutionaries in London," one man was heard to say, whilst trying to extract a cork from a magnum bottle of *Canard-Duchêne Grande Cuvée Charles VII* champagne.

"I have never seen such an ineffective tide of effeminate revolutionaries before in my life," said Stanford.

"I agree," stated Beardsley, "I have seen more concentrated and unremitting terror in Bond Street on a Sunday morning than that which we have been compelled to endure here today!"

"However, their failed revolution has given me quite a thirst!" said Sargent, as two waiters were restraining one of the last of the bearded fanatics.

"Why are we subject to those persons' outbreaks of confidence and outrages each time we go abroad in the Metropolis?" I asked our new companions.

"But surely you know, you do not know?" asked Sargent.

"Know, know what?" asked Mahler.

"The Nihilists are on the rampage because of Oscar Wilde's play [2] in which they feel they have been slighted and their legitimate revolutionary cause diminished and turned into an object of ridicule. As a result of Wilde's deprecating their cause, they have turned from being an ineffective lower middle class concern, into a *concentration* of Nihilists, who consider themselves now by way of being revolutionaries.

The fact that Wilde's play continues to receive great critical acclaim, has further acerbated their unbridled fury. In addition, their wrath is given manifestation in the form of their avowed intention to, 'correct, with vigor and determination, the inequalities of a society which is terrorized by the over indulgent upper classes augmented by the even less practical *bourgeoisie*.' In their all-embracing quest, to remove all privations from society, the Nihilists will annihilate all extravagances, which are practiced by the profligate and carefree privileged upper classes.

Their sole aim is to dispatch forthwith the upper classes to oblivion, and they will achieve this by organizing major inconveniences and incommoding the upper classes in their sacred places of entertainment, and, as it were, '*wage ceaseless agitation against the mindless privileged few*,' as they see us!" said Aubrey Beardsley, whilst pouring vintage *Perrier-Jouët* champagne into his throat.

"But, neither my friend here Friedrich, nor I are *bourgeoisie*; simply because we are subjects of Franz Joseph's Austro-Hungarian Empire!" complained Mahler.

"That may be so, but the Nihilists see themselves as an international brotherhood sworn to incommode the upper classes on any continent; and it is certain that they will have an opinion or two, to offer your Emperor Franz Joseph," said Sargent.

"I cannot believe this," said Mahler, "we avail ourselves of a varnished Landau carriage to deliver us here to the Criterion Bar for lunch and our sensibilities are assailed by a ruthless pack of malcontents, from the lower orders; it is beyond the plausible."

"I am afraid Nihilists make no distinction. The fact of your arriving in a Landau carriage, highly varnished or not, probably inflamed their dislike for you further. You must remember, they have all been indoctrinated, as it were, operating as they do, from that town house in Bergen Avenue. And, it is from such an innocuous address, itself located in an affluent district, that the Nihilists are turned into fanatical automatons.

Propelled by this unreasoned monomania, they will be agitated into committing the most *outré* of acts, against the upper classes. In exporting to the known society their avowed intentions, they are galvanized by a peculiar individual, an ex theater manager of sorts, the name of whom escapes me. But, he is said to have a considerable hold over the Nihilists, by subjecting them to a mindless trance imbued by his charismatic cult personality. They even say that he is able to turn innocuous members of the lower middle classes into fanatical and formidable Nihilists, dedicated to the overthrow of the upper classes. In so doing, he mesmerizes his cult followers into causing the most reckless of acts and outrageous inconveniences, all designed purposely to incommode, often at considerable risks to their persons and freedom," advised Sargent.

"We have had to tolerate these Nihilists of late," said Beardsley, "as a result of Oscar's play, but today's invasion marks a new level of inconvenience. Normally they confine themselves to lurking in the background, in the shadows and never daring to show their faces, hence the beards they wear. Usually, they cannot quite get the critical numbers of agitators up; always too short, to become a formidable *concentration* of Nihilists able to launch whatever outrage they have in mind. Today, they obviously achieved that critical number; and with inordinate confidence, attempted to effect an expedition into our Criterion Bar!"

"That is indeed news of great import;" said Charles Villiers Stanford, "gentlemen, I advise you to abandoned the Metropolis!"

"The Nihilists," continued Sargent, "have developed a sinister means to attempt to instill abject terror into the very souls of the privileged and indeed, the ordinary public. One is their avowed intention to promote the *ennuyeux* [3] into becoming the unchallenged arbiters of taste and ideas. And the other sworn aim is to convert society into a lower middle class order! Can you imagine the unremitting homogenized purgatory that would be unleashed upon us privileged few? A society where the lower middle classes, petrified of calling each other by their surname, define behavior!"

"Apparently, in a concerted effort to achieve their aim," said Beardsley, "they have taken to carrying about their persons, in public for all to see, black painted bowls used in playing that very lower middle class game of *bowls*. When challenged by the constabulary in the street for carrying what looks like an *infernal device*, a bomb if you will; their stock reply is that they are taking their *bowl* to have it re-varnished!"

1 A black painted replication of a bomb made of *papier-mâché*.
2 The play *Vere and the Nihilists*.
3 Persons of a boring disposition.

Chapter 26

The Vision and the Passion

Our experiences in the Criterion Bar were as illuminating as they were enjoyable. In this respect, whilst we had been subjected to outrages instigated by these disaffected persons, the Nihilists; their attempted expedition into the Criterion Bar resulted in our becoming friends with Beardsley, Stanford and Sargent. We also discovered the reason why the Nihilists were so agitated as a result of Wilde's play '*Vere and the Nihilists*'. It was as much as Mahler and I could do to get back to the St. Pancras Hotel later that evening, but somehow we did. The following morning I made my way down to the Grand Dining Room to take break-fast. As usual Mahler was there seated at the table.

"I cannot help feeling, you know Gustav, that we have turned a corner in our lives. The performance in the Café Royal, I think was instructive. At first it could appear inquisitorial and indeed vicious; but I think it had the effect of making me certainly, and you possibly, sort our priorities out. What is important to us, the people we love or our aspirations? As they say in Vienna, the best steel must go through fire.

But, in so doing, I think you came out stronger in yourself but weaker in your concepts, that may in itself allow you to re-focus and concentrate on aspects of life that you cherish. The *finale* to your huge Eighth posed questions that you, whilst testing them with other intelligent people, have answered. My being with you meant that I too have benefitted from these *impromptu* discourses.

As your friend, would you agree with what I have said, Gustav?" I asked.

"I want to express so much to humanity in my symphonies – express the power of life – its positive and negative aspects. But, more importantly, its sheer pleasure; not every silver lining, my dear friend Friedrich, has a dark cloud!" said Gustav.

I do love the beauty of life, as conveyed in my *Lieder* – of the world, the lakes and woods. I was born in Moravia, but accepted, later in my life, the Catholic faith. In becoming so, I think that I understand the concept of eternity as being able to behold the face of Christ. It could be for a fraction of a second or, all eternity; since time must in such a concept ceased to exist or exert a dimension.

It is the soul, and not the mind, that could experience this concept of eternity. It is the soul within us that is capable of receiving the breath of God and gives us that life above the mortal. It is the ability to receive that gift from God that must give us meaning for existence. It is a non intellectual *rationale* to existence that I try to project in my symphonies reflecting that life, however we find it, is a celebration," replied Mahler, in a very reflective mood.

"That may well be the intellectual case, but I think we need something more tangible if we are to possess our souls and deal with the *concièrge* at the main reception; for we are due to vacate our Hotel this morning and catch the Simplon Orient Express back to Vienna," I reminded Mahler.

Our ordeal at the reception desk and in particular with the surly *concièrge* was not as daunting as we had imagined it might be. However, he did display a fixed grin on his face, as though he were pleased at our quitting his Hotel.

"Will we be seeing you both again sir?" he inquired, as though to challenge us.

And with that *Parthian* shot, he again turned on his heels, abandoning us in the process. It was just as well, as we had a journey to undertake and so headed outside to call a carriage. We left the reception in the main Entrance Hall, and walked through the honey coloured Ancaster stone framed doorway, flanked by columns of polished green and pink limestone. We stepped smartly down into the *Porte Cochere* and approached a waiting Phäeton carriage.

"Victoria Station wherever that is," I said to the liveried carriage driver.

"It is in Victoria, or at least so I have been reliably told," answered the coachman, without a discernible change of facial expression.

We clambered aboard and with a flick of his whip, the horse pulled us out of the covered *Porte Cochere* and into bright sun light streaming down from the heavens. Our eyes blinked in this welcome sunlight, which also shone brightly on the front of the St. Pancras Hotel. This of course was the first time I had seen the Hotel in all its glory, now released from the shrouds of fog that had held it in its grip for the last three days. I was impressed with the structure and its Romantic outline expressed in its masonry.

As our Phäeton carriage progressed along the front of the building we both continued to look up. We did so, almost in awe, as we witnessed the majestic spectacle and splendor of the front of this huge Hotel, with its

St. Pancras Hotel

magnificent phäntasmagoric *façade*.   Clearly, the St.
Pancras Hotel represented a fusion of functionality and
monumentalism.   Both were expressed as a mass of
decorated stone and red brick, assembled to create an
ostentatious High Victorian Gothic edifice to Romanticism, complete with pinnacle, turrets and towers.

Eventually our Phäeton carriage progressed along the
Euston Road, I think, and out of sight of the Hotel. Our
journey to Victoria was interesting, in that it afforded
both Mahler and myself views of the London Metropolis,

that up until now had been denied us, due to the pervasive fog. My impression of the Metropolis, coming from Vienna, was that London is not what I would call a beautiful city, but rather a powerful city. It is easy to see its *rôle* at the center of its Empire, the wealth of which is easily recognized and reflected in the imperial buildings of which this city is comprised.

Our Phäeton carriage took us along the Euston Road over the Portland Road and past the bronze bust of a dead President shaded by an apple tree bearing late fruit, and then made its way into Portland Place. It was down this broad *boulevard* of a road that we clattered. Portland Place, in turn, led into Langham Place and in between the Queen's Hall and Langham Hotel. I noticed Mahler smile at scenes of his, baptism of fire, his metamorphosis.

We were of course heading south down the Regent's Street; an impressive street with much to catch one's attention. However, on this occasion our attention was caught by something very worthwhile. We had by now progressed down the Regent's Street, but our carriage had stopped due to a commotion of sorts that had erupted in the carriageway in front of us. It was only when we began to recognize our immediate surroundings that we realized that we were stationary outside the Café Royal.

The commotion seemed to involve a group of persons, including four uniformed constables. They appeared to be attempting to intervene, or apprehend an individual in the midst of a group of gentlemen.

Then the reason for our carriage having been stopped became evident. A police wagon was making its way in the carriageway, against our flow of traffic, toward the commotion outside the Café Royal.

It was only on the arrival of the police wagon that the

constables acted determinedly; and suddenly pulled a stout fellow wearing a checked patterned suit from the small crowd of gentlemen, and handed him what was clearly a summons or warrant. Both Mahler and I, of course, up until now were disinterested in this *mêlée* in a London street. That is until we recognized who the stout fellow in the checked suit was. We could not believe our eyes, except by now they were watering with tears of laughter!

It was with great reluctance that we allowed our carriage driver to continue on to Victoria, but at length the police wagon clattered off with its prize, so we too continued accordingly to Victoria Railroad Station. In so doing our liveried coachman took his carriage down the Regent's Street and then waited to turn left into Burlington Street.

Whilst we waited to cross the carriageway, my attention was arrested by the presence of a building called Vigo House. I now remembered why the building had an immediate impact on me, and everyone else, for that matter.

I took this opportunity to look up at the familiar *façade* of Vigo House. We had good reason to remember this building and the *bizarre* practices that took place in the circular domed structure on its roof! Although I have always considered the edifice to be basically Neo-Classic in style, it is the way the entablature progresses upward from the roofline architrave that suggests to me repressed monumentalism.

By the time we arrived at Victoria, we had exhausted ourselves laughing to such an extent, I felt obliged to tip our Phäeton carriage driver generously, lest he think he had delivered two deranged persons.

Mahler purchased the train tickets for our Simplon Orient Express to Vienna, from a ticket office represent-

Vigo House, Regent Street

ing the *South-Eastern & Chatham Railway* and the *London, Brighton & South Coast Railway.*

I purchased some newspapers for our journey from an adjacent *kiosk.*

"Yes," I distinctly heard Mahler say to the ticket clerk, "I want two tickets for travel on the Orient for Vienna."

"Do you want the *Brighton Line?*" I overheard the clerk asking Mahler.

"The *Brighton Line?*" asked Mahler, "the line is immaterial!"

"If you say so sir," insisted the ticket clerk, "but line one carries the Continental Express to Folkestone, and then by steamer to Calais and thence onto Paris, to the Gare de l'Est. There you will connect with the *Express d'Orient* to Vienna."

Whilst this encounter was going on in the station I had quick look at one of the papers I had just purchased. It was an article in 'Stop Press' margin of *The Daily Telegraph* and I naturally read it, but could not believe the account. A warrant had been issued for Wilde's immediate arrest, apparently for some irregularity involving a libel action in court. Who, I wondered had Wilde, in his loquacious exuberance, libeled? The laughter came back to me and could hardly contain myself or wait to show Mahler, that is, if he ever emerged from the ticket office with our tickets!

Still waiting for my friend, I glimpsed at a Viennese paper, the *Neue Freie Presse* and naturally opened it in the usual place eager for *any* news of Vienna. There another article caught my attention. It was syndicated from the European press. I could not believe it, but resolved to show Mahler, only when we had secured our seats in the privacy of a carriage on the train, in case he should re-act in a public place.

We made our way to the platform gate; there we showed our tickets to a railroad *employé* wearing his distinctive black velveteen uniform with red piping. After a cursory glance, he let us through. As the passengers alighting from other trains subsided, we in turn made our way in the other direction along the platform in search of a 1st. Class compartment. The usual performance attended our boarding the train, but at length we secured a 1st. Class compartment and made our selves comfortable on the heavily patterned green *brocade* covered seats, complemented by intricately designed, white cotton *antimacassars*.

I produced the *Neue Freie Presse*, and having got my friend's attention, pointed to the relevant article with my index finger.

"Gustav, there is a newspaper report that you ought to know about," I said with evident tremor in my voice, which immediately alerted his sensibilities.

"Let me see it," said Mahler, "no, Friedrich, you read it out aloud to me. I can bear the news if it comes from you."

"Well my friend, it comes from a Vienna newspaper, the *Neue Freie Presse* and has been syndicated from Vienna and Berlin to London.

The article reads:

> 'Bruckner, not Brahms was the rightful successor to the Austro-Germanic symphonic tradition. That tradition, going back through Schumann, Schubert and Haydn to Mozart, is continued now in the person of Gustav Mahler.
>
> He takes his deserved place in the Pantheon of our great composers and his Eighth Symphony merits his honor in that august place.
>
> That the Eighth Symphony and some of the earlier symphonies are difficult and challenging in many respects can never be in

doubt. This is in part due to the *tonal* and possibly even *diatonically* aspects of his works; which require the listener to recognize the innovations of his variation structures and shifting chromatic *tone*, and the ability and skill in applying these to his polyphonic thematic compositions.

Such are the great innovative achievements in the arts, which invariably challenge and make demands upon our sensibilities. As we have experienced in the past, age ameliorates the impact of new ideas; and will allow this Symphony, his Eighth, in his continuous creation and development of the symphonic form, to take its place in the *repertoire* of all the great orchestras, for the benefit of mankind.'

We both sat back on our green *brocade* covered benches in silence. Even the cacophony outside on the busy platform appeared to diminish, in acknowledgement of our welcome news. Under circumstances such as these, words simply cannot do justice to the moment. It was a moment I had wanted to share with Mahler, but always doubted in my heart this could be so. And yet, as we all of us know, vindication never needs qualification.

Our thoughts were brought down to earth, as it was with a severe jolt that at length the train began to traverse down the side of the platform and eventually burst out from beneath the iron and glass roof of Victoria Station, and into bright sun light.

"Gustav," I said, "there is more news that you might find just a little upsetting, for it does alas concern a friend of ours."

I then handed over *The Daily Telegraph* to Mahler,

pointing to the *Stop Press* article about the warrant being issued for Wilde's immediate arrest. Mahler read the report with genuine concern upon his facial features. Gradually those stern features gave way to a more relaxed countenance. That in turn resolved itself into audible laughter, the depths of which reverberated around the carriage, but such was its infection, that I too joined in.

It was during this second bout of loud, almost manic laughter, with tears in our eyes, that we rocked ourselves back and forth in our seats in syncopation with the swaying from side to side of our carriage, as its steel wheels pounded the rails of the permanent way below us. It was under these somewhat unusual circumstances that the guard made his entrance into our 1st. Class compartment.

The ticket inspector introduced himself well enough with the injunction:

"Tickets please gentlemen!"

Mahler reached into his inside pocket and produced with a flourish a leather wallet containing our 1st. Class tickets, which he had purchased, for our journey from London to Folkestone and onto the continent back to Vienna. Mahler, without a second thought or look, but still laughing, at our news regarding Wilde being incommoded, with confidence, handed the tickets to the guard. I continued to chortle to myself whilst surveying, through the carriage window, views of the suburban Metropolis fleeting by.

"Just a remark," said the guard, "but are you two enjoying yourselves in this 1st. Class carriage?"

We were somewhat taken aback by the guard's confidence in addressing us.

"The reason I ask," continued the guard, "is because these tickets are for 3rd. Class accommodation, not 1st. Class.

I am afraid these tickets do not entitle you to occupy this carriage and therefore must ask you to remove yourself to the 3rd. Class carriage located at the end of this train. There you shall be accommodated in the style and dignity befitting the class of ticket you hold!"

At this juncture I intervened.

"I appreciate fully your concern," he continued, stifling my protest, "and the lack of a cotton *antimacassar* covered headrest on your un-upholstered seats; but the timber benches are of English elm and will suffice for your needs. In addition, for your comfort, the London, Brighton & South Coast Railway now covers, with a rain proof membrane, our 3rd. Class carriage!"

"But this is outrageous," I protested.

"It may well be," said the guard, "but you should have consulted the information contained in that most excellent of pocket books *Bäedeker's* guide to London, which I highly recommend you purchase, read and apply its uplifting and expedient information regarding purchasing the correct railroad ticket!

Availing yourselves of that useful book might help you appreciate the class of ticket you hold, together with your proper location on a train, and thus avoid being in embarrassing situations, as this one!"

And with that *Parthian* shot, invited us to follow him down to the 3rd. Class carriage for completion of our journey on this non-stop express train to Folkestone. Needless to say the embarrassment and ignominy of our being escorted by this velveteen uniformed supercilious guard through twelve packed carriages to the rear 3rd. Class carriage was too much for us to bear.

All of a sudden it started to rain from a cloud that did not have a silver lining.

THE END

Index

Aalto, Alvar 173
Abschieds Symphonie 277
Acropolis 10, 11, 286
Aëolian Hall 19
Aëolian pianola 28, 125, 134, 137, 267, 282
Allgemeine Elecktrizitäts GmbH AEG 84, 101
Alma-Tadema, Laurence 121
Also Sprach Zarathustra 56, 190, 275
Alt, Rudolf von 168
Antheil, George 124, 131, 138, 149, 167, 189, 190, 192, 198, 202, 225, 227, 292
Astarta Syriaca 90
Astarte 90
Auferstehung 3, 14, 164, 190, 242, 243
Austro-Germanic Symphonic Tradition 321
Aztec Building 39, 40

Bäedeker's Guide to London 34, 36, 70, 219, 324
Baker Street, London 36, 41
Balakirev, Mily 43
Ballet Mecanique 125, 126, 136, 189, 192
Balzac, Honoré de 177
Bauer-Lechner, Natalie 57
Bayreuth Festival 175

Beardsley, Aubrey 78, 121, 167, 172, 173, 298, 299, 301, 302, 304, 305, 312
Beata Beatrix 90
Beckford, William 229
Bechstein Hall - Wigmore Street 232, 233, 234, 237, 238
Benediction 71
Bénédiction de Dieu dans la solitude 28
Berg, Alban 46, 85, 246
Berlin 3, 56, 159, 170, 321
Berliner, Arnold 84
Bergen Avenue 250, 251, 279, 280, 283, 284, 292, 311
Bizet, Georges 179
Böcklin, Arnold 171, 292
Bond Street, London 19
Borodin, Alexander 43
Bradshaw's Railway Guide 176
Brahms, Johannes 5, 6, 141, 165, 321
Bruckner, Anton 44, 141, 151, 154, 155, 162, 244, 274, 321
Budapest Opera 6
Bülow, Hans von 4, 28
Burne-Jones, Sir Edward 121, 133, 134, 227
Byron, Lord 177

Café Royal, London 72, 73, 82, 121, 149, 177, 189, 225, 290, 299, 313, 317

Camden Town Group 291
Carlyle, Thomas 133
Catholicism 5, 104, 146, 147, 165, 220, 314
Charing Cross Railway Station 15
Chevalley, Heinrich 208
Chicago, World Columbian Exposition 234
Chopin, Frederic 78, 152
Colony Room Club, London 221, 222, 223, 224
Covent Garden Opera House 36, 179, 221, 291
Crane, Walter 302, 303
Criterion Bar, London 285, 286, 288, 303, 306, 311, 313
Cui, César 43

Daily Chronicle 43
Daily News 43, 45, 47, 53, 90, 206
Daily Telegraph 23, 49, 204, 205, 320, 322
Dante Symphony 130
Dante's Devine Comedy 223
Das Klagende Lied 5, 267
Das Liebesverbot, opera 30, 31
Das Lied von der Erde 267
Das Rheingold, opera 258, 266, 284, 301
Death and Transfiguration 165
Delius, Frederick 275
Delville, Jean 302
Der Einsame im Herbst 52
Der Ring des Nibulungen, operas 31, 51, 157, 158, 169, 15, 175, 284, 293, 300
Der Rosenkavalier, opera 127
Der Titan 128, 141, 158, 191, 294
Der Tod in Venedig 176
Der trunkene in Frühling 52
Der Zeit ihre Kunst-und ihre Freiheit 169
Des Knaben Wunderhorn 14, 50, 132, 158
Deserted House, the 88, 89

Devonshire Place, London 211, 212, 217
Die Entführung aus dem Serail, opera 236
Die Frau Ohne Schatten, opera 127
Die Meistersingers von Nürnburg, 132, 209
Die Music 166
Die Tote Stadt, opera 12
Disraeli, Benjamin 178, 180
Don Giovanni, opera 6, 7
Doré, Gustave 15
Doyle, Conan 177
Dresden 140, 152
Dublin 82, 84, 179
Dumb-Mute, the 218, 219, 220, 224, 225, 231
Dunkel ist das leben, ist der Tod 52,
Dvořák, Antonín 70, 71, 151, 233, 244

Earl's Court, Exhibition Hall 34, 36, 37, 39, 40, 129
Echo, The 43, 49, 54, 206
Echoes of Valhalla 282
Egyptian Avenue of the Dead, 113, 114, 118
Ein Deutsches Requiem 165
Ein Heldenleben, 157
Electrical Musical Industries - EMI 262
Elgar, Sir Edward 101, 187, 188, 189, 228
Emperor, Franz Joseph I 38, 263, 310
Enigma Variations 82, 188

Faust 144, 146, 147
Feuersnot, opera 47, 161
Folies-Bergère, Paris 74
Fonthill Abbey 229, 230
Fourth Estate 3, 41, 54, 59, 83, 135, 204
Frankfurt-am-Main 10

Freud, Sigmund 2, 47, 172, 173, 210, 213, 216, 275

Fusion of the Arts 167, 168, 169, 171, 173, 291, 293, 295

Futurists Movement 135, 138, 197, 200, 209, 236, 240, 241, 248, 273, 276, 286

General Electric Company GEC 84

German Expressionism 173

Globe, The 42, 204

Goethe, Johann 45, 46, 80, 101, 139, 146, 162, 163

Götterdämmerung, opera 4, 45, 121, 229

Great Marlborough Street, London 71

Grimshaw, Atkinson 78, 80, 86, 124, 228

Gropius, Walter 101, 173

Gurrelieder 47, 174

Hall of Machines 24, 25

Hamburg Opera 28, 201, 207

Hanslick, Hans 157

Harmonies, Poétique et Religieuses 71

Haydn, Joseph 321

Hegel, Georg 46, 152, 165

Hell, Theodor 127

Herzfeld, Victor von 6, 7

Hetherington, Dot 267

Highgate Cemetery 101, 102, 105, 117, 121

Hirschfeld, Robert 47

Hoffmann, Nina Anna 175

Hoffmann, Joseph 169, 175

Hoffmann, Josef 168, 169, 171

Hofmannsthal, Hugo von 127, 168

Holmes, Sherlock 177, 178, 228

Hungerford Palace of Varieties 271, 291

Hunt, Holman 93

Ich bin der Welt abhanden gekommen 12, 245, 246

Imperial Austria-Hungarian Exposition 33, 38

Imperial Theater 271

Interpretation of Dreams 47

Isle of the Dead 292

Joyce, James 84, 93, 156, 167

Kandinsky, Wassily 83, 86, 154, 159, 161

Kettner's Restaurant, London 82, 285

Kindertotenlieder 52, 126, 233, 243, 244, 245, 246

Klimt, Gustav 167, 170, 171, 172

Klimnger, Max 171

Klopstock, Friedrich 4, 14, 164, 190

Köln 10

Korngold, Erich 12, 158, 172

Korngold, Julius 160

Kössler, Hans 6, 7, 209

Kraff-Ebing, Richard von 210, 302

Kroyer, Theodor 159

Kurtzweil, Max 168

Ländler 12, 164

Langham Hotel, London 41, 42, 317

Langtry, Lily 61, 101, 272

Lawrence, Katie 267

Lehár, Franz 260

Lehmann, Lilli 232, 235, 236, 237, 245, 267

Leipzig 141

Leitmotiv 72, 157

Leverson, Ada 304

Lieder eines fahrenden Gesellen 130, 245, 267

Lipiner, Siegfried 54

Liszt, Abbé 28, 71, 130, 152

Lloyd, Marie 267

Lob des hohen Verstandes 132

Lodge, Michael William 243, 248, 250, 253, 257, 258, 261, 265, 268,

273, 274, 277, 279, 281, 283, 284, 292

Lohengrin, sacred music drama 31, 121, 152, 158, 207, 229, 293

Löhr, Friedrich 18, 83, 173, 215, 216, 220, 253, 257

London 15, 16, 179, 202, 210, 219, 225, 234, 316, 317, 324

London, Brighton & South Coast Rly 319, 324

London Chronicle 49, 243

London, Midland & Scottish Railway 2, 3, 226

London Post, the 202

London Symphony Orchestra 52

Lost Chord 109

Lützow, Count 38

Lyrische Symphonie 128

Madame Butterfly 179

Mahler, Almanée Schindler 52, 169

Mahler, Gustav 1, 3, 18, 43, 92, 131, 146, 161, 189, 195, 198, 213, 232, 253, 283, 321

Mahler, portrait 6

Mahler, portrait 296

Maiernigg am Wörthersee. 1, 7, 9, 57, 159, 210, 239

Mann, Thomas 176

Marinetti, Filippo 197, 236

Mausoleum at Joensuu 48

Metropolitan Music Hall, 291

Metropolitan Opera House 232, 233

Metropolitan Railway 34, 35, 37, 41

Millais, Sir John Everett 94, 97, 120, 227, 272

Moll, Carl 51, 52, 167, 168, 169, 174

Moore, Albert 121, 303

Morning Post, the 42, 50, 203

Morris, William & Jane 91, 94, 134

Moser, Koloman 168, 171

Moulin Rouge, Paris 74

Moussorgsky, Modeste 43, 293

Mozart, Amadeus 6, 60, 152, 153, 236, 275, 293, 321

München 1, 40, 144, 157, 158, 183, 200, 270, 290

München Ausstellungs Halle 39, 174, 270

Music of the Future 124, 131, 137, 189, 201

Musicvereinssaal 160, 268

Neue Freie Presse 160, 320, 321

Neues Pestor Journal 6, 209

Neuschwanstein Schloß 229

New York 232, 233, 246

New York Daily Tribune 246

New York Sun 246

New York Times 246

Newman, Robert 62, 69, 183, 184, 190, 193, 194, 198, 200, 221, 223, 224, 237

Nietzsche, Friedrich 50, 57, 190, 191, 275

Nihilists 30, 138, 198, 200, 204, 206, 209, 235, 240, 241, 244, 248, 273, 276, 286, 303, 306, 312

Nodnagel, Ernst Otto 158

Nürnburg 10

Olbrich, Joseph Maria 169

Old Compton Street, Soho 72

Ophelia 94, 97

Pall Mall Gazette 52, 126

Panathenäenzug 157

Parsifal, sacred music drama 31, 121, 130, 152, 157, 229, 293, 302

Phenomenology of Spirit 46

Picture of Dorain Gray 143, 176, 178, 180, 303

Pictures from an Exhibition 293

Plesse, Edward 282

Pollini, Bernhard 8, 54, 200, 201, 207, 208, 209, 240

Pomp and Circumstance Marches 188

Portland Road, London 70, 317

Pound, Ezra 133, 192

Pre-Raphaelites 81, 90, 94, 120, 121, 132, 133, 138, 168, 227, 291, 302
Pringsheim, Klaus 45
Promenade Concerts 8, 62, 180
Puccini, Giacomo 179

Queen's Hall 8, 19, 29, 59, 183, 190, 194, 200, 202, 204, 205, 234, 237, 240, 258, 273, 317
Queens' Hall Orchestra 8, 29, 63, 186, 189

Rachmaninov, Sergei 292
Rackham, Arthur 301, 303
Rättig, Theodor 155
Ravel, Maurice 275
Red House, the 91, 92, 95, 96, 99, 102, 122, 134, 136
Regensberg 10, 150
Resurrection Symphony 3, 14, 50, 164
Richter, Hans 31, 52, 188
Richter, Jean Paul 53, 128, 129, 191, 294
Richter, Johanne 129, 131, 140
Ricketts Charles 78, 91, 124, 167
Rimsky-Korsakov, Nicholas 43
Roller, Alfred 57, 58
Ross, Robert 143, 144
Rossetti, Dante Gabriel 90, 91, 95, 98, 100, 102, 132, 134, 136, 167, 221, 227, 292
Rott, Hans 54, 140, 141, 142, 155, 284
Royal Albert Hall 29, 31, 32, 52, 139, 250, 258, 267, 272, 276
Royal Aquarium Building 270, 271, 272, 276
Royal Court Theaters - Vienna 54
Rückert Lieder 233, 245, 246
Rückert, Freidrich 12, 233, 243, 245
Ruskin, John 80, 133
Russolo, Luigi 232, 235, 236

Saarinen, Eliel 47, 48
Salomé, play 163, 301, 302, 304

Salomé, opera 163
Sargent, John Singer 79, 90, 167, 298, 299, 309, 313
Schaupielhaus, Berlin 56, 159
Schindler, Alma   see Mahler Alma 11, 82, 167, 172
Schindler, Emil 45, 167
Schlesinger, Bruno 8
Schreker, Franz 158
Schönberg, Arnold 2, 46, 52, 172, 174, 240
Schönbrunn Schloß 263
Schopenhauer, Arthur 305
Schröder-Hanfstängl, Marie 207
Schubert, Franz 151, 244, 275, 321
Schumann, Robert 321
Secession Building, Vienna 169
Šechtl, Jindřich 38
Sibelius, Jean 47
Sickert, Walter 285, 286, 289, 290, 291, 293, 295
Siddal, Elizabeth 90, 92, 93, 94, 95, 99, 102, 108, 120, 123, 136 167, 172, 173, 177
Sign of Four 178
Simplon Orient Express 314, 319
Slaughter Bench of Humanity 152, 165
Soho 72, 73, 221, 285
South Eastern Railway 15
South-Eastern & Chatham Railway 319
Sporting Life, the 57, 126
St James' Concert Hall 70
St. George's Hall 268
St. James' Gazette. 53, 143, 144, 162
St. Pancras Hotel 16, 17, 23, 26, 33, 41, 118, 202, 217, 221, 224, 226, 230, 233, 248, 249, 258, 283, 315, 316
St. Pancras Railroad Station 21
St. Vitus' Dance 218, 264
Stanford, Sir Charles Villiers 82, 98, 102, 124, 135, 144, 154, 285, 292, 298, 312, 313

Stansfield House, Hampstead 93
Stoclet Palace, Brussels 171
Strauss, Rickard 7, 47, 85, 127, 156, 157, 158, 161, 163, 293
Sullivan, Sir Arthur 272
Swinburne, Algernon 91
Symphony No. 1 in D major(1888) 14, 29, 30, 32, 33, 125, 128, 129, 139, 160, 164, 241
Symphony No. 2 in C minor(1894) 3, 4, 7, 14, 50, 160, 163, 164, 165, 166, 190, 191, 243
Symphony No. 3 in D minor(1895) 14, 49, 56, 159, 160, 161
Symphony No. 4 in G major(1900) 14, 158, 159, 160, 162
Symphony No. 5 in C # minor (1902) 10, 11, 14, 132, 162
Symphony No. 6 in A minor(1904) 14, 45, 46, 162, 191, 192, 244
Symphony No. 7 in E minor(1905) 14
Symphony No. 8 in E ♭ major (1907) 1, 2, 7, 14, 16, 19, 33, 41, 143, 144, 174, 183, 190, 195, 206, 220, 239, 313, 321
Symphony No. 9 in D major(1909) 83, 85, 101, 244, 248, 250, 267, 268
Symphonie der Tausend 3, 43, 145, 195
Symphony in E major 141, 282

Tantum Ergo 71
Telemann, Georg 153
Temple of Erechtheion 286
Three Pintos, opera 127
Times, The 33, 43, 205
Titan Symphony 5, 14, 29, 52, 125, 128, 162, 191
Tod und Verklärung 85, 157, 164, 165
Tone Poem 85, 86, 157, 292
Toscanini, Arturo 237
Totenfeier 28
Tragische Sinfonie 45, 47, 191, 192

Trinity College, Dublin 179
Trinklied von Jammer der Erde 52
Tristan und Isolda, opera 157, 229, 304
Twelve Tone 2, 174

University of Cambridge 82
University of Oxford 127
University of Vienna 179

Valhalla 10, 166
Veni Creatus Spiritus 144, 145, 146, 195
Verdi, Giuseppe 179, 293, 294
Vere and the Nihilists 139, 313
Verkläte Nacht 47
Victoria 266, 267, 269, 315, 316, 318
Victoria Railroad Station 315, 318, 322
Vienna 1, 16, 46, 154, 160, 170, 174, 194, 233, 235, 314, 317, 320, 321
Vienna Conservatory 141, 179
Vienna Court Opera. 5, 54, 179
Vienna University 84
Viennese Secession 167, 169, 170, 291, 292
Vier Letzte Lieder 86
Vigo House, London 318, 319
Visions of Architecture 121, 226, 228
Visions of Architecture Drawing 256, 257
Vivian Gray 178, 179, 180
Völsunga Saga 175, 293, 301

Wagner, Otto 170
Wagner, Rickard 4, 30, 44, 72, 132, 152, 156, 157, 175, 179, 188, 229, 266, 284, 293, 300
Walter, Bruno 49
Watts, George Frederick 101
Weber, Carl Maria von 44, 70, 127, 140, 153
Webern, Anton 245

Wesondonk Lieder 229

Whistler, James 78, 80, 85, 86, 95, 124, 167, 172, 292

Wiener Abendpost, the 47, 192

Wiener Werkstatte Gruppe 171, 172

Wilde, Oscar 78, 95, 107, 124, 149, 153, 161, 167, 181, 189, 225, 285, 292, 299, 304, 313, 320, 323

Wings of Eternity 115, 116

Wood, Sir Henry 8, 29, 62, 183, 194, 200

World as Will and Representation 305

Wunderhorn Symphonies 14, 241

Zemlinsky, Alexander von 82, 124, 128, 129, 140, 144, 149, 172, 174

Zichy, Count Gezé 207

Zinne, Wilhelm 57, 98